LOST CAUSES

AN ELEMENTS NOVEL

MIA MARSHALL

For those fighting
their own invisible battles

CHAPTER 1

I never dreamed of falling. When I slept, I didn't imagine taking a test I hadn't studied for or showing up in public naked. At night, I saw only flames. I smelled smoke and the sickening odor of burning flesh. I watched a man die, and I felt my mind unhinge, again and again.

It was safe to say I wasn't sleeping much.

"Another nightmare?" Sera asked.

I blinked, letting my eyes adjust to the darkness, and didn't bother answering. I'd woken to the sound of my own screams and was covered in sweat. The answer seemed self-evident. "How long did I sleep?"

"Two hours." Sera stood at the window, peering through a gap in the curtains to the parking lot below. It was still night, and I could make out little more than her silhouette. She wasn't tall, but she was strong. She had the curvy, compact muscles of a skater, plus an impressive amount of fire magic, but those weren't her real strengths. Sera was a fighter. She never gave up, and she expected the same from everyone around her.

I was trying. I reached for yesterday's jeans. "Two hours more than the night before."

Sera glanced over her shoulder. "We're getting you some Ambien."

I made a face. We both knew the problem with sleeping pills was they, well, put you to sleep. Great if you needed eight hours of uninterrupted shut-eye. Bad if you were running for your lives and the people chasing you got a little closer every day. There were already too many times I needed to be knocked out. We couldn't risk adding to that.

"Vivian figure out where we're heading tomorrow?" I tried to sound optimistic. It wasn't Vivian's fault that our search for the other dual magic had stalled more times than a '78 Gremlin. Not only did we know nothing about this person, but he or she would have a strong desire to remain hidden, what with the whole death penalty for duals thing.

"She found something in New Mexico she wants to check out. Northwest, near the Four Corners."

Neither of us mentioned that we'd already spent weeks scouring New Mexico. We'd found several desert elementals and a few stones in the mountains, but that was it. No sign of a dual magic.

Duals were the only elementals who could control two elements. Very few existed, because they could only be born from the union of two full elementals, each with a different magic. Fulls weren't especially fertile—a built-in counterbalance to our longevity—and they tended to stay with their own, so such births were extremely rare. We only knew of four living duals. Trent Pond was trapped in a mental institution on the California coast. One had supposedly been spotted on the Prince's Islands near Istanbul. Another had been tracked to the American Southwest, which explained why we'd spent the last three months looking under every rock and cactus.

I was the fourth one.

Though I'd have preferred to find the dual we sought months ago, in truth their rarity was a blessing. After using both elements one time too many, duals were the only elementals who could be driven mad by their magic. A "destroy cities for shits and giggles" kind of madness.

I had yet to raze an entire town. Other than that, madness was a problem I understood a little too well.

"Is Mac still out?" I asked. It was a rhetorical question. If Mac was there, he'd be at my side, dark brown eyes watching for any sign I was about to lose it.

"He texted fifteen minutes ago to say they're on their way back. He made it ten miles and at least an hour this time."

"Damn it." Mac and I had been conducting small experiments over the last few months, learning how far we could separate before the bond we shared snapped, forcing him to return before he became ill. We'd hoped that, if we pushed the distance a bit further each time, the magic would adapt the way a muscle pushed to failure grew stronger. Instead, we were as tied to each other as we'd ever been. If he left me, he grew ill. If he stayed away too long, it became life-threatening.

There was one exception. If my magic was shut down, the connection vanished. When my mind turned black and my friends chemically silenced my power, Mac could travel as far as he wanted. It was the only solution we'd found, and spending large chunks of my life comatose wasn't much of a solution.

"Did you shower? Your hair is looking a little more deranged than usual."

Sera shook her head until black curls fell in front of her eyes. "This is the freshly fucked look," she said. "You should try it sometime."

The problem with sisters is they know all your weak spots, including how long you've been celibate. "It's complicated," I muttered. It always was with me and Mac. "Go. I'll take over guard duty. The only reason we're in a motel tonight is Simon insisted on hot showers for everyone. Might as well take advantage."

She hesitated.

"Get Miriam over here and give her a syringe if you're scared to leave me alone." I couldn't be angry. After all, I'd given them plenty of reason to believe I couldn't control myself.

Sera wanted to trust me. I knew she did. But she'd witnessed what happened when I used both sides of my magic. When I called fire and water, when I let their power consume me, people got hurt. Sometimes people died.

The door shook with three heavy knocks. Sera opened it a crack, and Miriam shoved it open until it smacked against the wall.

"We gotta go."

We gaped at her, hoping she didn't mean what we thought she did. She exploded that hope right away.

"They found us." When we still didn't move, she barged into the room and picked up the bags we never bothered to unpack. "The goddamn council finally caught up. The blond bastards are downstairs, so stop catching flies and move your asses."

We didn't argue. I shoved my feet into my blue Converse, grabbed my bag from Miriam, and began running.

"This way." Simon appeared before us. Unlike Miriam, the cat shifter knew how to be stealthy. "Take the eastern stairs to the ground floor, then walk south two hundred feet."

Sera and I waited. Simon rolled his eyes.

"Turn left, go down, then turn right. Stop when you see the vehicles. Someday, you must learn to navigate without the sun's guidance. Please bring my clothes with you."

One moment, a good-looking man in his early twenties with black hair and startling green eyes stood next to us. The next, a small black cat with green eyes leapt onto the railing, and from there to the roof, where his black coat vanished against the night sky.

We followed his instructions, meeting Vivian on the stairs. Despite getting no more sleep than the rest of us, she was alert.

"Do you know what's happening?" I asked.

"Simon saw visitors in the motel office," Vivian said. "Tall, skinny blonds in designer clothes. He's getting a closer look now, but he thought it was Deborah and Michael."

I feared he was right. The description sounded like either the water council or wealthy Scandinavian tourists exploring the finest truck stops of the American Southwest. The first option was the more probable one, in many ways.

"How the hell did they find us? Viv, weren't you keeping an eye on the satellite images of the hotel?" Sera demanded.

Vivian reached up to tug on one of her dreads. She avoided our eyes. "There was a glitch. I'm doing what I can out here, but it's not always a strong connection."

Sera grumbled, but I said nothing. Knowing Vivian, she was madder at herself than we could ever be.

At the bottom of the stairs, I peered around the corner. No light came from any of the rooms. Sera moved in the darkest shadows of the hallway. Vivian and I followed. Miriam brought up the rear.

The path took us off the motel property. Simon failed to mention we would climb through a broken chain link fence to reach the closed car wash behind the motel. As soon as the Airstream was in sight, we sprinted. Mac was already at the Bronco's wheel. His locked jaw relaxed when I came into view. Carmichael flung the trailer door open and we leapt inside. We'd barely closed it behind us before we began moving. The Bronco swung into the empty street, pulling the Airstream behind it. We headed in the opposite direction of the motel.

"Johnson already took the camper?" I asked Carmichael. The two FBI agents were traveling with us. They said it was their duty as the official paranormal liaisons of Lake Tahoe. Neither seemed to consider it relevant that they hadn't seen Tahoe in months.

"He left about thirty seconds before we did. We'll catch up with him soon."

There was a heavy thump above us. I slid the sunroof open, letting Simon in. He shifted back to human. As usual, Simon was unconcerned about his lack of clothes. "They were still in the office. We were lucky to find an especially stupid and greedy clerk at this motel. He cannot quite remember us, but he wants more money for the little he knows."

I dropped onto the Airstream's small couch, my breath coming a bit easier.

"You're sure it was the council?"

He confirmed this, and I bit back a curse. Simon knew their faces. He wouldn't confuse them for anyone else.

Deborah Rivers and Michael Bay were all that remained of the water council, but they were more than strong enough to hurt us. I could match their power—if I was willing to tap into both sides of my magic and slide further into the darkest part of my mind. I didn't have much further to go before I could no longer see the way out.

Our best option was to keep running, and we were getting pretty good at it.

———

FIVE MINUTES LATER, WE WERE SPEEDING DOWN THE FREEWAY. Well, speeding as fast as a camper van and an old Bronco pulling an Airstream trailer could go—which is to say, moving at a pace some turtles might call sedate.

The busy interstate was too exposed and we took the first exit off the freeway. The offramp dropped us onto a narrow two-lane road that didn't seem to lead anywhere in particular.

Agent Carmichael poked at the keyboard on his clunky government-issued laptop, deep lines forming around his mouth. He was a handsome man, all chiseled jaw and high cheekbones, but the last month had taken its toll. The circles beneath his eyes were nearly purple and his jaw was covered in dark blond stubble. It was a shocking look for such a meticulous man.

"I don't understand how they found you. Johnson and I asked the Bureau to lock down any information that might appear in a database. Your IDs and vehicle info should be covered by the highest security protocols."

Sera stood on the bed, watching the road through the rear window. Her voice carried through the trailer. "It shouldn't matter. We change plates and IDs every few days. We paid cash at the motel. I didn't master this shit as a teenage delinquent to get caught now by a bunch of watery technophobes."

Vivian worked next to Carmichael, her fingers flying over two separate keyboards. Unlike his government issued computer, her laptops were the latest model, and then she'd upgraded them until they had the power to launch missile strikes in foreign countries. She'd already worn the letters off most of the keys from constant use.

"I wrote a script that deleted us entirely," she said. "According to the federal government, we don't even exist."

Carmichael scrubbed his hand over his face. "I'm going to pretend I didn't just hear you admit to hacking FBI computers."

Vivian didn't even attempt to look contrite. "If I could break through your security, theoretically they also could. It made sense to remove it altogether. High security doesn't mean much." Vivian was a weak earth elemental, with far more human blood than magic. As a computer mastermind, she was the scariest thing I'd ever seen. "Though that is very theoretical. They are old ones, after all."

Elementals lived a long time, and the more magic they possessed, the longer they lived. A few chose to adapt as they moved through the centuries or even millennia, but most couldn't be bothered to do more than the minimum. The world changed too fast to keep up with every passing fad, and few saw any reason to master a skill they believed would soon become obsolete—"soon," to an elemental, being a subjective term. Many of our race were unconvinced computers were here to stay.

By elemental standards, I was young at sixty-five years old, but even I could barely work my smart phone. The decade I spent hiding from the outside world hadn't helped. Sera was about ten years younger than me, and she had no difficulty functioning in a technology-obsessed world.

My sister joined us in the main room. "What about ISP tracking? That's a thing, right?"

Without lifting her eyes from the screens, Vivian pointed to a small metal box on the table. It was black and sleek, one of those mysterious technical things I knew as a doodad or a thingamajig.

"Mobile wi-fi, run through multiple VPNs." She must have known we had no idea what she was talking about, because she elaborated. "Virtual private networks. One should be enough to hide our ISP and, therefore, our location. I'm running our data through several different ones, each set to ping me if there are any disruptions. There haven't been. Plus, yesterday I used our credit card at the Four Seasons in Boston, so if they were looking anywhere, it should have been New England."

"Then how…" Sera began.

"I don't know!"

Seeing Vivian flustered was almost as unsettling as having the council on our tail. Earths were calm and stable. They didn't panic.

"I don't know how they keep finding us." Vivian aimed for a calmer tone and mostly succeeded. "I'm pulling up real-time satellite maps of the area."

"Is it possible they are using the same footage?" Simon had found pants at some point. He sat on the Airstream's small couch, and for once he hadn't folded his legs beneath him. His feet remained planted on the floor, and his fingers curled around the edge of the sofa.

Vivian punched keys until she accessed a clear image of the desert. "Consumer satellite images aren't available in real time. For that, they'd need to access government equipment, and we're talking about a group of people who don't even use email."

Carmichael gave up on his own search and peered at Vivian's screen. "I *am* using a government account and your image is three times as clear."

"Okay, I think we're…" Vivian didn't finish the sentence.

Carmichael swore and returned to his computer. "Can you see the license plate?"

Dread pooled in my stomach.

There we were, clear as day on the map—a beat-up

camper van a hundred feet ahead of a Bronco pulling an Airstream.

Two miles behind us was a black luxury sedan we couldn't seem to escape.

Sera grabbed the walkie-talkie we'd been using in isolated areas and hit the button. It crackled for a moment, then went dead, its batteries exhausted. She hurled it against a wall and yanked her phone from her pocket. "Damn it. No bars. We've got to let them know."

Simon returned to his feline form. Using Sera's shoulder as a springboard, he leapt through the open sunroof. Light footsteps above us, then the cat landed on the Bronco's roof. He slithered through the open passenger window with some contortionist ninja moves the rest of us had no hope of replicating.

The Bronco took a hard right, and we lurched against the trailer's wall as the Airstream left the road. The camper followed suit. Several times, Mac swerved to avoid the piles of rocks decorating the landscape, and the trailer would tilt onto two wheels for several heart-stopping seconds. The huge vehicles aimed for a stretch of red rocks in the distance. They were tall enough to hide us, if we made it in time.

Their sedan could hit ninety without breaking a sweat. The council was closing the gap.

Carmichael's eyes were glued to Vivian's screen. "We should get to the rocks, but they'll see where we turned off." The desert was dry and still, with no rain or wind to cover up the tell-tale tire tracks.

I swallowed. "No, they won't."

I'd barely tapped into my magic the last couple weeks, only using enough to recharge and heal myself. Recharging through my element was so instinctive that most of the time I wasn't even aware I was doing it.

The water magic I'd known all my life, the power that once comforted and fueled me, wasn't the same. It was sharper now, covered in edges that would slice at my mind if I let my guard down for even a moment.

And I always let my guard down.

I'd tried after we escaped my family's island. I tried to use my water magic as I had for decades. It wasn't meant to be a passive power, and it chafed against the restraints. I thought I'd be safe, so long as I felt none of the rage that pushed me toward darkness.

But every time I reached for it, I found the rage already waiting and the monster that lived inside me eager to escape. I only needed to lose focus for a fraction of a second for the madness to dig its claws deeper into my mind.

Too many times over the last few months, I'd forced my friends to inject me with the drug that was both my bane and my savior.

Created by another dual and refined by many others with their own agendas, the serum suppressed magic. Neither elementals nor shifters were meant to live without their magic. Our bodies' natural defense was to fall into a coma until the drug worked its way out of our system. At best, the drug was a delay, not a cure.

We didn't know anything about the long-term effects, and our supply was rapidly dwindling. It was irresponsible to put myself in a position where we had to use more.

But those following us didn't only threaten my life. Our laws promised a century of incarceration to any elemental who helped conceal a dual magic. My mother and Grams were already enjoying the hospitality of the elemental penal system. They'd been sentenced a month after I escaped my family's island. They were in prison because of me, and I was too busy running for my life to help.

With three-quarters elemental blood in her veins, Sera

would live for at least a thousand years. She would consider the punishment worth it. Vivian was another story. She had so little earth blood that she'd die in captivity.

The shifters didn't fall under elemental rule, but it was impossible to predict what would happen to Mac, Simon, and Miriam. When large swathes of the elemental population considered them an abomination, due process might seem like a quaint notion to those pursuing us.

My friends were here because they were trying to save me, no matter the cost to their own lives. I had to at least try to save them in return.

I reached for the water magic in my core. As always, it was coiled around the fire. I tugged at the fire's knots to free it, letting my water rise to the surface.

The fire churned, eager for release. Once, I would have fought against it, refused to allow it freedom. It was too late for that. The fire was part of me. It might help drive me to madness, but it wasn't the enemy.

It couldn't be, not when the enemy was behind us.

The water magic hummed under my skin. Not long ago, it had felt pure and energetic, a crystal stream pouring down a mountain. These days, it was more like a lake at midnight, dark and full of secrets.

I sent it from my body to look for water and knew its frustration when it found none. A southwest desert in late August was pretty much the definition of dry heat.

"How much time do we have?" I asked.

Vivian's intent eyes never left the computer screen. "Their car is about half a mile away."

"Hope no one's thirsty later." I twisted the faucet in the tiny galley kitchen and summoned the magic back to me. It attached itself, one molecule at a time, to the water flowing into the sink.

Sera's panicked voice reached me, but not her words.

I took long, deep breaths, striving for the kind of focus a Zen master would envy. Nothing existed but the magic.

I grabbed the stream of water from the sink and sent it arcing through the sunroof toward the tire tracks.

It wasn't moving fast enough. It would never eliminate the evidence before the council reached us.

I knew only one way to boost its strength. Centering myself and hoping that was enough, I added the fire's power to the water.

The water flew from me, well beyond the hundred-foot radius that limited other elementals. Two hundred feet, then three, and then five hundred. I released it, the water dropping onto the dusty ground and washing away the tracks. I did it again, this time pushing it one thousand feet, all the way to the edge of the road.

The wet ground would give us away as surely as any tire marks. I recalled my water magic but let the fire remain. Heat rose, devouring any sign of the rainstorm.

On the computer screens, the black sedan continued down the road, missing the turnoff.

My skin hummed, and my focus cracked. "Let's go get them. We can end this now."

I faced the others. They looked small. They occupied such a finite amount of space, and their lives were so fragile. They would never be more than what I saw now.

Dual magics were different. I was only beginning to understand how much.

"Aidan."

My lips twisted, resisting the command in that voice. I turned to the speaker and saw the syringe in her hand.

The magic hissed in fear and anger. For a moment it considered attacking, but fire couldn't hurt that woman and there wasn't enough water left to drown her.

Also, it was Sera. I didn't hurt Sera.

I stumbled backwards as reason slammed into me. I wrenched the threads of power back to me. They twisted in my core, displeased, but at least I controlled them. It had so nearly been the other way around.

Sera's movements were hesitant, as if she approached a wild beast, but her eyes were as determined as ever.

"I'm back," I said. My face was red and my heart pounded like I'd sprinted a mile, but I'd come back. This time, at least, I'd come back.

Sera studied my face for a long, silent moment. She returned the syringe to the black case and tucked that into one of the kitchenette's drawers.

Carmichael and Vivian watched me as they would a stranger. A stranger who might try to eat their liver with fava beans and a nice Chianti.

"Really, it's me. So long as I'm not using the magic, I'm still Aidan. I didn't slide any further down the sanity slope."

They looked unconvinced.

"We can't use the drug every time." I attempted logic. "It knocks me out for days, and we can't afford that."

"I'm all for knocking you out, but we don't have enough left to do it whenever you're an idiot." That might have been Sera agreeing with me.

I gave her a shaky smile. She slapped my face.

"Hey!" It only stung a little, but allowing her to slap me whenever she thought I was stupid wasn't a precedent I wanted to set.

"That's for using your magic. We agreed. As little as possible until we find the other dual, remember?"

"But the tracks…"

"Don't even start. If they caught us, we'd have dealt with it. We're handling this, Ade, and you're going to let us. You don't get to be the hero this time." Her eyes blazed with anger and fear.

I nodded. It was all I could do. After all, I didn't actually want to go off the deep end. I wanted a life with my friends. I wanted Mac. And maybe, if it was even possible, I wanted a chance to make up for the things I'd done.

"Good." She spoke between gritted teeth. I suspected I hadn't heard the end of her anger on this one. "Now let's get far away from those elemental fuckers and figure out what we do next."

CHAPTER 2

We headed northeast, taking little-used roads that added hours to our trip. We drove across a land of red rocks that gave way to pale brown desert and scrub as we approached New Mexico. The sun crept toward the western horizon, but there weren't any trees or structures tall enough to cast long shadows. We kept all the windows in the Airstream open for a cross-breeze, but that only helped so much when it felt like the air itself could leave scorch marks.

When we stopped for the night, everyone tumbled from the various vehicles, but there was none of the usual stretching and groaning that accompanied the end of a long drive. Our eyes were watchful, scanning the flat land in all directions.

"It's clear." Vivian still held her laptop. Sometimes, I thought it was fused to her hand. "I've been tracking their car. They stopped in Flagstaff thirty minutes after we lost them and haven't moved."

That put almost four hundred miles between us and the council.

The mood instantly lifted. Agent Johnson stepped toward Carmichael and grasped his partner's shoulder in a strong, manly show of solidarity. Where Carmichael had dark blond hair and blue eyes and looked like he could be cast as Captain America's uptight brother, Johnson was taller, darker, and stronger. Despite these physical differences, both men were serious agents who only wanted to help the good guys and catch the bad ones—even if those lines weren't as clear as they used to be.

Miriam popped the back of the Bronco open and pulled a bottle from the cooler. If we were done driving, it was beer o'clock. She smacked it against the trailer hitch to open it.

Mac did what he'd done every day since we started running. He walked to me with fear in his eyes.

"You okay?" He wasn't scared of me, though I sometimes thought he should be. He was scared we wouldn't find a cure in time. They all were.

"I'm good." I forced a smile I knew he wouldn't believe.

It was crazy to think Mac could fear anything. He was somewhere between huge and freaking enormous, and that was in his human form. When he was a bear, he got to add claws and teeth to the whole intimidation package. The fact that he also had thick dark hair and melting brown eyes and a wide, handsome face—and was honest and loyal to a fault—just meant I'd never really had a chance. I'd started falling for him the first day we'd met.

We'd never put a name to what was between us. If we'd been humans, we'd have been dating for months now. We certainly would have enjoyed some naked fun time, maybe talked about moving in together.

Instead, we'd spent our days trying to solve murders or find kidnapped children while I slid toward madness. It hadn't made for a conventional courtship.

Even so, the cord that tied us together was stronger than it had ever been, and it wasn't just the tiny bit of my magic that now lived within him, permanently entwined with his shifter power. I was his, whatever that was worth, and I was pretty sure he felt the same about me. Most days, that was enough.

Besides, it was hard to move a relationship forward while surrounded by so many helpful friends.

"She's pissing me off, Mac," Sera called. "Control your woman."

I made a face at her, and she only raised an eyebrow in reply. Mac waited for an explanation.

"I might have tapped into my magic but only for a few seconds and that's why we're not having a battle with evil elementals right now but I won't do it again." I spoke into the collar of my shirt. When there was no response, I forced myself to raise my eyes.

I was hoping for frustrated, maybe exasperated, but that wasn't what I got. Thunderstorms had fewer clouds than Mac wore on his face.

"We'll talk later," he bit off, then disappeared into the Airstream. When he returned, he carried a five-gallon container of gas for the Bronco. He filled the tank without meeting my eyes.

The awkward silence was interrupted by a booming voice. Miriam's vocals had two settings: loud and blow your eardrums. "At the risk of stating the obvious, we're even more in the middle of nowhere than we were this morning. Please tell me one of you fuckers has a plan that doesn't involve running from elementals for the next ten years." While the words were sharp, she spoke with the hint of a smile. It took a lot more than being lost in the middle of a desert to freak Miriam out.

Vivian dropped to the ground out of habit, though she required rich soil rather than a dry desert to recharge. "Well, we know they're not tracking the cars. If so, they'd have followed us."

"Except they were in a sedan," Carmichael noted. "They couldn't have followed us far off-road, even if they were tracking us."

Sera disagreed, which was to be expected. The two of them had an unspoken competition, though no one else seemed to understand the rules. "That sedan could go anywhere the camper could. Plus, we checked the cars last week, same time we switched to new burner phones. We've been careful."

"A lot happens in a week," Simon reminded her.

"From now on, daily checks," I said.

We knelt on the ground and peered into each wheel well, and when we found nothing Miriam brought out a flashlight to be extra thorough. It wouldn't have been the first time someone used a GPS device to track us.

I almost hoped we'd find something. A nice, easily smashable electronic, and then we'd be free again.

Each vehicle was clean.

"Could they be in touch with local law enforcement? I mean, Stephen Grant is an ice, but he's also a cop in Tahoe. Maybe they're getting some local help?" I was thinking aloud, trying to fit the pieces together.

Again, Sera disagreed. "The help would need to be a desert or stone. There aren't any waters out here, and we know they haven't told anyone else they let a dual escape. If they had, every damn elemental in the world would be looking for us."

"What about that glitch at the motel?" I looked at Vivian's laptop with distrust.

Vivian didn't look worried. "That was patchy internet. It happens."

Sera hesitated. Sera never hesitated, so she had to be carefully considering her next words. "But on the extreme off-chance that someone is finding us electronically, would it hurt to go off-grid for a little bit? As a test, Vivian."

Vivian's lips thinned. "It won't make any difference."

Miriam threw her cell phone battery into the middle of

the group. "I always hated these fucking things anyway," she grinned, doing her best to break the tension.

We all followed suit. Anything that sent or received signals was turned off.

Vivian watched the electronic carnage with displeasure. "It's not me. It would be easier for them to access bank records than track this computer."

"Good point. Cash only." I pulled out my wallet and counted the money. "Twenty-three dollars," I announced.

"I've got five." Sera held up a single bill.

"Forty-six cents." Miriam's contribution fit in the palm of her hand.

"Two hundred seventy-six dollars." We all blinked at Simon. "One never knows when a high-quality sushi meal will be required."

Sera plucked the bills from his hand, adding them to the pot. "Sushi can wait. This will last us while we confirm they're not finding us through any computers."

Vivian mumbled something about how she was already setting false money trails, but no one was listening. It felt good to take any action, even an unnecessary one.

Mac replaced the empty fuel can in the Airstream, then leaned against the hood of the Bronco, eyes closed. He wasn't relaxing. Mac might not talk a lot, at least compared to the rest of us, but I knew he was listening, sifting through the possibilities and finding the truth in his own time. When he spoke, it was usually because he had something worth saying. "What if they're using the same system we are?"

Two lines formed between Sera's brows. "But we've been relying mostly on the info we found in Josiah's files. He had years of research on this other dual."

She rushed through the sentence. We never wanted to forget our father—couldn't if we tried—but it hurt to say his name. He'd been amoral and manipulative, with absolutely no respect for personal boundaries, but he was our father, and he shouldn't be dead.

I dragged my mind back from the dark thoughts. Remembering Josiah's death and the events it triggered was a surefire way to rouse the cruelest part of my magic.

I focused on Mac. "That's not what you meant, though."

He met my eyes for only a second, then looked away. Yeah, he was still mad. "The East Texas address we found in Josiah's file was a bust, so we started looking at all the other possibilities he found. Every town that's had some unexplained incident, anything that might have been the work of an elemental. What's to stop the council from following that same trail? Once they figured out what we were doing, it would be easy enough."

Sera considered it, fingers tapping against her leg to release excess energy. "Somehow, the old ones always find a way to track public magic use."

Johnson looked less convinced. "It's a pretty big leap. What would draw them to the southwest in the first place? You could just as likely be hiding in Tasmania, or Outer Mongolia. Or the Prince's Islands, where Josiah thought there was another dual."

"Why did we not look for that dual?" Simon asked. "It is a much smaller area to explore, and I understand the Turks are fond of cats."

"A Homeland Security system that even Vivian didn't want to hack."

"I'd prefer to stay out of a terrorist detention facility, if it's all the same to you," she agreed.

"We can sail there," I reminded Simon. "It would only take a month or two."

I thought he actually turned green.

"We're here because it was the best choice at the time.

We had an address. Then we had a forwarding address," I said.

Sera leaned against the Airstream. She didn't even notice the scorching metal. "And then we were lost. Hell, maybe we should go to Turkey. Why not?"

Carmichael fidgeted. That was definitely outside his jurisdiction.

"No." I hadn't meant to be quite so loud. I lowered my voice. "It's a long way to go. And it's a long way back if we don't find anything." I didn't finish the thought, but we all knew. I was already living on borrowed time. "At least we have another lead, right? Something in New Mexico? It doesn't matter if they're finding us by following our path or using bloodhounds or if they hired their own traveling psychic. It changes nothing. Our only hope of finding the answers I need is to find another dual. It's all we've got."

Miriam chucked the empty bottle into the recycling container next to the cooler. "You said northwest New Mexico, Vivian?"

Vivian's gaze was fixed to her computer, and her fingers stroked the keys as it powered down. "That was the last possibility I found. I won't be able to get our next location if we're offline, you know. Plus, this will delay me looking into that whole boy-in-car thing. I think I was making progress, too."

"We need to leave it for now." Sera ground out the words. I wasn't much happier. We still didn't know the full reason David killed Josiah. All we had to go on was the stone's quiet statement that Josiah murdered his mother and he'd been "the boy in the car."

Still, if we could only find one answer at a time, one was more time sensitive than the other. "Let's go," I said, trying to sound more upbeat than any of us felt.

No one argued. We'd chosen to run, and we would

keep running until we found what we needed, or until we were caught.

Those were our only options.

WE NEEDED TO REPLACE THE WATER I'D USED DURING OUR escape, so our small caravan crept back toward civilization, though we drove parallel to the highway as much as possible. We found an old truck stop not far from the state line. It had a single security camera, which was disabled when a black cat perched atop it and drooped his front paws across the lens.

While the others filled the trailer with water and loaded up on supplies, I sought out Sera.

She sat at the small table in the Airstream, the black case resting on the laminate surface. I slid onto the bench across from her.

Sera raised her eyes and we looked at each other for a long time. We'd always been able to have long conversations without speaking, but these days we had so many unexpressed thoughts that even our silent discussions were filled with double meanings and uncertainty.

When the silence veered from loaded to downright awkward, she moved to the freezer tucked under the counter. Holding a kitchen towel in one hand, she filled it with ice and twisted it closed.

"Here." She handed it to me and returned to her seat. "Put it on your face. You should use as little magic as you can, even to heal."

I waved it off. She hadn't hit me hard enough to bruise, and I suspected she knew that. "Is this your version of an apology?"

"Did you hear me use either the words 'I'm' or 'sorry'? Then no."

I wasn't ready to apologize, either. "What else could I have done?"

"Nothing! You do nothing, Aidan. Damn it. I've lost too many people already. Our father. Christopher. Hell, I've been losing people my whole life."

She paused, swallowing whatever she'd been about to say. Sera rarely spoke of her mother, who died when she was thirteen. Elementals were long-lived, but we weren't immortal. Any sudden trauma would kill us as easily as it would a human.

When she spoke again, her words were measured. "I'm not losing anyone else. I don't care if I have to burn those council assholes myself."

"You're not a killer, Sera. You'd never be the same."

She held my eyes, her own so serious I barely recognized them. "But I'd be sane. Can you say the same thing?"

She was right, and at the same time she was so very wrong. "You know who you sound like?"

One side of her mouth quirked in the tiniest of smiles. "What can I say? Like father, like daughter."

"Daughters," I corrected. "And if we're not careful, we're all going to die in our efforts to protect each other."

Like Josiah already had.

Sera's jaw was set, her expression as rigid as her thoughts. "You proved I was innocent when the council was ready to execute me. You already protected me. Now it's my turn." She opened the case. Nearly all the syringes were empty.

It was a harsh reminder of how many times I'd lost myself over the last three months. Each time the madness threatened to overpower me, I felt a sharp prick in my neck and I lost days. When I awoke, it felt like I'd been trampled by a herd of buffalo, or possibly a herd of eighteen-wheelers, but the madness would have receded… for a little while.

"What's the plan, Sera? Keep me drugged until we find this dual?" I meant it as a joke.

She didn't laugh.

"We don't have enough," I said.

I tried not to show my agitation. I knew the drug was the only thing holding me together, but I hated it. Every time I came to after a dose, I felt different. Duller. The serum hadn't exactly gone through rigorous FDA testing. We had no idea what the long-term effects might be.

Sera withdrew one needle. The liquid inside was a pale gold, and as the late afternoon sun glinted off it, it seemed to glow. Something about the syringe was different, but before I could articulate what it was, Sera leaned across the table and stabbed me, hitting the plunger in the same motion.

She watched me. I gave her credit for that. She didn't turn from my look of shock and betrayal.

"I wasn't out of control," I protested. Already I was dissolving, my words slurring as the magic slid away.

"You almost were this morning. It's time for preventative measures."

"It was…" My tongue was thick in my mouth and the words stuck, but I realized what was different. There'd only been a small amount of liquid in the syringe.

"A tiny dose, yeah. We're nearly out of the full ones, so I'm hoping a few drops will block your magic for a couple days without knocking you out. Maybe get us to Turkey after all."

I tried to glare, but my heavy eyes and slack jaw made that difficult. I slid off the plastic seat and became a puddle on the floor.

"Well, that didn't work," Sera muttered, just before I lost consciousness.

CHAPTER 3

One would think the after-effects of a quarter dose of the drug would be less painful than a full dose. One would be wrong.

I swallowed. Even that tiny movement caused a wave of nausea that radiated outward from my stomach until it seemed my entire body wanted to retch.

The nausea receded at last, likely because the pounding in my head now demanded my full attention. I groaned, and even that hurt.

I waited, letting my body return to some facsimile of equilibrium. When I thought I might be able to move without dying, I pried my eyes open.

It was still night, though I didn't think dawn was far off. Someone had moved me to the bed after Sera drugged me.

I sat up halfway and stopped, unable to even scream as every nerve ending in my body lit up. There was hurt, and then there was agony, and then there was this. Tears slid down my cheeks as my body cycled through one stabbing pain after another, tiny needles cutting into each cell.

I stared at the glowing green numbers of the digital alarm clock without blinking, focusing all my attention outside my body. The numbers turned over ten times. At last, the pain ebbed and became something I could manage with the help of an entire bottle of Advil.

It had taken too long. Last time, I'd struggled for about

six minutes. It was getting worse.

Sera had a hell of a lot of explaining to do.

I pushed back the thin cotton sheet and eased first one leg, then the other to the floor. I swayed as I stood, and I needed to wait another two minutes before I dared move again.

With each staggering step toward the trailer door, the pain decreased and righteous anger took its place. Sera was my sister and my best friend, and she'd done this to me.

I threw the door open. The clanging of the aluminum door against the side of the trailer sounded unnaturally loud on the flat terrain, which had no trees or water to absorb the noise. It would wake everyone up, but I didn't care. I already planned to do that.

"What the hell is wrong with you?" I shouted as I stepped outside.

My fury increased when I realized I was talking to myself.

The group sometimes fell asleep around the fire pit. As hot as it was during the day, the temperature could drop thirty degrees at night. There were still a few embers glowing in the makeshift fire pit, but no one was gathered around it.

"You're kidding me. Sera, get out here." There was no reply. I glanced through the window of the Bronco, still hooked up to the trailer. It was empty. "Don't even try to avoid this. First you slap me, then you drug me when I was completely fine. I expect groveling."

I rounded the trailer and froze.

"This may not be the best time for a heartfelt apology." Her tone was dry, but her dark eyes held no hint of humor. They weren't focused on me, either. All her attention was reserved for the tall man with a gun standing about twenty feet away from me.

Most people would see the man himself as a threat. Though not as big as Mac, he was several inches over six feet and well-built. His jeans outlined long, ropey muscles and the biceps peeking out of his t-shirt were three times the size of any water's arms, but his physical strength didn't concern me. The weapon he held was another matter.

I knew little about firearms. They were one of the few ways to instantly kill an elemental, even an old one, so we tended to be big believers in gun control. It was a handgun, rather than a shotgun, and it didn't look like one of the modern blocks of metal I saw in most action movies. If anything, it looked more like the six-shooters from old westerns.

My friends were gathered before him. Vivian, Miriam, and Sera lay in their sleeping bags. The agents had pulled themselves to standing, but they'd clearly been caught off-guard. They wore sweatpants and t-shirts, and neither had their weapon. Simon crouched on top of the van, still in cat form. Mac had been sleeping apart from the others, and now he stood a full thirty feet away, too far to rush an armed man without finding a new bullet hole in his chest. Even so, I didn't think he'd ruled that option out.

The stranger slid his eyes to me, though the weapon never wavered. He was outnumbered, and my appearance only tilted the scales further in our favor, but he showed no sign of nerves. "Come on, then. Join your friends."

A growl rumbled through the night.

The man was smart enough to move his eyes toward Mac. "You're weighing the odds right now, aren't you? Figuring out how fast you can move versus how fast I can pull the trigger. I'll give you a hint." He swung the gun to his right until the barrel pointed straight at me. "Not fast enough."

The growl didn't subside, but Mac remained where he was.

The man had no room for mistakes. We tracked his every move, waiting for an opening.

Miriam didn't bother waiting. "Are you stupid?"

His attention turned to the brunette pulling her legs from the sleeping bag. His brow furrowed, either in surprise that she wasn't cowed by his threats or in confusion that he was being insulted by one of the world's most adorable women. Miriam was an otter shifter, and though she'd proven many times that she was a grade-A badass, I still wanted to coo over her enormous brown eyes and button nose.

"What?" he asked.

"Seemed a straight-forward question to me." She stood, ignoring the gun now pointed in her direction. "You don't have that slack-jawed idiot look, but maybe you just aren't good at math. There's one of you and one of that cute penis substitute you're holding. Looks like it holds six bullets, and there are eight of us. So I guess the real question is, how fast can you shoot?" She took a step toward him.

With his attention diverted by Miriam, I moved forward. I had no idea what I was going to do, but I damn sure wasn't going to cower in the corner while an armed man threatened my friends.

He caught my movement in his peripheral vision and turned toward me. Mac took advantage of the distraction to step closer. We came at him from three sides, taking advantage of our greater numbers.

Even so, the man's expression remained relaxed, even confident. "If you lot are willing to sacrifice one of yourselves, well, that might work. Course, one of you will be dead afterwards, so that plan does have its downside. The other option, now, is to talk like reasonable people."

"I'd feel a lot more reasonable if you weren't holding us at gunpoint," I said.

He laughed. "And I'd feel a lot safer if a pissed-off giant wasn't creeping toward me, but we don't always get what we want."

He pointed the handgun at Mac, who didn't even seem to notice. The stranger sighed and swung it toward me. Mac froze.

"Yeah, I thought it might be like that." For the first time, he really looked at me.

He reached into his pocket. A second later, I recoiled from the harsh glare of a flashlight. I shielded my eyes, but the light had already moved on. It paused on each of us for a few seconds, even swinging upwards to where Simon crouched on the camper's roof.

"Now, this is interesting. A fire," he nodded at Sera. "That might make sense in a desert, but I'd be more likely to find a cat in a rocking chair factory than a water out here in the middle of August."

I met Sera's eyes. For him to know what we were by looking at us, he had to be an elemental himself. It meant he also had to know how strong we were, because only those with dominant elemental blood had the traditional coloring.

He knew how powerful we were and still wasn't scared.

"Fair's fair. Show yourself." My voice didn't waver, and it wasn't even false bravado. I was just done being afraid of people threatening to kill me. The novelty had worn off long ago.

"And blind myself with my own light? I'm thinking that's not a great idea."

"What's your plan?" Sera asked, following Miriam's lead and pulling herself from the sleeping bag.

"I'm interested in learning what you're doing here. We're smack dab in the middle of nowhere. I don't get a lot of visitors out this way."

I shook my head. "We're only passing through. How about this? We get in our vehicles and drive away. You never see us again, and we don't get shot. Everyone wins." I thought that was a fair compromise.

He didn't seem to agree. "It's too late for that. You've already seen me. Your name, blondie."

That was the final straw for Mac. Hold guns on his friends, that was bad. Give me a disparaging nickname, and someone had to bleed.

Mac's clothes ripped in half, falling from his body in shreds as the bear emerged. At least he was only wearing boxers and a t-shirt for sleeping. Mac's temper meant he had a higher clothes budget than the rest of us.

The man swung the gun toward him, eyes widening in shock and fear. Mac as a human was intimidating as hell. As a bear, he could make grown men wet themselves.

Unfortunately, we'd stumbled upon one of the few who was either too brave or too stupid to flee for his life when faced with an enormous black bear.

His finger tightened on the trigger. Panicked, I reached for what little magic I could access.

There was nothing there. The drug was still exiting my system, leaving me powerless.

I launched myself toward the man, no thought in my head but to somehow defy all laws of physics and reach him before he sent a bullet into Mac. As soon as I started running, Mac raced for me, trying to head me off before I reached the other elemental.

Sera chose the more dramatic solution and set the stranger's hand on fire.

"The bullets will explode!" I yelled back to her.

"Not hot enough," she assured me, though she pulled back on the flames a little.

"Still pretty damn risky," the man said, undisturbed. The fire disappeared, but he didn't drop the heated metal.

Only another fire would be immune to that heat—or to anything else Sera could throw at him.

It also meant he couldn't hurt me or Sera, not with magic. Even in the limited light I could see he didn't have the dark coloring of a strong fire. He was much too tall, as well. He was more human than elemental, but he still had enough power to hurt our friends.

I was ten feet away when he sent a fireball straight at me. It hit the center of my chest and my body absorbed it. Energy filled me as my fire magic fed. The man's eyes narrowed, calculating.

My plan wasn't fancy. I would run at the man, and then I would tackle him. We'd figure out the rest later.

I never made it. With only two feet to go, the ground rose to greet me, the desert sand swirling around me. It flew into my ears and mouth, my nostrils and eyes, until I could only gasp and choke. I fell to my knees, retching.

The attack ceased as soon as I stopped moving. I expelled the last of the sand from my throat and cleared my eyes.

When I looked up, all was silent. Everyone stared at the newcomer. Even Mac studied him, his furry head tilted to the side as he considered this new information. No one moved, not even the stranger. He seemed as surprised by his actions as the rest of us were.

"People," I managed, the words raspy, "it looks like we found the other dual magic."

CHAPTER 4

"A what?" For the first time, he didn't sound like a cocky bastard.

I should have moved away from him, what with the tendency dual magics had to lose control, but my feet carried me toward him without bothering to consult my brain.

It wasn't only because we'd been looking for him for months now, though I was plenty happy for our search to come to an end. It wasn't even that he might have information I needed.

I was drawn to him for the simplest reason. If he was like me, that meant I wasn't alone. I wasn't the only one.

The night was retreating, allowing dawn to creep over the horizon. With the growing light, I could make out features that had been hidden before. He had a strong face with sloping cheekbones and a straight nose, a solid jaw currently clenched until a small muscle twitched in his left cheek. It wasn't a harsh face, though. If anything, the long lashes and the dimple in his chin softened his appearance. I wondered if he minded when people called him pretty.

Like me, he didn't have the traditional fire coloring of black hair and eyes. On the outside, I was a perfect water, and he appeared to be nothing more than a desert. His hair was a medium sandy blond, his gold-flecked eyes closer to amber than brown. Even his skin was tanned to a burnished gold. He reminded me of a rancher accustomed to spending days in the sun, but without the leathery skin that tended to come with such work. Our extended lifespan was possible thanks to our high-octane healing powers. Sun damage really wasn't a concern.

The man was still trying to look innocent. It wasn't an expression that suited him.

"Well, you controlled desert and fire," I said. "If you have some explanation for how that's possible other than you being a dual, we'd love to hear it. Perhaps someone's hiding nearby?" I gestured at the flat landscape surrounding us.

I could practically see his mind racing, though his words were slow and lazy. "I'm a desert, sure. Don't know what you're talking about with the fire."

Sera didn't bother to remind him that his hand was unburnt. Instead, she hurled a ball of fire at him. He didn't have a chance to duck.

He also didn't burn.

"Good thing you were right," muttered Vivian.

The man studied each of us, his face wary. He ended on me, and he considered me for quite a while. Long enough for the sky to lighten another degree and for whatever thoughts churned behind his eyes to settle. At last, he lowered his gun, though I noticed he still kept his finger near the trigger. "You're a bit more than what you seem, too. Aren't you?"

I inclined my head, acknowledging the truth. He'd seen my watery-looking self absorb my own ball of fire. There was little point arguing.

"You're not here to kill me." He stated it as a fact.

"No."

"You gonna try telling me that a couple of old-as-sin waters appearing in the southwest same time as you is a coincidence?"

It was my turn to try looking innocent. He snorted.

"Right. So what are you doing here?"

I smiled with a bit too much enthusiasm. I much preferred talking to standoffs with firearms. "You. I mean, we didn't know who you were, only what. So we were searching for the abstract you, not the specific you, if that makes sense. I'm Aidan Brook, by the way," I added as an afterthought.

He wasn't impressed by my explanation, though the last bit caught his attention. "Brook. That's one of the old names. I imagine a dual from one of those families would attract a fair bit of attention. You probably should find a different name."

"Is that what you did?" Sera asked.

"It's harder to find someone who doesn't exist."

"Who were you originally?" Vivian asked. I knew she itched to power up her computer and examine every identity he'd ever had to learn why he'd been so difficult to find.

The man tutted at her, as though she'd asked a naughty question.

"It doesn't matter," I assured him. "Though I'm curious to learn if you've been running so no one would discover you're crazy. Are you, by the way? Crazy?" Why ignore the elephant in the room when you can climb on its back and go for a ride?

"Are you?" he countered.

"Only sometimes." I was opening my mouth to share my entire life story when Mac appeared at my elbow, a gentle reminder to shut the hell up. He'd shifted back and pulled on a pair of jeans.

"What's your name?" Mac asked, eyes narrowed.

The man spun his gun once and slid it into a hip holster. He hooked the thumb of his other hand into a belt loop of his jeans and raised one side of his mouth, more smirk than smile. If we'd ordered a hot cowboy from Central Casting, we couldn't have done any better.

"Luke."

"No way."

He glanced at me, eyebrows raised. "You don't believe me?"

"There's no way you're named Luke. Or Colt or Jed or any other perfect cowboy name. You were born a Frederick, admit it."

His mouth widened in a grin, displaying straight white teeth against tanned skin. He raised his hand to his forehead, tipping an imaginary hat. "You can call me anything you want, darlin'."

I gripped Mac's forearm before he could call Luke a few choice names himself. "It's better than blondie," I whispered.

Luke watched Mac, unconcerned. "Well, with two duals here, any fight will be mutually assured destruction. So how's about we all put up our arms—" Luke gave Mac's biceps a pointed look, "—and head inside before the day gets too hot for anyone who's not a desert or a fire. I've got a little place about half a mile up the road."

He headed northeast, following a trail no one else could see.

We waited several seconds, having as many conversations as we could through loaded looks and emphatic gestures, but it was pointless. He was the reason we'd spent nearly three months driving around the southwest and most of Texas. Of course we were going to follow him.

We were halfway to his house before I realized he never said whether he was crazy.

———

House was a generous description of the structure. It had four walls and a roof, but my version of a house had conveniences like soft beds, internet access, and indoor plumbing.

Instead, we found a structure that appeared to have risen from the desert floor itself, the walls bleached from constant exposure to the merciless sun. A covered well and several large buckets stood on the hut's east side. I stretched my magic into the depths of the well to greet the water gathered at the bottom. It was stagnant and lacked the vibrance of the lakes and rivers in the Tahoe area.

I ignored the pang of homesickness. It had been too many months since I fed from either Lake Tahoe or the Truckee River. Other than a quick trip to the Gulf Coast and another to the Rio Grande, I'd been limited to flat, still lakes. Since we started running in June, I'd recharged where I could, because I needed to, but it never felt like home.

It wasn't just the fresh, vibrant water I missed. I missed the A-frame cabin, with its living room covered in floor pillows and the ugliest orange curtains this side of the 1970s. I missed the upside down teddy bear wallpaper and the spiral staircase that took me to my small bedroom, where Vivian sometimes lived across the hall and Simon slept upstairs. When I cracked the window, I could hear the river rumbling by. I didn't sleep as well anywhere else as I did in that cabin.

Home meant safety. I had to believe I'd see it again.

For now, I fed off the stale well water, and soon the last residue of the drug exited my system. My power remained dull, but I was getting used to it. It was the cost of using the serum, and I tried not to think about whether that cost was permanent.

Luke's home didn't have a door so much as a heavy

piece of wood covering a large opening. He grabbed it on either side and easily moved it out of the way. Next to me, Miriam made an appreciative sound.

I slid my eyes toward her.

"What? Being a dual doesn't mean he can't be hot. You better hope that's true, at least."

I couldn't deny she had a point. While I'd developed an appreciation for men built like small trucks, Luke's lean body held a certain appeal, particularly when his back and shoulder muscles flexed under his cotton shirt.

Heat filled me that had nothing to do with the attractive stranger or the rising temperature. Even before I faced him, I knew Mac stared at me. His expression was opaque. Before I could say anything, he walked away, joining the agents as they pulled up in the vehicles.

"You're going to need to move those." Luke told them. "There's a decent-sized ridge five miles north of here. The overhang should hide them."

Sera glanced into the dark room. "No."

"This isn't a discussion." Luke drew a bucket of water from the well. As his biceps bulged and released, I was pretty sure I heard Miriam whimper.

Sera wasn't so easily distracted. "Ten minutes ago, you were pointing a gun at us. We're going to keep our escape route open."

He grabbed the full bucket off the rope, then faced Sera.

Carmichael stepped closer, and I resisted the urge to yank him back. The agent hadn't always shown sound judgment when interacting with the magical world. Placing himself between two ludicrously powerful elementals was a terrible idea, but he might not figure that out before he was dead.

Luke set the bucket on the ground and leaned against

the adobe wall. From a distance, it was a casual, even relaxed pose, but tension thrummed through his body. He was prepared for a fight.

"For the last eight weeks, everywhere I go I've gotta worry that some old one's gonna turn up. I've been keeping a low profile for a damn long time, and up until recently, it wasn't that hard. All the old ones, anyone who might know what I am or what's supposed to happen to someone like me, I knew where they were. Now I've got strangers traveling around every place I've ever lived, and you lot show up out of the blue in all the same places."

I felt a stab of guilt. He was safe until we decided to find him.

Sera didn't appear to feel the same. Her eyes flashed and her fingers tapped against her thigh.

"Of course it's not a coincidence." I spoke in a rush to intercept whatever Sera was about to say. "But we already said we don't want to kill you. We're here for information, and dead people don't answer questions. But while you don't know us, we don't know you, either. Until we're sure you don't have some medieval torture chamber in there," I waved toward the inside of the hut, "we're taking your word that you won't kill us."

A clever woman would have stopped there. "By the way, how are you doing with that whole sanity thing?" I offered my brightest, most helpful smile, the smile of a woman who'd never thought of hurting another, and I ignored the shadow stirring to life now that the drug had worn off.

Luke offered an inarticulate shrug, though a smile played on his lips as he watched me, through pure force of will, stop talking.

"It's not up for discussion," he repeated. "This is my secret home. It has no records, and it's impossible to see on any map or satellite. Even someone in a helicopter would have a tough job finding it. If you want to learn whatever you're here to learn, you'll move those shiny heaps of metal where they can't be seen."

He disappeared into the hut.

"Let's move them," I decided. "We can't ask him to trust us if we won't do the same."

"And if he tries something, I'll take him." Miriam grinned, possibly hoping it came to that.

Mac scowled, but he didn't argue when Johnson climbed into the camper van and Miriam slid behind the wheel of the Bronco. We watched them drive off until they were out of sight, then moved toward Luke's home.

I stepped into the darkness.

THE INSIDE DID NOTHING TO DISPEL MY FIRST IMPRESSIONS. It was, at most, fifteen feet in either direction. The floor was packed earth, the walls unpainted adobe. The only furniture was a cabinet that doubled as a counter, a large cooler, and a twin mattress held off the ground by a crude wooden bed frame.

The cooler was the only thing that didn't look like it was cobbled together from items found on the side of the road. It was high end, the sort that might keep food cold for several days despite the heat. Most elementals had more than their share of money—live long enough, and even a conservative investor would became wealthy enough to buy a small island—but the cooler was the only sign Luke hadn't gambled his fortune away one drunken night in Vegas.

The room was barely large enough to hold all of us, and there were no chairs. Mac claimed one corner, where he could best observe the entire room. Sera perched on the edge of the mattress and Carmichael followed, keeping several inches of space between them.

Simon had assumed his human form for the walk to Luke's home. He glanced around the dark room, unimpressed. A second later, he returned to his cat self. He strode outside, a tiny bundle of pure grace, then ruined the effect by flopping on the ground with his belly exposed to the sun.

Luke watched the transformation, his expression somewhere between shock and amusement. "If we're trading answers here, I'd appreciate it if one of you lot could explain why people keep turning into animals. I heard rumors, but figured that's all they were."

I couldn't help smiling at his confusion. Many fulls weren't taught about shifters, though we shared a similar origin story.

Both races were born from the earth's first magic, but whereas we were born of humans and magic, they'd been born of animals and magic. The old ones tended to find this, to use the technical term, icky. Many of them preferred to deny shifters existed rather than share their origin story with creatures they considered polluted. The original magic that created shifters lived for a while in human form, which was why shifters could assume both human and animal shapes, but that made no difference to the old ones.

"I'll let Simon fill you in. He loves correcting elementals' ignorance." Luke nodded his thanks and moved to the counter, pulling bowls and utensils from the cupboard. He seemed to consider my response good enough for now. Whatever else he was, the man wasn't easily ruffled.

I wished I could say the same. I bent to pick up Simon's discarded clothes but saw no place to put them. Instead, I folded them and set the neat pile back on the ground.

Luke dipped a glass measuring cup into the bucket of water he'd drawn from the well, then held his fingers to the cup. A few seconds later, he poured boiling water over a bunch of eggs and into a large French press filled with ground coffee.

No one seemed inclined to speak.

"Is this some sort of Walden Pond, go back to nature thing?" I asked to break the silence.

Luke pulled out a loaf of crusty bread and cut several thick pieces. It was one of those artisanal loaves, the sort that went stale in a day. He might live here, but he still visited civilization on a regular basis to collect supplies.

All eyes were on the serrated blade he'd used to slice the bread. He replied while gesturing with the knife, big sweeping motions that didn't come near any of our bodies. I didn't feel threatened. I thought he was messing with us.

"Well, I can't say it's a bad idea to get away from the concrete and air conditioning, but if I recall, Walden Pond was all about deliberate solitude. Being here isn't a choice I made." He ended with a pointed look at me, both eyebrows raised, but he also set the knife down. "So, care to tell me why a dual, a strong fire, a…" He looked at Vivian, who sat cross-legged in the corner. "…An earth?"

She confirmed his guess. Vivian was too weak to have the traditional physical characteristics that strongly marked both me and Sera—or Luke, for that matter. Powerful earths' hair and eyes were nearly the same shade, the deep brown of the richest soil, and Vivian's eyes were hazel. However, she was also too damn calm and grounded to be anything else.

"Okay then. Why are several elementals, a couple of humans, and some people who turn into animals all looking for me if they don't want to capture or kill me?"

It looked like the small talk was over. "I'm trying to

understand what I am. The dual part, I mean. I don't know any others."

Luke's expression softened a bit. "You won't find any others, darlin'. So far as I've been able to tell, they're all dead. The old ones made sure of that."

Mac's eyes darkened. I feared, if Luke didn't start calling me by my actual name, or perhaps "Ms. Brook, the woman I'm not even a little interested in," he'd find himself with claw marks in unexpected places.

"Because of the crazy."

Luke took a bite of buttered bread and swallowed before answering. "Because of the crazy. Most don't learn to control it. I only knew one other, about a hundred years ago. He hid it as best as he could, but our kind of nuts doesn't sit quietly in a corner. Eventually, it needs to be heard, and the kind of destruction that happens then… let's just say it draws attention."

Excitement rose. I was only in my sixties, though few would peg me as being older than my early twenties. Still, for a full, I was practically a baby. If Luke was already more than a century, there might be hope.

"How old was the other one?" Carmichael asked.

"Forty."

Damn.

Still, he'd said most don't know how to control it, and most wasn't the same as all.

It was a start. I turned to Mac, who'd moved closer to me. He no longer had murder in his eyes. Instead, they held the same hope I was allowing myself to feel.

"But it can be controlled?" The words came out higher than expected. Sera learned forward, elbows on her knees. Sparks flew from her fingers. She tucked her hands under her thighs to hide the agitation.

Luke hadn't expected the intensity of our response.

"You don't know? I guess you wouldn't, if you never met any others." He smiled at me, and again I was aware of our connection. It wasn't physical, not even emotional. It felt like I'd found one of my people.

"No one knew what I was. Except my father, and he never..." I stopped, remembering Josiah's last moments, dead on the floor of a library, and I remembered my response. The death I'd caused, not out of self-defense or by accident, but out of the need for retribution. In a life of questionable choices, it was the only thing I'd done that was truly unforgivable.

I reached for the cup of coffee Luke handed me. I rarely drank it, preferring tea, but the simple act of stirring in milk and a bit of sugar was calming. I handed the cup to Sera. She preferred it black, but she never turned down morning coffee.

Sera finished my thought. "Our father never found a cure."

Luke's eyes flicked between us, seeing no family resemblance, but he shrugged and kept going. "Well, it's not common knowledge, to be fair. I didn't know there was a cure until I stumbled right into it. I guess I got lucky." He didn't sound certain.

"What is it? How do I get it? Can we do it today?" The words rushed out, and only Luke's pained expression kept me from badgering him further.

Luke rolled one of the boiled eggs on a table to crack it, then peeled off the shell. He sprinkled salt on the top, then bit off half.

If I was a suspicious sort, I'd say he was stalling.

He finished the egg and washed it down with a sip of coffee. "Are you that far gone? No other options?"

The madness writhed within me. Most of the time, I could hold it at bay, but it was always there, always looking for opportunities to escape.

It always found one.

"No," I said, with absolute certainty. "No other options."

He nodded, as if he expected that response. "Right. Well, I can help you with some basic stuff to get through the day. But if you want a permanent solution…"

"Yes," I interrupted. "Permanent, yes." I could barely contain myself. It was more than I'd dared to dream. If I could control myself, maybe even learn how other duals could be cured, I could reason with the council. I could convince the old ones I wasn't a threat.

Maybe they'd let me live.

"It's not going to be easy," he began. "In fact, it may be the hardest thing you've ever done. And I'll tell you what to do, but I won't go with you. Information's all you're getting. First, you'll need…"

He didn't finish. Simon rushed in, once again wearing skin, and began yanking on clothes. "Don't you hear it?"

He scowled, frustrated by our limited hearing.

Mac went still, listening. "It's the Bronco. It's coming back, fast. There's a second vehicle right behind it." He moved to my side, as if he could protect me through his bulk alone. "It's not the camper."

Sera and Carmichael stood, faces set. His gun was already drawn, and Sera's fingers sparked as her fire roared to life.

Luke calmly took another bite, then crouched by his bed and withdrew a well-worn canvas messenger bag. He slung this over his neck and arranged it so the bag was well-balanced. He unholstered his gun. "Suppose I knew I couldn't hide forever. Any chance this isn't the waters that've been following you?"

As much as I wanted to tell him there was a chance, it

would be a lie.

"Then I guess we're fighting our way out of this." He looked at me, and to my surprise his lips quirked. "You wanna be Butch or Sundance?"

Before I could respond, he stepped outside to face the council members who wanted us dead.

CHAPTER 5

The Bronco roared up with Miriam at the wheel and Johnson beside her. She always managed to cajole a bit more from the engine, and the SUV careened toward us at an unnatural speed. The camper van and Airstream were nowhere in sight.

The passenger door swung open before they came to a complete stop. Johnson jumped out. I'd only seen him and Carmichael in their capacity as FBI agents, which so far as I could tell required them to ask a lot of questions while wearing pained expressions. Though I knew Johnson had a military background, I was still surprised by how effortlessly he moved. He landed on the balls of his feet and spun, pulling the rear door open.

"Get in," hollered Miriam through the open window.

We rushed to obey, but it was too late. Miriam could only break so many laws of physics, and there was no way an old Bronco could outrun a brand new SUV at full acceleration. The council's new ride was a top of the line four-wheel drive with a big old performance engine. It drew to a rumbling stop in front of the Bronco.

Miriam reversed, making it a full hundred feet before she realized no one was attempting to escape with her. It was pointless. If we drove away, they'd follow us—and they were faster. She hit the brakes, but she didn't turn off the engine or step outside the vehicle.

The SUV's doors opened, and two elementals exited.

We'd known it was them. Simon had confirmed it. Even so, until they stood a few feet from me, I'd hoped he was wrong and it was two random waters chasing us across the desert. Maybe Deborah's and Michael's descendants, elementals with the same faces but a fraction of their power.

It was a foolish hope. Asking others to hunt me down would require the council to tell them what I was, and they wished to keep my existence secret. I was evidence of their failure, the dual magic who'd hidden under their collective noses for decades. They'd prefer to eradicate their failure with as few witnesses as possible.

Deborah Rivers was probably the oldest and most powerful water in the world, and she wasn't my biggest fan. Considering she'd seen me go batshit crazy and immolate a man while in the depths of madness, I couldn't really blame her.

Next to her stood Michael Bay, a man I remembered mainly for his unfortunate name and strong desire to run away from trouble rather than toward it. Despite this, he was an old one, and you didn't get to be his age without gathering a tremendous amount of power. He was nervous, and had likely hoped they never found us, but he could still drown my friends in a heartbeat, even in the middle of the desert.

They were the only remaining members of a governing body that should have held six members, a single representative from each of the old families. Three members had died. The sixth spot technically belonged to Grams, but she couldn't fulfill her duties while incarcerated. The slot should go to my great-grandmother or one of my aunts, but there'd been no effort to fill it. It would be a while before another Brook was welcome on the council.

Deborah appeared wary, but she wasn't afraid, and that worried me more than anything. They might be two of the strongest waters in the world, but that strength wasn't a guarantee against our ragtag group of magic, claws, and firearms.

My friends seemed to have a silent agreement to appear non-threatening. There was no reason to escalate things before we had to. Johnson, Carmichael, and Luke all held guns at their side, but they kept the safeties on. Simon and Mac remained in their human forms. Vivian stood next to Simon, seeking the comfort of her best friend. If it did come to a fight, she had no weapon of her own, and Simon could do little more than claw someone and run away. Miriam stood near them, her hard expression an unsettling contrast against her soft features.

As for Sera, she knew better than to summon any flames the others could extinguish with a thought. Instead, she tried to destroy them with a glare.

Deborah and Michael gave the others a cursory glance and saved their close scrutiny for me. I thought they were checking for signs of madness, and I resisted the urge to cross my eyes and have a conversation with myself. That might be considered escalating the situation.

"No lackeys?" I asked, pointing at the two of them, then gesturing to the nine of us. "Feeling that confident?"

Deborah took a step toward me, though Michael remained by the car.

She didn't look at me like I was a threat. Rather, she studied me with a curled lip, as though I was a bug she very much wanted to squash.

"I'm aware that you can destroy both of us with ease, Ms. Brook." The polite address was delivered with a sneer. "However, our deaths would cost you dearly."

Fear settled in my chest, a heavy weight, and I struggled to take a full breath. "You may not believe this, but I wasn't planning on hurting you or anyone else. Not again." Unbidden, the image of David writhing in a circle of flames rose to greet me.

I pushed the thought away. The madness might live in me, but I couldn't afford to live in it.

Deborah studied me. I doubted she missed a single expression on a face that had always been too transparent for my own good.

"Regardless of your intent, I believed insurance was necessary." She held out an unsealed envelope. It was large, the sort used to mail documents that shouldn't be folded.

I glanced at the others, seeing my uncertainty reflected in their eyes. I didn't want to play the game on her terms, but I saw no other option. I took the envelope and upended it, sliding its contents into my hand. It didn't contain documents. It held photos.

I flipped through them, then again more slowly, needing time to understand what I was seeing. With each image, my anger rose and the tight rein I kept on my power frayed.

The first photo was of the Rat Trap, a bar Sera and I knew well. As undergrads, we'd passed many drunken hours beneath its roof. It was owned by Frank, a human and a good man who had nothing to do with any of this. He wasn't even aware elementals existed. The front door was barred, a government sign in the windows informing me that the building was closed for health violations.

I moved to the next image. It featured an oversized monstrosity, a McMansion built in front of the Tahoe National Forest. The ugly home was little more than a gateway to that forest, where Carmen Avila shifted into a mountain lion and claimed the woods as her own.

The next photo was of a wooden house built sometime in the sixties. It was the home of Mac's uncle. Will had taken Mac in when he chose civilization over the feral life of a bear and left his father and brother behind in the forest. Mac's teenaged cousins also lived there, only one of whom was a shifter. Not all the children of shifters were born with the changing gene. They grew up as humans in a magical world. Without any power of his own, Brandon would be even more vulnerable to the elementals' attacks than the others.

Sera's beloved red Mustang was parked in front of the house. We'd asked Will to liberate it from the clutches of airport parking once it became obvious we wouldn't be returning anytime soon. The car's presence confirmed this was a recent picture.

The final image held two blond elementals I'd never seen before. The women held five-gallon cans of gasoline and a lighter. They smiled at the camera, the threat explicit. Do as we say, or be the cause of your friends' deaths.

I took careful note of their faces. I never wanted to kill again, but if I ran into them down the road, I could give them one hell of a wedgie.

Besides, what I wanted meant little to the madness. It studied the images too, full of hungry malevolence. The longer I stood before the council, the more agitated it grew. It craved release. It demanded that I buy my freedom with death.

I dug my fingernails into my palm, forcing myself to remain present.

Maybe the others sensed it. Sera moved to my left side and Mac stood behind me. The power I'd given him rose to the surface, seeking to connect with my own. I took the comfort and stillness he offered.

Mac reached over my shoulder, grabbed the photos, and ripped them in two.

My voice was level when I spoke at last. "Most people would avoid angering a dual. I thought you were smarter than this, Deborah."

She ignored my jibe. "This is only the beginning, of course. How old are you now? In your sixties? You left your island home a mere fifteen years ago, but that is long enough to meet people and make connections. You also are familiar with a weak ice, are you not? A local policeman. We would not hurt innocent elementals, of course, but he has a human wife. Human co-workers. This bear…" She paused for a moment, as if unwilling to acknowledge Mac's presence. "He still has family in the forest, doesn't he? Wildfires are so common in late summer."

Deborah continued, unaware of my growing turmoil. "If you are as stable as you claim to be, I'm certain you would do anything to prevent harm befalling those you care about."

"What do you want?" I spoke through gritted teeth. I was hanging on by a thread.

"I wish for you to return with us, of course. It is impossible for a dual magic to be loose. The damage you could cause is unimaginable."

Luke shuffled his feet, and I fought the urge to glance at him. He'd received nothing more than a cursory examination when they first saw him. Either they hadn't figured out what we were searching for in the desert or they didn't realize we'd already found it.

"And then you'll execute me." It wasn't a question.

Deborah's voice was so gentle it could almost be described as kind. "Aidan, I know how you were raised. I have met your family. You were brought up by good people who instilled a sense of honor and responsibility in you. Even now, it pains me to keep your mother and grandmother locked up."

I winced. It didn't just pain me. It tore at me every day.

"Exactly," Deborah said. "You still feel compassion. Though you hope you will not murder again, it is inevitable. If you live, it will be as a monster. Come with us. You can end your life in relative peace, on your terms. Those you love will remain safe."

A low growl rumbled behind me, and I thought Sera actually hissed.

The problem was Deborah wasn't wrong. Not entirely.

However, I'd had months to consider my options. Sure, the first had been "run for your life and never get caught," but that option came with too many downsides. There was another possibility, though, one on which I'd pinned all my hopes.

"What if I learn to control it? If I can prove I'm not a threat to anyone?"

Deborah shook her head. "Duals wreaked havoc for hundreds of years before we decided to eliminate them. There is no reason to believe you will find a solution when others did not."

"But what if I could. Give me a month, Deborah. Like you said, I'm in my sixties. That's a whole lot of time spent not harming people. I can manage another thirty days. If I figure out how to do it, imagine what would change. Full-blooded elementals with different magics could have children together without the fear of sending more duals into the world. You're already keeping Trent Pond alive, experimenting with the drug. Why not let me live, too? One month. That's all I ask."

When I started speaking, I presented a reasonable argument. By the end, I was begging. Pride was for people who didn't have a death sentence hanging over their heads.

Michael's eyes darted between us. "That seems like a good compromise, Deborah. We can go now." He climbed into the driver's seat, more than ready to leave us far behind. Michael hadn't grown a backbone since our last encounter.

Deborah moved to the car and opened the rear door, gesturing me inside. "I do not consent to your terms. We will not allow you to be loose in the world."

I caught a flash of dark blue against the car's black interior. Another person. One with a needle in hand, I'd guess. The council would have replenished their supply after we left my family's island.

My feet were glued to the ground. "Thirty days," I repeated. It was becoming a mantra. I needed more time. We hadn't been through everything—my friends hadn't uprooted their lives, my family hadn't sacrificed their freedom—for it to end like this. Not when Luke had been seconds from telling me how to control it.

Deborah saw my resistance. "At most, we can offer you the same chance at life Trent currently has. You will be contained while your associates pursue this mythical cure. If you come with us now, we can discuss that possibility."

The words came too easily. I didn't believe them, and neither did my rage. It crawled toward the surface, gleeful and determined. Deborah took an involuntary step back when the anger reached my eyes.

"Oh, hell." Sera glared daggers at the woman. "You couldn't give her thirty days? Miriam, tell me you brought the case with you."

Just a little, whispered my fire side. If I only used a little, I could maintain control.

I threw a wall of fire outside the Bronco's door, blocking Miriam's exit. "I don't need drugs," I insisted, stalking toward Deborah.

The woman used those I loved as bargaining chips. She couldn't be allowed to harm them, and I couldn't let her continue to pursue me.

For the first time, Deborah looked afraid. She was so old and powerful, so unaccustomed to being threatened, that perhaps she'd never truly believed I would harm her. It's why she chose to meet me in the desert with nothing but a few photos as defense.

Michael turned the ignition, ready to flee.

Deborah hurried into the passenger seat and slammed the door shut.

One moment we stared at each other through the glass, and the next the car lurched forward, aiming straight for the nearest person—who happened to be the other dual.

Luke leapt out of the way, performing a neat roll as he landed. Michael made a narrow u-turn and headed back.

Elementals could only die in a car accident if we were killed instantly, unable to access the healing powers of our element. Based on Michael's grim face and the speed with which he approached, it seemed instant death was very much the plan.

"Don't you dare, Ade. Don't you fucking dare." Sera's voice cut through the growing rage, reminding me what a bad idea this was. How much I needed to fight the worst part of myself.

That was all the time Sera needed. A second later, her own wall of fire surrounded the car, blocking the driver's view.

The fire was instantly extinguished—not by the elementals inside, but by the man who also controlled fire. "I'm thinking an exploding gas tank isn't the best idea," Luke suggested.

As the car hurtled toward them, Johnson and Carmichael placed themselves in front of it. Their warning shot was ignored, and the next three ricocheted off the windshield. The shots reverberated across the high desert, the sound deafening.

The agents leapt out of the SUV's path before it could mow them down. "Bulletproof glass," Carmichael shouted to his partner.

The SUV spun around again, this time racing straight toward me.

It was twenty feet away when another shot rang out.

Luke stood behind the vehicle as it swerved to the left. Michael struggled with the wheel, fighting to pull it back to center.

Luke pulled the trigger again, and the second rear tire blew. With grim smiles, the agents raised their weapons and took out the two front tires. The vehicle swung in a circle, completely out of control, then drew to a stop. Deborah and Michael wouldn't be going anywhere soon.

Grinning, Luke whirled the gun around his finger once, then blew on the barrel before holstering it. Normally, I'd mock him for that, but he'd earned it.

"You're the first elemental I've met who liked guns, but right now I'm pretty glad of it," I told him.

"Darlin', I was born in Texas in 1875. They put this in the cradle with me."

"What now?" asked Vivian.

With the threat neutralized, I was at last able to gain full control of my rage. I walked toward the car and waited until Deborah rolled the window down a crack.

"Thirty days. That's all. If I don't find an answer in that time, I will turn myself in, because you're right. I don't want to be a monster." She nodded in eager agreement, but it wasn't enough. Her compliance would last only so long as she felt scared. "You threatened my friends. Let me return the favor." Her eyes widened a fraction. "If you harm any of them, not only will I refuse to turn myself in, I'll stop trying to control myself. How old are you, Deborah? I bet you've grown close to a lot of people over the past millennium or two. It would be a shame if anything happened to them."

I let the fire rise a bit, let it darken my gray eyes until they were the color of ashes. I didn't think I meant my threats, but Deborah couldn't know that.

When she nodded, I almost believed her.

"Good choice," I said. I let the fire drop, so when I turned back to my friends, they only saw my water side. "We're done here. Let's go."

No one argued. We claimed to be the good guys. That meant not killing the council, no matter how much we didn't like them. Deborah and Michael could use the well to recharge their magic, and they would have cell phones. The phones might even get reception out here. They'd live.

One by one, we piled into the Bronco. It would have been a more dignified escape if we hadn't needed to sit on each other's laps to all fit.

I found myself squished next to Luke. "I maybe forgot to mention that life with us could be a little dangerous," I told him.

"A little?"

"This was the first time anyone's tried to run us over, so I give them points for originality."

He smiled, but it seemed like his mind was already elsewhere. "Back there... you began to lose it, didn't you?" He saw the answer in my eyes. "Damn it. Well, I couldn't much live with myself if I sent you out in the world like that. Not if I think I can help you."

Luke glanced around the crowded Bronco. He paid no attention to Mac, glowering next to me. "I'm not much for groups."

"Most groups aren't as awesome as we are. We almost

never hold sing-alongs or braid each other's hair."

Reluctance gave way to amusement. There might be hope for him yet.

"Welcome to the gang, Luke. Try not to be a psychopath, okay?"

CHAPTER 6

"You're kidding, right?" Sera circled the vehicle as if unable to believe it was real, or that there would be any circumstance in this world that might convince her to step inside.

"You got a better idea?" Luke sat on the hood of an avocado green Ford Pinto that was missing all its doors.

The junkyard was full of such treasures. A powder blue Cadillac limousine. A rusted-out El Camino with a kiddie pool in the rear. A pickup truck and an old Volkswagen Beetle welded together by the automotive equivalent of a mad scientist.

And an old school bus, painted gray, with "First Baptist Summer Camp" stenciled on its side.

"She has a point." I examined the bus alongside Sera. "There's a good chance we'll be struck by lightning if we even step foot onto this thing."

Miriam slammed the hood shut and wiped sweat from her brow, leaving a thick grease stain behind. "It's in decent shape. Has all its parts, at least, which is more than I can say for most of the cars here. Needs some oil, but it'll run."

Sera was unconvinced. "And when the waters catch up to us? Do we ask them to wait while we get out and push? It could reach a whole thirty miles an hour if we all work together." She pointed toward a couple of old muscle cars in the corner. "You guys do what you want. I'm taking the

Chevelle."

"I kind of put the fear of, well, me into them," I said. "Maybe they'll leave us alone for the next month." The group was silent, but not a thoughtful silence. More a "let's humor the delusional woman" kind of silence.

"I guess it's possible," said Vivian. It would have been more convincing if her voice hadn't risen on the last syllable.

Simon made no effort to indulge me. "They cannot let you dictate the terms of your own capture. Or your own escape, for that matter. It will make them feel weak and ineffectual, and that would be unacceptable to ones as old and powerful as they are."

"Fine," I grumbled. "But we still need to switch cars. The only way they could have followed us to Luke's super-secret hideaway is some kind of satellite imaging. You said it's unlikely, Vivian, but it's the only possible solution. We change cars and maybe buy some time while they keep searching for the Airstream."

Vivian grumbled. She was crouched on a bucket seat that hadn't seen the inside of a car in a long time, using the shade from the bus to stay marginally cooler in the sweltering heat. "Let me check. Give me ten minutes with my laptop and I'll find a way to block any satellite access they may have." Her hand was already moving toward her computer bag.

Sera shook her head. "Why risk it?"

I took a hesitant step inside the bus. Simon followed, examining the worn vinyl seats with the air of a man who'd lost all hope. "Is it too much to ask that, someday in the future, we no longer live in a state of squalor?"

I still hoped that, someday in the future, we all got to live, but I doubted that needed to be said aloud. "Regretting that you didn't stay with Carmen and the other Tahoe shifters?"

His scornful expression suggested only a fool would question his judgment. "Of course not. I would not mind a few of the pleasures of home, however." He hooked a finger under a strip of duct tape that kept the thin stuffing from escaping one of the seats. "Carmen's house may lack personality, but at least it is not held together with tape. Also, my room had a walk-in closet."

A shadow fell over me as a man large enough to block most of the front window joined us. "You assume her house is still standing."

"It is," I said. "If the house was already burnt, they wouldn't be able to threaten us with its destruction. We need to give them a heads up, though. At least make sure their insurance is up to date. Sera has their number."

Simon took advantage of the excuse to leave the musty-smelling bus. He delivered the message to Sera, who still stared at the vehicle with an expression somewhere between horror and amusement. She dug through her bag and found the notebook with everyone's phone numbers. We'd call the Tahoe shifters as soon as we reached a gas station with a payphone.

I knelt on a seat and pushed the window down. It made it half an inch before becoming irrevocably stuck. "Carmichael, any chance you're friends with someone who can help erase some bogus health violations? Frank could probably use some help with the Rat Trap."

He seemed dubious, but he and Johnson conferred.

I returned to the aisle and found my way blocked. Mac had that determined look, the one that suggested I wasn't going anywhere until he'd said what he needed to say.

I began with an apology, hoping to save a bit of time. "I'm sorry this is happening. I know what your uncle means to you."

"It'll take more than a fire to hurt Will."

"And I'm sorry about the whole using magic thing, though let's be honest, Sera already punished me for that."

He kept watching me. I couldn't think of anything else I needed to be sorry about.

"I'm not so mad about that. Not right now."

It took me a second to realize that his determined look wasn't so much about what he wanted to say as what he wanted to do.

Though the windows were grimy, they weren't opaque. We were visible to anyone who cared to peer inside. I squirmed backwards, putting space between us.

Intent brown eyes followed my every movement.

I tried distracting him. "They're threatening to hurt shifters. Your people. You aren't okay with that."

"They'll be fine. Even if they get the buildings, the shifters will be safe. We'll make sure of it. They can always rebuild. Are you really saying I should give you to a council that wants to kill you to protect a few pieces of wood?"

"When you say it like that, you make it sound crazy." I raised my eyebrows, daring him to laugh.

He rolled his eyes. Close enough.

"What's your opinion on the new guy?"

The hint of humor vanished. "We need to be careful. All we're sure of is he's a dual magic, and that makes him dangerous. He said there's a cure, but hasn't given us any information about it."

To be fair, Luke hadn't ridden with us. When we'd picked up the Airstream and camper from the overhang near his hut, he reclaimed an old Indian motorcycle, a black cruiser with a low seat. From there, he'd led us to this automobile graveyard.

We were all itching to learn more, but our first priority needed to be ditching the council—and that meant changing vehicles.

"Hey, I'm dangerous, too." I stood tall and tried to channel a fraction of Sera or Miriam's badassery. I suspected there were fluffy bunnies who appeared more threatening than I did at the moment. "Well, I can be."

Mac placed his hands on my hips and drew me against his chest. One hand wrapped around my waist, and the other threaded through my hair. His body put off as much heat as any furnace. Although the outside temperature was transitioning from "unbearable" to "hotter than the devil in a Texas sauna," I felt no desire to move.

"And being dangerous is the worst thing for you. You don't need to be that woman, Aidan. Let me be dangerous, instead."

Some primitive part of me responded to his vow of protection, but another, much louder part disliked being told to be weaker than I was. Mac was wrong. Until we were all safe again, I did need to be dangerous. I just needed to figure out how to do that without endangering myself as well.

"What is it?" The words were whispered into my ear, the breath warm.

I ignored the question. I might not be able to hide my transparent face, but that didn't mean I wasn't allowed some private thoughts.

"You two planning on breaking it in already?"

Mac bent his knees slightly, positioning himself to see out of the filthy windows. Luke still leaned against the Pinto.

"We're coming out now," I said, glad for the distraction.

Instead of moving toward the door, Mac turned his head and captured my lips with his own. My breath stopped for a moment as I forgot where I was or who might be watching, then a melting warmth that had nothing to do with the day's heat poured through my body. I wrapped both arms around his waist and slipped my hands beneath his t-shirt to feel his back, thickly muscled and damp with sweat. I dug my nails into his skin.

Mac tilted my head, adjusting the angle, and deepened the kiss. He resisted my efforts to pull him closer, to push the pace into something a bit more frantic, a bit hungrier. Instead, he chose a slow, lazy exploration, and only his hand tightening around my waist hinted at the need building within him.

My magic rose, fire and water together, and met the small piece I'd left behind the night I healed Mac. They mingled and fed off each other as our lips did the same. Most of the time, I felt fractured, but not with Mac. When Mac touched me, I was whole.

He ended the kiss, pulling back enough to see me clearly. We wore matching expressions of affection and longing, but there was another emotion on his face, one I knew wasn't mirrored on mine.

The bastard looked smug.

I stepped back, out of arm's reach. "What, was peeing on me too messy?" I pointedly didn't check to see if Luke was watching.

He had the grace not to act confused. "I thought this would be more pleasant." He smiled. "Are you complaining?"

I wasn't entirely sure. The modern feminist side of me was annoyed that he wanted to assert a claim. The primitive side thought it was kind of hot.

"Have you finished marking your territory?" I said.

His eyes flashed. "Not even close." He stepped toward me, erasing the small space I'd bought for myself. "If you check my back, you'll notice you also marked me."

I blew out my breath, hoping to expel some of the rampant lust. "Maybe we can make Miriam steal a van for us."

"The kind with curtains in the windows?"

"And shag carpeting. Hell, yes." I grinned, almost wishing we weren't joking.

Mac and I slept together most nights, but that's all it was—sleep. In the past, we'd come close to doing a lot more, but that was before I started losing my mind on a regular basis. Until we found a cure, any loss of control, even the good kind, wasn't an option. I knew Mac agreed. Neither of us made any effort to sneak away from the others for more than a quick word or a few rushed kisses.

It was the right decision, and it sucked.

"We should join the others." I needed to get away from Mac before my libido decided it didn't give a damn what was going on in my brain.

Mac blocked the aisle. I pushed him lightly toward the door. He didn't budge, but he wouldn't have if I'd put my full strength behind the move.

He threaded a hand through my hair and pulled me in for another kiss, hard and fast. This one had nothing to do with Luke and everything to do with the two of us. "Soon. Soon you'll be cured, and the minute that happens, we're going to discover what we've been missing all this time." Before I could catch my breath, he headed for the door.

Once my knees were again able to support the rest of my body, I followed.

I'd only been outside a second before I heard a heartfelt "Damn it!"

I spun in surprise, unaccustomed to Vivian raising her voice, let alone swearing.

"What is it?" I asked. "Oh, Vivian. Didn't we agree…?"

"You agreed," she said. Her fingers flew across the keyboard, typing commands the rest of us couldn't hope to understand.

"Viv?" Sera came running. "What's wrong?"

"Damn it. Damn it!"

"Is it Olivia?" I was almost afraid to ask about Vivian's ex-girlfriend, the woman she'd left behind to help us find a cure. "Is the council going after her?"

"No, no, not that… fuck."

Now I was worried. "We're going to need some verbs, Vivian."

She glanced up from her laptop for a second, long enough to find Sera. "You were right. They were using satellite maps to track us."

Normally, I didn't understand the numbers and images that scrolled across the screen while she worked. At that moment, I knew exactly what I was seeing.

It was a low-quality picture of Vivian, a bit blurry around the edges. The sort of quality found on a photo taken in a moving vehicle. It had been badly Photoshopped so it looked like Vivian was holding a tablet. The tablet screen faced the camera, and the screen held a satellite map. The map indicated our current location.

"What the fuck, Vivian?" I thought Miriam spoke for all of us. "I thought you said they couldn't access real-time satellites."

"None of the ones I was monitoring," Vivian's voice rose in a panic. "I think… this shouldn't be possible, but they accessed Homeland Security." Her eyes were wild. "That's not the worst part. They sent this image to me. To *my* computer. Whoever did this broke through every protection I set up."

Miriam shook her head. "Tell me you're fucking kidding. Didn't we count on the council barely understanding how to turn their damn computers on?"

Vivian gnawed on her lip as the flipped through one screen after another. "It was a reasonable guess. Other than their Swiss bank account, there's no evidence the council ever went online."

"You hacked a Swiss bank account?" Luke gave a low whistle.

If they knew where we were, we needed to hurry. I imagined the council had already formed a plan B after the disastrous confrontation outside Luke's hut. "The flash of blue."

The others stayed silent, waiting for me to make sense.

"In the SUV. I thought I saw someone when they opened the door. The person wore blue. Then the council tried to run us over and I kind of forgot about it."

Vivian slammed her palm against the ground. "They hired their own freaking hacker. I can do this. I'll anonymously alert Homeland Security and they'll break the connection for us. As soon as I figure out how they even got in. Simon, get me another battery pack."

"Are they on their way? Do we need to run?" Carmichael's eyes darted around the yard, perhaps expecting the council to leap out from behind a retired limousine.

Vivian glanced at another window on her screen. "They're still fifty miles away. Maybe Aidan scared them enough to give us some space, but they're telling us we're not getting a lot of space."

While Vivian worked, the rest of us grabbed supplies from the Airstream and camper and loaded up the school bus with several duffel bags. We'd already been traveling light. Now we aimed for spartan.

Miriam shoved a cooler under the dashboard. It was filled with sandwiches and fruit and, if I knew Miriam, several six-packs of beer. I didn't argue. We all had our own definition of "necessities."

"Hide the vehicles over there." I pointed. "The Airstream can fit between the moving truck and the pile of…

whatever those are. If we pull some sheet metal around it, it can stay hidden for a bit."

"No." Mac was certain.

"We have to," I began. "It's your home, but…"

"No," he repeated. "They've already seen where we are, so they'll expect us to switch vehicles. We need to prove them wrong."

"We'll do it." Carmichael called over his shoulder to Vivian. "Give us ten minutes before you shut them down."

"We're setting a false trail," Mac explained, loud enough for all to hear. "Maybe they'll buy it, maybe they won't, but they'll at least need to follow the Bronco to be sure we're not in it."

"Good thinking, bear." Miriam tossed the Bronco's keys to Johnson. He caught them one-handed.

I was less certain. "We split up, we're less powerful," I argued. "And these two will be sitting ducks. Sorry, guys."

Carmichael wasn't offended. He'd seen what elementals could do. "And if they do catch us, we're humans and FBI agents. Agents who check in regularly with our higher-ups. If we disappear, the Bureau will want to learn why. From what you've told us, elementals avoid anything that could draw the attention of human authorities."

"If the agents return to Tahoe, they would be in a better position to protect our friends," Simon pointed out. "Even if those friends do not trust humans. Or the FBI. And they may remember that Carmichael almost killed Mac."

"No, they should go." I wished that wasn't true. "Give us a few minutes to grab some items."

Vivian's face was strained. "I can't hold the connection very long."

In the end, there were no long goodbyes. There were a few handshakes, an overly enthusiastic hug from Miriam for Johnson, and a complicated look between Carmichael

and Sera. Carmichael drove the camper van, while Johnson took the Bronco and Airstream. The men adjusted
their seats and mirrors, waved goodbye, and pulled out of
the junkyard. We saw them turn north, and then they were
gone.

Vivian waited long enough for them to hit the highway,
then sent the alert that would have our nation's primary
security agency scrambling to shut down the elementals'
connection. If we were really lucky, they'd also find themselves being interrogated for several days in a windowless
room.

Vivian stood, stretching her muscles for the first time
since we arrived at the junkyard. "They may find another
connection, but we'll be far away by then." Her satisfied
smile lasted only so long as it took her computer to emit a
single loud beep.

"No no no," she whispered, crouching by the machine.
"No."

We'd thought she was panicked before. We were wrong.

Her movements were both tiny and frantic. Eyes
scanned the screen left to right while her fingers flew
across the keys. Windows opened and closed as Vivian typed commands in a language none of us knew. It
only took a few minutes, but Vivian grew more desperate
with every passing second. When she finally sat back, she
looked as exhausted as any marathon runner. Worse, she
looked ashamed.

"I'm sorry. I should have seen it."

We all worked very hard not to rush her in any way.

Well, most of us did. "Vivian, you're killing us," I said.

She forced herself to meet my gaze. "The picture, the
satellite map, it was all a distraction. While I was working on shutting it down, they snuck in and burnt through
my encryption in minutes. I don't know how. They down-

loaded Josiah's files."

I could practically feel the group fight against despair—and lose. Those files had been guiding most of our movements since we escaped my family's island.

"All of them?" Sera's voice was quiet, but she practically vibrated with agitation.

"I stopped the transfer before they got it all, but they grabbed a lot. I can't even say what files they found. I haven't read all of it yet, because I was focused on finding Luke." She met his gaze. "If they didn't know about another dual before, they do now."

At most, Luke appeared mildly chagrined, and even that passed. "Well, I've already been running quite a while. Least this time I'll have company." He shrugged and stepped onto the bus.

Miriam followed. She crouched beneath the steering wheel, smacked the dash in a carefully chosen spot, and pulled out several wires. She peeled off their casings with a pocket knife.

The motor stuttered several times, but at last it roared to life. Well, whimpered to life.

"We'll need to stop for gas at the first station," Miriam called. "Right now we don't have enough to get us to… where the hell are we going, cowboy?"

He directed his answer to me. "Someplace you don't want to go. You're sure you have no other choice?"

I was sure.

"The good news is we're heading somewhere that probably isn't in any of those files. The bad news is we're going someplace so awful you might prefer to meet the council again."

CHAPTER 7

We drove until sunset, retracing our steps through the largely uninhabited land along the Arizona-Utah border.

Luke rode in front of us. His ride was a lot sweeter than ours, but I didn't mind. It seemed like a good idea to keep him and Mac at least a hundred feet apart until Mac recovered from his unexpected case of the alpha males.

We'd passed Monument Valley but not yet reached the rich water of Lake Powell when we stopped for the night.

The little-used campground had a lake, of sorts, a pool of stagnant water surrounded by low red hills anemically populated with thin trees.

No one spoke much while we set up camp. I tried once more to broach the subject of a cure with Luke, but he shook his head.

"Tomorrow," he told me. "I'll give you what I know tomorrow."

For now, that had to be good enough.

It had been a stressful couple of days, and we all needed to recharge. Vivian hadn't touched her computer since we left the junkyard, and I feared she was approaching a catatonic state after being out-hacked. She spent hours flat against the red earth, trying to soak up power from the unfamiliar source.

Miriam had her clothes off even before she exited the bus, and soon a Tahoe river otter was swimming in an Arizona desert lake.

Mac took off, needing the space to roam. He didn't like changing in unfamiliar areas, particularly those with a high rate of gun ownership among the population, but shifters had to change. He headed into the spindly trees. I doubted he'd be gone long.

Sera and Luke started a fire, then plunged their hands into its core. I didn't actively reach toward it, but I felt myself strengthen from proximity to the flames.

Simon had spent most of the drive sleeping on duffle bags in the rear of the bus. He woke up long enough to move toward the fire's warmth before settling down for another nap.

I sat in the water, listening to the camp sounds behind me lessen and eventually cease as the others fell asleep. Soon after, a warm bear nose nudged my shoulder and I crawled onto the shore to join him. There was no reason to make up a bed. Mac would be a far better mattress than a lumpy pile of blankets.

Mac shifted in the dark and pulled on a thin pair of sweatpants. He wrapped his arms around me, drawing me close, and I rested my head against his chest. Spending hours as a bear made him feel more at home in his own skin, but he wasn't finished. As we lay together, I pulled on the lake water and sent its power along the connection we shared. We didn't need to consciously reach for the other for his magic to feed, but I enjoyed exploring the bond. I loved feeling the water heal the day's aches and pains, but that was a prelude to the main event, when the magic repaired all the aging Mac had done that day. So long as Mac had access to my power, he had access to my longevity, and in those moments I could pretend we'd have centuries together.

We fell asleep, finding something close to safety in

each other's arms.

I woke gasping, images of flames still dancing behind my eyes and David's screams echoing in my ears. I must not have cried out. Mac still slept, facedown in the dirt. One arm was draped across my side, the hand curling around my waist.

I inched away, careful not to disturb him. He grumbled once and turned over, but he didn't wake.

I slipped on my shoes, rose to my feet and began running, moving beyond the camp radius before anyone could spot me, then I picked up the pace. My legs pounded against the earth as I bolted across the desert, putting miles between myself and the others. Hell, putting distance between me and the rest of the world. If I had a spaceship, I probably would have used that instead.

My whole life, I'd hated exercise, but my fire side felt differently. It demanded movement. I told no one about this change. I snuck in my runs and push-ups when I was alone. If my friends heard I now craved physical activity, they'd probably assume I'd already gone off the deep end. I tugged on my t-shirt, hoping the sleeves were long enough to hide my newly discovered biceps.

At last, I drew to a stop and bent over, hands braced on my knees as I gasped for breath. There was no water to access here. I couldn't speed the healing, so I had to do it the old-fashioned human way.

A fire appeared two feet from me. "Use that," Luke said.

I didn't need to be told. I was already gobbling its power. "You're up early." Not even a strip of light shone on the horizon.

"I wanted to grab you before the others woke up. I'd like to show you something."

I raised an eyebrow and, with great effort, didn't make

an inappropriate remark. "What?"

Luke dangled the keys to his bike. "My past."

"I'M STILL NOT SURE WHAT WE'RE DOING HERE." I MEANT TO sound annoyed, but as I was holding a cup of actual black tea laced with half-and-half, it came out sounding deeply grateful.

We sat in a diner on the main street of one of those towns you'd miss if you closed your eyes for twenty seconds while driving through. It was about forty-five minutes south of the campsite where we'd spent the night.

Luke had claimed a booth next to the front windows. The street had everything you could need, so long as you didn't want many choices. It wasn't a wealthy town, and I suspected it scraped by on money from the tourists driving to and from the Grand Canyon. It was the kind of place filled with people who worked full days and woke up early, even on weekends. Though it was barely six-thirty, stores were already opening, the town coming to life.

After the last few days, it felt like the height of civilization. This was my favorite sort of diner, a place where the coffee cups were always full and the pancakes were the size of your head. Once I confirmed Luke was paying, I ordered two plates.

Luke stared out the window, like he had since we arrived. He hadn't flirted with me once. "I used to live here. About twenty minutes east, cause town was a little too busy for me, but I'd come in often enough to do my shopping or see a movie."

I tried hard to stay quiet, figuring he would tell the story in his own time. I started fidgeting after thirty seconds. "And what, you craved some hash browns this morning?"

"This isn't a breakfast date, Aidan, though I suppose

you already figured that out. We both know it's not like that between us. Still, no reason to tell your boyfriend that. I know you aren't supposed to poke an angry bear, but he just makes it too easy." He winked at me, then went back to staring out the window.

I tried pulling his attention to the matter at hand. "So, about that cure…"

"Right there." Luke placed his left index finger against the window. The touch was gentle, almost loving, as if he feared breaking the glass. "That was my reason for living here."

I followed his gaze. Across the street, a slim elderly woman walked down the sidewalk. Her white hair was thin and wispy, and her face was marked with the wrinkles of a long life.

She took care with each step, but her spine was straight and she didn't use a cane or walker. The sign on the building behind her proclaimed it an elder care facility, and I assumed she'd stepped out of their front door. I hadn't been paying attention, but Luke clearly had.

"How long ago did you live here?"

"Fifty-six years, eight months." He glanced away from the older woman, and I thought it pained him to tear his eyes from her for even a few moments. "Sixteen days."

For once, I had nothing to say, and I waited.

When he began to talk, his voice sounded distant, as if he spoke from another place—or another time. "Nora and I, we had one of those relationships. You know the kind. Loud fights, loud making up. She drove me crazy, and I was crazy about her. I think it was mutual, too, but I let all the bullshit get in my mind sometimes. I drank more than I should some nights. Lot of people did back then, so I thought it was okay. One night, I'd had a little too much of a bottle of rye, and I started wondering where Nora was.

She was out later than she said she'd be. I got to thinking she was with another guy. Some human guy who didn't have to keep secrets like I did. At the time, I only knew I was half desert, but that was plenty. She didn't understand why I wouldn't drive to the ocean or why I refused to take her on a cruise."

The words grew strained as they fought past the lump in his throat. He drank coffee until his voice was steady again. "Anyway, that night I sat on the couch, waiting for her to come home, and I was drinking and getting angry, and the more I drank, the angrier I got."

Nora stepped into a convenience store on the corner, completely unaware of the man across from me and the effect she had on him.

"She goes to that store every day for the newspaper. Refuses to get a subscription. Nora says delivery is for old people who can't walk a hundred feet to get the news. On Sundays, she buys an apple danish, too."

"How often do you come here?" I swallowed a bite of pancakes and barely tasted them.

"Whenever I need to remember."

The door swung open and Nora stepped back into the street, newspaper tucked under her arm. I could see the side of her face that had been hidden before.

My fork clattered against the plate.

The left side of Nora's face was deformed. Thick scars ran from her temple to her chin. They pulled at the corners of her eyes and mouth, tilting both down so that she appeared perpetually sad.

Luke's eyes remained locked on the woman. "Maybe if I was a human, we would have thrown some dishes, said some ugly things, and been done with it. As heated as we got, I didn't lay a hand on her. I'd never do that. But that dual nature had other plans. I hadn't known what I was until I was burning our house down around us. The ceiling fell on her and crushed her legs. She begged me for help, and I only watched her, trying to think past the haze of alcohol and magic. I couldn't remember who I was for a couple minutes, and that was too long. Her legs were broken. That's all it took for her to be disfigured for life."

Nora returned to the elder care building. Luke continued to gaze at the closed door, perhaps finding his way back to the present. When he turned to me, his eyes were wet, and he made no effort to hide it. "I did that, Aidan. I did that to the woman I love."

"I'm so sorry." I knew the words were inadequate, but I hoped he understood how much I meant them.

"Yeah, well. Now you know." He gulped his coffee, now lukewarm, then threw two twenties on the table, far more than the meal cost. Luke strode to the front door and held it open for me. "Let's get out of here."

We'd parked behind the diner. Luke glanced over his shoulder twice as we left, but he didn't mention Nora again.

In the parking lot, he jumped up and down, like he was trying to shake off memories that would never leave. "I'm sure you can guess I don't show that to many others. You're the first person I told cause you have to understand. Nora is why I needed the cure. What I did to her, that broke me, and I think I would have given in to madness rather than live with what I'd done. I didn't even go looking for the cure, didn't know it existed, but it was a damn good thing it found me. I would have done some terrible things without it. But the cure itself, Aidan... it's awful. After Nora, it's the worst thing that's ever happened to me. It's gonna be awful for you, too, more than I can ever explain. So, are you absolutely sure you can't function anymore? Cause if it's not too bad, maybe I can help you control it."

"I killed a man." I saw no need to sugarcoat it.

"Any chance he deserved it?" Luke looked almost hopeful.

"Does it matter?"

"I suppose not."

"There were others, too." The story came pouring out, the dam broken. "Times I would have killed, but someone interrupted. They wouldn't have deserved it either. One was self-defense, but maybe I could have stopped him some other way. I didn't even try. It's getting worse, Luke. The madness is winning."

He gazed up at the cloudless sky, deciding. "All right, Aidan Brook. I'll help you upend your entire life if that's what you want."

"You're a little late for that."

"It's dangerous."

I snorted. Given what my life had become, I couldn't even pretend to take him seriously.

We reached the bike. Luke chucked the spare helmet to me with a little too much force. "Do I look like a wimp to you? I'm not scared of a lot, so trust me when I say it's risky as hell."

I didn't pat his head in a condescending manner. I considered that a win. "Over the last few months, I've dealt with a homicidal dual magic determined to make me his love slave and brood mare and a shifter doing her best to kick off a magical race war in Lake Tahoe. My house has been firebombed and someone sent the car I was in rocketing over the side of a mountain. I've seen people suffocate, burn, and outright explode, so unless the solution to my madness involves me being shot from a cannon through a ring of acid and landing in a pit of tarantulas, I'm telling you this: fucking bring it."

He sat on the bike and watched me a little too intently.

"You need a first magic."

I'm sure he expected a reaction. I'd give him one, as soon as I got over my shock. "A what?" I managed.

He didn't repeat himself.

"You mean... the creatures born from the earth's original magic? The ones from whom all elementals and shifters are descended?"

He raised both eyebrows and waited for me to believe him. It was going to take a while.

"They don't exist anymore. Okay, there were a few rumors, but people claim to spot Elvis more often than elementals talk of the first magics."

"There were rumors about shifters. How did that turn out?"

"That's different. That was more of a deliberate lie told by the old ones who hoped, if they repeated it often enough, it would become true. If part of our creation myth was still walking the earth, someone would have said something." I shook my head, ready to believe that Luke was insane after all. Except, instead of being homicidal, he now believed in fairies and unicorns. "You're talking about the first creatures in all of existence. They're pure magic." I emphasized the last two words, not sure he understood what he was saying.

"I know our history." His voice was dry.

"But... what do they look like? Even a full-blooded elemental is half human, though they rarely admit it. And they're so old. They're as old as the earth itself, which is... okay, I don't know. I slept through science. But that's really, really old. How did you even find one?"

"Like I said, I got lucky." His expression told me he didn't believe that for a moment. "And now it's your turn."

CHAPTER 8

"So, new plan." I swung off the bike and pretended like that didn't make me feel cool as hell.

The others had already packed up and were ready to go. I got the feeling they'd been waiting a while. Only Simon was still half-naked while he dug through his duffel bag, searching for clean clothes.

Simon and Vivian looked relieved when I appeared. Sera was angry, and Mac was closer to murderous. Seeing me pull up with my hands wrapped around Luke's lean waist probably didn't help.

"Where the hell have you been?" Sera rushed at me, then stood on tiptoe to peer into my eyes, checking for madness like a parent might look for signs of drug use.

I jerked away. "There was something we had to do."

"You left? Without the case? What if something went wrong?"

"It didn't." I'd heard teenagers offer the same argument. That didn't make it less true. "You can't control everything, Sera."

She didn't seem to hear me. No one did. They were too busy listening to all the things they wanted to say, about responsibility and consideration and not running off with the hot guy on a motorcycle. That last part was mainly from Mac, though he phrased it a bit differently.

Luke and I exchanged glances and waited them out.

It was a long wait. "When you're done, we should get

moving. We're hunting a mythological creature that even scares Luke. Who's in?"

That shut them up. After I explained, they remained quiet, this time with slack jaws.

Miriam found her voice. "No way. The firsts are part of our creation myth, like Adam and Eve with fewer fig leaves. Whatever you think you found, it was something else. "

Sera's face was impassive, as it always was when her mind churned. "Luke, you're not giving us a lot of reason to believe in your sanity here."

Luke wasn't offended. "I'm telling you what I know, but I'm also telling you I think it's a terrible idea. The one I knew was unpredictable on her good days and downright volatile the rest of the time. We can't walk up and expect an ancient being to listen to a reasoned argument."

"Care to fill us in?" Carmichael's tinny voice came from Sera's right hand.

I raised an eyebrow.

"He was checking in." Sera put the phone on speaker.

I spoke loud enough for Carmichael to hear. "It's where we all come from. Well, not you, but the rest of us. Even Johnson can trace his ancestry to the original ones, what with his tiny hint of elemental blood. When the earth was created, it produced magic. Or maybe magic produced the earth, no one's really sure. All we know is life is creation, and creation is a form of magic. The firsts existed from the dawn of time, at least as far back as we can measure it, and they stayed with the landscapes to which they were connected—earth, water, glaciers, volcanoes, stone, desert, or beach. It was this way for millennia, at least until humans started claiming the land for their own. That's when the original magic chose to take human shape and mate with the men. Call it the 'if you can't beat 'em, join 'em' approach. Most of the mothers grew too attached to their children to leave once they were born."

Miriam chucked a heavy duffle bag into the bus. "And those that didn't care for their new human bodies became animals, and that's where shifters come from—the mix of magic, animals, and the memory of humanity. Can't really blame the firsts for that, but it's why I thought it was just myth. The whole thing smacked of Zeus becoming a swan and all of that."

Simon frowned. "The Greeks stole that from us."

I hurried to finish the tale. "The official elemental story is that some of them chose not to permanently become humans or animals. Instead, they disappeared into the wilds, never to be seen again."

Miriam swung the second duffle bag on top of the other one, arm muscles flexing under its weight. "Didn't you get this in the info package, Carmichael?"

"He's a bit slow," Sera stage-whispered. She wasn't entirely wrong. Carmichael wasn't stupid, not at all. He just needed to hear about magical things at least three times before he started to believe them.

The agent didn't rise to the bait. "If these are your ancestors, won't they be willing to help you?"

Luke laughed, a short bark with little humor. "Don't ever think the firsts will act as you'd expect a normal person to act. Full-blooded elementals are half-human. These things… well, they're pure magic. That's it."

Simon finally found a t-shirt that passed his rigorous smell test and pulled it over his head. "So we find one of these creatures and save Aidan, then we return to living like civilized people capable of wearing clean clothes on a regular basis. I support this plan."

Mac sounded like he didn't believe a single word of Luke's story. "How will a first cure Aidan?"

Luke held his gaze. "She'll let the first mess with her power and hope it eventually decides to heal her. That's all Aidan can do, and it's a hell of a long shot."

He really wasn't filling me with hope and confidence.

Sera looked about as certain as I felt. "Is there any other cure?"

"Not that I know. Not permanently."

Mac's fingers contorted, the nails growing hard and sharp. "If you're lying…"

"I know, I know. You'll disembowel me while singing a jaunty tune. I got the message. Believe me, if there was another choice, I wouldn't be going anywhere near this thing."

"What's so dangerous about it?" Mac asked.

Luke exhaled. "She plays with elementals and their magic. She's controlling and demanding, and she won't help Aidan out of the goodness of her heart. Hell, she may trap her forever."

"She?" I asked.

"The first takes a female form when she wishes to appear."

With Luke's description, my friends seemed even more nervous about this course of action.

To forestall further debate, I found the black case and showed them its contents, reminding them how little of the drug remained. "We're out of choices. No matter how dangerous it is, it's better than the alternative."

Sera's mouth twisted in displeasure. "Then I guess we better start searching for a mythological being."

I refused to share the others' concerns. "Hell, we used to believe shifters and duals didn't exist, and look at us now. I bet we could find Yeti and the Loch Ness monster without even trying."

"Where are we going, Luke?" Miriam already sat in the

driver's seat.

"North, across the Utah border. I'll get you there, but I'm not meeting with that thing again. You get to do that on your own."

My friends stared at Luke, suspicion writ large across their faces.

He was unmoved. "I've been trapped by that thing, and I won't go through it again. I'm not exaggerating about how awful it'll be. You'll be lucky to escape at all. I got away once. I'm not fool enough to think I'll do it twice. This is your risk, not mine." Luke put his helmet on and revved the bike's engine, forestalling any further questions.

Mac crept behind me. "Why are we following him again?"

I gave his wrist a quick squeeze. "Because it's a risk worth taking."

That wasn't the real reason I wanted to believe Luke told the truth. In so many ways, we were the same. Trusting him meant I could trust myself, and I very much needed to trust myself for a while longer.

TWO HOURS LATER, LUKE PULLED THE BIKE OVER AND JOINED us. He pointed to my destination. "You'll need to walk. The bus won't make it."

He wasn't kidding. The landscape had really begun showing off the closer we got to the Utah border. Everywhere I looked, I saw another setting begging to be photographed. Red rocks erupted from the ground. Some were flat and thick, oversized stepping stones guiding us across the land. Some formed sharp spires, their pointed tips stretching to meet the sky. About two hundred feet from the road, there was a red hill with sloping sides leading to a flat top. If Luke was correct, that's where a first waited. From here, I couldn't see anything but the few trees blocking our view of the top.

Sera pointed at the steam rising from the overheated engine. "There's a chance this beast won't be making it anywhere ever again. You got this, Miriam?"

"On it." Miriam was already digging tools and jugs of water from beneath the seats.

I grabbed a gallon of water as she passed. I might need it for the hike, but mainly I felt better holding my element like a liquid security blanket. "Only one way to find out what's up there." I took a step toward the door.

Mac, Sera, and Luke grabbed me.

"Aidan…" Luke stopped, taking a few seconds to think about what he'd say next. His expression was earnest, without a hint of his usual humor. "If you go up there, you may not come down. You definitely won't come back the same."

"I got the doom and gloom memo. I have to try. You can come with me. Another dual would be a huge help."

Luke's eyes grew wild with fear. "That's the one thing I can't do. Aidan, there were five of us when I was there, all strong as hell. That's her world. She's in charge. Escape isn't impossible, but it's damned unlikely."

"I'm going." Everything depended on it. My sanity. My friend's safety. My family's freedom. If I was cured, I might have some negotiating power with the council. It might only be a pipe dream, but it was a pipe dream that kept me going.

"Not alone." Mac spoke in that low growl he used whenever I did something he considered risky—which was pretty much everything.

My voice rose in frustration. I knew they'd consider my anger proof they were right, which only pissed me off more. "Will you stop that? I still make my own decisions, and I've decided if this is as dangerous as Luke says, I'm going by myself. I'm the only one who needs the cure."

My friends' vise-like grips didn't give an inch. I pried off Mac's right hand. He replaced it as soon as I removed his left one. I switched to logic. "If it's a trap, someone will need to rescue me when I inevitably put my foot in it. And someone else needs to man the getaway vehicle." I smiled winningly. They weren't won over.

Sera had a different plan. "Vivian will drive. Simon and Miriam can rescue. That okay with you, Simon?"

Miriam slammed the hood shut, making Luke wince. The man wasn't on edge. He was tiptoeing across a razor.

"Luke, what the hell should I expect up there? You said earlier that it'll try to play with my magic. Now would be a really good time to offer a few specifics."

Miriam interrupted before he could answer. "I'm good with rescue duty, but Simon might be a problem. If you're going to ask him, you'll have to speak a little louder." She pointed at the slope leading to the top of the hill, where a small black cat started his climb.

"Damn it," I swore. "When will you people stop acting like a bunch of heroic idiots?"

Mac and Sera were distracted enough by Simon that I was able to wrench myself loose. I raced off the bus and sprinted toward the hilltop. Footsteps pounded after me, but my secret morning runs gave me a boost they couldn't match.

So much for approaching the first in a calm, organized manner.

I hit the top twenty feet ahead of Mac and Sera. I leapt over the edge, prepared to pick up speed on the flat surface.

Instead, I drew to a panicked stop, barely avoiding falling into the giant pit at the top. I peered into its depths. Parts of my soul seemed to freeze at the horror below me.

Simon's voice was thin. "I wished to scout."

Sera and Mac clambered over the edge. Sera was cursing, her words overloud and inappropriate. I saw her enraged face inches below mine but couldn't process what she said.

I pointed a shaking hand and watched the same mix of shock and terror I felt appear on their faces.

We stood on the edge of a mass grave.

There was no other word for it. Bodies lay upon bodies in various stages of decomposition. Some had half their flesh, the rest eaten away by desert animals. Some were only skeletons, the bones bleached by the merciless sun. Some bones were broken or twisted. I wanted to believe that occurred after death, when the bodies were thrown into the pit, but I wasn't sure even my capacity for denial extended that far. However these people had died, it hadn't been peaceful.

"How many?" Sera asked in a whisper. "How many are there?"

Mac crouched low to the ground so that he could peer into the pit without falling in. "At least ten."

I took a deep breath to calm my surging magic and nearly gagged on the stench of decomposing bodies.

Madness whispered to me. It had no interest in the corpses, for in death they were nothing but bones. No, the madness promised me distance. The ability to gaze upon a pile of dead bodies and feel nothing.

I'd never been so tempted to let it in. If I stopped fighting, all the pain and suffering would belong to others.

"Ade. Aidan!"

My head snapped up, and the darkness retreated. "I'm here," I said, and it was mostly true. "Who are they?"

Sera shook her head. "Can't say for sure, though the coloring on a few of them suggests they were deserts. A couple of fires, too. One that might be an ice, though I can't begin to say what an ice would be doing in Utah."

"The height was about right, too," I said, reluctantly recalling the image. Fires tended to be on the short side, while deserts were often like Luke, tall and rangy.

Luke. He'd said he was scared of this place, but he could have been more detailed about why. He told us she kept people. I'd pictured hostages, not corpses. Somehow, he'd escaped this fate.

"Head back to the others, Sera."

Her jaw set, braced for a fight I had no energy to start.

I gestured around us. "There's nothing else here. Nothing you can protect me from, unless we believe in zombies now. Mac will be with me. We'll head down as soon as I explore. Feel free to interrogate Luke without me. Or to stick his head in some fast-moving engine parts. There were a few gaps in his story."

Too late, I worried that my belief in our connection had put us all at risk. Someone who leads you to a pile of dead bodies might not have your best interests at heart.

Sera didn't want to leave, but neither did she trust Luke with the others. Reluctantly, she and Simon stepped over the edge, leaving me and Mac alone. Alone, except for the decaying corpses at our feet.

I stepped around the pit, putting at least ten feet between me and its edge.

About five hundred feet in the distance, the hill sloped upward again, but until then it was a perfectly flat surface. The grave only took up about ten feet of that area. The rest was hard red rock. Luke said the first magic kept people, but there was nothing to support his story. There were no buildings, no structures of any kind where these people would have lived.

I walked across the flat surface, then returned in widening circles that allowed me to explore every foot of the space.

"Mac," I pointed at a square of charred ground, about fifteen feet long on each side.

"A building?" He knelt and ran his hand along the ground, then sniffed his fingers. "Burned."

My fire already knew that. Perhaps Luke had told us the truth, or at least some version of it.

Mac walked ahead of me, staring at the ground. "There was another here, also burned. The marks are about the same age."

"You picking up any scents?" My senses were as limited as any human's. With the stench of decaying flesh filling my nostrils, I was doing my best not to inhale at all.

Mac lifted his head and took a long breath, pulling air deeply into his lungs. His tanned skin paled. He wasn't immune to the smell of death. "Ashes. Small animals. And ozone." He glanced up at the clear sky and shivered. "Is there supposed to be a storm?"

I felt it then. Icy fingers trailing along my arm, cold breath against my neck.

Mac lurched forwards, pulled by invisible puppet strings.

No one spoke, and no words reached my ears, and still I heard the voice, high and clear and pure, a sound free of the limitations of humanity's vocal chords. A voice that didn't require lips and teeth and tongue, that had never been restrained by such earthly concerns.

It spoke a single word that rang inside my skull, and when Mac's head jerked up, I knew he heard it, too.

"Mine," it said.

CHAPTER 9

The cold claimed me. It touched every cell in my body. It slid from my throat to my shoulders and arms, traveling through me in seconds.

I'd felt something similar before, when an ice elemental used his power to subdue me. I'd never have expected to find an ice in the desert.

Something reached for my magic with grasping fingers, its touch greedy and demanding. It gripped the strong threads of both fire and water and tugged, its hold merciless. I resisted, but between the ongoing side effects from the drug and the icy touch slithering through me, I was too weak. Bit by bit, my magic was torn from me.

Luke said it played with magic. I should have insisted on more information. This thing didn't want to toy with me. It wanted to devour me.

I saw nothing. I only sensed a hunger, a gaping, cavernous hunger that could never be satisfied.

Panic swelled as my fire and water were inexorably drawn from me.

Mac stood next to me. Whatever had controlled him a moment ago now seemed focused on me.

"Aidan!" His nostrils flared, shifter senses working overtime to find anything he could fight.

I tried speaking, but my tongue was frozen.

Mac roared, the beast replacing the man. His human side might be capable of logic and cunning, but the bear possessed a feral instinct for survival that trumped anything the man could offer.

The cold vanished, and while my magic wasn't released, it was no longer drawn from my body. I still felt the voracious hunger, but it wasn't directed at me.

Mac's face slid between bear and man over and over, but the transformation was wrong. During a normal shift, each feature would reform as the lines of his face built themselves into the desired shape.

Now the bear slid from his face like a mask being removed to reveal the human underneath. Mac reclaimed it each time, and his teeth would sharpen and fur would darken his skin, but the attacker was insistent.

I couldn't see anything, but I sensed its emotions. Not just hunger, but frustration when Mac resisted. A determination to triumph.

I narrowed my entire focus onto my fire half and wrenched that thread from the distracted being that held it. The fire recoiled, slamming into my core.

My bid for freedom didn't go unnoticed. It resumed its assault on me, twice as strong as before, but the thing released Mac. I thought it could only manage a direct attack on one of us at a time.

I crumpled to my knees, holding on to my power with all my remaining strength. There was nothing I could battle, no countermeasures either of us could take. I could only play defense, and I was losing.

Once again, it tried to rip my fire loose. Though the threads remained anchored within me, my opponent held the other ends of both fire and water. The magic was strung between us. Fingers caressed my power, the touch covetous and eager. When I continued to fight for my fire magic, the creature dropped that thread entirely, doubling its assault on my water side.

I rocked back and forth, unable to do anything more than whimper.

Mac wrapped his left arm around my waist. He hauled me against his left side, my legs dangling. It was a rough hold that would leave bruises, but it kept his right half free to battle—though there was nothing for him to hit.

The first released me.

I allowed myself a second to go limp.

"Aidan!" Though his face was mostly human, hard claws dug into my skin.

"Still here." My power had been returned, though I didn't understand why.

"It's here, too," Mac confirmed. "I can smell the ozone." He spun in a slow circle, following the thing as it moved. "You ready to run?"

Desert sand spun around us, an impromptu tornado summoned from the ground.

I squeezed my eyes shut and pressed my lips together in a tight seal, then pinched my nostrils closed with the hand that wasn't trapped against Mac. The sand still found me. It climbed into my ears until I heard only a dull echo of the outside world. It slid under my fingernails, pushing with unnatural force against my skin.

I clutched Mac, desperate to keep our connection as my senses were stolen and my nerve endings howled in pain.

I'd never battled a desert. Hell, before this summer I hadn't even visited one.

Sometimes, you have to learn on the job.

I grasped my water magic and sent it from me in a rush, hoping to find anything to wash away the sand. There was only the gallon of water I'd brought with me. I gathered it in a large ball and waited. I couldn't smell the creature like Mac could, but the thing emitted an emotional signature

I could follow. Greed and determination and, underlying it all, a desperation so acute it brushed against fear. When all that need settled in a single spot, I flung the water at it.

The hot sand fell to the ground, abandoned by the first.

The second we were clear, Mac slung me across his shoulder and began running.

The landscape reformed, the flat surface rising and falling in an ever-changing obstacle course. Mac leapt across three new mounds of earth. The fourth rose as he flew over it, knocking his legs from under him.

He rolled as we landed, but my right side landed wrong. I heard the sickening snap of my arm breaking.

The thing was right above me. I felt its pleasure. Its satisfaction.

I didn't know what I was doing. I didn't know if such a being could be defeated. I only knew I wasn't going to die without using every weapon I possessed.

When I reached for the magic, I didn't use one to boost the other as I had in the past. I was too exhausted for such finesse. I could only slam them together and hope they found a way to strengthen the other.

They collided in a crash that resonated throughout my body.

I slid across the ground, the impact knocking me backwards. The blast rocketed toward the first above me.

I laughed, loud and wild.

As the explosion spread across the hilltop, the first magic appeared.

As Luke said, it took the form of a woman, perhaps a leftover from the days when the firsts mated with human men, but it looked like no elemental I'd ever seen.

It looked like every elemental I'd ever seen.

Its eyes were a golden brown until it blinked, when they became the arctic blue of an ice, then the near black of a true fire. Its skin changed colors as it moved and the light hit the bones in new ways, turning it from bronze to gold to a pale white in the space of a heartbeat. The wild hair was black and brown and the lightest blond, all threaded together. It was like staring at a hologram, where multiple images existed simultaneously, and what you saw depended entirely on where you stood.

She was horrible, and she was also magnificent, and it was beyond me to look away.

"Mine." This time the word was audible, her lips curving awkwardly around the single syllable.

The magic blast I created was already settling, and with it the flesh and blood creature began to fade.

Mac didn't give her a chance to vanish. From his hands and knees, he launched himself at her. Though he wore skin, there was nothing human about the movement. A foot from the first, his hand sprouted rich black hair and the claws sharpened. He pulled back his right arm and swung.

The claws scraped across her chest, splitting the flesh wide open. Within the wounds I saw flashes of light, a tiny glimpse of the pure magic from which she was formed. More unexpected was the very mortal blood dripping from the cuts.

She paused, transfixed by the red stream sliding down her stomach.

"Time to go," Mac said. He pulled me up by my good arm. I stumbled for several steps, but he didn't slow down, and he didn't let go.

The ledge approached. Two hundred feet, then one hundred. With only fifty feet to go, we dug deeper, finding reserves of speed to push us forward.

We needed only three more steps to launch ourselves over the ridge and begin the downhill sprint when we slammed to a stop.

A slab of ice stood between us and escape. I'd witnessed a similar trick before, but that had been in rainy Oregon. Not even a full ice could find enough moisture in the middle of a desert to build such a barrier.

It didn't matter how she'd done it. I wrapped flames around it.

I blinked, and it melted. I wasn't strong enough to do that on my own.

The wall vanished, revealing Sera.

I'd seen her angry, and I'd seen her use her power, but I'd never seen this avenging goddess. Fire didn't spark from her fingers, and she didn't hold fireballs in her palms. Sera was made of fire as she stepped toward us, every inch of her skin alight.

The first magic appeared between us, still visible. Sera pushed all her flames toward it. The thing absorbed the warmth, and for a moment her eyes and hair stopped shifting with each movement and became the black of a fire elemental. That was its only reaction.

Sera had thrown all her power at the creature, and it reacted with less interest than most people showed at a mosquito bite.

The first magic studied the newcomer, her expression more curious than threatened. Her mouth moved. Seconds later, the words reached us. "I do not need you."

A flick of her hand, and Sera flew beyond the ridge. I screamed, and in my fear and rage I found my strength.

This time, when my magics collided, I knew what to expect. I tried to ignore the maniacal glee that poured through me, how parts of myself shifted like tectonic plates. The explosion hit the creature square in the chest. More cracks appeared in her skin, more flashes of light.

She touched her wounds, the movement uncertain. We

didn't wait to see what happened when the effect wore off. Mac and I stumbled over the edge and let gravity propel us forward. Sera was already rising to meet us, her face bloody.

"Go, go!" I shouted.

She glanced past me. Whatever she saw convinced her. She raced ahead of us.

Sera leapt onto the bus, skipping two steps. Mac and I followed. Miriam was already at the wheel, the engine running. Before the door closed, the bus pulled into the road.

We didn't make it ten feet before Miriam swerved to avoid the crackling wall of flames. She evaded that, only to spin the wheel away from the sheet of ice improbably rising from the scorching ground. Next, she slammed on the brakes before we crashed into a pile of red rocks.

The first was turning us in a circle, forcing us back to her.

I raced down the aisle, peering through the front window. The thing stood atop the hill, arms wide in a cruel parody of a welcoming gesture.

"I'll help." Luke's voice shook. His bike was parked on the side of the road, but he'd been waiting on the bus with the others. "I can neutralize the desert, at least."

I didn't trust him, but I could accuse him of half-truths and treachery later—say, when we weren't escaping a creature that made me feel downright sane by comparison.

When the desert sands started to spin again, Luke pulled them to the ground, clearing our vision. With hundreds of feet between us, I felt the thing's anger rise.

My magic felt wrong. It struggled to rebuild itself as it was before I created the explosions, but it was too sluggish to make any progress.

I knew how to recharge it. "Miriam, get us on the road.

Sera, get a needle ready. Don't even fucking argue." I gave into the pure calm I found in both my magics.

The first had desert, fire, and ice, but I'd found no evidence she controlled water.

The bottles in the bus exploded, the liquid rushing toward me and through an open window. I added my fire side to the mix, using it to boost my power. The two threads intertwined and flew toward the creature. The water spun in a circle around her.

I felt her grasping, trying to claim my water half once more, but the magic moved too fast. Fueled by the fire, it spun around her. I increased my attack until the water was nothing but a blur.

Already, she was turning it to ice and melting it. I wrenched my power to me before she could grab hold again.

Miriam made the old bus fly.

Soon a thousand feet separated us from the hill, then fifteen hundred. No further barriers stood in our way.

An enraged scream echoed through my head. We all cringed and covered our ears, though the voice was inescapable.

With another thousand feet, the sound faded.

"Will she follow?" Vivian whispered, but her voice rang through the quiet and nervous bus.

Luke dropped into a seat, his face ashen. He looked like a man who'd woken from a nightmare and was trying to convince himself it wasn't real. "She can't. The firsts are trapped on the land where they were born. It's the only reason I could escape before. She wouldn't have let me go. If I'd gone up with you…" He didn't finish, but the utter terror in his voice filled in the blanks.

Mac walked to Luke and picked him up by his throat until his head was pressed against the roof. Luke didn't struggle. "Give me one reason we don't throw you off the bus right now."

Luke twisted his head toward me, and the others followed.

I held a ball of water in one hand, a ball of flames in the other, and with calm detachment debated the best method to kill this man.

"Because I'm the guy who knows how her power works."

The needle slid into my neck, and I didn't fight it. I'd be awake soon enough, and the magic would be waiting.

CHAPTER 10

When I woke, the pounding inside my skull made a good argument for a head transplant.

They'd created a makeshift cot for me at the back of the bus, several blankets in the aisle softening the hard floor beneath me. Mac watched me from above.

After blinking and groaning for fifteen minutes, I managed to push myself onto my elbows. "How long?"

"A day." He hadn't changed his clothes since I lost consciousness.

"You there?" I tried to ask if he'd watched over me, but two-word sentences seemed about my limit.

He tilted his head, working to interpret my question. "Yes, I'm here."

I grunted and bent my right leg, then my left. At this rate, I might be standing by Christmas.

I attempted to clarify my point. "No babysitter."

"Then stop acting crazy." Sera's head popped up from the seat in front of us.

I swallowed, but my mouth was dry, the movement rough. Sera threw a canteen down to me. I gulped the water, though it was lukewarm and tasted slightly metallic, and I began to feel less wretched. More like death warmed over than death itself. At least my broken arm had healed while I slept.

I pushed myself up fully, then took a moment to catch my breath. "How much did you use?"

Sera studied me, watching for any change. "Only a few drops. We've got to make it last as long as we can."

"Did you kill Luke while I was out?"

"No." Mac's statement might have been more promising if he hadn't added "Not yet" under his breath.

"You interrogate him?"

"Nope," said Sera. "We thought you should be there for that. Miriam's been guarding him, though that may be an excuse to drool over his muscles."

I pulled myself to standing. The world wobbled a bit, then settled. After a while, my stomach did the same. Steadying myself with both hands on the seat backs, I shuffled toward the front of the bus and stepped outside. The sun was setting, streaks of red and orange fighting a losing battle against the encroaching darkness.

"Where are we?"

Vivian was perched on a rock, fingers on her laptop keyboard. "Smack dab in the middle of nowhere. Don't worry. I'm not connected to anything." The anger in her voice wasn't directed at anyone else. The rest of us had already forgiven Vivian for her overconfidence. She hadn't caught up with us yet.

Simon sat next to her. "We do not seem to have a destination right now."

That was an understatement. We'd found the dual, and we'd found the promised cure, and we'd barely escaped with our lives. It was safe to say our current plan had some flaws.

"Where is he?" Sera said.

Vivian pointed to a small group of trees, where Miriam and Luke competed to see who could lasso the highest branch.

"Wasn't she supposed to tie him up?" Mac asked.

"Let's get this over with." I forced my body to take

long, confident strides toward the pair. "So, Luke. It turns out that thing was a homicidal nutcase who attacked first and asked questions never. Something you forgot to mention?"

He dropped the rope and turned to face me, looking both resigned and defensive.

"I gave you what I knew. I… it's a long story."

It was a weak response, and the unimpressed faces surrounding him seemed to agree.

"And yet," I said, "I'm pretty sure we can squeeze story time in between our busy schedule of running for our lives and driving aimlessly around the desert."

He nodded, just once. "I'll tell you, under one condition."

I waited. I wasn't particularly inclined to agree to his terms.

"No matter what you think of me right now, you keep me with you." He met my eyes, and his own were determined. "I've picked up a bit of wisdom over the years, and you need it."

Despite everything, I wasn't ready to walk away from the only dual who understood how to control his power. "Okay."

"No." Both of us turned to Mac. His ears were rounding, teeth elongating. "You're a lying bastard who damn near killed us all. You gave us no warning what to expect up there."

"I didn't know!" He looked at all of us in turn, hoping to find a sympathetic face. "I was about to tell you what the cure would entail, but the damn cat was too impatient."

Simon bristled, but he couldn't argue.

"I swear, when I left, she was unstable, but unstable like unpredictable, moody. Not mass grave unstable."

"Left?" Sera stepped closer. "I thought you said you

escaped."

"I did! She doesn't let people go. And I said that could happen to you, too. I warned you she would play with your magic and try to keep you."

I took a step closer, fighting for calm. "I could have survived being a prisoner. I could have even dealt with a creature who viewed my power as her personal entertainment system. That's not what happened. She tried to steal our magic. She ripped it from our bodies."

Luke swallowed. "I didn't know," he said again. "She only fed a little, one or two sips. Easy to replenish. Nothing like what you're describing."

I wanted to believe him, but there were still too many holes in the story.

Sera picked up a desert rock. She threw it in the air, and each time she caught it her grip was a little tighter. "Was she sipping from the ice, too? Cause I'm not understanding how an ice could replenish itself in the middle of a desert." Her voice was dangerously calm.

"There was one elemental she didn't feed from, another desert. The creature fed her instead, giving her sips of magic. I guess it was like a drug, cause she worshipped the first. She went on our supply runs, because we knew she'd always return. She brought food, clothes, and bags of ice, enough to refuel the ice's magic. That's why some elementals sought the first out. They'd heard stories from that desert of a mystical, generous creature."

Simon gave Luke the kind of disdainful look only a cat could manage. "I am trying to care about any of this. I am not succeeding. Tell us about the cure so we can decide whether you are of any use. You will not be interrupted you this time."

Luke met my eyes. "Learning about the cure isn't enough. Not without a first."

We waited, keeping Simon's promise not to interrupt.

"The thing is, you've been wrong, Aidan. Separating the threads isn't the cure. You need to join them, and join them permanently. Only a first can do that. So if you're gonna try this again, maybe you all oughta care what I went through."

Luke glared at the cat shifter. Simon gave him a slow, lazy blink.

"You wanna know what happened to me? Firsts control magic. You discovered that for yourselves. Well, she'd never met a dual before I stumbled into her lair. She played with both my fire and desert every day. She pulled the threads apart and stitched them back together. Whenever she ripped them apart, I thought I was dying. When she joined them, I was reborn, though that was its own torment. I was mad or sane depending on her whims. She enjoyed putting it together the most. She watched me, and though it's hard to call anything they do human, she felt smug. Really damn pleased with herself, like she had a secret. And when I got used to being whole, she'd rip it apart. Some days she let me wallow in memories. Sometimes she stripped my humanity and demanded I fight another of her pets. Once, I killed another fire, and she rewarded me by fusing the magic together right away so I could stand over the corpse of the man I'd suffocated with desert sand."

Each word was coated in bitterness. It was impossible to say how much of his hatred was for the first and how much was for himself.

Luke shook his head, forcing himself back to the present. "Anyway. That day, she'd just finished putting the threads together. I felt her glee, as usual, but I also felt her hunger. Fewer visitors were coming those days, and she'd been taking a bit more from each of us when she fed. That's when a stone elemental appeared out of the blue, drawn by the rumors of a pure, glorious creature. Her joy at having a new element after so long distracted her. I didn't waste my chance. I ran as fast as I've ever run in my life. Three of us did. Two didn't made it off that slope."

He rolled his shoulders to release the tension that built while he was telling his story.

"That was twenty years ago. Because I left when my magic was joined, I got to stay sane." He grimaced. "More or less."

"That's the cure, then? Let one of those ancient fuckers mess with Ade's magic?" Sera's words were level, but her anger rose. Anger and fear. She threw the rock she'd been holding. It flew so close to Luke's ear it lifted his hair as it passed. He didn't flinch.

"I tried to tell you. You didn't want to hear it, not really." He exhaled. "And maybe I didn't want to relive it. That's on me. I should have tried harder. I guess I thought Aidan had a chance, more than I did. She's in better shape than I was when I stumbled onto the first, and she has you guys."

"We're not going back there." Mac's tone left no room for argument, though no one was inclined to disagree.

Miriam pursed her lips in thought. "Luke, did you get anything else from her, like where the others are? Or if they're all batshit crazy?"

"That first is the only one I ever heard about, and I don't think they learn about each other. In their own way, they're more trapped than I ever was. Another first might not be as far gone. This one was in better shape when I was with her, though she was already growing hungry. The bodies suggest she progressed to starving. She probably consumed all their power to fuel herself. Other firsts might not be so awful, not if they're feeding regularly."

It was a huge risk. The others could be even worse than

what we'd found on the Utah hilltop. No reasonable person would seek out another of those creatures.

I didn't get to be a reasonable person. "So we need to find another ancient creature born of the earth's first magic and hope this one won't try to kill us on sight. No big deal," I said.

Sera snorted, and for a moment things felt normal, like we weren't planning a course of action that led to death and destruction.

"Does anyone have any idea where to even begin looking?" I wasn't too optimistic, and I wasn't sure I heard correctly when Vivian spoke up.

"I do."

I didn't think she wanted to continue. Vivian enjoyed helping, but she preferred to do it behind a computer, from the comfort of her office. Generally, she wasn't a fan of situations that led to chaos and bloodshed. She wasn't timid. She just wasn't as stupid as the rest of us.

Despite her reluctance, she squared her shoulders and finished her thought. "I know where another first is."

"Hawaii? Seriously?" Sera hadn't said much else since Vivian delivered the news.

She paced up and down the aisle of the bus, now heading west. It was Mac's turn to drive, which meant, for once, we weren't traveling at a speed that threatened to make the bus implode around us.

The minute Vivian informed us another first lived near Sera's home, my sister demanded we start driving and debate the merits of this new plan along the way. That was her version of patiently waiting for more information.

"Where? I grew up there. My family's compound is there. I never heard anything about this."

"There are lots of islands," I said.

"Not that many." She sat down in a huff. "You're telling me the thing we needed was right under Josiah's nose and he had no clue?"

Sera stared at the roof, considering. She was so familiar with the islands she could navigate them with her eyes closed. "There's Niihau, which is almost completely cut off from the public. Population of about six hundred. Kahoolawe is uninhabited, but that's cause there's no fresh water and the U.S. Navy liked to shoot guns there. A gathering of elementals would be noticed in either place."

"You're kidding me, right?" Miriam stared at Sera, incredulous. "You elementals are constantly hiding in plain sight. From what you've told me, your family compound is underneath a damn volcano, yet somehow no vulcanologist or tourist has ever found a bit of evidence. Brook's family has an island right out in the open, yet somehow it disappears from any map the minute it's found."

I acknowledged the point. "We're pretty much a cartographer's urban legend."

Sera wasn't convinced. "Are we pretending this first has Vivian-level computer skills and can erase herself from existence?"

Vivian was offended at the mere suggestion. "Of course not. I don't understand it, but this island has found a way to stay hidden."

Sera plopped down on the seat across from Vivian. "Right. What have you got?"

Vivian nudged Sera with her laptop, asking her to look at the map.

"Right there. Josiah gave latitude and longitude, though I had to work through several layers of encryption to find this. The man intended for this to remain a secret. I'm almost positive this is where the other first lives."

Simon studied it over her shoulder. "Correct me if I am wrong, but that spot does not appear to be an island."

I sat behind Vivian and adjusted my position so I could also see the map. The spot she indicated was, in fact, in the middle of the ocean.

Vivian clicked and brought up another map. "This image is archived from a year ago. Check again." This time, there was a tiny blur in the same spot.

I squinted. It wasn't as defined as the other islands on the map, but we were definitely looking at something. "An island that appears and disappears? Please tell me we aren't searching for Brigadoon."

"What makes you believe a first is there?" Sera asked.

It was a fair question. Josiah wouldn't have kept a map with an arrow and "First magic here" scrawled in red ink.

Vivian reclaimed her computer and pressed a few buttons, then leaned back, posture rigid. She watched Sera the way one might watch a ticking bomb. "There's nothing in the files to indicate Josiah was aware of the connection between firsts and the cure." Vivian took a long drink of water. "Sera, I'm not sure how to tell you this."

"Tell me what? Vivian, you're not Simon. Stop drawing this out."

In a single breath, Vivian did just that. "He wasn't trying to find the first magic. He was looking for your mother."

Sera didn't pale or shout or even blink. She stood up, gripped the seat backs on either side of the aisle, and watched Vivian with blazing black eyes.

"Explain."

Instead of speaking, Vivian punched another button to pull up a photo. Sera stood next to me, still refusing to sit. Together, we stared at a picture we'd never seen before.

It was a scanned photo of a small sailboat, taken by someone standing on the dock as it pulled out of the harbor. One woman hoisted the sails while the other sat in the boat's stern, watching the land recede. Both their faces were alight with joy. I didn't recognize the one doing the work. She had blond hair and blue-green eyes and looked like a strong beach, maybe even a full.

I'd hadn't met the woman at the railing, but I didn't need to be told who she was. Her skin was a lighter shade of bronze than some fires, due to being half human, but her hair was a wild mass of curls and her eyes turned up at the corners like the woman standing next to me. Sera's mom wore a v-neck sundress with oversized flowers on the skirt, and the other had flared white pants with a patterned wrap top. The photo had yellowed with time.

"Viv, when was this photo taken?" The words were strangled.

Vivian's eyes were too soft, too full of pity. "According to Josiah's notes, 1973. Two days before her death. Her official death, that is."

Sera said nothing, but two seats near Mac burst into flames.

Miriam sauntered to the front of the bus. She grabbed the fire extinguisher and doused the flames as casually as she would water plants.

I watched Sera, hoping the entire bus wouldn't explode when Vivian answered my next question. I reached for my fire side, just in case. "Is she still alive?"

Vivian didn't stammer or hesitate. "I can't say. I only know that she didn't die when you were told she did."

Tiny sparks flew from Sera's fingers faster than any Fourth of July firework. "How is this possible? I went to her funeral. I was there when the body was lowered into the volcano to rest with her ancestors. She was dead."

Vivian pressed a key. "I didn't find her by searching for Aidan's cure." She said nothing more, letting us put the pieces together ourselves.

It was another photo, this time of a woman with gray eyes and curly brown hair. She leaned against a railing with a close-mouthed smile. A small boy with slate gray eyes and brown hair stood next to her, face somber. Two stone elementals in a family portrait.

The truth was right in front of me, but I didn't want to acknowledge it. He couldn't have. Yes, his morals were flexible, but this would have been a step too far, even for him.

"The boy in the car," Simon murmured.

It was a photo of David, taken years before. The stone I'd murdered. The man who claimed Josiah killed his mother. The man who'd hated my father since he was ten years old, hated him so much he spent decades following Josiah, trying to find any weakness that would allow him to kill the oldest fire in the world.

The same man who told my father that he was "the boy in the car" right before he stabbed him.

It shouldn't have been true. No one would do that to an innocent. Even Josiah wouldn't protect his daughter if it meant ruining another child's life.

Except we both knew better. Josiah would have wiped out a continent to protect his children.

The stone was the right height, and her build was similar. Like fires, stones were muscular, if not as curvy. Her hair was lighter, but a bit of dye would have sorted that out quickly. If she was disfigured in a horrible accident…

Miriam rejoined us and studied the photos. "Vivian, how the hell did she die?"

Vivian didn't have a chance to speak before Sera bit out the answer. "Her car drove over a cliff. Near the volcano, right?"

Vivian waited. She didn't contradict anything Sera said.

"And David was in the backseat. He watched Josiah take his mother, because my father needed a corpse to bury. He murdered her and destroyed her son, then hid it from me my entire life. The fucking bastard." The last words burst from her, each syllable a small explosion. She paced up and down the aisle, the movement growing faster and more agitated. "How do I find out if she's alive, Viv?"

"The last time anyone saw her, she was headed for the first's island. You'll need to start there."

Sera didn't need any more information. She spun around and took long strides to the front of the bus. "Move."

Mac's shifter ears had picked up the entire conversation, and he didn't argue. He barely managed to pull the bus to the side of the road before she tugged at his arm, demanding he move from the driver's seat. As soon as Sera took his place, she pressed the accelerator to the floor. The engine groaned in protest, but even it couldn't resist Sera's will. Tires squealed as we pulled onto the road, leaving black rubber behind.

I kept my voice low, though I doubted Sera even heard the rest of our conversation. All her attention was focused on a small island thousands of miles away.

"How is Sera's mom connected to the first?"

"This folder is all about Helen Blais, from about a year before her supposed death. There are notes from investigators, photos, that sort of thing. Josiah was paranoid, but this time it was justified. She planned to leave him."

Vivian showed me another photo, this one of her mother sitting at a cafe with the blond woman. Their heads were bent together, as if they didn't wish to be overheard. Another showed them on a park bench. They were intimate pictures, but they looked more like two women who shared a secret than shared a bed.

"What are we supposed to be seeing?" Mac asked.

He'd moved next to me. I welcomed the solid warmth of his body. It felt wrong to be comforted while Sera's world was unravelling, but I was okay with wrong when it came in a Mac-shaped package.

"Nothing, yet." She swiped the trackpad, and a hand-written note appeared. The ink had faded, but it was still legible. It was addressed to Sera's mom.

Helen, I cannot believe I'm writing this at last, but I found proof. The first magics do exist, and I've found one. It's so close! Only two days by boat. We can witness this miracle and return before anyone notices we're gone! Tell Josiah and Sera you're visiting family on Oahu. I will wait for your response. Kathy.

It was dated a week before Sera's mom officially died in a car accident.

"But why would he lie?" I asked. "Why not tell Sera her mother left? Many parents try to protect their kids from grief, but his solution was unthinkable."

I slid my fingers through Mac's hand, gripping his palm. He held me as tightly, as if afraid I might slip away.

"I didn't know Josiah well," he said, "but I don't think he'd have protected Sera from the grief of her mother leaving. Wouldn't that still be better than believing she died? He might even like being the 'good' parent in her eyes, the one who stuck around."

"Then what..." I didn't need to finish.

Josiah was making sure Sera never went looking for her mother. Never followed her.

Sera's mom and her friend had willingly traveled to the island for a short visit. As far as we knew, they hadn't returned.

And we were about to do the same thing.

CHAPTER 11

"**N**o." Simon stared at the immense metal beast rising above him. I thought I actually saw his hackles rise. "Not again."

"Only way across the ocean."

"Airplane." He spoke the word with absolute certainty, as though I'd asked him the sum of two plus two, a question to which there was only one possible answer.

I wished he was right. I'd rather be at the airport than watching a container ship load in Long Beach, California.

Flying would be a hell of a lot faster, and while I dreaded what waited for us in the middle of the Pacific Ocean, any further delay could cost us dearly. Sera had parceled out the drug as much as she could, filling four syringes with a few drops each. We'd run out of time.

Vivian stood next to Simon, studying the vessel with only a little less dread. Just as waters weren't overly fond of the desert and fires didn't vacation in the Arctic Circle, earths would find pretty much any excuse to avoid boats—particularly when the boat wouldn't be near land for the next five days.

"We can't fly." She'd already said this, but Vivian needed to remind herself. "Even if we were willing to risk a connection, it would be stupid to break into the TSA's system. If I left any footprint behind in the current political climate, deleted footage would raise too many eyebrows. And that other hacker... he's good. If we fly openly, he'll find us."

I'd never heard Vivian express doubt before. A week ago, she would have scoffed at the idea of being caught or outmaneuvered. If I ever met that blue-shirted bastard, I'd give him my nastiest look. Then, when he started laughing, I'd ask Miriam to beat him up.

Sera strode down the gangway, returning from her discussion with the captain. Her movements were even more determined than usual, her eyes more intent.

"Did you figure it out?" I called when she was within earshot.

"Yeah. He's got a couple of no shows. If the captain sticks us in their cabins, he can keep us off the books, which means he also gets to keep all our money. I do mean all our money, too. If the agents hadn't arranged that nice anonymous transfer, we'd be screwed. I was only able to keep a hundred or so."

"One-way trip, then?"

The question had multiple meanings, and Sera ignored the scarier one. "My family has a small armada. They won't notice if we take a few."

Simon hadn't moved his eyes from the ship. He seemed to think, if he stared at it hard enough, it might transform into a plane or perhaps an especially long bridge.

"A week surrounded by the ocean on that... thing, and then we transfer to smaller boats? I do not plan to speak to any of you for the foreseeable future."

"It's not an issue. You're not going." I didn't realize I'd made the decision until I spoke, but as soon as the words were out of my mouth, I realized it was the only possible choice.

They yelled at me simultaneously, voices rising to be heard over each other. Together, they accused me of being stubborn, of trying to handle too much on my own, of refusing their help. Miriam added a few anatomically impossible suggestions for what I could do with that particular idea.

"She's right," Sera said. "It's too dangerous. You're not going."

Mac already stood next to me, but at her words he wrapped an arm around my shoulder.

Sera rolled her eyes. "Don't worry. You have a ticket, Mac."

Vivian's fingers curled into fists. "You already made the decision for the rest of us?"

For as long as I'd known her, Vivian didn't get mad. At most, she became a bit peeved. Watching her face darken, I thought this trip might have pushed her over the edge.

She continued to glare at us. "I'm here because I wanted to be with you and help however I can. Don't you dare take that choice away from me."

"You're not thinking, Brook." Miriam said. "Are you really planning on infiltrating the home of some homicidal magic bitch without Simon's spy skills? Or maybe an otter who can sneak onto shore in a way no boat can?" She glared at me, trying to force her words into my thick skull. "Plus, sailors have nothing to do but gamble. Give me a week, and we'll be flush. I might also be a happier woman after a week with sailors."

I hesitated. Her libido aside, there was truth to Miriam's words.

It didn't matter. I couldn't shake the memory of that mass grave. The image had woven itself into the tapestry of my nightmares. When I'd slept the night before, I dreamed of bodies rising from the pit, begging me to help them even as I smothered them with flames.

If anything like that waited for us on the island, my friends needed to stay behind. I couldn't risk their lives, not if there was another option.

"You weren't there. You didn't see, didn't feel…" I struggled to express the terror that had overcome me at the first's touch. I didn't think there were words in our language that could capture such fear. "We were her puppets, her fuel, her playthings, and if I hadn't figured out a new way to use my power, Mac and I would be dead."

Vivian lifted her chin. I'd forgotten how stubborn earths could be once they'd made up their minds. "It's my choice."

Sera grabbed Vivian's bag from the bus and chucked it to her. "I arranged your passage, Viv. You're coming."

Vivian and I wore matching surprised expressions.

"She has to," Sera reminded me. "The council has seen her with us. She's an elemental and subject to our rules, including the one where she gets locked up for a hundred years for helping you. You want her to share a cell with your mom and grandma?"

Sera understood exactly what button to push. It was horrible enough that I could do nothing to free my family. I wouldn't allow Vivian to suffer the same fate.

My earth friend swung the bag onto her shoulder. "I'm defenseless on my own. I wouldn't have a chance if they came for me." She sounded almost happy about that.

I grumbled something that might be interpreted as acknowledgement of Sera's point. Vivian had thrown her lot in with us, and we needed to protect her—though taking her toward a homicidal creature seemed an odd way to do that.

"Besides," Sera added, "if they catch Vivian, you'll have another reason to feel guilty. I'm already bored of your martyr complex." Her expression was bland, daring me to take offense. "You need a new schtick."

"There's nothing wrong with my schtick," I muttered.

"That's what he said." Miriam waggled her eyebrows. "Now, if we're done being serious, let's get our asses on that boat."

"You and Simon aren't going. That's final." I said. "Before you all accuse me of being stubborn, well, shut up. More people at risk means more I need to worry about—and more chances for me to lose control. You'd be in danger if you went, but so would I, because I'd flip out if anything happened to you. Also, you're needed in Tahoe. The council is threatening our friends. We can't leave them to fend for themselves, not when we caused this mess. And you know the agents will be lucky if even one shifter takes them seriously."

They wanted to argue, but for once I'd used actual logic.

"Good." I felt the weight of responsibility lift. "Simon, contact the bears and mountain lions when you get home. Carmen is stubborn, but Will should listen. They're going to want to fight the elementals, so remind them how powerful the old ones are. Anything weird happens, make a note and fill us in later. There probably won't be cell reception on the island, so we'll be out of touch for a while."

No one spoke. They were too busy looking really depressed.

"We'll see each other soon," I insisted.

"What about me?" Luke stood apart from us, leaning against the hood of the school bus with his thumbs hooked into the belt loops of his worn jeans. The pose should have appeared studied, but it had the opposite effect. It made me think that every man who'd ever posed as a cowboy for a book cover or beefcake calendar had taken his inspiration from Luke.

Sera fixed him with her trademark glare, the one that told him she might tolerate his presence, but she didn't plan to make it easy for him. "You're coming with us so you can teach Aidan everything you know. If she makes it to the island with all her gray matter working, maybe I'll forgive you for that whole Utah debacle."

Mac's jaw tightened, but he didn't argue.

The last of the shipping containers was lifted onto the vessel by the metal monsters lining the docks.

We said goodbye, and the words carried more than a hint of desperation. Sera handed Miriam the last hundred dollars to cover their fuel costs.

Simon rubbed his cheek against my shoulder. "Come back. I am quite fond of you."

I blinked away the tears that came with Simon's version of unconditional love.

Miriam wrapped all of us in enthusiastic hugs, including Luke. She managed not to grab his ass, though the wicked smile told me she considered it.

Sera's face was impassive, but she swallowed several times. "One last thing. Friends don't let friends ride in a Sunday school bus." She pulled three cans of spray paint from underneath a seat. "Don't worry, I didn't spend money. I stole them."

Vivian protested. Miriam nodded her approval.

"I'm keeping track of all my thievery, Viv. I'll pay them back when people aren't trying to kill my sister, okay?"

As she spoke, she coated the side of the bus in thick black paint, obliterating the stenciled letters proclaiming the bus transportation for the faithful. Over the black, she used orange paint to create crackling flames. As a final touch, she grabbed the red can to write, in strong block letters, "Hell on wheels."

"That," she said, stepping back to admire her work, "is an improvement."

I stood next to her, welcoming the brief moment of

normalcy. Whatever doubts and questions she had about her mother, they weren't consuming her, not yet. And I hadn't gone mad, not yet. Things could be worse.

"Much less conspicuous," I said.

Sera chucked the empty cans onto the bus. "Once they're far from us, they won't matter to the council. Making any effort to capture them would require acknowledging shifters even exist. They'll leave them alone."

"As much as they're leaving any of our shifter friends alone," I reminded her. We both grimaced, but sending them away was our best choice. "I know most elementals don't believe in the Christian god, but maybe we should hedge our bets."

"Pfft. Sometimes, you need to remind the universe to relax and enjoy the joke."

I grabbed her hand for a quick squeeze.

And then we were done. Miriam and Simon waited till we boarded the ship, then they waited while it left the harbor. I stood at the railing and watched until they were nothing but tiny specks on the shore. Even then I didn't move. I fixed the land and my friends in my mind and imagined I was leaving a piece of myself behind, an anchor that would draw me back when our task was complete.

WE SPENT THE FIRST NIGHT EXPLORING AS MUCH OF THE SHIP as we were allowed to access.

Until that point, I thought I knew all about boats. When you're raised on an island by a bunch of strong waters, it's inevitable that you learn your way around every kind of yacht, sailboat, and canoe.

The cargo ship was something different altogether. Unlike a cruise ship, which felt like a glamorous floating city, this was block after block of industrial neighbor-hoods, nothing but metal and sharp edges. It wasn't dirty, but it was far from pristine. The containers were all faded shades of orange, gray, and brown, dull against the vibrant blue of the ocean.

We ate dinner with the crew. Somehow, I'd expected a bunch of surly longshoreman who resented our presence, but instead we found a gregarious bunch from enough different countries to hold their own international summit.

It was full dark before we made our way to the cab-ins. I'd pictured large rooms strung with hammocks, but it turned out that didn't exist in this century. The cabins were small and plain, but they were clean and provided all the basic necessities.

Sera had only been able to bargain for a couple of rooms. Both had two single beds too small for any of us to share comfortably. Vivian had the second cabin to herself, mainly because Sera and Mac wouldn't leave either me or Luke unsupervised.

The men claimed the floor, either because they were gentlemen or because they didn't want the other guy to look tougher. Sera and I didn't argue. Mac lay on the ground next to my bed. I suspect he would have done so even if there'd been enough beds to go around.

Luke lay down a few feet from Mac. Within minutes, his breathing deepened.

After months of sleeping either in a cramped trailer or on the ground, it was a luxury to have a soft mattress beneath me. My body was desperate for sleep, and for once I didn't fight it as I slid into unconsciousness.

Even without Mac's arms around me, I slept more soundly than I had for weeks. Being surrounded by the soothing whispers of my element after weeks in the desert helped. I woke once in the middle of the night, but the nightmare images faded quickly. I was able to sleep again, and my eyes remained closed until the dawn light peeked through the small cabin window.

The others slept, and I was in no hurry to get up. For a moment, I felt safe. In the middle of the ocean, we were free from the pursuing elementals and not yet facing the terror that awaited us. So long as we were on the ship, nothing could harm us.

My magic took greedy gulps from the feast surrounding us. For a few minutes, I pretended I was just a water. For the next week, I would keep that side of myself so sated it drowned out the fire.

An hour later, the others woke up. Sera filled the small coffee maker, looking somewhat disgusted by its inadequate size.

The room was too small for four people to shower and dress with any privacy, so we took turns, then joined the crew for breakfast. Once they began their work day, we were more or less left on our own. They likely expected us to read or play cards.

Instead, Luke decided it was a good opportunity to learn how to control my power.

"Are you sure this is safe?" Vivian perched atop a container. While the ship was capable of stacking ten containers—five above deck and five below—it didn't have a full load, and the final row had singles on either end. Sera and Vivian had climbed on top of one, mainly to get out of my and Luke's way.

The good thing about cargo ships, compared to most other vessels, was how small a crew worked on the enormous boat. Once the containers were loaded, the ship required little supervision. Only a dozen men were needed to keep us moving in the right direction, which meant no humans would happen upon some elementals flinging magic around the stern.

There was a narrow passageway between the rows. Luke and I stood there, with a container on either side. We hoped the metal would resist any accidental fires.

Mac, of course, was behind me, glaring at Luke. "You ever done this before?"

"Have I ever trained a dual, even though I only met one, and that before I knew what I was?"

"So you could make it worse."

Luke hesitated. That didn't fill me with confidence. "I suppose it's possible. We could wait, but that means Aidan will face the next first with no new information about her power. I've only got what I picked up before, during, and after my cure. I know how using both magics causes the separation, those two selves that make it so, eventually, she can't come back. It ain't much, but I'm offering it. You want me to share it or not?"

Mac grumbled. Sera held up one of the last syringes, reminding him of the stakes, and at last he acceded. "Please be careful," he said.

I'd have felt better if Luke had needled Mac a bit more. Instead, he was sincere when he said, "I'll do my best."

I took a deep breath and shook myself out like a sprinter before a race.

When I was ready, Luke began. "How's the sanity doing? Give it to me between one and ten, ten being destroy the world."

"A four?" I guessed.

Sera scoffed. "Even before this started, you were a three on a good day." Now that we were making progress toward our destination, to both my cure and information about her mother, she was relaxed enough to mock me. It was oddly comforting.

Being surrounded by my element meant it took almost

no effort to douse an annoying friend. Sera sputtered as a gallon of ocean water landed on her head.

"Four," I insisted.

Luke's pose was as relaxed as ever, but his eyes were serious. "How'd you come up with that number?"

"Well, I haven't tried to kill anyone in days, so that's a good sign, right?"

A muscle ticked in his jaw as he studied me. I got the feeling I wasn't his ideal student.

"Let's try again, without murderous intent being the litmus test. How much control do you have?"

"I…" I stopped. I couldn't bullshit my way out of this, not with Sera watching. She'd been the one to drug me whenever I lost control, and she knew exactly how often that had happened since we escaped my family's island. "Not enough," I conceded.

"What's your mind doing these days?" His voice was quiet, the words meant just for me.

I turned my focus inward, searching for the blackness I usually tried to avoid. It was there, as it always was, dormant but watching. Waiting.

I sometimes thought it was embedded so deeply within me that, even if I did learn how to remove it, I'd cut out large swathes of myself in the process.

"It's there," I said, the queen of understatement.

Luke didn't need more information. He understood.

"What happened when you lost it? Your dark part?" I asked.

His laugh held sympathy but little humor. "Oh, it's still there. Always will be, but it's a lot quieter these days. It belongs to me, not the other way round."

"That sounds okay." Even if there was a complete, irrevocable cure, I thought parts of my magic would always be covered in black from the lives it took, and I wasn't sure that was wrong.

Luke's amber eyes missed nothing. More than anyone ever would, he understood the ongoing horror of living with power that was both gift and traitor.

My friends inched toward me, concerned. The silence had stretched a minute too long for comfort.

When in doubt, make a bad joke. "So, how do you channel the darkness now? Do you listen to more Nine Inch Nails?"

"Only Johnny Cash's versions," he said, feigning offense.

Damn. A man who listened to country music, who had a dimple in his chin and eyes that crinkled when he smiled. If Mac didn't already hold my heart in his hands, I might have been tempted.

"It's kinda like driving an old car with a big hole in the passenger side footwell," Luke said. "It all runs fine, but it's a little broken, a little ugly, and sometimes it's louder than you want it to be. And we never get to trade it in for something new and shiny." He dropped the metaphor. "You and me, we get to live with our past for the rest of our lives."

"As it should be."

"Yep."

Before I could worry about the future, I needed to make sure I had one. "So, what do I need to do?"

"I can't say I've been a professor before. Feel like I need a pipe and tweed jacket. I'll try to keep it short. So, you've got the two magics. Based on those blond locks, I'd say you discovered the fire second."

I confirmed this.

"When did you find out? Five years ago?"

I blinked at him, too stunned to speak for several seconds. "Five months."

His eyebrows reached for the sky. "That's some accelerated crazy you've got there."

"Well, there's been some stress this year," I said, upgrading myself to the empress of understatement.

"Considering what we're heading into, we can't count on that changing, so let's do what we can. When you first learned the risks of being a dual, you kept them apart, right? Did whatever you could to stop the fire from interfering with the other side."

Again, I felt the thrill of speaking to someone who understood exactly what I'd gone through. A single conversation with Luke was better than years of therapy.

"Exactly. At first, I lost control whenever I deliberately called the fire, but then the water started joining in on its own. The first time I used both, it was okay. You know waters can heal, right? I was curing someone, and I got through it without incident."

"What she's failing to mention is he was dead and she ended up leaving some of her magic behind."

I'd almost forgotten Sera was there.

"Wait, what? Where is it now?"

Mac growled.

Luke rolled his eyes. "Of course."

I rushed to change the subject before Mac could respond. "So, yeah. When I was healing him, it was okay, even when I boosted the water with the fire. But once I figured out how that worked, I couldn't seem to stop."

"It's hard to put power back once you find it."

Not long ago, I'd intertwined both magics. They'd strengthened each other, and in that instant I'd believed I was the most powerful elemental alive. Sometimes, in my weakest moments, I missed that feeling.

I needed to derail that train of thought. "Anyway, that's where it is now. I was told using both would eventually create a schism, a split self. First I'd lose control, then I'd lose my sanity, and then I'd lose myself. That's pretty much been the path. I mean, there's normal me…"

Sera snorted. I was glad to see her sense of humor was as inappropriate as ever.

"And batshit crazy me is showing up more and more, but…"

"But for now, you know who you are, most of the time." Luke finished for me. "You weren't given bad information, but you weren't given the whole story, either. Damn good thing I'm here, isn't it?"

That carefree grin slid across his face, the dimple appearing. I couldn't help returning the smile.

My neck grew cold as the sun that had warmed me was blocked by a very large shifter moving even closer. I knew Mac misinterpreted my connection to Luke, but right then, soothing his ego fell lower on my priority list than "be less crazy." He could deal.

Luke didn't even glance at him. "It helps to think in chemistry terms. Sometimes a couple of things can be entirely harmless on their own, but put them together and you've got a toxic mixture."

Yeah, I knew a thing or two about that.

"That how it is with us. When the magics work together, it's like those chemicals. Harmless on their own, but together they create an explosion, and that causes your schism. Each explosion does a bit more damage, until I guess there's nothing left to destroy. I don't know how long that takes. It's not like there's a manual on this stuff. I learned this from trial and error and a really cruel teacher."

"So, what? I need to work harder to keep them separate, so there are fewer of these explosions?" Considering how quickly my control fled when anger took over my body, I might as well work on my ability to fly or walk through walls.

"Oh, it's too late for that. No, you've gotta start combining them on purpose."

CHAPTER 12

No one was impressed with Luke's suggestion.

"Won't that lead to more of those so-called explosions?" Sera pointed a sparking finger at Luke.

"If done incorrectly, yeah, which is why I'm talking Aidan through it." An edge crept into his words. "I'm not stupid or suicidal. There's a way to focus the magic, and she needs to know it. She may need to fight."

"And right now I only have a few fights left in me. If that." I eyed the syringe pointedly.

Sera gritted her teeth, but there was no comeback.

Luke waited for my answer.

"Tell me what to do."

His voice dropped. The others could probably hear, but he didn't care about them. "Think back to when you healed the bear. You said you were okay then?"

It wasn't hard to pull up that memory. I couldn't forget the night Mac died. The only reason he lived now was because of my dual nature, and for that alone I couldn't regret what I was.

"How was that different from the other times? Why didn't you lose control?"

I recalled that night, pulling apart the memory and examining it with new eyes. "I wasn't angry. I was scared." The emotions came in a rush, and I turned, needing to see Mac's face. "I was going to save him, no matter the cost."

"And?"

"And I was focused. I knew I couldn't lose control for even a second. A single slip, and that would be the end, and…" I managed a wobbly smile that Mac returned. "I couldn't let him go."

Luke waited. I made myself turn away from Mac.

"When the madness comes," I said, "it's not the same. The world shrinks, and I feel nothing but cold certainty, but that's not focus, not really. It's the opposite. I don't care what happens. Hell, I'll set anything on fire when it's at its worst. I feel in control, but I'm causing chaos."

"And?"

I grimaced, wondering at what point he'd make me wear the dunce cap. There was a detail I was missing, something so simple Luke would keep prodding until I found the solution on my own.

"How are your actions different when you lose control? Your motives?" he urged.

When the answer finally came to me, it was so clear, so beautifully simple, that I wanted to smack myself for not seeing it earlier. "When I called the magic to heal Mac, I didn't use it to destroy. I used it to create, to give life."

Luke smiled, a warm grin that offered none of his cocksure charm. Rather, it was congratulatory.

"Yep. There was still a reaction when the two halves joined. It would explain why some of it got left behind. But you were tapping into its original purpose. Creation. Life. That's all it really wants. You can't use it to destroy without destroying yourself at the same time. You figure out a way to channel your power into creation instead of ruin, and you might be okay for a bit. Might feel better in your own heart, too."

I pondered his words, weighing them against my experience. "One problem. Most of the time, I don't choose to call both magics. I get pissed off, and boom, there's the fire and water and a whole lot of crazy riding in the sidecar."

"And that's why we're in the middle of the ocean headed toward another first who may or may not kill us on sight. I'm just trying to help you get there with your brain working."

"Four tiny doses," Sera reminded me. "And another week on this boat."

"Maybe we can cut a day off that." Luke winked. "Feel like speeding things up a bit?"

"No." Sera, Mac, and Vivian spoke together.

"I need to practice. Better to do it in a controlled environment than the next time someone tries to kill me." I didn't wait for them to argue. "Tell me what to do."

"Think about something you've created. Let that be the source of your power. Now you're going to build a wave where none exists, but don't isolate the magics. Start with them fused together. You'll have that boost, but you'll avoid the explosion when they meet."

I reached for the threads coiled together in my core.

"Oh, and Aidan? Don't lose your focus, okay? Creation only."

No pressure there.

I imagined the threads of fire and water moving together. They knit themselves into a single force, the bond growing tighter and tighter until the dual parts of my power existed as one unit.

My friends' tension was almost palpable. No one seemed to breathe or even blink while they waited to see what I would do. I was a science experiment that could explode at any moment.

"You're really not helping," I said.

I blotted out everything else, concentrating only on the power and my intent. Even now, the madness hovered in the corners of my mind, eager to squeeze into the cracks if my attention slipped even a little.

Before I closed my eyes, I saw Luke gesture to Sera, asking her to toss down the syringe. Perhaps he wasn't quite as confident in my ability to stay non-murdery as he pretended.

I took my friends' fear and wrapped it around me, knowing they weren't concerned about themselves. They worried about my safety.

They worried because I was loved.

We'd made something together, a small family entirely separate from those to which we were born, and I'd been a part of that.

It wasn't much, but it was also everything.

Holding the thought of that family in my mind, that small group we'd created, I checked my magic. The bond was even tighter now, almost glowing with a newfound strength. I grinned to see it. Something so light might have a chance against the darkness.

Magic flowed through my skin, as strong as ever. I pictured the metal maze surrounding us and sent the threads rushing between the containers.

The water magic attached to the ocean's molecules and I made no effort to stop the fire from joining in and adding its strength.

I pushed it upwards, forming a twenty-foot swell. In the distance, I heard an alarmed shout, but there was no reason for concern. The wave didn't so much crash as slide into the ocean, gently nudging the ship forward.

I did it again, the wave a bit taller, a bit wider. To an outsider, it would look like nothing more than a freak weather phenomenon.

I decided to create something else. I imagined the ocean's flat surface, then I built upon that. Between two placid sections, I envisioned a current the ship could slip into, where it would move a little faster than the surrounding water. I'd barely had the thought before the ocean hurried to obey my request.

The cargo ship picked up speed. My friends murmured to each other, but I kept all my attention on the primordial magic I possessed, that power so old it predated speech.

It was the magic of creation, the same source that lived in every elemental and shifter. I could sculpt new worlds, using oceans and flames as my blades.

I wondered how many knew duals could do this. It would explain why we were feared. Our ability to destroy was horrible, but many would consider this power just as terrifying. If they wanted to, duals could change the very fabric of the world.

Most people reject change, or fear it, and I was a living symbol of that. Of course they wished to eliminate me. Destroy me.

My focus slipped, just a fraction, and I paused to rebuild it, placing my attention on the multiple streams.

Streams of water. Streams of life, each one created by a choice I made. I could have chosen the stagnant stream of isolation, or the quiet one where I avoided trouble rather than seeking it out. Perhaps I could have chosen a healing stream months before. If I'd gone to the compound when Josiah asked, maybe we would have found this creature already, and I'd have done so with my father at my side.

Josiah.

Somehow, it hadn't occurred to me before that a choice I'd made led to his death. The truth pulled at me, demanding my attention.

If I'd gone with him the day I learned what I was, all of this could have been avoided.

The memory rammed into me so hard I took a step backwards, hitting the hard wall of Mac's chest. It offered no comfort against the image of my father lying in a pool of blood in my grandmother's library.

The man had tried to save me so many times. He tried to save Sera from following her mother to an unknown danger. His actions were unforgivable, but he was our father.

I grasped at the creation magic as it slithered from me, but my hold was weak. Inky tentacles slid over my mind, obliterating the positive thoughts I'd built with such care. Memories of my family and friends were replaced with images of death. Josiah. David. Brian. Christopher.

The guilt was too strong. Madness promised freedom from the pain.

Wind whipped my hair around my face, the ship now racing across the Pacific.

"Aidan!" The single word reached me, screamed by a voice I knew.

Arms wrapped around me, muscle and sinew and flesh. They were immense, capable of uprooting entire trees, and they were also so fragile. Water crashed over us, forcing the arms to release.

Fifty-foot swells appeared under a clear sky. Panicked voices surrounded me.

A wave surged between the containers, catching the people perched atop one and dropping them onto the deck.

"Aidan!" A woman with black hair plastered to her skull screamed at me from ten feet away. "You have to stop."

Another woman spoke. She also had dark hair, though hers was dreadlocked and her skin was darker. Her eyes were more fearful, too. "Aidan, you're going to expose us. We can't hide this from the humans."

My power began to fizzle. I grasped at the threads, panicking. Months of that vile serum was taking its toll. I boosted my magic as much as possible, trying to sharpen the dull edges.

I refused to be weakened, and I refused to restrain my actions for a few humans. My laugh was cruel, incredulous. "Humans can be thrown overboard."

Once more, the muscled arms grabbed me. I reached for another swell, a stronger one capable of pushing my captor so far he'd never grab me again.

But it was a trap. I saw it a fraction of a second too late. The women hadn't been trying to reason with me. They'd only needed to keep my attention while another man moved behind me.

I howled my anger and covered my attacker in fire before I remembered it couldn't hurt him.

The needle found my neck.

The blackest part of my mind screamed. It had been so close. Another minute, another death, and it would have claimed me forever.

Instead, it withdrew, pulsating with malice and bile, and I slid into unconsciousness. Oblivion was so easy. So comforting.

Before I slept, I saw the faces that surrounded me. They were worried, an expression I'd seen too often recently, but there was more.

They no longer looked at a friend. The hurt eyes that stared back at me saw only a stranger.

WHEN I AWOKE, I WAS STILL ON A BOAT. I KNEW THIS BECAUSE I sensed the ocean on all sides, not because I could see a damn thing. The room was nearly pitch black. Only a thin strip of light appeared beneath a door.

I reached instinctively toward the ocean to heal my pounding headache. The headache had other plans, preferring to hang out with the nausea. My skin prickled, tiny needles jabbing my stomach. My hearing was muffled, as if my ears were plugged with cotton.

I examined my mind, looking for weaknesses and injuries the same way I'd explore my physical body after an accident. My memory was intact, and I winced at what I found. My friends' faces as they saw what I was truly capable of doing. It was a mirror, reflecting my own horror of what I might become.

The magic was a little duller than it had been before. A little weaker.

Self-assessment complete, if unsatisfactory, I turned my attention to my surroundings. I was on a particularly uncomfortable bed, the mattress unforgiving and short enough that my feet hung off the end. The air smelled musty, as if the room hadn't been aired out in many months.

The boat rocked with the undulating waves in a way the cargo ship never would. We'd switched to a far smaller vessel. I doubted it belonged to Sera's family. Josiah wouldn't have allowed anything he owned to be described as musty.

I pushed the thought away, terrified to even remember his name after what happened on the ship.

I didn't want to move. I wanted to stay below deck, possibly for the next twenty years or so. Perhaps my friends would have forgiven me by then.

Bracing myself for the pain of sitting, I dug my elbows into the lumpy mattress and pressed myself up.

I drew to a sudden stop when restraints tugged on my wrists and ankles.

"Hello?" I called. My voice was so weak it was almost inaudible. I coughed and tried again.

"Aidan?" Mac answered immediately. He was right on

the other side of the door.

"Of course it's me. Are you tying up so many women you're confused?"

My attempt at humor was met with silence. I could practically see his jaw tightening in frustration.

"Where are we? When did we switch boats?" They'd only given me a few drops, enough to put me out for a day or two.

He didn't answer. Not me, at least. I heard a low murmur as he conferred with someone else.

"How long are you keeping me here? Are we heading to the island?" I tried for a conversational tone that gave away none of my trepidation.

"Where else would we be going?"

He sounded so confused I didn't mention that, for a second, I wondered if they were finding a nice place to dump the body when I lost control for the final time.

"I thought… it's not important. But if I'm plummeting over the cliffs of insanity, restraints aren't going to make a difference. I can access my magic without them." I didn't know if I was helping my cause or not.

"Are you accessing any now?"

"To heal." I drew a little more water toward me. My headache downgraded from screaming jackhammer to a dull throb.

Someone whispered to Mac. I thought it was Vivian, but the words were too muffled for me to be sure. His response was equally quiet. They didn't seem to be arguing. Rather, it sounded like they were in perfect agreement about the need to keep me locked up.

"You're not moving, Aidan. You're staying in that room until we hit the island."

I grumbled several unflattering things about domineering men, knowing his shifter ears would pick up every word.

"Complain all you want. Spend the next twenty-four hours thinking of new ways to insult me, but you're not leaving this room." I tried finding a hint of softness in the words, but there was none.

"Back there, on the boat, I didn't mean…" I had no idea how to end that sentence. For those few moments, I'd meant it all. "You know I'd never really hurt you, right?" I had to believe that was true.

He didn't respond.

"Mac?"

Instead, I heard heavy footsteps moving away, and the next voice was Sera's.

"Stop apologizing. Hell, stop talking. None of this is up for discussion, Ade. I can't believe you're even considering joining us right now. You should be begging us to move you to a sensory deprivation chamber. Are you trying to lose it completely?"

I thought it was a rhetorical question, but she paused, waiting.

"Do you really need to ask that?"

"After the last month? Yeah, I do. But I don't care if you're done fighting. We're not. We're getting you to that fucking island, and we're getting you there with your brain still working. It's one more day, Aidan. We used every last drop of the drug to get you this far. We're out. So, for the next twenty-four hours, there will be no stimuli, no conversation, nothing that could possibly push you over the edge."

"Sera…"

"We'll be there tomorrow morning," she said. It was her only answer, and though I didn't hear any footsteps, she didn't speak to me again.

CHAPTER 13

I woke to loud swearing. "Damn it, Ade. What part of 'don't use your magic' was open to interpretation?"

Sera stood in the door. She was distorted, her body undulating in waves. It made sense, considering I stared at her through several feet of water.

"I didn't mean to," I said, though I wasn't sure she could hear me. It was true. The day before, my thoughts had instinctively skittered away from memories with negative associations, anything that could cause stress. Instead, I'd replayed what Luke taught me, picking the words apart and imagining all the things I could create. I made a mental list, in case I ever needed to redirect my energy away from destruction in a hurry. Waterslides that criss-crossed mountains. Natural sprinklers on dry grass. Reservoirs in drought-plagued areas. The last thing I remembered before falling asleep was an image of a perfectly square pool held together with magic instead of walls.

I might not talk in my sleep, but it seemed I now accessed my power while dreaming.

I'd filled the room with a pool that rose well above my body, and I'd done so in a completely new way. Normally, I'd pull water through an open window or door, but this room had no such openings. The others would have noticed if I'd directed ocean waves below deck.

I'd created this from nothing. I tried telling her that.

"I can't hear you. Which is good, cause if I can't hear

you offering some weak-ass excuse, I'll be less tempted to dump you overboard. You're tilting the whole damn boat."

I offered my winning smile. She scowled with no humor, and I looked closer. There were dark circles under Sera's eyes, her bronze skin was ashen, and she'd lost weight in the last few days.

She wasn't accessing fire to heal herself. Not when I was so close.

I pulled against the restraints, then glanced pointedly around my watery cage. If she wanted to hear me, I needed to dispel the water I'd created while I slept.

"Nope. No magic, not when we're so close. And let's face it, you aren't saying anything that important."

I struggled, mouthing words at her. Considering that my most mature comment was "You're not the boss of me," it was for the best she couldn't hear.

Her smile wasn't the mocking one I might have expected. It was relieved. "You're still there."

With that, I stopped fighting and let her see me. Scared and uncertain, but me.

"Good. Don't ever do that again."

I nodded, though we both knew it wasn't a promise I could keep.

Heavy steps moved toward us, Mac joining Sera in the doorway. His jaw tightened when he saw the pool I'd created, and he was no more moved by my smile than Sera was. Unlike Sera, he stepped into the water, and with a surprisingly graceful combination of swimming and walking, he reached the restraints and untied them. We floated upwards, facing each other. When he stood on the bed, Mac's head rose just above the water line.

His white t-shirt clung to his body, and the water increased his hair's natural wave. Even staring at me with a mix of concern and fear, he was damn hot.

"Hi," I said.

He said nothing.

"Sorry I tried to kill everyone?"

He closed his eyes. His sharp exhale stirred the water. "Sera, can you give us a minute?"

I heard her leave, but all my attention was on Mac. I waited for either anger or forgiveness. I wasn't even sure which I'd prefer.

He gave me neither. "We're here."

"That's good, right?"

"I don't know about good, but it's necessary. After..." He swallowed and didn't finish. "It's our last chance, and we're going to make it work. That's the only option."

"I want this, too. I'll do anything."

"That's a lie."

"It isn't! I messed up on the boat, but I was trying. You have to know that's true." The surface of the water churned, doing its best to contradict my words.

"That's not what I'm talking about, though that was a disaster. Luke pushed you too fast."

"We had to try," I insisted.

"Maybe." He grimaced. "My point is, you say you'll do anything to save yourself, but you keep trying to save the rest of us. Sera talked to you about this already. You act like your life is secondary to ours. If one of us is in danger, you don't even hesitate. You grab your magic without considering other options. The drug's gone, Aidan. You don't get another chance, so you've got to stop doing that."

He was right, but not entirely. "My life *doesn't* matter more than yours. More than any of yours. I'm stronger than you and Sera. If it takes my power to save you, then I'm going to use it, and I'll pay the cost, no matter what it is."

His fingers gripped my upper arms, squeezing a little

too hard. "It's not that simple. If I die, that's it. It's one death, and it's okay. But if you lose this battle against yourself, there's no telling what damage you'll cause. Remember the stories about out-of-control duals raining death and destruction? This isn't about us anymore."

I shook my head so fast wet hair slapped my cheeks. "No. It's definitely not okay if you die. I deserve to have some say in this, and I say no. I'm the reason we're all here, and I will not have a single one of you dying on my account. If I do cross over, one of you needs to kill me. That's my choice."

The warmth seeped from his brown eyes. "Even if Sera could do it, she'll be distracted learning what she can about her mother. Vivian's not going. Luke's an unknown. We can't count on him."

"Mac…"

"What would you do if I gave you a gun and told you to shoot me?"

My shudder shook the water.

"Exactly. I would drown myself a thousand times before I hurt you, Aidan. Any version of you. Don't ask me to do the one thing in this world I'll never be able to do."

I threaded the fingers of my left hand through his thick hair and tugged him toward me. His forehead met mine and our breath mingled. "Then don't ask me to do the same. You and Sera, you've been hovering over me for months now. Telling me where I can go, what I can do. It drives me insane—okay, bad choice of words, but there's some irony here. Your need to keep me safe and calm pisses me off. I've let it slide because I understand it comes from fear and I've given you plenty of reason to be afraid, but I'm not letting this slide. You don't get to tell me that I should let you die."

We remained like that for quite a while, neither of us

willing to bend.

Finally he pulled back. His eyes were dark and full of unexpressed emotion. "Then you better stay in control for a few more days." It wasn't a request. It was a proclamation made by an enormous bear who would destroy anything that dared cross him. He was growling to the universe, daring it to interfere with his plans.

"I will." My words carried the same determination.

I pulled him to me, demanding more. He nipped my lower lip once, then slid his mouth across mine. I climbed his body and twined my legs around his waist. The water rose with me.

We separated only when I pulled the water too high. Mac sputtered and scowled at the offending pool.

"Yes," he said. "You damn well better stay in control."

He wrapped my hand in his and squeezed.

"What are we going to do with this?" I gestured behind me as we left the room.

"You controlling it?"

"Nope."

He shrugged. "Then apparently you created a square pool that doesn't need any walls. We'll deal with it later."

The others were already gathered on the deck. Luke and Sera held four bags total. Vivian stood at the railing, gazing longingly toward land. Her laptop remained in her bag. I felt like she was missing an appendage.

"Why don't the rest of you remain with Vivian? Keep her company until we discover how dangerous it is?"

I had to try.

Sera rolled her eyes. "Because my mother might be on that island. Luke knows a bit about these firsts, and he's actually feeling brave enough to come with us. You could lock Mac in a trunk and drop it in the ocean and he'd find a way to get to you. Viv will be here in case there are any problems, but that's it."

I read between the lines. Vivian was staying on the boat because, if we didn't return, there needed to be someone alive to tell the others what happened.

We approached the island from the south. It was a little more than half a mile wide. It was impossible to guess the length, but a small mountain jutted toward the cloudless sky about a mile from the boat. The island was large enough that, by now, it should have been discovered. The first would need to shoot down satellites, bribe cartographers, and hire advanced hackers to keep it hidden. It made no sense.

The boat inched toward a short strip of sand. Beyond the narrow beach, there was nothing but wilderness. Tangled vines and palm trees and rich ground cover obscured any possible paths. It would probably take an hour to force our way from one end of the island to the other.

Somewhere within that impenetrable vegetation, we'd find answers. "Let's go," I said.

Our goodbyes to Vivian were perfunctory. We pretended like we'd see each other that evening. You know, take a tour of the island, meet the first for tea, get cured, and come right back. That sort of thing.

Sera chucked the bags into a small rowboat and climbed down.

I followed, balancing out her weight. "Where did you find this boat?"

"I stole it. We didn't have time to get to my family's slips. It's okay. Vivian made me leave an IOU."

Luke followed us. The rowboat dipped when Mac took his seat at the oars, but it held.

We moved toward land.

"I agree with him."

I stared at her, hoping she didn't mean what I thought

she did.

"Your sanity matters more than our lives. That's a fact. So before you do anything stupid for the gazillionth time, try to remember that the rest of us aren't wimps."

"I will, if you can remember that I'm still a fucking grownup."

"Still? You were before?"

With great effort, I did not soak her. "My cure matters, but so does finding your mom, or at least finding answers. I'll do whatever I can to help."

"You don't have to. That's my point. I'm an incredibly strong elemental. Luke is a dual who's actually in control of his powers. Mac turns into a seven-foot bear who can break people by waving his paws about. We can handle ourselves, and you're going to let us."

"You're the supernatural Avengers?" I had to ask.

"With less spandex." She studied the island as we drew closer. "Let's save the world, H2O. Or at least save you, which is kind of the same thing to me."

THE FOUR OF US STEPPED ONTO THE EMPTY BEACH BAREFOOT, holding our shoes. I wore cut-offs, but the others were in jeans soaked from the knees down. They weren't exactly the type to wear board shorts, regardless of the weather.

I chucked my Converse several feet ahead of me and dug my toes into the sand.

It was hot, but nothing like the raging temperatures of the desert. Where that was a dry heat, this was humid, the air so thick and heavy it settled across my skin like a blanket. None of us complained. Luke, Sera, and I were all part fire, and we welcomed any heat. Mac probably wouldn't complain if someone held a match to his skin.

I wasn't allowed to touch my magic, but I didn't need

LOST CAUSES 145

to. It rose up, more exuberant than ever before. Energy flowed through me, every nerve ending waking up.

"Do you feel that?" My eyes widened and my mouth formed a small, surprised O. "Is that energy put out by a first? When they're not trying to consume you, I mean?"

Luke looked as amazed as I felt. "It's new to me."

Sera scanned the vegetation for any threats, but she found time to laugh at us. "You guys are crap fires. It's the volcano."

Mac, Luke and I looked up, seeing nothing but tree-tops, blue sky, and a green, unvolcanic mountain.

"I take it back. You're really crap fires. It's a seamount, an underwater volcano. Someday it'll rise above the water, but for now it's hanging out below the ocean floor. They're all over Hawaii. How do you not know this?"

"I was an English major."

"I skipped college."

Luke and I nodded, more than willing to support each other's ignorance.

I inhaled, sensing a force as majestic as the ocean at my back. I was pretty much in dual heaven—if I'd been allowed to access both my magics.

There was something else. A power I'd never felt before, but it was warm and giving, and it soothed me in a way I hadn't felt in months. The blackness receded, just a tiny bit.

I'd expected to find the same desolate silence that we discovered on the Utah hilltop, but instead the island was filled with sound. The lap of the waves behind us, the calls of birds, the rustle of palm trees as the wind passed through their fronds, the exuberant leaves of the hala trees whispered to each other. The hilltop had been death. This place teemed with life.

Hope stirred. It was so vibrant, so very alive, that I

couldn't believe cruelty or evil waited for us beyond the tree line.

A dart shot past my shoulder.

You'd think, after all this time, I'd get used to being wrong.

"Get down!" I shouted.

We flung ourselves onto the sand, raising our heads an inch to search for the threat.

The dart had flown past us and landed in the rowboat. Another soon joined it. At least whoever was aiming was a crap shot.

"Where's it coming from?" I kept my voice low.

Mac studied the angle of the trees, measuring them against the darts' position in the boat. He raised a finger to test the wind, calculating their likely trajectory. His gaze moved from one spot to another as he performed mental geometry. At last, he nodded toward a thick hala tree a hundred feet away that marked where the beach ended and the vegetation began.

A second later, Sera was up and running in a crouch. I tried joining her, instincts kicking in before I remembered everyone's insistence that I do nothing. A large hand hauled me to the ground with more force than necessary.

"Don't even think about it," Mac warned.

"Still a grownup," I reminded him. A foolish grownup, sure, but one who was sick of being ordered around.

A second later, a tree burst into flames.

It didn't take long for Sera to cut off all escape routes. As one tree after another lit up, figures emerged from the tropical forest, coughing and swatting at the small sparks on their clothes and hair. As soon as the forest was clear, Sera extinguished the fire, limiting the damage as best she could.

Water magic stretched toward the ocean behind me,

absorbing its healing power.

My fear receded. This wasn't an ambush by the invisible first. No, this was the devil we already knew.

I leapt to my feet and strode toward Deborah, who managed to maintain her dignity despite her singed clothes and sweating face.

"Are you fucking kidding me?"

Michael stood next to her, his shaking hands holding an enormous device I'd only seen on nature shows when zoologists tranquilized elephants. It still contained several darts.

"Thirty days. Thirty days in which you weren't supposed to track, ambush, and/or drug me." I eyed the darts, hoping they didn't hold anything more permanent than the anti-magic serum. "You couldn't even do that. How the hell did you find us?"

I blinked as a spear of light hit my eyes, then vanished. A small woman attempted to hide behind the trunk of a palm tree. She'd wrapped her fingers around the metal necklace that had given away her presence. She straightened her shoulders and lifted her chin, trying to hide her fear.

She appeared to be in her late twenties, and she was small. Barefoot, she'd be lucky to reach five feet, and her weight might not cross into triple digits. Though her hair and eyes were both black, I picked up no hint of fire magic. I did, however, spot a rectangular bag resting on her hip—the kind Vivian always carried with her. Unlike Vivian's bag, hers was decorated with a large Hello Kitty patch. She wore purple instead of blue, but I had no doubt it was the same person I'd spotted in the SUV outside Luke's hut.

"Josiah's files. You're the one who took them."

She managed a weak smile.

Sera closed the distance between them. She didn't often get to look down on people, and she took full advantage of the intimidating position. "Considering that you're helping them find us so they can execute my sister, you should stop smiling."

The woman hurried to obey.

The stranger wasn't important. She'd already done all the damage she could. The real threat stood before me.

"What was the plan? Knock me out or kill me?"

Deborah didn't answer. Michael looked more than moderately terrified when Mac moved closer.

"Not kill," Michael turned the gun so we could view the darts in greater detail. "We wouldn't do that, not with…" His eyes jumped from Mac to Sera to Luke. They wouldn't harm me, not with my powerful friends watching.

"How much of that stuff do you have?" I asked.

Deborah's expression never changed. "We constructed a laboratory to produce large batches of the drug. It ensured we had enough for Trent Pond's daily dose."

"You drug him every day?" It was a horrifying thought. If my power felt dull after three months of semi-regular doses, his must seem like it had been ground to dust.

The sides of Deborah's mouth quirked upwards, her version of a grin. "A single drop. That's all."

"And?" I asked.

Behind Deborah, the ferns twitched. Sera's eyes followed mine, her muscles tensing.

"The results are promising," Deborah said.

My attention snapped back to the council leader. We'd never tried such a tiny dose. I struggled to control my voice. "What does promising mean? Could it really work, in the right formula and the right dosage? Deborah, if there's a real chance, this can end right here."

Her lips tightened, a red slash across her face. "Trent Pond never murdered anyone. You have. The punishment for killing another elemental, regardless of the circumstances, is well known. Besides, we already offered you the opportunity to live as Trent does. You rejected it."

I took a deep breath and prepared to deliver an argument worthy of Perry Mason, though likely with more babbling. Something about how I couldn't be responsible for the murder if I wasn't sane, and I couldn't be destroyed for being a dual if there was any hope of a cure, and even humans were merciful enough to allow an insanity defense. Sure, the argument had a few holes, but it was all I had.

Before I could speak the first word, Deborah's knees buckled and she stumbled to the ground. Michael followed, whimpering as a brown rock smacked against the back of his skull.

I was shoved behind a Mac-shaped wall. I peered around him to see who was attacking, and more to the point, how we could convince them to stop throwing rocks.

Except they weren't rocks. Whoever was hidden in the trees was throwing coconuts at us.

Mac grunted as one of the projectiles hit him in his left shoulder, but that was the only sign he felt pain.

The others weren't doing so well. Deborah and Michael were crawling to the safety of the ocean. Most of the coconuts missed them, but more than a few made contact. Michael abandoned the tranquilizer gun in favor of speed.

Sera and Luke darted from side to side, champion players in the game of coconut dodgeball.

I goggled at the sight. "Someone please tell me we're not being attacked with fruit."

They'd told me I couldn't access my magic. No one said I couldn't use my utter lack of self-preservation instincts.

"Stop!" I darted around Mac before he could stop me. I needed to swerve and duck more than once, and one husk scraped my ear. "We don't mean any harm," I called.

That was exactly what movie aliens would say before they took over a planet, so I tried again.

"Okay, some of them do. If they're dressed in white Calvin Klein, they obviously don't belong on the island. Completely inappropriate wardrobe. I have no idea why they're here, so feel free to use a coconut cannon on them." Yes. That was much better. "The rest of us, we want to talk to the one who has long called this home."

I dodged two more coconuts, but they weren't thrown with quite as much enthusiasm. "I understand she can help me." At that, the assault stopped completely.

"The island does not accept fulls." A disembodied voice floated from the trees. It was husky, and it could have belonged to either a man or a woman.

"They're the only fulls!" I pointed at the two council members, now standing knee-high in the water. "You can totally reject them."

The voice didn't speak again.

"The fire is three-quarters. The tall brown-haired man isn't an elemental. I have no idea what the short woman is, so do whatever you want with her."

The short woman sent me a dark glare. I smiled.

"My name is Jet," she told me, her spine straight. "If you're willing to doom me, at least use my name."

The silence grew heavy, waiting. I'd hoped they wouldn't notice my omissions. Luke gave me an almost imperceptible nod.

"The other man and I are duals." I braced for a reaction.

I'd expected gasps of horror. Instead, an average-sized woman stepped forward. Her expression contained far more curiosity than concern.

She had a medium build, and her bright blue-green eyes and light blond hair marked her as a strong beach. She also appeared healthy, well-fed, and not even a little like she'd been trapped and abused for decades.

"Really?" Her head swiveled between me and Luke. She paid no attention to the others. "How fascinating. I've only heard stories. Can you show me?"

"Ade," Sera warned.

Luke hurried to my side, a ball of fire already forming in his palm. A second later, the air changed, becoming as dry and scorching as any desert breeze.

The woman's face lifted in wonder. "My goodness. You're the same?"

"I'm water instead of desert, but yes."

"They can't be here." The husky voice spoke again. "They're fulls. They should all be sent from here immediately."

"It's a technicality," I insisted. "We're really two halves." I hoped the islanders weren't taught basic fractions.

The blond tapped her finger against her chin. "Eila will want to judge for herself. They're powerful. That could benefit all of us."

"It's too risky."

I squinted through the vegetation, trying to catch sight of the person so determined to get rid of us.

"It's not your decision." The blond peered over my shoulder. "It's hers."

I spun around—and froze.

Someone new had joined our group. Someone with ever-changing eyes and hair, who seemed to hold ancient power while simultaneously appearing light enough to float away on a strong breeze.

The woman—the creature—who held my life in her

hands.

And she looked pissed.

CHAPTER 14

Like the one in Utah, the creature's appearance constantly altered, but it was more of a steady dissolve than the manic switches I'd seen before. Her hair fell in shifting streaks of gold and black. I thought her eyes were gray until I spotted the black ring around her irises. The colors traded places, and soon charcoal eyes were outlined by the gray of river stones. The other elements all had their turn. Though her coloring varied, her body looked human and solid.

My muscles tensed, waiting for an assault. It never came.

Instead, she stared at Deborah and Michael, still standing in the ocean.

Tendrils of water gripped their thighs and hauled them backwards. The council flew through the air, landing at least five hundred feet out to sea. Whatever countermeasures two of the most powerful elementals in the world were using, they weren't working.

That was unsettling.

On the other hand, they were now so far away that they were no longer a threat. It was just me, my friends, a bunch of coconut-throwing locals, and a first that could cure or kill me.

For now, she wasn't interested in us. "Fulls." The anger I sensed earlier had faded into resignation. "They are not welcome."

The islanders didn't react. They'd heard the proclamation before.

She never spoke with a single voice. A gentle chorus emerged from her throat, soprano and alto and contralto all harmonizing. It was closer to music than speech. It was beautiful, but also alien, and the words themselves sounded strained, like she needed to run each syllable through a translator before she could speak.

The first watched the council members bobbing in the ocean. A rush of power flew past me, and they moved further out to sea.

"Eila?" The blond woman approached. She didn't show even a hint of fear. "Their boat is on the western shore."

A minute later, it floated next to Michael and Deborah. The first observed them long enough to confirm they would take advantage of her generosity and sail away.

Only when the boat was out of sight did she speak again. "They were with you?"

The first didn't turn. One moment she gazed at the ocean, and the next she faced me, but I caught no movement between the two positions.

"No. Nope. Not at all. They arrived before us." I spoke in a rush, too overwhelmed with relief to make any sense. Not only had the first removed the bane of my existence, but she'd done it while not acting like a homicidal maniac. She even seemed to have a name, one that wasn't "Your Almighty Evilness."

"They sought you."

Note to self: don't lie to a creature of unknown abilities.

"They did, but trust me, we didn't seek them. You can kick them off the island as many times as you like." When she didn't interrupt me—or try to murder me—I decided to go for broke. "We're seeking you, actually."

She didn't respond.

Instead, Eila moved between me and my friends, studying each of us. To say she walked would grant her movement a human quality it simply didn't possess. She didn't glide or fly or anything like that. It was more that she willed herself to be in a new place and her body chose to comply in as little time as possible.

Jet dropped her eyes under the power of that gaze.

"Human." The first sounded puzzled. "You see me."

When Jet didn't contradict her, Eila stood before the blond, who put out her hands with no hesitation. Eila wrapped her fingers around the other woman's wrists.

The blond's expression became drawn, and the first began to disintegrate. I could make out her face and form, but it looked like she was made of particles rather than flesh and blood, countless specks of magic all shaped like a woman.

"Thank you, Tricia." There was no mouth to speak the words, but they rang across the beach.

The particles spread a hundred feet in either direction before falling to the ground. I couldn't see Eila anymore, but I could sense her. The ground below me grew rich with power, the land itself absorbing the magic she'd taken from Tricia.

When she was done, the first assumed her former shape and returned to Jet. Jet's eyes darted from one person to another as she struggled to grasp what was happening, but she gave no indication she saw the first standing directly before her. Eila nodded, satisfied.

The creature zapped to Sera next. My sister hadn't yielded in a staring contest in her life, and she wasn't about to end that streak now. She didn't lower her eyes. Eila's lips turned up, a movement so slight I wasn't certain I'd seen it.

"You are familiar." For at least a minute, the first was

motionless, lost in thoughts I couldn't begin to guess. "Please stay." She laid a hand on Sera's forearm, and in an instant my sister's confrontational glare softened into what I could only call pleasure.

When Eila reached Mac, there was no mistaking her reaction. She beamed, a smile so bright and pleased they could have used it in a toothpaste commercial. My spine stiffened and my fingers curled into claws. Only I got to look at Mac like that, and even I attempted to be a little subtle about it.

When she touched him, he didn't jerk away, not even when she slid her palms over his shoulders and gripped his biceps tighter than was really necessary. "Shifter," she sighed, her earlier joy increased exponentially. She continued to explore his muscles, eyes soft and unfocused as she traced his abdominals. I wouldn't have imagined the firsts were vulnerable to such a messy human weakness as lust, but she was doing her best to prove me wrong.

Her hands wandered lower, and I found myself having a protracted coughing fit.

She glanced at me, her ever-changing eyes seeing through my falsehood in a second, and she smiled. "You believe he is yours."

Mac's tense expression vanished, replaced by ecstasy.

I dug my nails into my palms to keep them from clawing at the creature's eyes.

After a short eternity, she released Mac and came to me and Luke. Her smile dropped and her eyes darkened. She examined our entire bodies, hair and bones and fingers. I was pretty sure she gave my cuticles a good assessment before she was done. I braced for the tendrils of magic, that invading touch I'd encountered in Utah, but nothing came.

"Two halves," she said to me.

She pressed a hand against Luke's chest, then yanked it backwards as if burned. "Whole." She grew agitated, her appearance changing faster and her body vibrating. "Unacceptable."

Eyes and hair so dark they seemed to swallow light, she placed her palms against his chest again. This time, the touch wasn't tentative.

From what I'd seen, Luke was pretty good at the whole stoic cowboy thing, but when Eila dug her fingers into his muscles, he screamed, high-pitched and desperate. I'd heard similar noises in the forest when prey didn't outrun the carnivores.

As quickly as she'd begun the torture, she released him. Luke staggered and fell, unable to support himself.

Eila was already there to catch him. He landed with his head in her lap like a child. With gentle touches, she soothed him. When he stopped shaking, she pressed all ten fingers against his cheeks until he felt the same bliss the others had.

"You are safe," she whispered, placing his head on the ground, the gentle movement a loving contrast to the agony she'd caused him.

I hurried to him and crouched at his side. "Luke?" I repeated his name, more frantically each time. At last he focused on my face. "Are you okay? What happened?"

Eila answered for him. "Two halves are acceptable."

I studied Luke, praying I'd misunderstood and his magic was still fused together. His small head shake disabused me of that hope. She'd taken the threads apart. We'd come here for one cure and within an hour we needed two. I wanted to scream.

I was the only one left to examine closely. I stood, drawing the movement out as long as I could.

"You are the reason." I sensed no malice from her, nor

the ravenous hunger I'd felt from the other creature. She was curious, perhaps, and pleased.

Then she wrapped both hands around my neck. It was possible I'd misjudged her intent.

Fingers kneaded my skin, testing the tendons and muscles and outlining the thick arteries. Mac growled, loud and insistent. She ignored him. All her attention was focused on my neck.

I struggled to fill my lungs, but already my airway was closing. Sera's fireball crashed into Eila's chest and dissolved.

I heard shouts and curses as the others fought to reach me. Sand crawled up their feet and gripped their ankles, the restraints as inescapable as any iron cuffs.

I couldn't access my power. Not when it would almost certainly be the last time I ever did so.

I gripped her wrists and yanked. Her hands didn't budge an inch.

My vision grew dark at the edges. I lashed out with my right foot, kicking wildly. It connected with her shin, and I didn't think she felt it. She moved with me, an easy step. We were dancing partners in a macabre waltz.

My legs turned leaden, all energy fled. I had nothing left.

Nothing except myself, and I placed the entirety of my will into my eyes before raising them to her. The creature's own eyes were now a pure gray, as cool and sedate as any water while she choked the life from me.

I squeezed my arms between hers and shoved, putting every ounce of strength I possessed into the fight.

I slammed into the ground, then gulped air as fast as I could, feeding my starving lungs. My friends yelled my name, unable to move toward me while the sand grasped their ankles. The first studied me, as I did her.

I hadn't freed myself. She'd let me go.

I stumbled to my feet. Whatever she had planned for me, I would meet it standing up.

"You wish to live." Her lips moved, but the words were inside my head.

"I want to do more than live." My voice was low and raspy, but it still sounded overloud. "I want to be whole."

I didn't know if that was the correct answer. Eila's face changed constantly, but it was impossible to read.

Eila stood before me. She ran her fingertips from my temple to my chin, the touch as soft as a butterfly's. My skin tingled, then all my pain disappeared. My breathing was no longer ragged, and though I couldn't see my neck, I knew it wouldn't bruise. My mind settled, my desires and fears and regrets growing quiet.

"Please stay. All of you." The words were melodious, even sweet.

"How long do people usually live on the island?" Sera's sharp voice cut through Eila's gentle tones.

She blinked at Sera, uncomprehending. "This is their home."

I caught Sera's eye, warning her to drop the subject.

"Now it is your home. The others will guide you."

The land opened before her. She stepped into the hole and floated downwards. The sand swirled, covering the small tunnel she'd created. There was no sign she'd ever been there.

It took longer than I expected to reach our destination. The vegetation increased as we walked inland. I lost count of how many different ferns and flowering plants I saw, the colors so lush and rich it seemed rude to just call them purple or red.

The residents might as well have been walking on flat linoleum. Sera was almost as at ease. She'd spent decades traversing similar islands. The rest of us stepped cautiously between plants. More than once, tiny geckos raced before us, their technicolor green bodies impossible to miss.

Jet had stayed behind. She'd watched us leave with confused and worried eyes. I felt sorry for her until I remembered she'd been the council's lapdog. Besides, she had access to all the coconuts she could eat. She wouldn't starve. If I was feeling generous, we might even grab her on our way off the island.

Despite Eila's ominous statement that this was now our home, I needed to believe we'd escape. Somehow.

We followed four of the residents. The leader was too far away for me to make out anything, but her movements were stiff with anger. I guessed she was the elemental who objected to our presence. She rushed through the trees as if she couldn't get away from us fast enough.

The guides in the middle cast furtive glances over their shoulders, attempting to study us without being too obvious and failing. Tricia, the beach elemental we'd met when we arrived, acted like our unofficial guide.

I wasn't surprised to encounter a beach in Hawaii, though overall they weren't very common. Beaches were a late addition to the elemental family. They didn't exist until the stones eroded and became sand, and by then the world's original creation magic was dimming. They were weaker than the rest of us, even the full-blooded ones.

Birds flew from branch to branch and various critters skittered away as we passed. "There are spiders here, aren't there?" I asked, stepping around yet another gigantic fern. "Really big hairy spiders."

Sera glanced back at me. "A few. I'd worry more about the teeny tiny ones. The sort that climb into your clothes and you don't even notice."

"Not helping."

I didn't talk much after that, preferring to listen to the strange noises of this unfamiliar place. It reminded me of the quiet found only during a blackout, when every electronic hum died and only the sounds of nature remained. We could hear the ocean and the trees, the small animals and our own soft steps, but that was it. Whoever lived here, they hadn't embraced the twentieth century, let alone the current one.

As we walked, the vegetation grew more orderly and we found ourselves walking between rows of lychee, papaya, and passionfruit trees. Mac snagged several as he passed, unable to resist the lure of fresh fruit after months of strawberry Pop-Tarts.

At last, Tricia pulled back a heavy veil of low-hanging branches, revealing an area that had been cleared of vegetation. It was an oval, at least a thousand feet long, and it was set in the shadow of the mountain. Tents of various shapes and sizes were spaced evenly around the edge. It was a motley collection of camping tents, lean-tos, and a few more permanent structures built of wood and canvas. There were two in the center that were almost the size of a big top from the circus, likely the communal areas. It was all decidedly less ethereal than I'd expect in the home of the world's original magic.

Sera paid no attention to the camp, only its residents. Her head was practically spinning as she catalogued every person. Most she dismissed quickly, their skin too pale or bodies too tall, but more than once she perked up at the sight of a black-haired woman, only to grimace in disappointment after a closer look. The island was full of strong fires who bore a vague resemblance to her mother.

"What about her?" I pointed to someone moving rapidly in the opposite direction. "I don't think she's brushed her hair in weeks. You could be related."

Before Sera could think of a decent comeback, the woman vanished into a nearby tent. Once again, Sera's face fell.

"Who was that?" I asked Tricia. "The woman with the dark curly hair?"

"Ani?" Vertical lines appeared between her brows. "She was the one who led us here. Do you know her?"

Sera scowled. "No. I guess not. I learned about this place from someone named Helen. Is she here?"

Tricia didn't even consider the question. "No, sorry. There are only about forty of us, so there are no strangers. There's no one by that name. Perhaps she was here before I arrived."

I squeezed Sera's hand. "We'll learn what happened."

Sera's lips tightened into a thin line.

"You'll be over here." Tricia waved us forward.

We were given one of the sturdier camp structures. It had a wooden foundation, and heavy canvas lined the walls and formed a peaked roof. From the outside, you couldn't see silhouettes like you could with the vinyl ones, and the opening flaps could be tied shut. It was the most privacy we could hope for.

Mac lifted a flap and peered inside. I nudged him into the tent, and the rest of us followed. Blankets folded atop thick beds of hala leaves made four distinct sleeping areas. It wasn't fancy, but it was clean.

"And the previous owners?" he asked. "Where are they?"

"Gone," said Tricia.

"They left?" I tried not to sound too pleased that was an option. Mac's pinch told me I wasn't successful.

"Oh no. Why would anyone leave? People arrive. If

they are welcomed, they stay. After a rich and fulfilling life, they die, as we all must."

"When did you get here?" Luke's voice was strained. The further removed we were from Eila's soothing touch, the more we remembered our many reasons to be concerned.

Tricia waved the question away. "Time means nothing here, as you will soon discover. Do you have any other questions before I leave you?"

I got the feeling she hoped the answer was no.

"Yeah. The woman. The first magic. Why do you call her Eila?"

"Because that's her name, of course." When we looked unsatisfied, she elaborated. "She changes it when it suits her. She says she evolves too much for a single identity, so when a favorite pet dies, she takes their name for a while."

Mac was horrified. "You're her pets? And you don't mind?"

"I admit it requires adjustment, but it isn't inaccurate. To her, our minds are as simple and limited as a dog's would be to us. Likely more so. And she cares about us and protects us as any devoted pet owner would. Give it a chance."

She said her farewells, and then we were alone.

"We're all squicked out by the word 'owner,' right?" I said.

Sera was disgusted. "I know we said we'd do anything to help Aidan, but I draw the line at fetching her slippers and newspaper."

There was hearty agreement on that point.

The canvas roof was low enough—and I was tall enough—that I couldn't stand upright under the peaked section of the tent. Luke and Mac also had to crouch. Only Sera was able to remain at her full height—all the better to pace the creaking wooden boards, which she started doing as soon as the flap dropped into place.

I fell onto a bed in the corner, stretching my legs before me.

"I'm not sure if this is going according to plan or not," I said.

Mac gathered the leaves from his side of the room and hauled them to my corner, creating the island version of a double bed. I knew it was mostly due to his desire to sleep next to me, but part of me wondered if he was reminding Luke I was taken. Luke and I knew it was unnecessary, but that didn't mean Mac had caught up with us yet.

Instead of being annoyed by the display, I was glad of it. I'd never considered that the first creatures would be sexual beings, although their unions with humans and animals were the entire reason we existed. The manner in which Eila gazed at Mac—and the expression of pure bliss she'd put on his face—told me I should rethink that opinion. Their meeting had disturbed me more than I wanted to admit. If Eila had been in the room, I'd have made a show of claiming Mac, too.

"Well, we're here," said Sera. "And she hasn't killed any of us yet. It's a start. How much time have we got before you start going mad, Luke?"

He didn't take offense. "I should be a mess. She completely separated the threads, but I'm all right. Weaker than I would be, but..."

"You're not hovering on the edge of madness, are you?" I finished his thought. "Same. It's not a cure, but I feel like, so long as we're on this island, I'll be okay. There's something about this place."

"If you're stable, we'll stay as long as we need to." Mac dropped his arm across my shoulders. He wasn't staking a claim. He wanted to be near me, and it was hard to argue with that.

"Eila felt different from the other one," I said. "I mean besides the not trying to kill us thing. She was softer. Maybe being around so many elementals makes her less homicidal."

Sera raised an eyebrow. "Yeah. She was a regular ray of sunshine when she undid Luke's cure and throttled you."

"Aidan's right," Mac said. "She didn't sound as harsh or smell like ozone. I don't know what it means, but she's different."

The light was already fading. Though it was summer, we were too close to the equator for the extended summer days we'd find up north. "Should we look for dinner?"

No one moved. Mac pulled four papayas from his backpack, then added three passionfruit and a generous pile of mountain apples. He parceled out the feast. I didn't miss how reluctantly he handed Luke his share.

After we ate, Luke stretched out on his bedding. A minute later, his breath was deep and even. The man definitely didn't struggle with insomnia.

"Start trusting him," I told the others. I whispered, though I didn't mind if Luke overheard. "Maybe he gave us reason to doubt him, but that's over now. He's broken now, because of us. Yeah, he has secrets and yes, Mac, he's hot, but that doesn't matter to me. He's doing what he can to help us, and I can't think of a single selfish reason why he would. He's here because he's chosen to be."

They both looked guilty. It was a start.

We talked some, but mostly we listened to the noises of camp. We picked out a few individual voices and learned what we could. There wasn't much. The conversations were mundane and domestic. It would be easy to believe we were hanging out a campground in Tahoe. They didn't sound like prisoners. They sounded happy, and if a few of the voices were a little shrill for true peace, I could tell myself I imagined it.

"I know I said I'm okay here." I spoke so quietly I could barely hear myself.

"But you're ready to go home," Sera said. She heard it, too.

"Yeah. Your mom, a fix for me and Luke, and then we move. Whatever it takes, we'll do it."

As soon as I spoke the words, I knew I'd come to regret them.

CHAPTER 15

Our plan to find a cure right away turned out to be a little optimistic. The first morning, we learned that the tents weren't the island's only similarity to camp. It also featured non-stop activities from dawn to dusk.

I was an early riser, but I preferred the sky to have lightened to at least a light purple before I climbed out of bed. Tricia had no such preference, which we discovered when she woke us an hour before sunrise with a cheery smile and the promise of breakfast.

I wasn't convinced I was even awake as we stumbled toward the largest building in camp. Though we still yawned and rubbed our eyes, I couldn't help but smile. This was the camp's center, which meant it was Eila's center. The sooner I spoke to her, the sooner I could start convincing her to cure me and Luke.

My shoulders slumped in defeat as soon as we stepped inside. The tent held only elementals, who gathered around four long tables. They shared a huge fruit salad, which was to be expected from a vegetarian race stuck on a tropical island. To my horror, I saw no one drinking anything that included caffeine.

Sera whimpered next to me, noticing the same thing. "Islands full of Kona beans and they're forcing me to drink juice."

"It's barbaric," I agreed.

Tricia wisely ignored us. "We break our fast together

every day." She indicated three waters carrying bowls to the far table. "This month, it's the waters' turn to prepare and clean. Because you're new, your turn won't come until next month. For now, you can just enjoy the meal."

Studying the room, I noticed details about the camp residents I'd missed the night before. Every type of elemental was represented. Some appeared strong enough to be nearly fulls, while others might be only twenty-five percent magic. That was more than enough to be considered an elemental, but they were weak in comparison to the others.

Most chattered happily. They were far too perky, considering the hour. There were a few quieter people, their solemn expressions a marked contrast against the cheery elementals surrounding them. One desert in particular studied Luke, and she didn't seem to like what she saw. For the most part, though, only friendly faces smiled back at me.

Each person wore a uniform. It was a simple one, as uniforms went, made of white cotton pants, skirts, and tees. It looked both comfortable and creepy.

As horrific as it was, it was time to face facts. We were in a commune. Sure, it was led by a creature of immeasurable power rather than a man in a tie-dyed shirt, but it was still a commune.

Sera swore. "If we're here another month, I'll go Jonestown on them myself."

Without her morning coffee, I feared it was a real possibility.

Tricia led us to an empty spot at one of the tables, and we slid onto the benches. I took a hesitant bite, unsure what I'd taste, but it was only fruit. Mac sniffed it, and only after his shifter's nose agreed with me did he eat, slowly at first and then with great enthusiasm. If they were trying to appeal to him through his stomach, loading him up with fruit was the way to go.

We bolted down our food, but before we could escape, Tricia appeared out of nowhere and led us into another section of the tent. This area held primitive laundry facilities—washboards and oversized tubs. Whirlpool dryers hadn't yet made it to the island. Here we found shelf after shelf of white clothing.

"Pants or skirt?" Tricia asked me and Sera.

We answered together. "Pants."

She studied our bodies, then handed us two pairs of well-worn drawstring trousers. The cotton was soft and clean, though I knew we weren't the first to wear them. There was also white cotton underwear and a basic t-shirt. Luke was given the man's version of the same outfit. He dangled the tighty whities from one finger, looking bemused.

"Where does this come from?" I checked the shirt's label. It was the only outside item I'd seen.

"There's a water who handles supply runs. It helps that she doesn't need a boat."

Luke and I exchanged glances. If his experience was repeated here, that would be the most drugged-out resident.

"Wouldn't it be easier to keep a boat on the island so anyone could make the run?" I asked.

Tricia was too busy sizing Mac up to respond. "I'm afraid some of the clothes will be too small for you. Eila says you may go without a shirt."

Eila said that, did she? Sure, Mac was built more like a mountain than a man, but I'd seen a large guy among the other pets whose shirt would have fit Mac.

He took the pants without a word.

"You may shower and change in there." Tricia pointed

to a stall with a basic shower head and an even more basic drainage system, little more than a channel that sloped downward and disappeared under the edge of the tent. At least it had a worn curtain I could draw for privacy and a short wooden stool to hold my clothes and the soap and towel Tricia handed me.

"I didn't expect indoor plumbing." I turned the faucet. Water came out in a steady trickle, about the same temperature as the warm air.

"Not exactly," Tricia said. "It's gathered in a cistern outside of camp."

It wasn't a relaxing shower, with only a thin curtain standing between my naked body and a bunch of strangers, but it was better than nothing.

That was the best I could say about the clothes, as well. I wasn't so endowed as to require a bra, so I discarded my worn one for the clean undershirt. The pants slid easily over my narrow hips, and the tee was too big. If someone had actively tried to make me look like a skinny boy, they couldn't have done a much better job.

Sera had the opposite problem. Her curvy body pushed the fabric to its limits. It was tight around her hips and upper thighs, then loose in the knees and calves. The t-shirt stretched across her chest, and even through two layers I could see her black bra. Unlike me, she had something to support.

Before I could say anything, she pointed at me. "I'm still making it work."

I scoffed. "I'm surprised they found something short enough for your itty-bitty legs."

Mac stepped out then, and I forgot to tease. Forgot my own name, really.

Some amazing sights one can get used to with enough exposure. I never seemed to get used to Mac's naked chest.

Each muscle was so well-defined he could serve as a model in an anatomy class. Biceps, deltoids, triceps, pectoral and abdominal muscles… they were all there, and all a bit larger than on any other man. The drawstring pants rested low on his hips, and I did my best not to follow the thin line of hair that disappeared under the waistband.

My best wasn't very good.

Mac's nostrils flared, the damn shifter nose picking up my interest. "Maybe I should thank Eila."

Hearing her name pulled me from my lust-induced stupor. "When do we get to see her?" I asked.

"Eila?" Tricia shook her head. "I can't say. No one can. She shows up when it's time. Her presence is a gift, never an obligation."

"Can we go to her?"

"We don't know where she is. She may take a human shape for our benefit, but you must remember what she is. She has no home, no regular schedule. When she vanishes, I'm not even sure she retains consciousness. Perhaps she returns to pure magic. She surrounds herself with elementals, but she isn't one of us, Aidan. Don't ever forget that."

If she hadn't beamed with such joy, I'd have thought she was warning us.

For the next eight hours, we were shown how to knock coconuts from trees, how to identify poisonous plants, where to find fresh water, and where to bathe if we didn't want to use the showers. We were introduced to every single person—none of whom were Sera's mother—then taken through every possible chore we'd be expected to perform.

We were not, at any time, left alone.

I knew we should have been frustrated, but there was a soothing quality to the camp's schedule. We were given jobs, we did them, and no one tried to stab us with a dart or threaten our friends. It was rather nice.

On the second day, we were separated. Luke and I were pulled to gather food and firewood while Sera and Mac were asked to repair tents. When we collapsed on our beds at the end of the day, we were all too exhausted to do anything but sleep.

The day after that, Luke and I were placed on sewing detail, mending small rips and tears in the uniforms until our fingers were sore and bloody from pricking them with needles.

Sera and Mac's work from the previous day was judged inadequate, possibly because Mac's stitches were crooked and uneven and Sera's were ridiculous long loops spread an inch apart. One might think she wasn't taking it seriously. They'd been reassigned to kitchen duty.

For three more days, we were summoned before dawn and guided through our schedule. Breakfast, then work. Lunch, then break time, during which everyone remained in the camp. Someone was always nearby, preventing any private conversations. Even when the storms came, the rain warm and heavy, no one sought shelter. The entire group sat in the rain and waited for it to pass.

When it was dry, we quietly entertained ourselves, along with the rest of the camp. There were a few old paperbacks people had brought to the island over the years, most so worn the pages threatened to fall out in your hand. I wanted to use the down time to write in my journal, but I couldn't trust that my thoughts would remain private. The camp was too small and the residents too curious. I got excited when I found a book of word games, only to discover they'd already been filled in, most with the wrong answer. I settled for making my own crosswords and anagrams, just to have something to do while we waited for the afternoon shift to begin. Sera laughed at me for being a giant dork, but she played whatever game I created.

When our word games didn't draw attention, we wrote notes with jumbled letters. Each day, we tried making plans. Plans to find her mother. Plans to get the cure. Plans to do anything other than work all day long. Then the afternoon shift began and whatever plan we'd been concocting fell apart.

After work, we went straight to dinner. Even if we'd had the energy to search for Sera's mom after eating, it was already dark.

They began keeping me and Luke separate from the others. We were summoned to breakfast first and given earlier lunch breaks, so soon we only saw Mac and Sera in passing or late at night. The island's residents remained friendly, but they kept their distance from me and Luke in a way they never did with our friends.

"Are they keeping an eye on the damned dirty duals?" I whispered to Luke one afternoon as I slid the needle through yet another tent. Somehow, we never reached the bottom of the mending pile. I was beginning to think they tore the seams every night.

Luke didn't glance up from his neat stitches. "They're doing something," he said. "But damned if I know what that is."

Before bed, we reported on the day's progress between yawns. Sera had spoken to half the people already. None could recollect a Helen ever living with them. Somehow, she managed to stay calm, despite hitting one dead end after another. To my frustration, my day was so structured and my schedule so unforgiving that I had no opportunity to help her.

After two weeks on the island, Luke and I were no

closer to a cure. The more we inquired about Eila, the more they isolated us, until we feared saying anything at all.

Sometimes, the first magic appeared during our breaks. She roamed amongst her pets, offering them quiet words or a soft touch. When her fingers stroked their skin, their eyes softened and their jaws grew slack, euphoria written across their features. Afterwards, they stared at her with reverence. Receiving magic was like a drug, Luke had said. I suspected some heroin addicts didn't love their needle as much as these elementals worshiped Eila's touch.

Of the four of us, she only came to Mac. His face locked as she approached, but it didn't matter how much he hardened himself. As soon as she touched him, he was overcome by bliss. Many times, he watched her walk away. At those moments, I didn't want to know what he was thinking.

As for the rest of us, she'd given us a taste on the beach, then appeared to forget we existed. Whenever I moved toward her, she managed to be somewhere else.

During our third week, I made a half-hearted attempt to sneak away while the others ate lunch. A young desert whose name I didn't know caught up to me and peppered me with questions. I'd have thought it unfortunate timing, but the next day several people spread themselves around the border of the camp at regular intervals.

"Are we prisoners?"

"Of course not." Tricia worked alongside me and Luke, as she often did. She kept her eyes on the needle as it dipped in and out of the fabric.

"Then why haven't we been able to leave camp?"

The needle didn't pause. It made six neat stitches before Tricia replied. "Do you wish to leave? I thought you were here to see Eila."

"I am. We are. But she seems like a very busy first magic. Full schedule and all that."

"You'll see her."

"When?" Luke asked.

Her needle dipped again. "When Eila decides. Everyone on this island shares. We give, and we receive. Right now, you only wish to receive."

"The way you gave her your power?"

"Exactly. We each donate our magic to Eila." There was something off. She spoke a little too fast, remained a little too interested in her stitches.

I completed a few stitches of my own. They were sloppier than my previous ones. "What does she do with those donations, exactly? She did something to the beach when we arrived."

Tricia relaxed into a genuine smile. "Wasn't that amazing? She feeds it into the land itself. So long as it holds enough power, only those with magic blood can find her. We're practically invisible to humans. She hadn't fed it that day, which was why the girl could see her."

I spared a thought for Jet, likely still waiting on the beach for the council to return. Someone really needed to check in with her soon.

Luke grew thoughtful. "I'm guessing it gives the island some calming effects too. Aidan and I haven't struggled with our dual natures since arriving."

He was right, and it wasn't only that my rage had quieted. Despite everything we needed to accomplish, all the reasons to feel anxious, our stress never lingered long. It was always replaced by a vague certainty that our problems could be dealt with the following day.

I wondered if the island had a similar effect on all its residents. You didn't need to put a sedative in the water if people walked on one all day.

It was the kind of thing that might make someone delay finding a cure they desperately needed. They might make only a half-hearted effort to discover news about their lost mother.

"You only gave her a bit of your energy on the beach. Is that really all it takes to keep the entire island hidden?" I asked.

If I hadn't been watching closely, I'd have missed the short intake of breath. "No. I mean, I can't say." She stood. "I have to go. Gerta is calling me."

If Gerta was calling Tricia, it was by freaking telepathy. Even so, Tricia rushed through the open flap, leaving me and Luke alone.

"That was interesting," he said drily.

"And totally not suspicious," I added.

He grinned at me, that easy smile that had probably led to the downfall of countless women.

"Out of curiosity, do you feel like you're being drugged into mindless complacency?"

He dropped his sewing. "I hope not, though it does explain some things. You?"

"Maybe? I keep forgetting to think about things I'm supposed to think about. But I already feel more awake, just in the last couple minutes. It's like knowing how the trick is done means it's harder to fool us."

Luke agreed, standing up and stretching until his hands hit the roof of the tent. "I'm wondering what these bastards will do if we play hooky. How about we see what happens if we forget to be complacent?" He winked at me. "We'll call it a mental health day."

We stepped into the sunshine, and I blinked against the bright light. Then I blinked again, because I didn't quite understand what I was seeing.

It appeared the soporific qualities of the island were no

longer affecting Sera, either. Considering the situation, I wasn't convinced that was a good thing.

Eila and Sera stood inches apart, and my sister pointed an angry finger in the face of one of the most powerful creatures in the world.

CHAPTER 16

"**W**here is she?" Sera made no effort to control her temper. Her fingers weren't just sparking. Full flames exploded from each tip. Her eyes blazed, and her hair was even wilder than the being she faced.

Sera's agitation had no effect on Eila. The first remained as placid as ever. Her coloring cycled regularly from one element to the next. She stretched a hand toward Sera. "Know peace, child."

Sera jumped backwards, avoiding the calming touch. "I'm not your child, and I asked you a question."

Eila's hair darkened to black and stayed there. Her voice was still musical, but it held hints of discord, a bow screeching across a single violin string. "You question me."

"Why not? I've questioned everyone else, and they all lied to me. This is your fucking island, so I'm asking you. What happened to Helen? Where the hell is my mother?"

Tricia tugged on Sera's arm. "There's no Helen here. I don't think there ever was." She was trying to defuse the situation, but her voice was too high-pitched to soothe anyone.

My sister waved a piece of white cloth in Eila's face. It was covered in writing I couldn't read it at this distance. "I found this tucked inside an old book. It's hers. I'd recognize her style anywhere. She's the one who taught me how to draw."

The wind caught the cloth, pulling it straight long

enough for me to see a black and white sketch of the beach with the ocean beyond. Not letters. A picture, like Sera always drew.

"Is she alive? Tell me!" The words were somewhere between a demand and a desperate plea.

Eila stood as immobile as any statue for a quite a while, though her hair settled into its usual rotating colors. When she spoke, her voice was again in perfect harmony.

"Your will is too strong." She tilted her head, contemplating Sera as if she were a puzzle to solve. Then, with an oddly human sigh, she raised her hands. "It is a pity."

I was too far, but I still tried running toward her. Luke restrained me.

"Wait." He jerked his chin towards Mac, who'd stepped between Sera and Eila before the first could act.

"You think that's an improvement?" I tried wrenching my arm from his grasp, but my newfound arm muscles weren't enough to overpower him.

To my surprise, Eila lowered her hands the moment Mac stood before her. Her eyes softened to a golden brown. "Shifter," she murmured.

"Sera is my friend. It would greatly upset me if anything happened to her." He looked down at Eila, a position she didn't seem to like. Her body expanded, rising until they were eye to eye.

"You do not need to be upset. You need never be upset." She didn't so much speak as purr.

"Some wounds are difficult to heal. This one would take a long time." He smiled, his eyes turning the soft brown I only saw when he looked at me.

My jaw dropped. My boyfriend was using his wiles on that ancient creature—and she seemed to be responding.

Well, she responded for a bit. "Time?" The word was foreign in her mouth.

The ground undulated, separating Mac from Sera. Once again, my sister stood exposed.

I inhaled, preparing to run or scream or dance a jig, anything to distract Eila.

"Stop!"

It wasn't me. A husky voice rang through the crowd. I'd heard it before. It was Ani, the woman who'd insisted we weren't allowed on the island.

I hadn't run into her since we arrived, which should have seemed unusual. In such a small camp, we met the same people day after day, but somehow I'd forgotten about her. It appeared complacency came in many forms.

We hadn't seen Ani's face on that first day, only her wild black hair. Now, she strode toward us. Her skin wasn't as bronze as a full fire, and her eyes weren't as dark as Sera's, but they tilted up the same way my sister's did, and the cheekbones and chin were identical.

Sera's mother stopped ten feet away. "I'm here. You've found me, so you can stop your ruckus. I'm disappointed to see you haven't learned self-control."

Even from this distance, I could see Sera's heart break. Mine did the same. This couldn't be the woman she'd mourned for more than forty years. No mother would be so cruel.

"You shouldn't have come. This is my home, not yours. I didn't want to be found." Ani's expression never changed as she spoke, and it didn't change when she turned her back on her daughter and walked away.

THAT NIGHT, EILA CAME FOR US.

Being an all-powerful magical being, she didn't politely knock on the door and wait for an invitation. Instead, she appeared while we were sound asleep and announced her presence by creating a giant ball of fire at least three feet in diameter. She hung it from the roof like a chandelier.

I jerked awake to find her staring down at me and Mac. "He won't love you if you go mad," she said.

I struggled into a sitting position. "Is that commentary, or do you have a solution?"

She didn't answer. She floated to Sera, already wide awake and crouched atop her bedding. "You have disturbed the camp."

I thought we settled things earlier that day. After her mom rejected her, Sera's fight drained from her. She left the camp, and though her spine was straight and proud, I knew it required every ounce of strength she possessed to walk to our tent without breaking down.

Eila had watched her leave and said nothing.

Now, Eila ran her fingers across Sera's cheek. My sister's expression melted into the pure pleasure I always saw when Eila shared her magic, but as soon as Eila released her, Sera grew wary. The first's coloring sped up.

"You cannot stay with us," she declared.

If I hadn't been fully awake before, that would have done it. "You're sending us away?"

"You must pay."

Mac moved closer to me. "Pay?" He tried using the soft tone Eila liked but couldn't hide the rough growl underneath.

"You have eaten. Slept in our beds. Worn our clothes. Taken power without returning it. There are costs."

I stood. If we were negotiating, resting on a mattress made of leaves didn't feel like the power position.

Mac stood with me. "We labored with the others. We contributed."

Eila stilled. I'd come to recognize that as her thinking pose. Her horribly unsettling thinking pose.

At last, she reached a decision. "Your labor will be payment for the food and shelter. The magic tithe is unpaid."

She took sips from everyone. We'd watched her do so many times, then observed as she fed that power into the island. No one appeared to be in pain while she withdrew their power, and they all healed soon after.

"We're okay with that."

Luke and Sera agreed. Mac couldn't offer the same, as shifter magic wasn't a renewable resource.

"But we didn't come here for a couple of weeks at camp," I said. "Luke and I can't exist in the outside world with our two halves separated. We won't leave until we're healed." Sweat ran down my spine. It was probably unwise to give Eila an ultimatum.

It didn't go unnoticed. "That is not your decision."

Luke shot me a warning glance. He forced himself to look at the first. "How about you decide then? What would be a fair trade for curing us?"

"You will increase your tithe?"

Across the room, Luke nodded. For once, Sera seemed uncertain.

"What is your price?" I asked.

"Him." She pointed at Mac.

I stopped myself before I throttled her, but I imagined it in vivid detail. "Nuh-uh. No way." I scowled. In that moment, I forgot what she was. All I saw was some bitch trying to steal my boyfriend.

My boyfriend who was considering her offer.

"What do you want from me?" he asked.

"I cannot feed from shifters as I do the others. Your power does not replenish. Instead, I will take you. I would feel a shifter."

I shook my head and kept shaking it. "No. No taking. No feeling of any kind."

Mac's hand grasped my wrist in silent warning.

Eila blinked. It wasn't natural, more like a memory of how a human should move. "You will lose him either way."

Every muscle in Mac's body tensed. Anger simmered below the surface, the bear waking up. His magic pulled on mine, grasping for stability, and I fed him the calm of my water side, though I didn't have much calm to spare.

"No," I said again.

"Go mad and lose him or give him to me. One way allows you to remain yourself."

"Your cost is too high." It wasn't just too high. It was unimaginable.

She waited. At least a full minute passed while we stared at each other. For the first time since I'd arrived, my rage began to stir. Whatever dampening effect the island had, it was nothing compared to the blind anger coiling through me. Only Mac's touch kept me grounded.

Eila gave nothing away. I'd started to think she'd entered a state of suspended animation when she spoke at last.

"He comes to me for a single night."

"No." I tried to remember other words. "No nights. No coming of any kind. A nice meal, we can do that. A long walk on the beach. That's it."

She gaped at me, and for a moment I thought I'd astounded a creature as old as time. "You negotiate?"

I locked my jaw, afraid of what I might say next.

Mac's fingers tightened around my wrist. "I'll do it."

I still had a hand free. I used it to punch his chest as hard as I could. He didn't even grunt, the bastard.

"No, he won't."

Mac spun me so I faced him. "Aidan, we already had this discussion. We get to make our own choices, and this isn't yours to make. If this fixes you, I'll do it. We agreed to do whatever it takes."

"But not this." My voice cracked. "This won't fix me, Mac. This will break me."

He closed his eyes, hiding his own pain. "But this way we get the chance to put you back together."

Sera's eyes implored me to accept the offer. It was only sex, after all. It wasn't like Mac was a virgin. I couldn't even say he was cheating on me, considering he was being coerced into it. Relationships had survived worse.

But when I remembered the ecstasy that crossed his face whenever Eila placed her hands on him, insanity seemed like a better option.

Mac studied Eila. "I have conditions."

She glided toward him, looking both covetous and fascinated. "State them."

"You heal both Aidan and Luke."

She didn't hesitate. "Acceptable."

"Sera is given an hour alone to speak with her mother. With Ani."

Eila rushed to agree.

Mac's voice remained as steady as if he were negotiating a business deal he was still willing to walk away from. "Also, Aidan needs to be cured before I'll do anything, and it needs to be permanent. When her magic isn't threatening her sanity, then I'll go with you. Only then."

His sentences were precise as he tried to close any possible loophole.

"Yes." Eila answered so eagerly I wasn't certain she'd even listened.

Mac relaxed. "As soon as those conditions are met, I'll go to you. After that, we leave the island. As you wanted."

She rested her fingertips against his chest once more. I gritted my teeth. He fought the pleasure she offered, but it never mattered. Her touch overpowered his will.

"You are giving yourself to me," she confirmed.

"I have one other condition." He grew larger, the bear just below the surface. "You don't forget, not for a single second, that I don't want this. Whatever you do with your touch, whatever magic you control, it doesn't change my heart. My heart will never want you."

Eila only smiled. "It is unimportant. You are willing. That is what matters."

My teeth ground together, but I managed to stay quiet.

"It will not be instant. They may resist the cure. You must be patient, but I will change them." Eila spoke of me and Luke, but her eyes were fixed on Mac, black and gray and brown all at once. "Afterwards, I will change you," she promised him.

Somehow, I didn't explode into a giant ball of rage.

There was nothing else to discuss. Eila blurred around the edges and her skin faded. It took seconds for her to dissipate and become part of the air. The fireball chandelier vanished with her, leaving us in the dark.

Luke squinted at the spot Eila had just vacated. "If part of her is still here, you'll feel her magic."

Sera's power brushed past me. She probed the air, searching for any hint Eila remained.

"Nothing," she said. "She's gone."

I took in a deep gulp of air, willing my muscles to unclench. "I'm not a fan of slut-shaming, but I'm pretty sure I get to call her a skank for that."

"Agreed." Sera nodded at the man next to me. "Thank you, Mac. For everything."

Luke shuffled his feet. "That's a big thing you did. Don't think we don't know. And I swear, if I'd ever heard they were into that sort of thing, I'd have warned you. The only thing I ever saw the other one desire is…"

"Adoration," I finished. "They want to be surrounded

by worshipful pets. And now you get to do the adoring. You shouldn't have agreed. You shouldn't have said yes." I heard my voice thicken and despised it. I wasn't ready for him to see my tears.

He dipped his head, trying to meet my eyes as I looked everywhere but at him. "It was the only choice."

"We don't know that!" I wasn't quite shouting, but I was getting close.

"How long have we been searching, Aidan? More than once, we would have lost you without that damn drug. She was about to send us from the island. Our last chance would be gone. I wasn't going to stand here and waste more time when I didn't have to."

"We didn't try anything else. Maybe that was her opening bid. We could have asked. But it took you, what, two seconds to agree to her terms? Didn't have to debate very long, did you? Hell, you practically jumped at the chance."

The last sentence was coated in venom. Mac's eyes narrowed in anger. Anger that we were in this situation in the first place, but more than that. It was anger at me for doubting him, and maybe for being the reason he needed to make this choice. It was anger that I was willing to hurt him.

I didn't care. He should hurt.

The magic sizzled, reaching for my skin. It demanded release. I wanted to burn, to ruin, to explode. If I let it, I wouldn't make it to tomorrow.

I rushed toward the tent's opening. "Get out of my way."

Sera stepped to the side when she saw my face.

"Don't even think about following me," I whispered, knowing Mac would hear. "Don't you dare try to save me again."

CHAPTER 17

I tore through the trees with no idea where I was going. Power rose. It whispered to me, persuasive lies that promised certainty and peace if I only gave in.

If I let it loose, I would never be whole again.

The same was true if I lost Mac.

So I ran, plowing through ferns and dodging tree roots. My arms pumped and my breath came fast as I released energy the only safe way I knew. More than once I fell. Sometimes I caught myself, scraping my palms as I landed on rocks. Sometimes I crashed to the ground, making no effort to cushion the fall.

I didn't mind the pain. If the magic was working to heal me, it wasn't trying to destroy. Creation magic, I remembered. I had to create something.

I had to create a way off this damn island.

I changed course, running toward the ocean I felt on my left side. It was only a few hundred feet away. I burst through the trees onto the beach. My feet were bare, and my heels sank into the dry sand, slowing me. I pushed harder, sprinting toward the water.

It offered no resistance. The waves crashing over me were as comforting as a gentle shower, and once I passed through them to calm sea, I sank to the sandy bottom. I drew on the power of the water, seeking a calm I could only achieve through the element I knew best. I inhaled, letting the water fill my lungs. It entered my ears and nose and mouth, every pore opening to receive the water's strength.

People thought of the ocean as an empty, quiet place, but they were wrong. It teemed with life. Thick schools of fish swam past me, and a curious turtle visited with me for a while. The ocean floor was covered in bright coral and rock enclosures that small fish used to evade larger predators. It was an entire universe down here.

It was life. Creation.

I stayed underwater until the rage grew silent. As calm returned, I discovered that a second energy was feeding me—the rivers of magma far below the ocean's surface. The seamount wouldn't rise for centuries, but it wasn't stagnant. It was alive, as full of power as the water above it.

When I possessed some facsimile of control, I returned to shore.

The night air was as warm as the tropical water, and I didn't feel chilled. I felt nothing, really. Numb was a lot easier than trying to understand the contract Mac had made.

"What's wrong?"

I pushed damp hair out of my eyes and squinted toward a dark corner of the beach, where a dreadlocked woman in a t-shirt and cut-offs watched me.

It took several seconds to convince myself I wasn't hallucinating. "Vivian? What are you doing here?"

Vivian refused to be distracted. She'd seen me on the container ship. She knew I walked a line so thin I could be the tightrope act in a circus. "That's not important. Are you...?"

"I'm okay. Really."

"But not cured yet?"

"Soon. We made an arrangement." I groaned at the reminder. "Don't ask. But it will be a couple of days."

"That's too damn long. I'm done playing a *Gilligan's Island* reject."

I'd been so focused on Vivian that I'd missed the small woman sitting on a nearby rock. Jet was a little beat up after weeks playing castaway, but the changes were all cosmetic. She needed a shower and a large meal, but otherwise she was fine.

While I was glad to see the other hacker hadn't died of starvation, my pleasure was tempered somewhat by the tranquilizer gun she held.

Vivian glared at her. "Put that away. We don't need it."

Jet didn't budge. She wasn't pointing it at me, at least.

I considered the gun Michael had dropped during his unplanned escape. "How many doses are left?"

"Four," Jet answered. She looked willing to use them all.

"Better you guys keep it, in case the cure doesn't take. Especially since Luke isn't cured anymore either. Long story," I said, before they could ask questions. "Wait. Give me one for Sera to hold. Just in case." I held out my hand.

Jet didn't seem thrilled at the prospect, but she didn't argue. The dart was uncapped. I removed my t-shirt. I still wore the undershirt underneath. Without touching the sharp tip, I wrapped the dart in several layers of fabric.

"Now tell me why the hell you're not on the boat."

Vivian lifted her chin. "It's been almost three full weeks. How long was I supposed to wait?"

"You weren't. You were supposed to sail in the other direction."

Her jaw set. "I didn't like that plan."

One day, I was going to find a friend who was easy-going and pliable, but this was not that day. "Did you leave the boat floating in the middle of the ocean? How did you even get here?"

"I anchored it and brought an inflatable raft to shore. You're a water whose magic stretches further than anyone we know. You'll be even more powerful once you're cured. You can get it back."

"And if I'm not cured?" I threw my hands up in defeat. "Okay. Whatever. You're here now. What's the new plan?"

"Jet and I…"

I rubbed a finger against my ear to clear it. "We're trusting Jet now? The woman who helped Deborah try to kill me and out-hacked you?"

"She did not out-hack me."

"Did too," Jet answered. "Also, no one told me they planned to kill you. I probably wouldn't have helped them if I knew."

Vivian looked like she wanted to tear Jet's shiny hair from her head. "Regardless," she said through gritted teeth, "Jet isn't loyal to the council. Or to us. She's loyal to money, and I've promised her plenty of it."

"You didn't bother telling her we can't access our accounts while we're fugitives?" I whispered, but Jet overheard.

"Not anymore," she told me. "Even if Deborah could replace me—which is a ridiculous thought—I fixed it for you. You bank in the Cayman Islands now. Don't understand why you didn't do that sooner. You're really rich, by the way. I like that about you."

I felt like I was at least three steps behind. "Slow down. From the beginning."

Jet still spoke quickly. I wasn't sure she had a slow setting. "When Michael and Deborah were asked to leave, they didn't have a chance to grab their bags. I kept the computer equipment in payment. I expect you to cover the rest."

I didn't know what to say, so I raised both eyebrows

and blinked a lot.

"C'mon. Don't make this complicated. I was on their side. Now I'm on yours. It's pretty easy."

"For how long?"

Jet grimaced. "They left me behind on an island full of crazy people, with nothing to eat but coconuts and sushi. They'd have to promise a lot of money to buy me back. I'll give you a chance to match their offer if they do."

I thought that was Jet's idea of a fair deal.

"How did a human get involved with the council in the first place?"

"They wanted to track you. I wanted to not star in the next season of *Orange is the New Black*. A month or two ago, our interests converged."

"They bought the judge presiding over your case?"

Jet shrugged. "I didn't ask."

It didn't really matter, but it explained why the council had become much harder to avoid in late summer.

"You think Deborah will return to the island?" I said.

Jet pursed her lips, considering. "Probably not. She has a serious hard-on for you, but I don't think she really understood what she was getting into with that weird-ass disappearing woman. My guess is she's hoping you never leave this place. It'd make her life a lot easier."

If I didn't have sufficient motivation to get off the island before, that would do it. Anything that made Deborah unhappy would find an instant spot on my to-do list.

"So if you were able to move my accounts, you definitely sent email. Have you been in contact with the others? Did they get back safe?"

Vivian smiled, and I exhaled in relief.

"They're fine. We can't exchange detailed messages, though. We're on satellite internet now, and only for an hour or so each day. Need to save the batteries."

"But they're okay." For the first time in weeks—hell, months—a flicker of real hope bloomed in my chest. "Tell them to stay safe. We're getting off soon." A couple days to be healed, then another for Mac to go with Eila. I shoved that thought away.

"How confident are you

 she'll let you go?" Vivian dug through one of the bags.

I wanted to believe Eila would keep her promise to let us go. I also wanted to believe in leprechauns and the health benefits of an all-carb diet.

Then I remembered how she stared at Mac, and the way none of the residents ever left, and I couldn't help thinking our escape plan would hit some snags.

"About as confident as a seventh grader at their first school dance. I'm still going to find a way off this island."

"Take this." Vivian handed me a tiny metal disc. It was smaller and slimmer than a watch battery, except it had a pin along its back. "Hide it somewhere."

I worked the pin into the inside of my waistband and snapped it shut. "Tracker?"

Jet preened a little. "One of the best. Custom made."

"It was supposed to be stuck to you if the council ever got close enough," Vivian explained. "Jet says it picks up both heat and the energy of magic. Even if it was possible for a human to build that, which it's obviously not, it will help us narrow down your location if you're not back here in a few days."

I cast a longing look at the water behind me. It was far more appealing than what waited for me at camp. "I guess I should return. But Vivian? Be ready to go, okay?"

My friend grabbed a computer and powered it on. She had the kind of determination you only saw in people with something to prove.

"Don't worry. I've got this."

———

I RETURNED TO CAMP AT A FAR MORE SEDATE PACE. BETWEEN my sprint across the island and the time bonding with the ocean, I felt less inclined to rip someone's head off.

I tried to find any reason for optimism. Vivian was smart as hell and had her computer again. If Jet was helping, I had no doubt they'd figure out an escape plan.

But we couldn't attempt to leave until Mac held up his end of the bargain. Eila wouldn't let him go without keeping his promise, no matter what scheme the computer geniuses devised.

It was that last thought that kept me dragging my feet. I understood the reasoning behind his choice, but that didn't mean I'd ever be okay with it.

The island was only so big, and inevitably I arrived at camp. No one saw me approach—no one except the large bear shifter leaning against a tree a hundred yards from the tent.

I drew to a stop fifteen feet away. "What are you doing here?"

"You told me not to follow you," Mac said. "You didn't tell me not to wait." His eyes were hard, but they weren't cold, not even a little. He straightened, though he didn't close the distance between us.

"You're splitting hairs. I'm not ready to talk." I moved, planning to walk around him.

He stepped to the side, blocking me. "Then listen." His voice allowed no room for disagreement. He would follow me across the island, talking the whole time, if that's what it took to make me listen.

This was our reality. I didn't get to escape it.

Reality had a lot to answer for.

"Say what you need to say." I clutched the calm center I'd found at the beach, willing my voice to be steady.

"You're not the only one who gets to make sacrifices. How many times do we have to go over this?"

"Until you stop trying to save me!"

His black expression turned incredulous.

The words poured out, though I knew he wouldn't accept them. "Don't you get it? You and Sera shouldn't have to suffer. You didn't hurt anyone. I can't let you pay for my crimes."

The muscle in his jaw went into hyperdrive. "You're punishing yourself for David." It wasn't a question.

"I don't need to punish myself anymore. If you go with Eila, you're doing it for me." Anger and hurt rose to the surface, and I made no effort to hide them. "And as a bonus, you get to live with the memory that you whored yourself out for me. Who knows? Maybe you'll enjoy it. I've seen your face when she touches you."

"I can't help that, and it means nothing. There's no emotional connection, and you damn well know it. What does it mean when you and Luke run off together?"

"It means nothing!" I threw his words back at him.

Mac gazed upwards, staring at the canopy of leaves above us. He needed to calm himself, and he couldn't do that while looking at me. "I don't care. I don't care if you're jealous about Eila, or hot for Luke, or beating yourself up for things you can't change. That's all secondary to you finally, *finally* being cured. This is my turn to save you, you stubborn, ridiculous woman, and you better believe I'm taking it."

If that was supposed to make me feel better, it needed a few rewrites. "Ridiculous? Ridiculous?" My voice rose. I stopped long enough to rein in the anger. "It isn't ridiculous to expect that my boyfriend won't pimp himself out to a creature. Eila's not even human. What if she destroys you? She could pull a praying mantis and eat your damn head when she's done."

He waited to respond, watching me breathe and calm myself. When he spoke again, his voice vibrated with tension, as if the words themselves would explode at the slightest provocation. "We aren't certain fusing your magics will work, either, but we're trusting her with that. How is this different?"

"You know how. For me, there's no choice. It's this or crazy. It's our Hail Mary. You don't have to do this."

"This is part of the damned Hail Mary, Aidan. It's the price we need to pay."

"And we'll pay it for years. Decades. I'll never be able to forget, never get over that she…" I bit off the final words, unwilling to hear them spoken aloud.

"That she what?" He stepped toward me, a movement so contained, so perfect, I could only call it prowling.

I held my ground, but it was a struggle. "That she gets to be with you before I do!" And there was the anger again, the words bursting from me.

He continued to stalk toward me, his face darkening with each step. "You think that doesn't piss me off? That I won't even have a memory of us to hang onto? Because whatever she wants, she's not getting me. No matter what she does, I never think of her, Aidan. Her name is never on my lips. That part is yours and yours alone. It's been yours from the day I met you, and nothing is going to change that. But this will change everything else, won't it? When you touch me, this will always be between us. It won't be just the two of us, not for a long time. Damn it, Aidan!" His fist shot out, and a palm tree swayed at the impact. "Why did you always have an excuse?"

"That's not fair!" I didn't remember rushing toward

him, but suddenly I was close enough to shove him.

As usual, he didn't budge.

"I tried," I reminded him. "We were interrupted. Don't put this all on me."

"You could have tried harder!"

"So could you!"

"If we tried harder, you would have lost control!" Mac screamed in my face.

We glared daggers at each other, only inches apart. Our breath met, heavy and ragged.

We recognized the absurdity of the fight at the same moment. He gave a rueful laugh, shaking his head, and I suppressed an inappropriate attack of the giggles.

"Good thing we didn't lose control, huh?"

Mac ran a hand through his hair. "That was... not good, was it?"

"We've had better moments." I slid down the trunk of the nearest palm tree until I sat on the ground. With an oath, Mac dropped to my side. We gazed at each other, trying to find our way back.

I slid my hand into his, needing his skin against mine. "I'm not hot for Luke. Never have been."

"I know. I was being an asshole."

"It was going around." I squeezed his hand. "Maybe we could manage it. We have a few hours before dawn. If we went slow, it's possible I could handle it. And it's not like I'd be feeling any rage. If I don't lose myself completely, it could work."

Mac ran his eyes down my body, considering. In the end, he shook his head, though not without regret. "Aidan, I've imagined you in my bed since the day I met you. And on my table, and in the rear of the Bronco, and against a wall. Pretty much everywhere I've ever seen you, I've imagined what you would feel like beneath me. I didn't spend the last several months imagining it to leave you with even a shred of control when the time finally comes."

If I was lucky, I'd remember to breathe again this century.

He raised my hand to his lips and nipped the knuckle of my first finger. "We don't know what will happen, and there's no way we're taking that big a risk when we're so close."

"You're right. I know you're right. But..."

"But?" Mac prompted, blowing lightly across the same knuckle.

"There's a lot of room between nothing and everything."

"Mmm-hmm?" He turned my palm upwards and sank his teeth into the mound of flesh at the base of my thumb.

I leaned toward him. He'd grown a beard during our weeks on the island. The hair was the same rich brown as his fur. I rubbed my cheek against it, savoring the unfamiliar sensation. I moved my lips to his ear. "And time for a few more memories. A few more things to hold onto."

Mac took a slow inhale through his nose. "Did you have something in mind?"

In fact, I did. I pushed on his chest. He didn't resist, falling until he lay flat on his back. "You're in control," he said, and closed his eyes.

I knelt at his hip. For a while, I simply looked at him. My eyes roamed his entire body. Almost every inch was covered in muscle, but he never appeared bulky to me. He was just more. More man. More Mac.

At last, my gaze stopped on his face. Underneath the new beard, the wide cheekbones were still visible. I pressed the fingers of both hands to the bones, then ran my index fingers across them, following the circle of the bone to his brow, relearning all the contours of his face. I traced his hairline, and the ridge of his ears, and then his jaw and chin. I skimmed my fingers over the cords of his neck and the hard line of his clavicle.

Each caress was light, but I felt the heat wherever our skin met. Using only my right hand, I caressed the outside of his arm, feeling each muscle and the sharp bones of his elbows. When I came to his hands, I outlined each finger. They were thick and callused, the nails short. His mouth quirked when I hit the ticklish underside of his arm, but he didn't move, and I hid my own smile as my hand slid down his torso.

I outlined his waist, hips, and legs, but I paused at the top of his right thigh. Mac tensed and held his breath. I dropped that hand and repeated the study on the left half of his body. Again, I stroked every inch, not only exploring but marking. I coated him with my scent, claiming him. I made sure his entire body knew my touch, and I was patient, allowing him plenty of time to commit each moment to memory. I took as long as we both needed, because we weren't sure when we'd get another chance.

When I reached the top of the second thigh, I only hesitated for a second before cupping him. He jumped into my hand, hard and ready, and his growl was equal parts satisfaction and hunger.

I moved to the waistband, plucking at the tie. Mac grabbed my wrist, stopping me.

"It's okay if you lose control," I reminded him.

His lips curled into a devilish smile. "You're not getting off that easy."

That was the only warning I got before I was flat on my back with Mac crouched above me.

"I need to remember more than your touch," he murmured. "It's your turn."

I knew what he planned, but I still wasn't prepared for

the sensation of his fingers and palms tracing my body as thoroughly as I'd traced his. His hands were large and rough, but also gentle. Where his skin brushed against mine, each nerve ending flared to life, electricity sparking through my neck and shoulders, then across my hips and legs. My breasts grew heavy and heat pulsed in my center. Everything else disappeared until I was only aware of Mac and his touch.

When he cupped me between my legs as I had him, my groan was a pathetic, pleading thing. "More," I insisted.

Mac rested on top of me, giving me as much of his weight as I could handle. I squirmed when I felt his length press against my hip.

"We missed one part," he said.

"Does it involve removing clothes?"

He laughed, and I felt the vibration through my body. "Not this time."

He traced my lips with the pad of his index finger, and I did the same to him. When my tongue darted out to taste his skin, he mirrored the action, and when he drew the tip of my finger into his mouth, I pulled on his, sucking it into the warmth of my mouth.

He released a jagged breath and grabbed my wrists, pinning them to the ground. I arched my back in anticipation. Mac wrapped both his lips around my bottom one and tugged, then did the same for the top lip. Only after he'd explored them thoroughly did he deepen the kiss, sliding his tongue to meet mine.

It was slow and languorous. We couldn't go further, but neither of us wanted the night to end, so we stayed like that for a long time. We tried to pull the other into ourselves, to share each other's essence as we already shared magic.

At last, he rolled onto his side, pulling me with him, and

with our arms and legs intertwined we began to drowse. Though he remained hard and I ached to be filled, it didn't matter. For that moment, what we had was more than enough. It was everything.

CHAPTER 18

The camp was stirring to life when Mac and I returned to the tent to change into clean uniforms. While I transferred the tracker to the new clothes, I shared what I'd learned from Vivian.

"They're trying to help us. I don't know how, or if they even can, but be ready."

"Always am, darlin'," Luke drawled. For once, Mac didn't glare at him.

I handed the single dart to Sera. "Just in case."

It was still wrapped in my t-shirt. She tucked it into her waistband, using the drawstring to hold it in place. It made her look a little pregnant.

Together, we headed for breakfast.

We didn't make it.

Tricia seemed to appear out of nowhere. "Luke and Aidan will come with me." Her huge smile didn't reach her eyes.

"Where are they going?" Sera placed herself between me and the other woman.

Tricia was unprepared for her aggression. "I thought… I was told you expected this."

Mac tapped Sera's upper arm. "This is what we wanted."

I'm not sure any of us believed that, but Sera grudgingly stepped out of the way.

Luke rolled his shoulders and cracked his neck. "What

the hell. I got away from the other first, and she liked to
decorate with skeletons. This one provides cotton underwear and all the papayas you can eat. We'll be fine."

People were starting to pay attention. I ignored them.
I'd go when I was ready. First, I needed to gaze at Mac a
little longer.

"Stop that." He moved a strand of hair behind my ear.

"What?"

"Stop looking at me like you're trying to imprint me
onto your brain. You're coming right back."

I grasped his hand and squeezed once.

I embraced Sera, catching her by surprise. We weren't
exactly big huggers. I lowered my head so I could whisper
in her ear. "Give Ani a chance. Maybe she has a reason."

Sera tensed. I hoped that meant she would consider
my request.

I wasn't ready. I spun around and ran to Mac. I rose on
tiptoes, and he met me halfway in a short, fierce kiss.

There was nothing left to say. Luke and I followed Tricia out of camp.

She moved a heavy palm out of the way, revealing a
twisting path up the mountain. The trail was well-used.
The plants that once grew along it had stopped fighting
the steady flow of elemental feet long ago.

"Where are we going?" I asked.

Tricia's only answer was to gesture at the long, twisting
path that led to the top. It wouldn't take more than ninety
minutes, though Tricia carried a large bag. I supposed it
was too much to hope that she'd planned a picnic at the
end of our hike.

We walked in silence most of the way. As we neared the
top, my nerves got the better of me and I needed to break
the silence. "Why you?"

Tricia stumbled on her next step, but she sounded

cheerful. "Why me what?"

"Why have you been our guide? Why not any of the others? You're the only one who's been alone with us."

"We all have a role to play." She turned sharply to the left, then doubled back. I was starting to feel like she was leading us toward a cottage made of candy… and Luke and I without any stones to mark our path.

"And your role is what, exactly?" I pressed.

She never slowed down. "I'm the liaison."

"Between Eila and the rest of camp? But you don't deliver any messages from her. What the…"

I stopped mid-sentence as we reached the mountain's peak.

"I believe the phrase you're looking for, my dear, is 'what the ever-loving fuck.'" Luke's tone was as light as ever, but his expression was grim.

We now knew where Tricia was taking us, but the answer to that question raised so many more.

We were surrounded by elementals, all with the traditional coloring. There was a black-haired fire and a blond water, a brown-eyed earth and a beach with those distinctive blue-green eyes. All seven elements were represented, and none were free.

The stone, earth, and beach were strapped to towering koa trees more than a hundred feet above the ground. Thick braided vines wrapped around their bodies from shoulder to ankle. At that height, it would be impossible for them to access their element.

The fire and water were buried under cairns of stones about fifty feet from the trees. The cairns were well designed. They weren't so heavy as to crush their prisoners, but neither elemental could escape on their own. Fire would heat the stones, but never move them. The water's cage was sturdier, as she'd have regular access to her element through the humid air and rainstorms.

The ice and desert were almost ignored, their powers weak on a tropical island. Both were simply attached to nearby tree roots with the same braided vines used on the elementals above us. They were equidistant from those above us and those in the cairns, forming the third point of a triangle.

Their bodies were thin, and filthy clothes hung from their bones. Their faces spoke of a struggle long since lost.

Even so, a low thrum of power pulsed across the mountaintop.

"What the hell is wrong with you? What are you doing to them?" I whispered.

Tricia was no longer at my side. She stood by the trees, filling several buckets with items from her bag. Each was attached to a pulley system.

With a sharp tug on the rope, the bucket lurched upwards toward the earth elemental. Whoever had tied the woman had bent one arm at the elbow and placed her hand against her shoulder, allowing her enough wiggle room to stretch that hand into the bucket. Light returned to her dark brown eyes and her skin plumped, the lines around her eyes and mouth vanishing.

Tricia repeated the process, sending up pebbles and sand to the other two. Next, she lit a small fire near the cairn and doused the water with several gallons of her element, then took an insulated lunch sack from her bag and placed it atop the ice's left foot. She withdrew a large pouch for the desert and draped it over her shin. It molded to her leg, and I assumed it was filled with some imported sand. Neither of them was allowed a free hand.

They were all given about fifteen minutes with their elements. All but the desert fed greedily. She stared at Tricia with heavy eyes filled with hate.

Once they'd refueled, Tricia gave each one a peeled banana. Those in the trees strained to maneuver the fruit to their mouths, but they managed.

Elementals needed at least some solid food to live, and most of them devoured the banana. The desert turned her face away.

"Please eat," Tricia begged.

The woman spat at her. "I'll die before I give that thing anything else. Tell her that, you traitor."

Tricia made no effort to defend herself.

She wasn't the liaison between the first and the camp residents. She was the liaison between these poor souls and Eila.

Everyone on the island played their part. This was hers. What I didn't understand was why—why she would be part of such a horror show, and why Eila required it.

"This is bad," I murmured.

Luke was close enough that I heard him swallow. "Beats a mass grave, right?"

Barely.

"Why are you showing us this?" I made no effort to hide my suspicion. "Why would you do this to them? Why don't you help them?" The words came out in a rush, demanding she answer each question, ideally at the same time.

"Eila is our god. She requires tribute." The sentences were delivered in a monotone.

"We're elementals. We don't have a freaking god." I managed to keep my voice low. I had little experience with those who positioned themselves as gods, but I suspected they didn't like to hear their existence questioned.

"What is a god but the creator, the one from which all else sprung? We are her children as much as Christians believe they were created by their God." Unlike me, Tricia spoke in a loud, clear voice, like she wanted to be heard.

"Let's assume you're right," I said. "Last I checked, followers of the Christian god had free will and didn't need to exist in a perpetual state of agony and denial."

"They feed their god with faith and prayer. We feed ours with magic. She returns the gift in kind. Those who now feed Eila were fed richly by her before they were chosen."

I studied each elemental. No one's eyes, not even Tricia's, shone with any kind of religious fervor. Virgins heading toward the volcano had been more willing sacrifices than these.

They weren't sacrificing their lives. They were sacrificing their magic. They might recuperate, if given enough access to their element, but that obviously wasn't happening.

"How long will they be here?" Luke's voice was strained.

Tricia wouldn't meet his eyes. "It varies."

The desert laughed. Her voice was barely a rasp. "Until you're replaced or you die. Well, you die either way. I've been trying to kill myself for a year now." For the first time, she seemed to notice Luke. Her voice hardened. "But maybe I don't have to worry about that anymore."

The water watched me with wide, terrified eyes.

"She does more than feed herself," Tricia hurried to explain. "Eila shares her power with the rest of us. It's why she's able to infuse the island with enough power to keep us safe."

It was a sickening irony. These poor souls gave Eila the magic she used to feed the island—a magic that established an ongoing sense of complacency. A complacency that prevented the residents from helping the tortured souls above them.

I couldn't tell how much Tricia believed what she said and how much she wished to believe, but I didn't care, either.

"How the hell can you be a part of this?" I no longer bothered to be quiet. I half wished Eila were here so I could yell at her. I'd likely die a horrible death, but I'd least I'd go out on a righteous high.

Tricia didn't avoid the question. She met my eyes, letting me see her shame, and gave me the simplest and most horrible answer. "Because I'm a stronger beach than she is."

"But why…?" Luke began. He didn't need to finish. His sharp inhalation told me he'd come to the same conclusion I had.

"Because only the strongest are used as food, aren't they? If you weren't useful in another way, you'd be up there instead."

Tricia didn't deny it.

"What happens when one is replaced?" I asked. They couldn't return to camp, not with the stories they'd be able to tell. There was a big difference between deliberate ignorance and seeing the evidence of PTSD each morning at breakfast. That kind of god would be a lot harder to worship.

I studied each sacrifice with new eyes. Many of the residents were powerful, but none were stronger than those before me.

Except for Sera. She was definitely stronger than the fire. Stronger than her mother, as well.

And Luke and I were stronger than any of them.

"Let me guess." Luke's ironic drawl was firmly in place, but it overlaid a grit I hadn't heard before. The hair on the back of my neck rose at the sound. After weeks in his company, I'd almost forgotten how much power he commanded. "The last one replaced was named Eila."

"They receive the greatest honor. They are given immortality. They become part of the purest magic." The words were pushed past a tight throat and a quivering lip, and her eyes were wet with unshed tears. I wasn't sure I had enough kindness left in me for pity.

"You mean she eats them." The grit in Luke's voice roughened to gravel.

Elemental magic worked like a generator. It wasn't a finite source of power. So long as it received fuel, it could run indefinitely. The only reason we died at all was the human blood we possessed. Eila could drink deep from those before me, and they would continue to live if they were given at least some access to their element.

To become part of Eila meant she consumed them. Those who were replaced were treated as batteries rather than generators. One use—one feeding—and their lives ended. It was what the creature in Utah had almost certainly done to the bodies in the pit. It was what she'd tried to do to me.

Luke's fire rose, and I assumed his desert side was doing the same. Tricia stepped back in a hurry. As a beach, she wouldn't feel his magic, but only a fool would miss his anger. The sparks flying from his fingertips probably helped.

I lay a hand on Luke's forearm. I didn't care what he did to Tricia, but I wouldn't lose him to this island.

"We need a new plan." I whispered, so only Luke could hear it. "I think we're about to be the next course in this macabre meal. Eila doesn't plan to keep the promises she made."

"Of course I do." The voice came from behind me, as light and delicate as a spiderweb. I was pretty sure Luke and I were the flies. "I will stop your madness."

"You said we would leave the island afterward," I reminded her, turning. No one was there.

"You will." Again, the speaker was behind me. I whirled to face it, only to find empty space.

"As soon as we were healed. That was the agreement."

"It was not."

"Yes," I insisted.

"No."

I blinked, unsure how to argue with someone using the debating techniques of a toddler.

"It was one of Mac's conditions." Desperation fueled my words. I'd known it was risky to trust Eila, but it was a risk we'd needed to take. "He said you had to let us go after he… after he went with you."

"And I replied." Eila gathered before me, slowly assuming the appearance of a calm water with just a hint of a steady stone.

"You did. You said…" I squeezed my eyes shut, fighting a wave of nausea. She never agreed on a time we would leave. Coming from a creature for whom a century passed in the blink of an eye, that was worrying. "But you said Sera had to leave camp."

I parsed her promises from the night before, and once again my stomach threatened to revolt. Sera was the strongest fire on the island. If Eila didn't consider the mountaintop part of camp, Sera might soon find herself under a cairn of her own.

Mac had tried to cover every loophole when he negotiated. He'd missed a few big ones.

Perhaps this first creature had a code of honor, but that code was very literal.

"What do you want?" I tried for bravado. I did a great job, if bravado looked a lot like despair.

"I will remove the possibility of your madness."

Eila stilled. I doubted I wanted to know her thoughts.

Tricia stood before the first, fidgeting. "Eila? Should I prepare for the desert and water to join you?"

Eila blinked to life. "That will not be necessary. I continue to need them."

They both looked relieved. The desert might seek death, but I thought she'd rather starve herself than live in Eila forever.

"The duals will not be able to replace them."

Luke understood before I did. He rushed toward Eila. It was a suicidal attack. He knew that. He no longer cared.

Eila had no intention of feeding off our magic. She planned to take it.

She flung Luke backwards with the force of the water in the air. Her hair coiled black.

"You desired a cure. This is it. You cannot go mad from dual magic if you do not possess both magics."

EILA POSITIONED HERSELF IN THE MIDDLE OF THE TRIANGLE formed by the various elementals and relaxed her human form. Her features and the lines of her body blurred against the sun.

There were no dramatic gestures. She didn't fling her arms outward or throw her head back. She stood in one spot with her eyes closed while her captives writhed in pain.

I moved toward her before I realized what I was doing. I didn't know how effective tackling a half-corporeal first creature would be, but it was better than doing nothing while she drained the prisoners.

Only Luke's tight grip on my upper arm kept me from doing so. "They'll live," he said. "If you do what I think you're planning to do, you might not."

He was right. We knew she didn't steal their power permanently. Even so, these weren't the quick sips she claimed from the others. Up here, she swallowed in long, demanding gulps.

With her form half translucent, I could witness the process. Eila drew their magic into what remained of her body, letting it cycle through each particle of her being. She claimed their energy for herself before returning the source to its hosts, where it would be recharged through limited exposure to the elements.

"That's not living," I told him. Luke didn't argue.

All at once, it stopped. The magic vanished. The prisoners' heads dropped forward, their chins hitting their chests, and all was quiet.

Eila was now as corporeal as the rest of us, though she appeared more vibrant than I ever would. Her eyes flashed with the colors of every element and her hair was a prism of different shades that changed with each brush of the wind. She was solid, but there was nothing stable about her.

"Removing magic is not easy. I must be strong." I didn't know if she spoke to us or to herself.

"About that whole removing magic thing. That seems like overkill. I was thinking you could fuse them together, like Luke's was when he arrived. He was all sane and healthy then, remember? It looked like a nice, quick process. Just a bit of glue on the two threads and send us on our way. That works for me. Let's get started."

I smiled cheerily.

Eila took a moment to understand me. I supposed I should be proud that I'd confused a being as old as time with my reasoning.

"No." Then again, she sounded really certain. "I will begin with the boy. I have already tasted him."

Luke's eyes were wild, filled with the same terror the other first had inspired. This was his worst nightmare, and I'd brought it to him.

I stepped forward. "Start with me."

Eila gave no indication she heard me.

Luke managed a shaky smile. "I don't think we get to be picky about how it's done. If we live, that'll be good enough."

I didn't know if he was right, but I wasn't given a chance to argue. Luke screamed, the sound impossibly loud. The others raised heavy eyelids, and those still capable of pity winced. No animals moved, and even the wind quieted enough to witness Luke's agony. It went on and on, the scream growing rawer but no less urgent.

Eila's expression transformed, moving from cool certainty to determination to anger. She released him with a grimace of disgust. Luke stumbled, falling across some tree roots. He turned his head and threw up in the bushes.

I hurried to him. "Are you okay? How much did she take?"

He tried to answer, but his mouth opened and closed on silence.

"I took nothing. He fought me." Eila sounded displeased.

"Good." I bit off the single word.

Eila wrapped slim fingers around my wrist and yanked me up. I gasped at her strength. She threw me against the trunk of a nearby tree, then pinned me in place with her right hand on the center of my chest.

I was given no warning. One moment I felt only her touch. The next I felt agony.

Eila examined every cell. She began in my core, where my power lived, and traced a path through my arms and legs, my hips and shoulders and neck—everywhere the magic had been called. My physical body belonged to the magic, and so she claimed my body as her own. She ripped me apart without spilling a single drop of blood.

I screamed, wordless, desperate pleas, and still the torment continued for what felt like hours. Knives cut into my lungs and heart, slicing through blood vessels and across skin, until all I knew, all I could remember, was pain. It was who I was. It was all there had ever been.

And then it stopped, and its absence was so shocking I forgot how to function. My mind wasn't just empty; it was blank, a white wall of nothing. In that moment, I wasn't certain I existed.

My lungs didn't pull breath and my heart didn't beat. I lay beside Luke with no memory of falling.

I came back to myself slowly. When I remembered where I was, I reached for my power. Both threads were still there.

"You…" I struggled to stand. I didn't make it to my knees before crumbling onto my side. I tried again and managed to sit up. "Nothing is different."

"No." She turned away, apparently done.

"You said you would cure me. You promised." I sounded like a child protesting that the world wasn't fair, but it was all I had left.

"There is no point."

Tears came to my eyes, the frustration and pain too much. I didn't bother to blink them away. "I don't understand."

"You also fought me. You must give me your magic by choice, and you are unwilling to do that."

I grabbed onto a tree trunk and pulled myself up, using the sturdy wood for support. "I wasn't trying to fight. I need to be cured. Why can't you just fuse it? We know that works."

Eila's hair darkened. "That is impossible."

"I don't understand." I hated this creature, but I would beg. I would do anything.

"You are a killer." Her voice was as harsh as it was certain.

I felt her claim like a punch to the gut, but she wasn't wrong. My nightmares told me so every night. It was my stubborn friends who kept pretending it wasn't true, and I did my best to believe them.

For those friends, I'd try. I stepped away from the tree and stood on my own. Eila watched me without a flicker of interest.

"I killed when I lost control. You agreed to give me that control."

"Control is the last thing you need." Her eyes turned black in anger. She might pretend otherwise, but she wasn't disinterested in this conversation.

"I never wanted it. None of this." I tried appealing to the human emotions of a creature with no humanity.

"You lie to me as easily as you lie to yourself. Death follows you. Your attempts to stop it were weak. Ten years in exile before you returned, and then you pursued one victim after another." She knew, of course. She'd torn me apart. I doubted there was a single dark secret she hadn't uncovered.

"I didn't know I was at fault." It was the same explanation I gave myself whenever I tried to forgive what I'd done. It felt as false now as it ever did.

For months, I'd tried believing it was because I was a dual, unable to control myself when the fire and water worked together, but never in my life had I felt more certainty and control than when I chose to kill.

I'd spent weeks, months, years trying to forgive myself, and only now did I understand why it was impossible.

I hadn't earned forgiveness. I never would.

I didn't protest when Tricia led me to a flat spot near the others, or when she piled rocks on top of me. My breathing grew shallow under their weight, but I said nothing in my own defense.

I didn't fight when Eila stood before me and drew from both my magics until I was so weak my knees buckled and I sagged against my bonds.

Hope had been an illusion, and illusions fade. It was with something like relief that I closed my eyes and accepted the last punishment I'd ever receive.

Before I blacked out, Eila's voice resonated inside my head. "You still hope to live. I will change that. Only then will you be cured."

CHAPTER 19

Days passed. The sky grew dark and lightened. The wind rose one afternoon with a small storm that drenched the mountain and made the trees dance attendance before it vanished into a cloudless sky. Tricia returned, and Luke spoke to her. I didn't remember what was said. I kept my eyes closed and waited.

Eila appeared each day, sometimes more than once, though she didn't stay long. She repeated the names of the dead and called me a killer, then she destroyed me.

I grew to welcome those visits, when she would break me into a thousand jagged pieces. After running so long, I was ready to pay. And yet, when she grabbed my fire side, my instincts kicked in and I fought. My screams echoed in my ears, the mocking sound of my unplanned resistance.

When I lay weak and depleted, my magic recharging as best it could, she spoke.

"You oppose me when you should confess." I didn't know if she spoke aloud or inside my head. "You add to your burdens instead of releasing them."

Through the haze of pain coating my thoughts, I struggled to understand. I'd admitted the worst part of myself. I'd accepted the consequences. Confession brought peace, and that wasn't what I wanted.

"You do not deserve this magic. You must relinquish it if you wish to purge yourself of the crimes it has committed."

She made perfect sense, but somehow I kept fighting. A soft hiss slipped onto the ends of her words.

Then one day, she didn't come.

The sun dipped into the west before I realized we'd been left alone. I cracked my eyes open, blinking against the light. My neck protested when I moved my head, the muscles and tendons locked in place after days trapped beneath the stones.

"Luke?" My voice was a dry rasp. He'd been placed next to me and covered with his own set of stones.

His head lolled to the side. "It's 'bout time you came back to us, sunshine." Somehow, he managed a grin.

I tried to return it. It would have worked better if the guilt wasn't jumping up and down, demanding my attention. It wanted to remind me that Luke's life was ruined because he'd chosen to help me. I didn't want to make everything about me, but I was noticing a certain trend in my life. "I'm so sorry."

"For what?" He shrugged as best he could within his bindings. "This isn't the first time I've been held by a crazy first. We'll get out of here."

I didn't argue, but I didn't agree, either. "I'm not sure I like Eila's version of the cure."

Luke's laugh was low and rueful. "I'm not too fond of it either. I've got the feeling losing half our magic will come with some serious side effects, too. Would it be so difficult to sew us together like the other one did?"

"I guess she doesn't want us to be that strong. Especially since she believes I'm a killer." I tried sounding matter-of-fact.

Luke wasn't fooled. "You really buying what that creature's selling?"

"It's not her. I've known this for quite a while."

"What you're thinking, it ain't true. No, you don't manage your dual nature particularly well, but a killer wouldn't cross state lines in an effort to learn control."

I wished I could believe him, but what he was saying didn't ring true. "Most of that wasn't me. Sera and Mac led the charge. The others, too. If I'd been the one making decisions, I'd have been executed after I murdered David. Sometimes I think that would have been the best choice."

Luke exhaled, reining in his frustration. "For reference, how long do you plan to punish yourself? Cause I was hoping to make other plans."

"There's no set time. I don't get a probation hearing in twelve months."

"So you're done? This is it? A cairn for the rest of your life? You leave your friends down there, waiting for you indefinitely?"

Luke was determined to puncture my self-hatred with reason.

"Not indefinitely. Just until she pulls my fire side. Once they see I'm fixed, we'll find a way to leave."

"Of course. An ancient being who has no history of releasing people will build you a raft once you hand over half your magic and more than half your power."

"You've got a better idea?"

The cool desert cowboy disappeared, leaving nothing but fire in his wake. "We fight, Aidan. That's all we ever do. You're fighting right now without even trying. She's not trying to cleanse your soul with that whole confession deal. She's breaking you down. She needs you weak so you'll stop resisting her. You think you're the only one? She's got my memories like she's got yours, and she shows me a goddamn movie of Nora and the fire. She can only claim your magic if you're willing, and you'll only be willing if you've got nothing left to fight for. If she tries taking it before you're ready, she'll destroy you completely."

If she did that, the deal with Mac was off.

I squeezed my eyes shut. Mac required proof I was healed before holding up his end of the bargain. If she was growing impatient with me, there was a chance Mac was making her wait.

A tiny spark flared in my core. I tried to snuff it. I was being repentant, damn it. Penitents didn't get to recover from their guilt and horror in a couple days.

But twenty-four hours away from Eila's voracious appetite was time enough to be free of her influence, as well. The self-loathing she'd so carefully nurtured developed some cracks.

Over the last few days, a new truth had begun to take root, growing stronger as I fought for my magic. Penitence isn't what you do to prove how much you despise yourself. It's about finding a way to live with yourself again.

Sitting under a bunch of rocks while my friends worried below, while Sera was at risk of joining us, while Mac was being tempted daily by Eila's touch—well, that wasn't something I could live with.

Maybe I would stop fighting, but I'd do it on my own terms.

ANOTHER DAY PASSED, AND NO ONE CAME FOR US. WHEN night fell, the rustlings of the trees and small animals was punctuated by the weak moans of the captives, denied access to their elements for too many hours.

A row of bushes ten feet from my head went up in flames. While my eyes adjusted to the sudden light, my magic fed eagerly.

A short woman with wild hair stepped through the fire. "Sera?"

No, not Sera. The woman's movements were jerkier,

and when her face appeared in the circle of light, it was lined in a way Sera's wouldn't be for another thousand years. "Ani."

Ani studied me. "How much do you love her?" She wasn't talking about Eila.

"She's my sister. My family." I said that like it was explanation enough, because it was.

Ani winced. I was glad to see the barb hit home.

"You can't give in to her."

She moved from one thought to another with little explanation. "You mean Eila? I'm not sure I have a choice. She won't let me go until I relinquish my fire side. Won't let any of us go."

"She told Tricia to bring Sera tomorrow. She said she wished for a new fire."

Oh hell.

"But if you feed her your power regularly, as much as you can, she won't need Sera." The woman glowered at me, daring me to argue.

"To be clear, the mother who abandoned her daughter to follow a semi-mythological creature is now demanding I live on this mountain for a few centuries to save Sera?" I'd do it if necessary, but I wanted that said aloud.

"Yes."

Ani met my eyes. I'd give her this—the woman didn't deny her past.

It didn't make me like her any more. "Why don't you save her? You can volunteer to be Eila's caged pet."

I was being cruel, but Ani didn't even flinch. "I've been trying to get Sera away from this horrible place since you arrived. I tried to stop you at the beach. When that failed, I said words I can never take back, hoping Sera would give up on me and leave." It was hard to tell in the firelight, but I thought her eyes darkened. "And then she made me repeat them."

If my hands were free, I'd have used them to smack Ani. "You didn't. An hour with your daughter, and you spent it telling her you don't love her?"

"So she'd leave!" It was a desperate plea for understanding, though I thought she spoke to herself more than to me. "But she won't. Not without you."

"She's a little stubborn. If you'd stuck around, you would know that."

Ani sat on the rocks that covered me. "I didn't come to argue. I'd take Sera's place with no hesitation, but Eila wouldn't allow it. Sera is stronger than both me and the woman next to you. It's her turn next."

I softened a little, but I couldn't honor her request. "There's a whole sequence of events here. If I keep fighting, Sera, Vivian, and Mac will be stuck here forever, and Sera will still be in danger."

Ani's lips tightened. "That isn't an issue. The earth left the island and the bear is dying. Sera is all that matters now."

I jolted up, forgetting the pile of stones holding me in place. "What did you say?"

"He's dying. He doesn't accept any food or water. Eila has tried everything, and still he fades. She's with him now."

I clenched every muscle and forced myself upwards. One rock moved an inch.

"Free us."

Ani hesitated.

"Trust me, whatever you believe Eila might do to you, I'm thinking of something worse." I'd just spent days regretting my more murderous impulses, but at that moment I'd never been so glad for my dual nature. Whatever Ani saw in my eyes, it convinced her to start lifting rocks.

I hadn't thought Mac and I were that far apart as the crow flies, especially considering how far my power could stretch. I'd been wrong.

When I made the mistake of flying a thousand miles from Tahoe, Mac had grown ill from the moment I stepped on the plane. Our friends believed he was dying and brought him to me. The moment I drew into range and he could access my power, he recovered.

I was Mac's element, and he'd been denied it for too long.

Mac was not going to fucking die, not when the cure was so simple. The cure was me.

God, I'd been a selfish bitch. I'd been so determined to accept my punishment that I let myself forget everything else. Mac's illness, Sera's vulnerability, my family's incarceration—I could help fix those, but only if I got off this damn mountain.

"Faster," I ordered. Ani cursed at me, already moving as fast as she could. In that moment, she sounded a bit like Sera.

I needed more power. I grabbed all the water I could from the air, but it wasn't enough. We were almost a thousand feet above sea level, but I sent all I had flying to the ocean's surface—then I kept going. I punched through the water, and while half my magic feasted, the rest dug into the ocean's crust, seeking the pulsing magma below. I pushed it further from my body than it had ever been before, and I was rewarded with the purest source of energy I'd ever felt.

This, I realized, was why fires lived near volcanoes.

I didn't need Ani anymore. When I sat up, rocks as large as my head scattered like pebbles. "Work on him instead."

Luke was trying to free himself, but his desert side limited the power he could access. Plus, he didn't have that whole desperation thing working for him quite as hard.

"Luke, find me after you're free. After everyone is free."

"You got it. And Aidan?"

I was already running. I turned, my face twisting in frustration.

Luke didn't cower under my glare. "If you're going to save him at the cost of your own mind, you might as well leave him to die. He'd prefer it."

I took a ragged breath. He was right. If I barreled into that camp ready to burn things, the situation would only get worse.

Mac would hate for me to risk myself, so I wouldn't. Instead of arguing about which of us was allowed to die for the other, I'd make sure we both lived.

I raced downhill. I created small fires to light my path, and I never stumbled. I knew roughly where camp was, and my magic knew where its lost piece would be found. As I ran faster than I ever had, my mind cleared until I could see with a clarity I'd been denied—or denied myself—for too long.

I was guilty. That wasn't going to change.

But I was more than guilty. I was a friend and a lover, and I tried to help people, even if I often made a mess of it.

That could all change, but only if I let it. I had to be more than what I'd done. I needed to be the things I did now, and what I would do in the future.

As I ran down the mountain, I let that clarity finally bring a measure of peace—and for the first time, I thought I might deserve that peace.

To my surprise, when I finally released the guilt and torment I'd clung to for months, I freed up a whole lot of brain space I could now devote to planning how I could defeat Eila.

I burst into camp in the middle of the night with something resembling a plan. All the camp residents were asleep—all but one.

"Aidan!" Sera ran toward me, meeting me halfway. "Is it done? Are you cured?"

"Not yet. Where is he?"

She didn't ask how I knew, just pointed to a spot at the far end of camp. It was at least two hundred feet from the nearest tent.

I paused to check my control and took several deep breaths. Then I walked to the giant bed laid beneath the stars.

Like the others, it was made from leaves, but it was covered with piles of bedding and it looked soft and even. It was also large enough to hold an enormous bear shifter and an all-powerful first creature of magic.

She was wrapped around him more like a mother than a lover, and her expression was almost as desperate as mine.

Mac was covered in a thin film of sweat, and he'd definitely lost weight, but the color was already returning to his cheeks. He didn't look weak anymore.

"Let me go." He struggled against Eila's rigid bonds. "Don't touch me."

Her eyes widened. "You heal," she breathed.

"Aidan? Where's Aidan?" He fought to sit up, pushing at the hated creature's limbs.

I'd seen Mac angry before, seen him uproot trees and fling appliances into the ocean. Mac's anger could be enormous.

At that moment, it was a condensed ball of rage, and it was more powerful than any of his rampages. Even Eila recoiled under its force. He continued to scream my name.

"I told you. She is resisting, but it will happen. There is no reason for us to wait."

"I can think of a reason or two." I moved forward.

Eila didn't sputter or ask questions. She blinked at me, as if uncertain how I could be there when I was also on top of the mountain with her other food. "It is you."

I'd expected Mac to relax once he heard me, but instead he struggled harder. He forced both hands under her inflexible arms and pushed. When that yielded no results, both hands changed into paws. He dug sharp nails into her flesh.

Eila disappeared, only to reform next to me. "You," she repeated. This time, it was an accusation. "I tire of your interference."

"Well, I tire of your face." I brushed past her and crouched in front of Mac. He'd already swung his legs around so that he was sitting upright and was ready to move—or pounce—as necessary. "You okay?"

His fingers grasped mine, a rough touch. "I felt you coming when I started to heal. It had to be that. Otherwise…" He couldn't finish.

Otherwise, it meant I was dead, our bond permanently severed. The only time Mac was free of our connection was when my magic was silenced—and death was a pretty permanent way to do that.

"Not an option." I pushed a spark of power into him, strengthening our connection and giving him the energy to stand upright. After another minute of feeding our bond, he appeared recovered. If it wasn't for the unwashed hair and sweat-dampened clothes, no one would believe he'd been tapping on death's door only minutes before.

He scanned my body, performing a similar assessment. "You look the same, except dirtier. The cure?"

I glanced back at Eila. "Needs to be renegotiated."

"That is unnecessary." Eila kept her distance from us, though her ever-changing eyes watched our every move.

"I disagree," I said. "You gave me a few days to think and a fair bit of new information to process. Now, I can't say I understand it all, but I know a little more than I did before I went up the mountain."

"What do you believe you have learned?" Eila's voice didn't change from its usual music, but the words sounded more alien in her mouth than they had before, as if she needed to reach harder for her humanity. Her face gave nothing away.

I looked past her. Sera had joined us.

"I know you need to feed off elementals, though I don't know what happens if you miss a meal." I paused for an answer, though I didn't expect one. "I know you say giving up half my power is the cure, but I also know that if I hand over my fire side, you'll need to replace me with the next strongest fire—who happens to be my sister. Somehow, that didn't come up before. One might accuse you of negotiating in bad faith."

This time, Eila's face was a little easier to read. The black eyes and dark curling hair were a pretty decent hint.

"So if I've got this right, the old deal gave you half my magic, a new elemental food source, a vague promise to be allowed off the island sometime before the apocalypse, and a night with my boyfriend. That's a crappy deal. If we took it, Luke and I might have our sanity, but we'd be broken in a whole new way. I'm glad we didn't shake hands or do anything that would cause me to feel obligated to keep that deal, cause I'm about to break it."

Eila grew several inches taller. I rushed through the last of my speech before I either chickened out or she flung me so far into the Pacific I could see Tokyo. "You get one of those things." I looked at both Mac and Sera, certain they'd agree but needing confirmation. "You either get a new elemental plaything, a night with a shifter, or you get to devour my magic. In return, you heal Luke by fusing his threads together. Then you do the same for me, assuming you don't choose to consume my fire. That's the deal. No taking half our power and calling it a cure. We're duals, and we're going to remain duals. You heal us and we'll give you something in return. Whatever you choose, you let us leave the island with the next sunrise. What'll it be?"

The three of us had spent months arguing over who got to be noble and self-sacrificing. Nothing like putting your money where your mouth was.

Eila was dangerous and horrifying and probably three thousand other negative adjectives I didn't have time to list, but as far as I could tell, she wasn't a liar. In her own way, she'd kept her promises. We just hadn't been careful enough when extracting them from her. I hoped I'd done a better job.

And if I hadn't… well, there was always the backup plan.

I did my best to picture boring items. Beige paint chips. Vanilla custard. Seventies progressive rock. Anything to prevent my face from showing my actual thoughts as Eila sorted through my proposition.

"This is my island. You do not offer me choices."

"And yet that's what's happening. You don't have many options. Either you take our power, or we lose control, or you heal us. We have to agree to the first one unless we're weak, and I'm feeling pretty damn strong right now. Keeping our powers dampened indefinitely will require putting tons of energy into the land. That seems like a lot of work. And if we lose control…well, maybe you could stop us, but who knows what damage we'll do first? It could be Godzilla versus San Francisco levels of bad."

Eila didn't move while she considered my argument. "I do not understand what that means. I will kill you now."

"Okay, there is that option. But if you choose it, you won't get your night with the shifter, cause that whole willing thing is obviously important. You'll lose Sera, because trust me, if you kill her sister, that woman will starve herself before she'll feed you a single ounce of power. You'll get nothing. Is that what you want?"

I held my breath. That was all I had. The thin belief that Eila desired one of us so much she'd surrender a fraction of her control. We'd soon learn if I was wrong—or at least our next of kin would.

Eila's eyes settled on Mac, hungry as ever. "I will have the shifter."

He sighed with relief. "It's a single night," he said. "Better than Sera being food or you being torn in two. It'll be okay."

I agreed, but only because I'd been ninety-nine percent sure that would be her choice. "Done. Now cure Luke." I pointed to the far edge of camp. Luke was stumbling toward us, still weak. He hadn't stopped to heal himself.

Thankfully, he was alone. I suspected seeing all her food following him like the Pied Piper would have led to further contract negotiations.

"Afterwards." Eila hadn't removed her gaze from Mac.

"Yeah, that's not going to happen." I watched her carefully. It was only there for a second. If I hadn't been anticipating it, I'd have missed it. Fear.

I'd long assumed elementals' emotions came from our human halves rather than the magic. After meeting Eila, I was beginning to question that. Perhaps the world really had been built on love and fear and desire. It would explain a few things.

"Very well." The words were the sound of waves crashing. They contained only the barest hint of humanity. Eila undulated the ground, drawing Luke toward us. When he was closer, she began her assault.

My friend fell to the ground, though this time he didn't scream. I didn't think he could. His back arched and he threw his head back, and for several moments he shook uncontrollably. The pain was short-lived. Soon, the agony in his face melted, replaced with an expression I could only call bliss. His beatific smile suggested nothing but peace.

Before Luke opened his eyes, he flew through the air a hundred feet above us. An enormous wave caught him mid-air and dragged him backwards. In seconds, Luke was no longer on the island.

"He can swim, right?" Sera asked.

There was no time to answer her. No time to celebrate that my theory was correct. Eila already moved toward me, and with no warning, I was unmade.

CHAPTER 20

I was a full-blooded elemental. Fire and water might coil in my core, but magic lived in each cell of my body.

Eila gripped every drop of power I possessed and ripped it from its moorings. With each tear, my anguish increased. This wasn't the drug, silencing my power. This was violence, an assault on everything that made me what I was.

Luke's expression had transitioned from torment to peace within a minute.

Perhaps Luke really was insane.

This was the cure I'd crossed deserts and oceans to find. I'd fought and begged and connived my way to this moment. I should be celebrating.

Instead, I panicked. Eila grasped both threads and pulled them one way and then the other, stretching them like taffy, then compressing them into a tight ball. She was like a child playing with a new toy, except when I managed to crack my eyes long enough to see her, her face contained no innocence. It was focused and hard, only a step below cruel.

Magic was birth and creation, but it was also death and destruction.

There was a viciousness to her touch I hadn't seen when she cured Luke, and rising paranoia demanded I fight back. I wrenched my power toward me, desperate to reclaim it.

It didn't matter how fiercely I struggled to keep it. It was tug-of-war between a professional football player and a toddler.

With a final yank, she separated my magic from my body. The threads were loose, no longer tethered to my core. Rocks dug into my shoulders, and that was how I knew I'd collapsed to the ground.

Keening filled the night, an unearthly sound coming from my own throat. My face was soaked with tears. I was a fraction of a person, sliced into sharp pieces that didn't know how to work together. The magic connected my bones and muscles and organs as much as my blood and nerves did. I couldn't function without it. It was like asking a human to live without their heart.

Already, my blood slowed with nothing to push it through my veins. Gaps appeared between my heartbeats, each longer than the one before.

Eila paid me no attention as I forced air into lungs unwilling to expand. Her fingers made small, steady movements, as if conducting an unseen orchestra.

They ceased moving, but my magic wasn't returned.

"Not possible." She pointed at Mac and hauled him closer, using the earth to drag his feet toward her. She released him just out of my reach. He tried to get to me, but the earth tightened around his ankles.

Mac's eyes willed me to live. I'd do anything for him, but that request might be beyond my control.

We watched each other, and I saw the moment he began his own fight. Oblivion called, but I resisted. I forced my eyes open, though it was the only movement I could still make.

"Not possible," Eila repeated. "You must give it to me."

Mac shook his head, his jaw locked.

She'd found it. The residual water that lived inside

him, entangled with his own shifter power. The part missing from the threads she twisted between her hands.

"Do," I managed, my tongue heavy. We'd tried to retrieve that small piece once before, but the bear living inside him refused.

"I can't," he managed.

Eila's coloring sped up, cycling through each element in the space of a single second. "He is yours," she accused. "You have tainted him."

Mac's face relaxed the moment Eila stopped her exploration.

"I cannot finish." She waved a hand, dismissing both of us. "She will not be complete. It matters not. His animal is weakened. It protects the girl instead of himself. I have no use for such a creature."

"You promised." My voice disappeared on the last syllable.

"As did the shifter. We both spoke words without meaning."

Mac's roar suggested he wasn't impressed by her argument, and the enormous black bear that appeared in place of the man seemed to agree. The grasping ground released him as his feet became paws.

Eila did nothing, too fascinated to move.

Mac charged. A moment before he reached her, she dispersed, leaving him with nothing to attack. He lumbered around, as fast as a seven-foot bear could move, but it would never be fast enough.

I tried to hang on, but sometimes determination and denial aren't enough. If there were any tears left, I'd have cried then, knowing I was leaving Mac and Sera alone, but even that was beyond me. My eyes drifted shut.

It should have been my end, but magic had other plans.

Power slammed into me, and I woke with a gasp.

Eila was distracted. All her attention was on Mac fighting to reach her, and her gaze was more covetous than bothered. The threads she'd toyed with and bent and eventually sewn together had been forgotten, and they did what magic always does. They returned home.

I stretched every part of my body, down to the tips of my fingers and toes, letting the muscles and bones and blood return to life as power filled them.

I'd known strength before. Both sides of my magic were impressive on their own, and when I combined them I thought I was the most powerful creature alive.

That was a fraction of what I felt now. The fire and water were a single piece, no longer writhing against each other but connected, fused together until I couldn't tell one from the other.

I howled my victory to the night. The surrounding trees burst into flames, the fire so hot they were incinerated in moments.

A wave followed, twenty feet high. It crashed over everyone, drenching Eila. I found Luke swimming toward us and pulled him to shore.

The residents who'd been woken by the noise stopped halfway to us, watching from a safe distance.

This wasn't the cold madness I'd known before. This was hot and angry.

I couldn't burn Eila or drown her. I doubted she could be physically harmed, but I could destroy her home. I could burn their trees, flood their camp. I could hold every last person in my grip and send them to safety on another island.

They could be free. We all could.

As quickly as the power arrived, it settled. My knees buckled and I fell to the earth, my human side too weak. It seemed even a cured dual needed a few minutes to recover from a short case of death. I reached for the surrounding water and burning embers, needing to heal myself. Destruction of a psychotic first's home needed to drop down the priority list for a while.

Eila forced the water back to the ocean and extinguished any remaining flames. The wave grasped Luke as it slid past the beach and hauled him back out to sea. Like that, the chaos stopped.

"She lives. She is almost whole." Though Eila watched me, the words were meant for Mac. "Shift."

"What do you mean, almost?" Sera sounded like Eila could tell her the sky was blue and she'd still be suspicious of anything the creature said.

"I mean she is not whole." Eila was confused, as if the explanation should be self-evident. "The bear keeps the rest."

Mac shifted in a hurry. Eila's gaze locked on his naked form.

He gathered the remnants of his torn clothes and wrapped them around his waist. "Is this true, Aidan?"

I managed a shrug. "I feel pretty damn complete. Also, alive and sane. If I'm not struggling after the whole tsunami and bonfire combo, I think we're doing okay."

Eila ignored me. "She cannot be whole. The bonding was incomplete."

I checked the cord, looking for any holes or gaps. The fusion was flawless, the two magics inseparable.

Then I found it. It was minuscule, a tiny section of fire missing the matching water that resided in Mac's core. It was a loose thread, one I instinctively knew I must never pull.

"I'll be okay," I reassured Mac and Sera.

As soon as I spoke, I knew it was true. My magic didn't rule me. I controlled it, and I wouldn't touch that forbidden strand. I knew it as certainly as I knew my own name.

I stood. My legs were unsteady, but they held. "Now we get to leave."

Eila's attention was completely fixed on Mac. "They may depart. Though incomplete, she has deemed the cure acceptable. I did not lie. You cannot lie, either."

"I thought I was tainted," he reminded her. "You didn't want me."

"I was incorrect." The word sounded especially foreign in her mouth. "You possess the wildness of a shifter. She has not ruined you."

"Have so," I muttered.

"The agreement was made. You will come with me."

Mac laughed, a short bark with no humor. "We spoke words without meaning, remember?"

Her eyes flashed black. "You believe it is your choice."

His smile contained a hint of amusement. "I know it is. Unless you want an unwilling partner?"

Eila exploded, unable to contain her rage, then reformed an inch from Mac. She was as tall as he was, pitch black eyes meeting his brown ones. "You agreed. You agreed." She spoke as if the repetition was enough to make it true.

"Perhaps you've told us the whole truth, but I don't believe you." He narrowed his eyes. "Let them go. Aidan and Sera, Luke. Everyone in the camp who wants to leave. Let them go, and give them enough time to get away from you, however far that is. When you've done that, you will have what you want."

"I accept." She answered before he even finished speaking, flitting backwards. She no longer felt the need to loom over him.

"No, no, no." She couldn't have accepted his offer. It meant giving up everything—all her pets, all her food. We'd been so damn close. "Hell no. It's done, Mac. I'm good. Cured. See? Sane as a... really sane thing." I swallowed. "You can't stay."

Mac looked at me. His eyes held no doubt. "We got what we came for. This is the final cost. It's not even that high, and it will get us off the island. You really think we'll all make it by fighting our way off?"

"We're going to try," I argued. I would argue until the volcano below us rose to the surface before I let him follow through on that offer.

"Do you trust me?" he asked.

I trusted him more than I trusted the sun to rise, but I didn't trust her. I knew with a bone-deep certainty that if I left Mac with Eila, I'd never see him again.

Good thing I had another plan.

"Right back at you." I told him. "You've got to trust me, too. Did you really think I'd offer a deal where you spending a night with someone else was an option?"

I gave him what I hoped was a confident smile. It was time to test the theory I'd formed on my race down the mountain.

After all, there had to be a reason Eila was afraid to cure Luke, and a reason she'd flung him into the ocean the minute his power was fused. Deborah and Michael hadn't even been allowed to set foot on the island. She kept the strongest elementals as food sources, but none of them were fulls.

Somehow, fulls were Eila's weakness.

I'd been two halves. Now I was a full. One she'd allowed to stay a few minutes too long because of her desire for Mac—and her belief that I wouldn't figure this out so soon.

My strength built, the same irresistible energy I'd felt before. Sera's fire kindled and stretched toward me, her magic augmenting my own.

I'd planned to assault Eila, but Sera's touch distracted me. Behind us, the camp began to burn, though I was careful and gave the residents plenty of time to gather their few belongings and get to safety. They were already awake, drawn by our noise. No one would be harmed. I'd make sure of it.

There was only one woman on this island who needed to die.

But I didn't know how to kill her. She was pure magic, and magic had been around since the dawn of creation. I had no idea if it could be destroyed.

Still holding Sera's fire, I called to the ocean. I was feeling pretty damn immortal myself at that moment. I fueled the wave with a glorious burst of power and slammed every part of a full's strength against Eila. The first creature staggered under the assault, inhuman eyes widening. I was almost too astounded by my success to plan another attack. Eila struggled to recover from my assault.

She feared fulls because they could damage her.

My victory was short-lived. Eila stood, and with eyes dark as flint, she gathered her own power, everything she'd been given at her creation and everything she'd stolen from others, and she attacked in turn. The ground beneath my and Sera's feet erupted, launching us into the air. Eila's grin was pure malevolence. It was both the least and most human expression I'd ever seen on her face.

I struck, flames and waves battering her from every side. Nothing slowed her.

Ice shards encircled me and Sera. Sharp points stabbed us again and again, dozens of tiny wounds. I healed as fast as she cut me, and I melted the deadliest shards, but I was growing distracted, spending too much time defending when I needed to attack.

"You ask me to lower myself." Her voice echoed. It

sounded like the night itself spoke to us. "You play with agreements you do not keep. You believe you can trick me. You dare believe you can control a force older than the stars above us. You are nothing to me, and only when you become mine will your pale lives be given meaning."

"Eila." It was the first time Mac used her name. It was his final attempt at seduction.

She didn't even look at him. "Someday, you will come to me, shifter, and you will beg me to take you, because that is the only way you will ever join your incomplete woman."

Incomplete. Missing a piece. Not whole.

Cold understanding hit me like a slap to the face. I'd based this entire plan on whatever mystical control fulls held over Eila—and I wasn't a full. I was ninety-nine point nine percent elemental, but so long as Mac carried that final piece, it wasn't enough.

I'd made a huge mistake. We were going to lose.

Eila retrieved all the magic at her disposal and gathered it to her. Her hands circled each other, creating a smaller and smaller ball. As she touched each thread, she grew more solid, her body appearing to be formed of flesh and bone like the rest of us.

When she was done, an orb of pure magic hovered in the air. She didn't need to chuck it at us like a pitcher. She only needed to will it toward our bodies. Our human halves would be ripped apart, releasing pure magic. Magic that Eila would claim forever.

For the second time that day, I prepared to face death.

For the second time, death had other plans.

Eila vanished. One moment she towered above us, and the next there was only empty air. The ball of weaponized magic vanished with her.

"What the…" I muttered. I ran to the spot where she'd

just stood. It was empty, not even a hint of power.

Three large darts lay on the ground.

Three large tranquilizer darts, the sort that could hold a serum designed to neutralize magic.

"I said you would need a ninja. When will you learn I am always right?" I turned, a grin already forming, to find Simon standing a hundred feet away with a tranquilizer gun in his hands.

CHAPTER 21

"Is she dead?" I whispered, afraid any noise would summon her back.

"Ding dong." Sera stood next to me and tested the air. "No fire energy. Nothing."

"But the drug doesn't destroy magic," I said, uncertain. "It only turns it off for a bit."

Mac's brow creased in thought. "It could be different. She had no humanity."

"Literally or figuratively," I said. "It could wear off. It always did for me. How full were those darts?"

Vivian emerged from the trees, Jet trailing.

"I think the official term is a buttload," Jet said. "All we had left."

I kept checking the air, afraid Eila would reappear with no warning. "Maybe she's dead. Maybe not. We can't be sure. Which means…"

For approximately three seconds, my friends stared at each other, then we leapt into motion. We threw questions and answers back and forth, making plans with each step. We could have hours to escape, or we could have minutes.

For the second time, I retrieved Luke from the Pacific and brought him soaring lightly over the trees on a wave.

He landed on his feet and took in the chaos in a single glance. "What do you need me to do?"

"Where's Ani?"

"She took the elementals we freed, though one insisted

on coming with me to camp. The rest headed for the other side of the mountain. If you follow the coast, you'll meet up with them."

Sera didn't hesitate. "I'm not leaving her." She sprinted toward the northeast. At a steady clip, it was a thirty-minute walk. At the rate she was going, she'd be there in five.

The residents hadn't moved. They watched the chaos with equal parts shock and uncertainty.

"Can someone check on the camp? See who's going with us?" I asked.

Luke took off and Mac followed.

"Wait!" I called them back.

The residents watched from a distance, unsure about their next step.

I crouched and placed both hands on the ground. I probed until I found the fat veins of magic running through the land. With a grin, I drew on the single thread within me. It was going to be many years before I tired of finding fused power instead of broken pieces.

I wasn't capable of removing all the energy embedded in the ground. Only the fire and water belonged to me, but this was a Hawaiian island, and those were its dominant elements. I couldn't claim an elemental's power like a first could—but unlike people, land wasn't sentient. There was no battle of wills as I drew large swathes of magic, enriching myself and minimizing the island's hold on those who stood upon it.

I sat back, exhilarated, and watched free will return to people who'd long ago stopped looking for it. They studied each other and the burning camp, as if they were doubtful about where they were or how they got there.

"Now." I said. "Now they may be ready to go. Vivian, what's the plan for getting off?"

"We're anchored there." She indicated a spot to the

southeast. Jet adjusted her arm until it pointed due east.

I found the vessel with ease, but the anchor was no lightweight. This wasn't the same boat that brought us here. That one would have been hard-pressed to hold fifteen people, and only if they didn't have personal space issues.

I directed a little magic toward the ocean, telling it to loosen the sand that gripped the anchor. "Did you bring a freaking yacht? How many can it hold?"

"Everyone, of course." While the others ran around like mad, Simon strolled around the camp, examining the evidence of the final battle.

"You had a lot of faith in me."

"This was not our doing." Simon's lips curled upwards in a secret smile. "Though I am unsurprised to see you cured at last."

"How did you find us?"

Simon held up a tiny electronic screen with a red dot. Jet's tracker had done its job.

The anchor released in a sudden burst, the boat practically flying toward me.

I no longer controlled it. "Guys?"

Before they could answer, thunder rolled across the island.

It wasn't a storm. It was dozens of feet pounding toward me. A few of them carried bags, but most brought nothing but themselves. Packing would have slowed their escape. A steady stream of camp residents hurried past me, heading to a rescue most hadn't known they wanted.

Mac led the way, and Luke brought up the rear. Luke was in bare feet, and he'd lost his shirt during his repeated trips to the sea. Now he wore nothing but a pair of dripping cotton pants and a big old grin.

Behind Luke, Tricia supported the exhausted desert

who'd been on the mountain. They moved with a shuffling gait, as fast as they could with the woman's limited strength. Though the desert cast hateful glances at Tricia, she didn't reject her help.

"We're almost there," Tricia urged.

"Mama!" A desert fought against the tide of refugees. "They said… I couldn't believe."

It took me a moment to place her. I'd seen her at breakfast on our first day, the desert who didn't appear to like Luke. It made sense now. If he'd become Eila's new pet desert, her mother would have been devoured.

The daughter wrapped her mother in a tight hug. Neither of them was able to speak, but words weren't necessary. There was both joy and suffering in their reunion, and it was all I could do not to break down sobbing.

Tears ran in rivers down Tricia's cheeks.

The small family hobbled toward freedom.

I checked in with the beach elemental. "Is that everyone?"

"Yes. No one chose to stay."

"Good." I glanced over her shoulder at the abandoned camp in the distance. Any building that remained standing, I burned to the ground. "Let's go."

Tricia hesitated. "I think I'll stay."

I knew her expression well. I'd seen it in the mirror too many times to count. It was the look of someone who believed she was past redemption.

"What do you think that will accomplish? You can stay here and become Eila's only food source, or you can come with us and try to actually help these people. It's your decision, and I won't make it for you, but I should point out that you've already made enough bad choices for a lifetime. Maybe try something different." I spoke for both of us, and I believed every word.

She nodded once and followed the others. Maybe she only needed to hear one person say she'd be welcome.

When I arrived at the beach, the islanders were already being hauled over the railing. The boat was less than a hundred feet from shore.

Except boat wasn't the best word. It was a yacht worthy of a starring role in a 90s rap video. I half expected to see scantily-clad women drinking Cristal and dancing to a thumping beat.

Instead, I saw Grams.

"Aidan!" It was difficult to hear her at this distance and with all the surrounding noise, but every word was precious. "It's about time you got here," she said. "It's quite mean of you to make an old woman do all the work."

This day was just full of surprises. My face broke into a grin so wide they could view it from space.

Grams had transformed the ocean surface into a solid path that the islanders could walk on almost as easily as they could walk on land. While she might technically be old, she looked more like a well-maintained New York socialite than someone in her tenth century of life.

I cupped a hand around my mouth to amplify the sound and yelled to her. "I've been a little busy. Aren't you supposed to be in prison?"

"It was dull. I made other plans."

I urged Tricia ahead of me. She was the last person to cross, and Grams allowed the water to soften behind her, the pathway disappearing.

"Your turn, dear."

I didn't need to reach for my magic. It was just there, humming under my skin, more a part of me than ever before. I spread my arms wide and asked the water to push me forward. My heels skimmed across the surface, body flying to rejoin my friends and family.

"We've got to make a pickup," I told Grams, already pointing the yacht north. Working together, it took us five seconds to move two miles. Sera and Ani were already on the shore.

The freed elementals huddled behind them. They squinted at the approaching boat, unable to believe rescue had arrived.

"Get us as close as you can." I helped Grams create another path for Luke and Mac, and the three of us ran across the ocean.

We worked together with very few words. Mac took the stone and ice, throwing them over his shoulders in a fireman's hold. Luke grabbed a couple more. Only two were left. Sera supported the beach's left side and Ani did the same on the right, though she watched Sera the entire time. The water was easy. I told the sea to treat its child well, and it did the rest. The woman floated to the yacht, passing the others on the way.

We were done.

I wanted to do a victory dance, but that could wait. I signaled Grams to start moving toward open water. She knew I'd catch up.

I was fifteen feet from the boat when an invisible tether wrapped around my waist and hauled me backwards.

It was like being punched in the gut by a giant. The magic rushed to heal me as the tether drew me relentlessly toward shore.

Shouts came from the yacht, the words indecipherable but the panic clear. Mac dove into the ocean and began swimming, long strokes that would never reach me in time. Sera screamed, arms flailing in the universal symbol for "Turn this fucking thing around." When the boat didn't respond fast enough, she leapt in after Mac.

I pushed against my restraints. It did no good. The cord

wasn't only formed of water. It was also earth and ice and sand welded together, unbreakable.

A wall of fire erupted before me, a line of flames so immense even the Pacific Ocean couldn't extinguish them. I could no longer see the yacht, and those on it could no longer see me. Mac and Sera were caught on the other side.

Eila flung me onto the sand. I rolled, finding my feet. A heavy wad of earth struck my chest and I stumbled backwards. Sand wrapped around my legs, my chest, my neck.

The humanoid shape Eila assumed expanded and blurred, the edges fuzzy with crackling magic. She soared above me, inconceivable power stretching into the sky. When I was nothing but a bug before her, she crashed to the earth, shaking it so hard my head swung in every direction and my jaw snapped shut. Whiplash, I thought distantly. Chipped teeth. Blood ran from my mouth and trickled down my chin.

I spared no more energy for healing. I yanked a wave over my body, needing the ocean to draw the sand away.

I summoned every bit of strength I'd ever known, then searched for more. Now that I was healed, I was free to use all the power I possessed.

Luke thought creation magic was more powerful than destruction. It was time to test that theory.

The water spun and condensed as I shaped it into arms and legs, then built a torso and head. Its hair grew long and straight. Cheekbones emerged from its soft face. The hips narrowed and the limbs lengthened.

Fire slid inside the being and gave it life, making it glow with energy. Like the first, it was a creature of pure magic.

Eila swatted at it. I created another, and another, and soon a small army of my doppelgängers swarmed her.

They ripped at her with greedy hands, grabbing small pieces and feeding the power back to me.

Eila's cry wasn't human or animal. It came from a place of fear so primal I thought it might be the first terror the world had ever known. A fear of an oblivion so absolute that magic had created our world to escape its emptiness.

It was an oblivion to which Eila refused to return. She vibrated, a movement so quick there seemed to be two of her. My army fell from her body. She turned each one to ice, and they splintered as they hit the ground.

I tried building another, but something was wrong. Even surrounded by my elements, I couldn't maintain my strength. My army grew smaller and weaker. Months of exposure to a drug that weakened me was taking its toll.

Eila shrank to her former size, solidifying into the humanoid shape I knew and loathed. When she reached into me, I realized her earlier touches had been gentle. She burned me with anger and froze me with malice. It didn't matter how strong I was. It didn't even matter if I was the strongest elemental in the world. To her, I was a mouse battling a lion. "You are not whole. You cannot defeat me."

Eila grabbed that tiny thread, the loose fire that could undo me and send me spiraling into permanent darkness.

"Mine," she whispered. She tugged.

Then she vanished.

Sera's dark curls were plastered against her skull, and she'd kicked off her pants during her swim. They would have weighed her down.

"Who puts up a wall of flames to block a fire?" she asked. "These firsts may be all-powerful and such, but they aren't that bright, are they?"

She dropped the casing of the final dart. "Let's move."

Then again, I remembered, the mouse had outwitted the lion.

WHEN RUNNING FROM A CREATURE INTENT ON YOUR DEATH, with dozens of refugees and several fugitives along for the ride, it's best to lie low for a bit. Fortunately, staying hidden is one thing at which elementals excelled.

Fires raised the practice of concealment to an art form. While the rest of us lived on isolated islands and glaciers or deep in unmapped forests and deserts, they preferred to make like a Bond villain and live underneath a volcano.

The Blais family compound had been built so long ago no one knew whether the elementals had built their homes into the volcanoes or the volcanoes had formed around their children. The entrances were concealed, and once inside there was no sign of common construction materials like plaster or brick. There definitely wasn't any wood. Instead, the compound was a maze of curving tunnels. Some had been formed by the flow of magma, while others had been helped along by its inhabitants, but none were flat and orderly. Navigating the ups and downs of a single path would cover your thigh workout for the day.

Some of the tunnels opened up into immense caverns. Others shrank until my head brushed the ceiling. A generous person would say the Blais family was average height. I preferred calling Sera a short-ass. Whatever the case, she was able to slide through the corridors as easily as I navigated the ocean. Mac, Luke, and I, on the other hand, kept bumping our heads and cursing.

All the rooms had windows, but they didn't reveal the world above us. They showed only rivers of lava running past. Sometimes it was thick and sluggish, and sometimes it flowed as easily as water. It all depended on the mood of the fire in the room and how much elemental blood they possessed. I had no idea what building material could possibly withstand that heat, but Josiah had built it. If Josiah needed to travel to a distant galaxy to obtain an indestructible glass, he'd have found a way.

The place wasn't just hot. The surface of Venus might be a relaxing vacation spot compared to most of the compound. Lava marbled the floors, living crimson lines decorating each room. Luke and I felt comfortable. Sera moved through the halls at an easy jog. Everyone else wondered if it would be rude to lie on the ground and die of heat exposure for a bit.

At least Josiah hadn't been the sort to avoid either technological advances or other elementals. The entire place was wired for electricity, which meant the guest quarters and meeting rooms were air-conditioned. When he was shown to his room, Simon headed straight for the shower to wash off the sweat he'd accumulated on the short walk to the guest wing.

Vivian went for the high-speed internet connection.

"Will you tell them we're safe?" I said. "Miriam first."

Our otter friend hadn't joined us. Someone needed to stay in Tahoe, and she'd put the need to protect shifters ahead of her desire to kick some elemental ass. I knew that couldn't have been easy for her.

"Oh, and tell her I can create an army of mini-mes now."

Vivian looked horrified. It was probably the correct response.

The compound didn't have enough guest suites for all the camp residents. The fires were moved to the family side, since they could handle the heat, and the stones were placed on the lowest basement level. The rest bunked four or five to a room while they made arrangements to return to their families—those who had families to which they could return. People they weren't too ashamed to face.

Sera and I wandered into a small library filled with old leather books while the others settled in. The two of us needed to debrief.

"Have you spoken to her yet?" I asked, settling into a soft red armchair.

Sera made a face and perched on the edge of the desk. "I'm waiting to have something to say that doesn't involve screaming."

"That's fair."

"She left me, Aidan. She left me for that thing, and she didn't say goodbye. Not even a fucking note."

"That was awful. I don't deny it."

Sera spoke faster, spilling all the words she'd been holding in for days. "And the way she acted on the island? That was cruel. There's no other word for it, and I don't want to hear some crap about protection. She could have come and talked to me. Warned me like a goddamn grownup. Even when Mac arranged our hour together, she kept repeating that I didn't belong on the island, then she walked away. Again."

"Yeah, she screwed that up, too."

Sera heard what I didn't say. "But?"

"But you forgave me. You forgave me for everything." I tried not to push too hard. With parents, we all had to find our own way.

"That's cause you're you. You're my sister, and you always have been. I don't even know who that woman is." Her voice rose on the final sentence. She hopped off the desk and began wearing a hole in the carpet.

"You could ask her."

"I won't do it," Sera insisted.

I leaned forward in the chair, bracing my elbows on my

knees. "Yes, you will. Because even if she is a giant ass-hole, she's your mother, and we both know that matters to you. You may never like her, but you won't give up on her. It's not your style."

"Maybe. Someday. In the distant future. Damn it. I hate when you make sense." Sera flung herself into the armchair next to mine.

"I always make sense. You struggle to understand."

The corners of Sera's mouth quirked, but the humor didn't last long. "Is this really it, Ade? It's over?"

I suspected I'd be answering that question a lot, and it would probably require many sane years before everyone believed it. "Yeah. I mean, the council's still out there, and my mother's in prison, but I'm okay. I really am. It may take a while for the effects of the drug to wear off, if they ever do, but I can live with that."

"Good." There was a suspicious wetness in her eyes.

I'd have given her hell if I wasn't fighting the same ailment.

"You know, even with my magic dulled by the drug, I'm still a gazillion times stronger than you, right?"

"Just for that, I'm not sharing my inheritance with you. You weren't in the will."

I did what any big sister would do. I flipped her off.

"Blame the council," Sera said. "They kept your secret so well no one knows you're Josiah's daughter. It would be too risky to give you anything now. Tell you what. It'll be secretly half yours," she told me. "But to keep the secret, I get the master suite. The yacht's mine. I should have the private jet, just to be on the safe side. The Tahoe hotel, that's definitely mine. You and Mac can bunk in the Air-stream."

Nothing sounded better.

Before I could go in search of him, Grams poked her

head into the library. She beamed when she saw me. "I've been looking everywhere, dear. I break out of prison to rescue my own granddaughter and I don't even get a hug?"

I remedied that quickly. "How did you know I needed rescuing?"

"It was a council facility run by council guards. Bored council guards who liked to talk."

I raised my eyebrows, uncertain I wanted to learn the methods she'd used to get that information. "And they were so bored of their duties they let you go?"

"Psshh. It was barely a prison." She waved off the idea of incarceration. "A locked door. Maybe two. And the guards were very handsome." She arched her eyebrows.

I definitely didn't want to know what methods she'd used.

"And my mother?"

Grams' smile dropped. "That, my dear, will require more work, but she is being treated well, as was I. She broke the law, and she is receiving her punishment. To harm her in any way beyond her incarceration would only break a different law. In this case, Deborah's strict adherence to rules works in our favor. We'll free her. I'm certain of it. If you discovered a cure, I do believe anything is possible."

"Why are you so sure I'm cured? Everyone else asks for confirmation."

"It's obvious to any fool with eyes." Grams shook her head at the others' blindness. "Have you ever gazed through a streaked window into a lovely garden? The flowers are beautiful, but they are dull and flawed when seen through the streaks. That was you, and I didn't even realize it. It's like you've been washed clean, and now I see you as you truly are. You bloom, my dear."

Only Grams could compare me to a flower and get away

with it. She got a second hug before she left.

One person had been noticeably absent since we arrived at the compound. "Where is Mac staying?"

Sera pointed in the general direction. "The last door on the right. It's the room with the biggest bed, the thickest walls, and Barry White on the stereo."

I didn't offer even a token protest. "Thanks. I mean, not the Barry White, but the rest sounds pretty good." I stood, stretching until my fingers brushed against the low ceiling.

"He's not there," Sera said. "He went to the solarium a while ago."

She gave me directions I'd have no trouble following. This wasn't my home, but I felt a kinship with its intricate maze of black and red corridors. The compound was the path I didn't take, the life I didn't get to live. Separate, but still part of me.

"Keep in mind there are security cameras up there."

I rolled my eyes. "I wasn't planning on ravishing him immediately."

When I tried to step past her, Sera blocked my way. "After you shower." She wrinkled her nose in illustration.

I headed to my room, grumbling about interfering little sisters.

"Ade?" she called. "I'll make sure the cameras are turned off."

CHAPTER 22

Sera was right. I needed to rinse off not only the dirt, but the desperate days I'd spent under the cairn. I probably needed to wash off months of pain and fear, but that would take a while. For now, I started with a twenty-minute shower.

Someone had left fresh clothes on the bed. I unfolded a knee-length pale blue sundress covered in a white hibiscus pattern, the kind found in tourist shops across the islands. It wasn't the sort of thing I'd buy for myself, but it beat walking naked through the compound. I combed the tangles from my hair until the blond waves lay smooth against my back.

I didn't have the patience for anything else. As soon as I was dressed and presentable, I went in search of Mac. I kept a little dignity and didn't run toward him. I walked very fast, however.

The solarium was on the top floor. It had been built for visitors who didn't adapt well to the underground lifestyle, though the fires used it when they desired a break from their day-to-day life as crazy mole people. Tucked into an area tourists rarely visited, the room was cleverly designed to feel, as much as possible, like the outside world. Concealed vents fed in fresh air, and the floor was made of living grass and ferns atop rich soil. Discreet sprinklers kept them healthy and green. A few rocks of various sizes were scattered on the ground.

The best parts were the arching skylights that opened to the world above and the enormous windows that provided a view of the ocean. Both had covers set to automatically close if outside sensors picked up any movement, but at that moment they were wide open, revealing a choppy sea and a sunny sky beginning to darken with an approaching storm.

I wasn't surprised to find Mac here, far from the darkness and oppressive heat. He sat on a flat rock, staring out at the ocean. I joined him without speaking, kicking off my sandals and curling my legs underneath me. The sun had warmed the stone's surface. Any other day, sitting there would make me drowsy.

I was wide awake.

"Is it really over?" he asked, looking at the sea.

"So I'm prepared, how many times are you going to ask that?"

"Only once." He turned then, his eyes fixed on my face. He was making sure that, whatever I said, it was the entire truth.

"It's really over."

I wasn't prepared for the way his shoulders hunched, causing his huge body to seem almost small, or the way he covered his face with his hands, scrubbing so hard I thought he'd remove the top layer of skin.

"Is that a problem?"

His voice was muffled. "Of course not. Just give me a minute."

I waited, uncertain. "Wasn't this what you wanted?"

Mac's arm shot out and wrapped around my shoulder. He drew me to him and buried his face in my chest, rubbing his newly-shaved cheeks against skin the sundress failed to cover. I couldn't tell if he was scenting or marking me. When his shoulders shook and my neck grew damp from his tears, I knew it was neither. He sought comfort.

"Hey," I wrapped my arms around him. "I'm here. Look at me."

He kept his head down. "You only got worse."

I played with his hair, tugging on the thick strands.

"I kept trying to prepare myself. To lose you. All I could think about was how fast you were changing. How little time we had. I was never jealous of Luke, you know. Not like you thought I was. I knew you didn't want him. It was that he kept taking you away from me. Stealing the last time we'd ever have together, and I hated him for that."

By now, he wasn't the only one crying. "I didn't know."

Mac shook his head, the movement digging his chin into my collarbone. "I couldn't tell you. None of us could. We had to keep believing so you would do the same. But each time we knocked you out…" He fought to regain control of his voice. "And now you're telling me it's over, and I'm not going to lose you, and I don't know how to let go of a fear that's lived inside me for so long."

I gripped his head with both hands and tilted it to face me, then knit my fingers into his hair so he couldn't look away. "I'm here. I'm not going anywhere." I forced him to see the truth of my words, and when that wasn't enough, I leaned down to capture his mouth. As our lips met, he straightened, growing taller until I had to tilt my head to reach him. I leaned into him. Mac was warm and solid, and he wasn't going anywhere, either.

He drew back and rested his chin on top of my head. His arms remained locked around me. "What about the water magic I hold? Eila said she couldn't complete the fusion without it."

Tentatively, I brushed the unfinished end. It was still there, a tiny bit of unattached fire, but it had no water to explode against. The most twisted, most self-destructive part of me was fascinated. It tried to visit that loose thread the same way one would probe the gap left behind by a missing tooth.

That side was no longer in control. Maybe I would always have some darkness. Maybe a killer did live within me, but I had lots of reasons to keep that bitch at bay. She would never win again.

"It's okay," I said at last. "It really is. But you know, it's probably safer to keep your magic close. Just in case."

Mac pressed his lips to my forehead, my nose, my cheeks. "That," he said, "will not be a problem."

I grinned like an idiot.

"We should head inside." He didn't sound like he believed it. "There's a lot to talk about. We aren't in the clear yet." He stood and held out his hand.

I ignored it. "I don't think you heard what I said."

His brow furrowed. "Which part?"

"The part where I'm okay."

"Believe me, I heard that."

"The part where I'm in control."

"Yeah." He drew out the word, still not understanding.

"The part where it's safe to lose control," I nudged.

Mac glowered at me. "What are you talking about? You just told me you'd never do that. Why would you choose to give up control?" He stopped, swallowing. "Oh."

"Yes. Oh."

He inhaled sharply. "Tonight?"

"Absolutely."

His expression was somewhere between a smile and raw lust. "Then let's get these discussions over with."

I didn't move. "I meant tonight in *addition* to other times."

He froze. "Here? Now?"

"You have an objection?"

He didn't move. I began to fear he had other plans.

"I thought you'd need to settle in a bit," Mac said.

This wasn't going the way I'd imagined it. "Do you want to wait?" A year or two passed while I waited on his answer.

He shook his head, and I exhaled.

"I don't want to wait, either. I've already waited more than long enough. I've probably been waiting since I first met you, Connor MacMahon. Even when I was scared of you, or scared of myself, or maybe just scared of what we'd be together, I wanted you. I wanted you from the day I saw you throwing furniture into the trees. I'm done waiting."

That was all he needed to hear. Mac grabbed my wrist and tugged, pulling me to standing. Though the touch was gentle, it was also irresistible. I fell against him, my chest meeting his.

Our first kiss was almost sweet, just the tips of our tongues meeting. He drew back, resting his forehead against mine. Already, his breath was coming fast.

Mac's hands roamed down my back and over my hips and thighs. When he hit the hem of my dress he paused. His fingers toyed with the fabric, as if unsure what to do with it. Before I could make a suggestion, he released it. My protest cut off when he cupped my ass and lifted me until my feet dangled inches above the ground.

He plastered my body to his, and I squirmed in an attempt to get even closer. The muscles of his chest contracted beneath me as he adjusted his grip, now holding my ass with one hand. He wound the other through my hair, tilting my head to kiss me again. His tongue swept inside and I returned the stroke in kind. All I knew was his body, his lips and tongue. We were pure heat and desire, giving and taking with every touch until the barriers between us slid away.

When he put me down and stepped back, I protested.

Mac managed a shaky smile. "I'm trying to go slow here, Aidan. We shouldn't rush our first time." He took off his t-shirt and my temperature shot up several degrees. Instead of throwing it to the side, he lay it carefully across a soft patch of grass. "We shouldn't get stains on your dress."

I made sure he was watching, then I grabbed the dress and pulled it over my head. I wore nothing underneath.

Mac stared. When he at last managed to speak, his voice was ragged. "You had other plans?" he asked.

"You and I are going to have a lot of firsts, Mac. There will be the first time we wake together and you slide between my legs before either of us has spoken a word. There will be the first time you take me from behind, your hands gripped tight on my hips. There will be the first time it's rough, and the first time it's gentle, and all the times in between. But this is the first time you'll ever be inside me, and it won't be slow. We've had months of foreplay. I want you to fill me, and I want it now."

Mac exhaled once, hard, then ripped the button from his jeans in his hurry to undo them. The fabric slid over lean hips and that arrow of muscle pointing downward, then over muscled thighs and calves. I was only beginning to process the perfection of Mac with no clothes when he kicked them aside and strode to me.

He wrapped his arms around my waist and lifted me again. There was a lingering patch of sun, the one spot the clouds hadn't yet claimed, and he carried me to it. I touched him wherever I could and ran my lips across his neck and shoulders. He tasted of salt and warmth, and I inhaled the scent that belonged to him alone.

Mac was gentle when he placed me on the ground, but there was nothing hesitant in his movements. He sat back on his heels and gazed at me. I was completely exposed, but I never felt vulnerable under his scrutiny. I felt adored.

I studied him in turn. His chest I knew well, though it affected me as much as it ever did. His bare thighs looked the way I imagined they would, though imagination was a poor substitute for reality. Knowing his legs would be muscled and tan wasn't the same as tracing the line of his quadriceps with my eyes, or seeing the light dusting of dark hair that thinned as it approached the center of his body.

Mac ran his hands up both my legs from the ankles to the inner thighs. I groaned and undulated my hips, begging for more.

When his palms slid across my stomach to cup my breasts, I stopped him. I'd already told him what I needed, and this wasn't it.

I urged his hand down, pressing his fingers to my center. He closed his eyes when he found me slick and ready, and the sound that emerged was as much animal as human.

Mac crawled up my body. The soft hair of his chest and thighs brushed against me, and my skin roared to life at the delicate touch.

He positioned himself between my legs, but still he held, unmoving. Mac demanded I meet his gaze, and I did the same to him. Everything we felt, everything we were, we laid bare to the other.

I slid my palms across Mac's broad back, feeling each muscle flex beneath my palm. When I reached his buttocks, I gripped the tight flesh and pushed at the same moment I rose to meet him.

I gasped when my body accepted his for the first time, and he released a guttural groan as he seated himself fully inside me. He filled me, and I surrounded him, and when we moved, we did so together.

I wrapped my legs around his hips, pulling him closer, and he slid his right arm beneath me, lifting me to him. The other arm he braced on the ground for support, but I tugged him toward me. I welcomed his weight. I needed every inch of my body to know his touch.

Our skin grew slick with sweat, and we slid against each other until I could barely tell where I ended and he began, and still I tried to pull him nearer. I didn't think he could ever be close enough. I moved my legs, winding them around his, and embraced him as tightly as I could. I felt nothing but his skin, hot and damp and wanting.

His hips picked up speed and I rose to meet every thrust, abandoning a little more control with each movement. His face was only inches from mine, and I felt his breath on my cheek as it grew faster and more ragged. Mine was the same, but through my gasps I spoke words both unplanned and true. I begged for release and prayed it would never end and told him that he belonged inside me. He growled agreement, his gaze hot and possessive.

We didn't look away from each other, not until the very end when I threw back my head, crying out. He roared above me, the sound both primal and pure.

Afterwards, we lay together, our skin covered in sweat, and we said the same thing with our words that we'd said with our bodies, and we kept speaking with one voice and then the other for the rest of the afternoon.

CHAPTER 23

As much as I wished to lock our bedroom door and emerge a year or two later, there were several things we needed to take care of first.

We arranged transport for the camp residents. Tricia and Ani handled most of this. Ani had once been mistress of the compound, under another name and in another life, and she still knew her way around. Various boats sailed at regular intervals. There were never so many they would draw the attention of outsiders, but every few hours a former camp member was sent back to their old life—or given a chance to create a new one.

Some had people who missed them, who'd searched for them for years and had clung to hope when there was no reason for it. Others had lost all their loved ones during the centuries spent on the island. Some never had any family, which might explain why they found their way to Eila in the first place.

More than a few learned that those they left behind weren't ready to forgive. Those elementals clung to each other, the only family they now had. Ani was in the final group, though she didn't seek to bond with anyone.

Despite our talk, Sera was determined to ignore her mother for a while longer, and Ani gave no sign she planned to initiate that thorny conversation. But I caught Ani staring at Sera often, and while the woman's expression was as hard as it had ever been, it also contained no small measure of determination.

Two stubborn fires, each ready to burst with unspoken words. I hoped the rest of us were outside the blast range when they finally collided.

Even those with forgiving families were in for a shock. I'd felt lost when I came out of hiding and discovered the internet had rewritten our world. Many of these people had never seen electricity. They wasted hours flicking light switches off and on. One spent all day in the kitchen, blending things. The existence of rock music, space shuttles, and birthday cake-flavored M&Ms was going to blow their minds.

Tricia took on the responsibility of helping them acclimate, though she was as lost as the others. She met with either Vivian or Simon in the mornings, learning everything she could. In the afternoons, she taught those who didn't have a family to do it for them. The desert and her daughter attended those sessions, though they glared at Tricia the entire time.

It was the blind leading the blind, but Tricia didn't hesitate to offer her help. She had a long path before her, and she would find her own way to travel it. Despite all she'd done, I hoped she'd make it.

"Make sure to show them Wikipedia," I said. "It's amazing."

Tricia jotted that down.

We'd been at the compound a week, and by now most of the guests had been settled elsewhere. Only a few stragglers remained. Our new challenge was finding a place where they could remain together.

We sat in a large multipurpose room in the guest wing. It was furnished with comfortable reading chairs, tables of varying sizes, and a pool table no one was using. Floor-to-ceiling bookcases lined the walls. They were stuffed with paperbacks in every genre along with several board games, most of which had all their pieces.

My friends were gathered on the other side of the guest wing, where they debated the latest information and tried to devise a plan that didn't involve remaining under the volcano for the next several decades. I should be part of that discussion, but instead I'd slipped away while mumbling flimsy excuses.

I couldn't bear the thought of hopping back into constant fear and turmoil, not when I'd finally been given a moment of peace. The outside world would be there when I was ready to face it again. Until then, I was going to hang out with my Grams.

I snuggled deeper into my armchair and set aside the book I'd been reading. "Did you know the firsts existed?" I asked.

Grams drew a needle through her cross stitch project. "I had no idea. Perhaps we are too isolated up north."

I took a sip of tea. I was glad to hear this wasn't another secret they'd kept from me. My ignorance was shared, at least.

"What about the stories, the myths? It's obvious they held more than a little truth. You told me the firsts who chose not to remain with humans vanished into the world and were never seen again. Same with the ones who chose not to stay with animals." I made sure to add the second part. Elementals needed to stop forgetting these stories also featured shifters.

Another stitch, then she changed thread colors. "That's what your great-grandma taught me, dear. I've had no reason to doubt it."

"They did vanish." Tricia looked surprised, as if she hadn't quite expected to say that.

She sat at a square table with three of the remaining

waters. They'd been working on a five thousand piece jig-saw puzzle of a sunset, but the other three stopped trying to solve it when Tricia spoke. She hadn't talked about Eila since we arrived at the compound.

"How do you know?" I asked.

Her expression turned wry. "Three centuries with a creature who styles herself a god? You pick up a few things."

Grams set down her cross stitch. It was an inspirational sampler that sought to inspire with foul language. "Tell us, dear."

The former island residents watched Tricia nervously, unsure if this was wise. They'd been Eila's pets for too long to lose their fear of her in a single week.

"Most of the first magics went one of three ways. They bonded with humanity and created elementals, or they embraced their wild side and sired shifters. Those that didn't choose either path simply became one with the land again."

"Like Eila," I said.

Tricia was appalled. "Eila is nothing like them. She despised them, said they were weak. They weren't weak. They just didn't fight when it was their time to move on. Nothing is supposed to be eternal. Even the original magic is meant to fade. They once existed all across the planet. If they hadn't died, we'd constantly meet them. Most understood that their magic came from the earth, and it would always belong to the earth. They returned willingly. You can sometimes find those spots, I think. More of the magical races live in those places, and even the humans carry a bit of their own magic. They're the dreamers and artists."

"The creators." A wave of homesickness hit me. Some places in Tahoe were like that. I wondered how many firsts had blessed it with their power over the years.

"Exactly. Nothing really dies. It's just reborn as something else."

"Why didn't Eila return to the land?" The island would have worked much better as an artist commune than as the elemental version of a cult.

Tricia's jaw set. "She refused. Maybe she had an ego the other ones lacked, but she saw it as a return to nothing. That horrified her."

"That's all it took? Refusing? Oh. The food." Remembering the abused elementals made me wish all over again I'd found a way to destroy her.

Tricia winced at the memory. "Exactly. If she keeps her power high, she can prevent what she sees as death. It may be against all the laws of nature, but if she feeds, she lives. And because the firsts are connected to the land of their birth, she can't leave. The food needs to come to her."

I shivered, the memory of the grasping first in Utah still fresh. That creature hadn't just been hungry. It had been feral, in the grip of a desperate need. Without any food sources, it was dying.

Tricia's explanation made sense, though it didn't answer everything. "What was her thing with fulls? It was almost like she was scared of them. I thought it meant they could damage her, but my attempt to test that theory went a bit wrong."

Tricia shook her head. "All I know is they weren't allowed on the island. She never explained why."

I was still curious, but it didn't really matter. Not all questions have an answer, and I was more interested in a particular part of the story. "If no one else visits her, she has no food. She'll have no choice but to return to the land."

Tricia nodded, a small smile pulling at her lips.

With all Josiah's surveillance equipment and Vivian's access to satellite footage, it wouldn't be too hard to make sure no boats full of curious elementals landed on the island ever again. "We can do that. We'll need to make sure her myth doesn't spread further than it already has."

Eila's former pets exchanged long looks with each other. "Trust us," one said, "we won't be telling anyone."

ANOTHER WEEK PASSED. WE COULDN'T WAIT FOREVER, BUT WE didn't know what else to do. For now, Tahoe and the council seemed to be in a holding pattern. There were tiny signs that all wasn't as it should be—Miriam's otter home had been burned, forcing her to fight for new territory—but there was no proof the council was responsible. It was now early October and the winter rains had yet to come. Forest fires weren't uncommon, even if a fire right next to the Truckee River was a bit odd.

Mac's uncle reported that a dark sedan frequently parked within sight of his house. The council hadn't forgotten about him.

The threat would have been more effective if Will didn't scoff at their puny efforts. "A tiny blond woman who doesn't seem to have any idea what she's doing. I think I can handle myself."

Reminding him that the tiny blond woman might be a powerful old one only made Will laugh. After all, this was the same man who patted my head and called me "little water."

Carmen sent her younger daughter, who'd been born without the shifter gene, to stay with her father until things calmed. Neither she nor Will needed to worry about their older children—Pamela and James had run off to Los Angeles the day they graduated high school.

Another dark sedan stood watch over Carmen's enormous house. Each morning, she brought the driver a cup of coffee the woman was scared to drink after the first time, likely because it was laced with sedatives. Afterwards, Carmen shifted into her mountain lion form and spent the entire day in the forest, well hidden and beyond the reach of any elemental.

They were all okay—and none of them were safe.

The descriptions of the women outside the shifters' houses matched the photo Deborah had given me of two waters holding a gas can. I had yet to meet the women, but already I'd learned to hate them.

There was no sign of Deborah or Michael.

It was a stalemate. We couldn't come out of hiding until we were certain Deborah would agree to leave me alone. The council wasn't ready to abandon its position of power. And the shifters—well, they were waiting for any excuse to fuck with the elementals who insisted on harassing them.

It was a powder keg, and it was only a matter of time before it exploded.

PASSIVITY DIDN'T SUIT US.

Mac prowled the halls with no direction in mind. Vivian refreshed her email every five minutes, hoping there'd be some news we could act on. Grams and I tried turning our excess time toward freeing my mother, but her seduction skills weren't as effective on guards who worked thousands of miles away. When we hit one brick wall after another, I gave up and tried to read. I scanned the same passage over and over before closing the book in defeat. We played sloppy games of pool, not even bothering to line up our shots. Hours passed in which we didn't accomplish a thing.

Simon… well, Simon mostly napped, but even his naps were interrupted by unpleasant dreams.

The volcano might be Sera's home, but after two weeks underground, she was ready to crawl out of her skin. "What the fuck are we waiting for?" she asked.

No one had a good answer. What had begun as a welcome reprieve from nonstop chaos had turned into a prison.

After too many days of this, we at last gathered around an enormous wooden table in the conference room off Josiah's office. It was time to decide on a course of action. Even a flawed course of action was better than whatever the hell we were doing now.

The office was on the family side of the compound, which meant the room held the kind of heat that usually indicated a hell dimension or an excellent spot to destroy a magic ring. We'd brought in as many fans as we could find, and several people sat with their feet in bowls of ice.

Despite the heat, it was the best spot for this meeting. Depending on how generous one felt like being, Josiah was either a cautious, paranoid, or sociopathic man with a fondness for intrusive levels of surveillance, particularly where his daughters were concerned. In his smaller office, four television screens displayed rotating images. In the conference room, at least twenty screens lined an entire wall. They featured familiar locations.

On one screen, I saw the house where I'd been raised, on another island far to the north. In his own way, Josiah had watched me grow up. It was creepy as hell, but it was also Josiah's inappropriate manner of expressing love. I hadn't really known the man, and I couldn't say I would have learned to like him, but now I'd never have that chance. The pulsing anger I'd once felt had passed. These

days, there was just a small, constant sadness I expected to
live with for a long time.

Several other screens focused on locations around the
world. Two scanned the Princes' Islands in Turkey, where
he'd believed another dual hid.

Josiah had also set up a camera inside Allison Ash's
house. She was the current leader of the fire council, so of
course he would spy on her. We turned that off in a hurry.
There was information, and then there was voyeurism.

On the top row, one camera after another showed Tahoe,
including the shifters' homes and multiple angles of the
cabin. The Airstream was in one shot, and Mac's shoulders
sagged in relief to see it. We already knew the agents had
arrived safely with the Bronco and trailer intact, but it was
comforting to see our home waiting for us.

Another screen revealed the Rat Trap, once again open
for business thanks to Johnson and Carmichael. I wondered how long that camera had been in place. I rather
hoped Josiah hadn't installed it ten years ago, when Sera
and I found a new kind of trouble every weekend in that
bar.

It was a gross invasion of privacy, but I had no energy
left for indignation, and it would have made no difference
if I had. At the very least, it explained why Josiah seemed
to know everything.

"I guess we should start with what we've already got,"
I said.

Vivian considered that her cue. She had connected
her laptop to Josiah's surveillance system. With a couple
clicks, she brought up an image.

"What are we looking at here?" I asked. So far as I could
tell, it was the Truckee River. The water was lethargic, not
yet fattened from autumn storms.

Vivian used a red laser pointer to circle a small patch

of black. "This was Miriam's territory. She helps her sister raise her pups here when they're in otter form. She used to, that is. As we know, the whole area was scorched. There was no sign of arson."

I checked the time stamp. The photo was taken two days after we escaped the island.

Vivian dropped the laser pointer and turned back to the table. "For argument's sake, let's assume this was the council's work. What would they hope to accomplish by burning such a small piece of land?"

Sera tapped her fingers against the wood. "They're trying to get to Aidan, and they're assholes, so they think it's okay to do it through her friends."

Luke leaned back in his chair and studied the screen. "That doesn't sound right. They've had months to hurt your friends, so why now? I'm not seeing a good reason to think it's their work, 'specially without any proof."

"Unless they are trying to draw you out." Simon sounded a bit smug, as he often did when he believed he had an answer no one else did. "If they believe you left the island, they will wish to make contact with you again."

That sounded ominous. "But how the hell would they know that? Damn it, someone get Jet."

It didn't take long. She was standing outside with her ear pressed to the door.

"I was curious," she said, without a hint of apology.

I hit her with questions before she could sit down. "Would they be able to watch the island without you? Did you show them how?"

Jet laughed. "Deborah couldn't work Google maps without me, let alone a satellite system. She could have hired someone, I suppose." Her tone suggested it would be a fool's errand, as she was irreplaceable.

Simon considered the images. "Perhaps they heard

about it from one of the escapees or their families."

It was a possibility. Eila's ex-pets had sworn to never speak of the place or the creature that lived there, but the promise might have weakened with distance.

If Deborah was behind the fire, she'd just rung the bell to start the next round. "I guess we should be happy they gave us this much time," I muttered.

Jet perched on the edge of her chair. "What about the forest fire?"

Everyone turned to her.

"Didn't you hear? There was a huge one started a while back. It took them a week to put it out."

Vivian considered it for a moment, then shook her head. "I know what you're talking about, but fires in the Tahoe National Forest are common after a dry summer. Like the one at Miriam's, there's no proof. Plus, it's worth remembering that we're dealing with waters here—waters who've given no indication they want to involve other elements."

"If you say so." Jet sounded like she meant the exact opposite.

"Wait, didn't she threaten you with a forest fire when she showed up at my house?" Luke looked as if he was reconsidering his earlier doubts.

"Deborah had me pull up some footage of the area. She wanted to know what animals lived there," Jet said.

Mac grew very still. Only his hands shook as he fought the shift. His fingernails began to lengthen. "Show me."

Jet wheeled her chair over to Vivian and pushed her away from the computer. A moment later, a topographical map of Tahoe was projected against the far wall.

Mac's face grew black. "A lot of bears use that forest when they need to run. Some permanently live off-grid there."

His ears rounded. Mac's father and brothers lived wild in that forest.

I had to control this before Mac went full furry. "Let's end this. We arrange a meeting, show them that I'm not crazy anymore. We offer them what I've learned about a cure, so maybe they can help others, too."

The table studied me like I had the wit of an especially clever rock.

"They'll still want you punished for David," Sera reminded me.

"Plus," Luke noted, "They won't believe you. It's a hard one to prove, and too risky for them to take the chance that you're lying."

Damn bunch of negative nellies.

"So what does this mean? I hide out in Europe?" Maybe a few centuries in the south of France wouldn't be so bad.

Luke watched the thoughts play across my face. "There are worse options."

I let images of a lifetime frolicking naked in the Mediterranean with Mac fade. "If I keep running, they'll keep hurting my friends. So we either need to fill that damn school bus with everyone we know and drive it far out of town, or I need to meet with them. That's the only way this will stop."

Vivian reluctantly agreed. "They're chasing you because they fear you could be a remorseless monster, but they're also counting on your conscience to draw you out."

Sera jumped up and began pacing, fingers beating against her thigh so rapidly they blurred. "What if it isn't only about Aidan? She's actually not the center of the universe, whatever the last few months have felt like. If the council started that fire, they did it while we were on the island. Aidan might never have learned about it, so it couldn't have been about getting her attention."

I picked up the thought. "And the council hates shift-ers. They pretend they don't even exist, and that's harder to do when they dominate one of the largest forests in California. It's a two-fer. It would draw me out if I survived the island, plus they got to harm shifters."

"But shifters have always been there," Vivian argued. "Why now?"

Sera knew. "Josiah's gone. He lived there part-time since we started at the university. No one would dare cause trouble in his backyard."

Grams nodded in agreement. "There's a power vacuum. Elementals have always sought to claim their own spaces. Tahoe isn't as isolated as most of our homes, but it's been a beacon to our kind." She nodded at Mac. "I gather it's the same for shifters. For the last fifteen years or so, Tahoe has been Josiah's nearly as much as this compound was, at least according to elementals. Now it is unclaimed."

Realization didn't dawn. It slammed into me like a bul-let. "They didn't hit Stephen Grant, or anyone we know from school, or Vivian's apartment. They never even threatened them. Other than Frank and the Rat Trap, they've only gone after shifters."

The table lifted several inches when Mac gripped its edge. He shoved himself away and stood against the wall, fighting the urge to rampage.

Sera's pacing increased, her fingers sparking as fast as I'd ever seen. "Damn it. Damn it."

I looked at each person in the room, the elementals and shifters who'd proven they would lay down their lives for each other.

"Sera's right. It isn't all about me. I'm the bonus prize, or maybe Tahoe is. The point is, they want both. They're going after our home, and they're sending a message that shifters aren't welcome in the new Tahoe."

No one argued.

Sera stopped moving with no warning. She didn't sit, but she braced her hands on the table and stared at me, black eyes burning. "Tell the truth. Can you handle this? We're gonna need you, Aidan. The rest of us have a lot of power, but not more than the council. You and Luke are the only ones strong enough."

"I'm in." Luke answered the question before anyone could ask.

Once more, I reached for my magic, exploring the threads Eila had merged. I didn't do it because I doubted myself. I did it because I never tired of feeling the solid bond between fire and water.

Until I reached that tiny bit of loose fire Eila tried to rip free during our last battle. I studied it from every angle, searching for any new frays. I found none. It might not be a perfect cure, but it was the best I'd ever have. It was enough.

"I can handle it," I told the room.

"Good, cause we're done running," Sera said.

"It makes us look like prey." She said that to me long ago, when life had been much simpler. It didn't make it less true now.

I stood, and despite everything we'd just learned, I grinned. "We're going back to Tahoe."

CHAPTER 24

It took us another day to make arrangements. Josiah's private plane was in Seattle, and it needed to be diverted several times to ensure the council couldn't track it. They'd find out we were coming soon enough, but we'd rather they didn't shoot us out of the sky before we arrived.

Vivian and Jet worked together. One redirected the satellites while the other convinced air traffic control that the plane didn't exist. Basically, they performed Jedi mind tricks with a computer.

"Please don't get arrested," I told Vivian.

Jet gave me what could only be called an evil grin. "Impossible. I'm a ghost. If I don't want them to know I'm there, they won't."

Vivian grimaced. Jet had already proven that.

Jet continued. "The only time someone found me, it was cause they didn't think a fifteen-year-old should have access to the state pension funds. I've learned a lot in ten years."

Vivian tutted. "You got caught? Sloppy. No one noticed when I refinanced my mother's house when I was twelve. Also, didn't you say you worked for Deborah because she made some criminal charges go away?"

The other hacker's eyes narrowed. Jet typed faster.

There was no question about leaving Jet behind. She was helping. Plus, we weren't willing to let her out of our sight.

Grams would travel with us. Ani, however, wasn't invited.

"You're sure? I mean, you just found her."

Sera was sure. "It's been decades, Ade. You learn not to miss someone in forty years. I don't need her."

I let my doubts show. I had a lot of them.

"I don't," Sera insisted. "I needed to know if she was alive. I needed to know that she chose to leave me. I got that."

"Uh-huh."

She rolled her eyes. "You're not giving up until we have some happy Disney moment, are you?"

"I'll settle for a Hallmark movie," I told her. "I mean, Josiah was way worse in the grand scheme of things, and you liked him."

"Because Josiah was there."

I couldn't argue. The ones worth keeping are the ones who never leave in the first place.

"You got over it when I ran away," I reminded her.

"You left because you were scared and in pain and had the emotional maturity of a caterpillar. She left because she was more interested in meeting that thing than in being a mother."

"No matter what she did, you're not going to forget about her, so maybe try to talk? Or glare at her, but be in the same room when you do? There's still space on the plane. And caterpillar my ass. I was a beautiful fucking butterfly."

Sera snorted and sent a shower of sparks toward me. "Keep telling yourself that. Even if you're right—which is improbable, statistically speaking—now's not the time. I don't need the distraction. Let's settle things with the council and then I'll think about it. Will that get you to shut up?"

I took what I could get.

In the end, eight of us stepped onto the plane. A bear, a cat, and two hackers joined a water, a fire, and a couple of duals.

Hawaii to Northern California should have been a six-hour flight. Instead, we stopped in Los Angeles, where it was easier to get lost in the stream of private planes, then headed to Phoenix. After the sacrifices he'd made, it seemed polite to give Luke a day with his second element.

We skipped the small and easily tracked Tahoe airport and landed in Reno after midnight. No one knew we were coming, so no one was there to meet us. We arranged for two town cars to get us to Truckee.

We crossed the California state line an hour later. The streets were empty, just as they'd been when, months before, I arrived in the middle of the night with Sera, hurting and distant and with no idea what my life was about to become.

This time, I was returning home.

I WOKE EARLY THE NEXT DAY, SMILING BEFORE I EVEN OPENED my eyes. I'd dreamt of this moment, but over the past months I'd doubted it would ever happen. But here I was, curled in Mac's arms with my friends safe in the cabin behind us. I was going to savor every minute. Even knowing I'd need to face the council soon didn't take away from my happiness.

After a while, my magic grew restless. I slipped out of bed and dressed. The night before, I'd grabbed a clean outfit from my room and, when she wasn't looking, borrowed a couple items from Sera, as well. She was a lot shorter than I was, but that didn't matter much with spandex.

I pulled on the sports bra and covered it with a t-shirt. I didn't have any proper jogging shorts, but it was cool enough that sweatpants would work. My Converse weren't great running shoes, but so long as I could heal myself, I didn't need to worry about arch support.

I didn't run. I flew. I raced down the driveway and across the road, then darted through the thin patches of forest until the lake appeared before me like an old friend. It was seventy miles around all of Lake Tahoe, and I almost wished I had time to make the trip. Instead, I ran several miles north. It was early enough that there weren't any witnesses when I launched myself into the freezing lake and glided back toward the cabin without once coming up for air.

When I was done, I snuck through the trees. I still wasn't ready to admit I was exercising after decades of condemning any activity more strenuous than lifting a forkful of pancakes. They'd find out some day, and then I'd need to reassure them of my sanity all over again.

The trailer was empty. I took a quick shower and walked to the cabin. I entered through the rear door and blinked.

"Brook!"

I barely had time to turn toward the booming voice before I was engulfed in an enormous hug.

Miriam squeezed hard enough to draw a squeak before she released me. "I hear we won't be checking you into the nuthouse, after all."

I was drawn into another set of arms right away, an embrace both familiar and strange. "We're glad you're safe, little water," said Mac's uncle.

I tilted my head to gaze up at Will. The man bore such a strong resemblance to Mac that I was predisposed to like him. He had a rougher version of Mac's features, but they shared the same coloring and immense build. More than that, they were both protective and loyal to a fault. Will was a good man, though he made it a point not to take me seriously.

"You know I'm an all-powerful dual magic, right?"

He bopped my nose with his index finger and let me go.

A large banner hung across the far wall. It was decorated with storks and baby bottles and read "Congratulations, mom!" in large curving letters—except "mom" had been crossed out and rewritten in black Sharpie. The banner now read "Congratulations, sane person!"

The trellis dining table held a small feast, and the smell of maple syrup told me pancakes were hidden beneath one of the metal lids. There were more bagels and muffins for the carb-addicted elementals, but also some sausage, a plate of lox, and a bowl of apples and blackberries for the various shifters.

The cabin was full of them. Simon and Mac, Miriam and Will, even Carmen mingled with the elementals. The shifters might be used to me, Sera, and Vivian by now, but Luke and Grams were new.

Several months ago, they would have been on opposite sides of the room, preparing to reenact *West Side Story*. Now elementals and shifters milled about, chatting and sitting side by side on the floor pillows scattered throughout the living room—along with a couple of FBI agents and one human hacker.

Carmen greeted me with a smile that barely touched her eyes. While the rest of us hadn't bothered to do anything more strenuous than brush our hair and change into clean clothes, she wore full makeup, tastefully applied, and designer jeans. The mountain lion's coloring wasn't far off a desert's—amber eyes and sandy hair. She and Luke almost looked like they could be siblings—except a grin was never far from Luke's face, while a scowl was never far from Carmen's. We weren't so much friends as allies, but it had been a while since I thought she wanted to disembowel me. I considered that progress.

Vivian and Jet sat cross-legged on the floor, their laptops between them like they were playing a high-tech game of Battleship. For the first time since we started running, Vivian wore her own clothes. Her t-shirt read "Have you tried turning it off and on again?"

"Everything okay?" I asked.

Vivian flashed me a small smile, then returned her attention to her screen. "No new disasters, but they'll know we're here soon if they don't already. Even without tech, it's easy to monitor cars coming in and out of the cabin, and there were a bunch of those this morning."

"What are you working on now?" I peered over Jet's shoulder like the scrolling numbers meant a single damn thing.

"Math," they said in unison.

"Uh huh." It was the only possible response an English major could make.

Sera sat next to Carmichael, who looked a lot better after a shave and a few square meals. She rose when I appeared.

"What is this?"

"It's a welcome back to sanity party. We got you a cake." She pointed to a white sheet cake with red piping that read "We'll miss you."

I raised my eyebrows, and Sera shrugged. "You expect more from the Safeway bakery at four a.m.? And, though I protested quite loudly, your favorite music." I tilted my head toward the speakers, picking out Patsy Cline over the others' voices. The song, of course, was "Crazy."

"You know, based on this evidence, I might think you like me."

"Family obligation. That's all."

"Don't think I don't appreciate it, but—"

Sera didn't let me finish. "But we need a plan? We need to figure out how to get the council out of Tahoe before they burn something else? We need to put Deborah on a one-way rocket to Mars?"

It sounded like a good start.

She piled five pancakes on a plate and smothered them in maple syrup before thrusting the meal at me. "We'll get to it, but we've earned this. We need a few hours when no one is hunting us or doing their best to destroy everything we love. It's not asking for much. Besides, after the island, you're skinnier than usual. Eat these before your ass actually becomes concave."

She was right, and we did get a few hours before we were interrupted.

A tinny ring struggled to be heard above the music. Out of habit, we checked our pockets, but most of us didn't have phones. We'd left them behind during our flight across the desert and hadn't bothered to replace them yet.

The shifters held up blank screens. The ringing continued.

I followed the sound until I found an old flip phone tucked inside a planter. No one spoke as I held it up, but their apprehensive expressions told me they'd never seen the device before. I didn't recognize the number on the screen.

The room was silent, waiting. I opened the phone and held it to my ear. I didn't speak.

The caller didn't need me to. She only wanted me to

listen. "Have you visited Frank at the Rat Trap yet?"

Threat delivered, Deborah hung up.

CHAPTER 25

From the outside, everything appeared the same. We parked in the alley, then crept around the building, scanning for threats.

There was no electrical fire, no broken windows, not even another closure for health violations. The Rat Trap was already open, ready to welcome the dedicated drunks and the college students who believed hair of the dog was a valid lifestyle choice.

"So much for our plan to swoop in and save the day," I said.

Mac peered through the windows, but they were dirty and covered with too many neon signs to see much. "It's a bit late to mention this, but anyone else thinking this could be a trap?"

We all were, but it didn't matter. Frank was inside, and we couldn't abandon him to Deborah's evil plans. When Sera and I had been reckless undergrads, the owner of the Rat Trap took care of us. He made sure we received only the best booze, then he made sure we got home safely. Both Christopher and Brian had worked for him. A lot had happened since those wild college days, most of it bad, but once they'd been our second family. Of the three, Frank was the only one still alive. He needed to stay that way, no matter what waited for us inside.

The Rat Trap was the world's only combination lounge/dive/tiki bar, and for a few years it had practically been my and Sera's living room. At midnight, with the lights dimmed and beer goggles firmly in place, it felt like a glorious land of possibility.

At ten in the morning, with the sun streaming through the dirty windows, it was barely recognizable. The dark red vinyl booths were cheap plastic, and the tiki artifacts on the walls likely had a "Made in China" label. Instead of being packed with healthy young coeds, a few old-timers ringed the bar, the sort of men who showed up early to fight the shakes and didn't leave until they were numb or broke, whichever came first.

The place was ugly as sin, but at that moment it looked beautiful. It was standing, and so was Frank—and the council was nowhere in sight.

Frank stood behind the bar, watering a listless potted ivy. He'd always tried to keep a few living plants. He said it gave the place a bit of warmth. The fact that they all died within a month never dissuaded him.

"Aidan, my beauty!" he called out, earning startled glances from the old-timers. "And Sera, too? Tell me what I've done to deserve this, and I'll be sure to do it again."

Frank was short, skinny, and hirsute, with features too heavy to be handsome. He was also an unrepentant flirt, and his enthusiasm and ability to make every woman feel special made him a surprisingly successful one. Frank was also devoted to his long-suffering wife, so no one took his frequent declarations of love seriously. Mac didn't even growl when Frank smiled at me.

Frank considered the enormous man at my side. "Don't tell me this is your type. It's no wonder I didn't have a shot."

"Please. A charmer like you always has a shot."

Frank winked, then looked over my shoulder at the others. In addition to Mac and Sera, Vivian had insisted on coming.

"I like Frank," she'd said, and that was that.

Some of the others stayed at the cabin while Will and Carmen returned to their homes to check on both the buildings and the people inside. With the council escalating their threats, I regretted that there was no equivalent of the compound in Tahoe. We could really use an underground bunker right about now.

Frank picked up a rag and rubbed down the already clean counter. "Don't think I'm not pleased to see you, but I don't remember you lot being morning drinkers."

"We're not here to drink," Sera said.

Though it had taken twenty minutes to drive to the Rat Trap, we'd been too panicked about what we might discover to bother coming up with a plausible explanation for our visit. I wasn't sure we had time to be subtle, anyway. "You have to leave. It's not safe here."

Frank's considerable eyebrows stretched toward his hairline. They didn't have far to go. "I only got the damned place open again after a bureaucratic nightmare you wouldn't believe."

"We'll pay for the lost business. I can't go into the details, but you really are in danger." I hoped for once my transparent face worked in my favor and Frank could see my sincerity.

Whatever he saw, it wasn't enough. "I'm going to need more information than that, Aidan."

I tried again. "I can't. You've known me for years, Frank. Maybe I didn't always make the best decisions, but I'm not a liar. Please believe me."

Frank braced both hands on the bar and leaned forward, tilting his head up to meet my gaze. "And you know me. I'm not running for no reason."

My voice rose. "There is a reason! I just can't tell you!"

Frank matched my glare, and I struggled to think of a reasonable explanation for my request.

"Ahem." When Sera had Frank's attention, she nodded at the ivy he'd been watering a minute before.

Before his eyes, the brown leaves turned a rich green, the thin stems strengthening and sprouting new leaves. Vivian's face was tight, all her limited power focused on this demonstration.

"What on earth?" Frank's eyes darted between the plant and Vivian.

I stared at Vivian, torn between shock and admiration. My friend was becoming a rule breaker.

She'd also made things a lot easier for us.

"Exactly. Vivian's an earth. Sera's fire. I'm complicated. But we can flood this place or burn it down with a thought, and we're not the only ones. Right now, people who really don't like us are threatening to hurt those we care about. So will you close the bar now?"

It wasn't like we could get in more trouble by that point.

Frank's mouth opened and closed with no sound. The old-timers considered the plant, then their drinks, trying to decide if there was a connection.

Mac suggested they finish their drinks and move on. They didn't argue. Then it was just us, waiting on Frank's answer.

"You're an earth?" He said the word like he'd never heard it before. He turned his dazed eyes on me and Sera. "You two... does this have anything to do with the way you haven't aged in fifteen years?"

Sera leaned toward him. "We'll answer all your questions as soon as we're somewhere else."

Frank seemed dazed, but he managed a nod. "Let me get my coat."

He was walking back to us when the front of the bar exploded.

Glass flew toward us, thin slivers and heavy shards alike as the front windows shattered. I barely registered what was happening before I found myself on the floor, struggling under Mac's immovable form.

I turned my head enough to see Sera under a table, her eyes black as she counteracted the spreading flames. If they reached the bottles of alcohol lined up behind the bar, the whole place would go up. I threw my power in with hers, and together we extinguished the fires.

Before we could relax, a second explosion rocked the building, louder than the first. The roof crumbled, chunks of plaster falling to the floor. Mac twitched as a large piece landed on his shoulders. He wrapped himself tighter around me.

"I can't see," My ears rang. I shouted, but my voice sounded tiny and distant. "Let me up."

He ignored me.

We waited, fearing a third explosion, but nothing came. I gave Mac's shoulder a hard shove, and finally he moved.

Sera was unhurt, but Vivian wasn't doing as well. Her back was braced against the bar. She held her right arm at an awkward angle, and her dark complexion had grown ashen.

I crawled to her. "Oh hell, Vivian. Let me see."

I expected to see fear in her eyes, or despair at finding herself in this situation yet again. Instead, I saw only strength. "I'm fine."

Sera's broken sob reminded me that Vivian wasn't the only one who required help.

A six-inch piece of glass jutted from Frank's neck. If that wasn't enough to kill him, the layers of roofing pressing against his chest would finish the job.

"Hell no. Oh hell no." It was all I could say, and I kept repeating it as I knelt at Frank's side. I didn't waste time focusing. Frank needed to live, and I could only heal him if I moved fast.

My magic shot past Frank's skin and attached to the water molecules that form so much of the human body. I was rewarded with a tiny flicker of life. So long as his heart beat, he could be saved.

Creation magic, I reminded myself.

I pushed the embedded glass outward, knitting the arteries and tissue as I went. It was unexpectedly easy. Life wanted to triumph, and Frank didn't fight me.

Sirens wailed in the distance. I moved as fast as I dared, expanding Frank's lungs and stopping the internal bleeding. Above us, Mac lifted layer after layer of the ceiling, lessening the pressure on Frank's chest.

Sera tapped my shoulder. "You've stabilized him. Let's go."

"We can't leave him."

"You hear that? It's an ambulance, and it'll be here in thirty seconds. If the cops following them see us, we'll be answering questions all day when we should be figuring out how to end Deborah once and for all. Now move your fucking ass."

Reluctantly, I withdrew the threads of magic from Frank. His breathing remained labored and a sheen of sweat covered his forehead, but he was alive.

Vivian leaned on Mac for support. She kept a hand on her broken arm, holding it in place. Sera and I followed them through the small kitchen. I glanced back at Frank once. I would remember what they'd done to him. What they would continue to do if we didn't end this.

We burst out into the empty alley and ran to the Bronco. We pulled into the street just as the fire truck arrived. Ste-

phen Grant, the local police who was also an ice elemental, was right behind them. We passed him on our way out.
His eyes widened when he saw, then he nodded in understanding. Stephen would fix it so no one ever knew we
were there. No one except the council.

DESPITE EVERYTHING WE NEEDED TO DISCUSS, OR PERHAPS
because of it, we were silent as we returned to the cabin.
Tahoe was our home, and they were taking it from us a
piece at a time… and they'd keep doing it until I capit-
ulated to their demands. This was starting to feel like a
lose/lose situation.

I couldn't get the stench of smoke out of my nose. It
taunted me, a lingering reminder of how easily Deborah
had manipulated us.

The smell grew stronger. Mac's eyes met mine, matching expressions of panic on our faces, then he punched the
accelerator.

He pulled to a screeching stop before the smoldering
ruins of the cabin.

We fell from the SUV and ran toward the remains of
our home.

The ground floor was burnt but recognizable. Scorched
walls outlined each room, though nothing within the walls
had been spared. The second floor was only rubble, and
the third floor loft was missing altogether. Thick plumes
of black smoke rose from the wreckage.

The explosion at the Rat Trap hadn't been intended to
harm us so much as distract us. Deborah had used Frank's
business and his life as nothing more than a diversion, and
we fell for it like actors in a script she wrote just for us.
She'd separated us with ease so the council could attack
where it would hurt the most.

This was my home. It was all of our homes—and it hadn't been empty.

"Simon!" I screamed. "Miriam! Grams!" I yelled their names until my throat was raw.

For too many heartbreaking moments, the only other sound was the river pouring over rocks, then an adorable head poked above the river's surface. A small cat with singed fur emerged from the nearby forest.

My knees buckled in relief and I fell to the ground. My friends shifted to their human forms, and for the first time since I'd known them, they didn't look comfortable naked. They looked exposed.

"Grams?" I asked them.

"She and Jet went with Will. She said she wanted to meet the children of shifters."

Of course she did.

"Call her. She's better at healing than I am, so she should fix Vivian's arm. It broke when the bar exploded and now the cabin's gone. It's gone. Call everyone and tell them the council is done waiting. They've started breaking things." A sob escaped before I could stop it, and another soon followed. "Everything's broken. Everything."

Mac crawled to me while I fought for control. I couldn't afford to break down, not yet.

I gripped his hand, fearing his despair and rage matched my own. The cabin was the only thing his mother left him, and now it was rubble. But when his eyes caught mine, his expression was more fierce than angry. "This was them, not you."

"I don't know. Burning houses have become a theme in my life." I tried for a wry smile before I realized Miriam and Simon remained tense and angry, and one person was noticeably absent. "Wait, where's Luke?"

I wasn't concerned. I was pissed. Luke should have

been here. If he'd controlled the flames, the cabin would still be standing.

Miriam glowered. "They took him. Pretty little thing walked right up to him, and he smiled and flirted as she stabbed him with a fucking needle."

I drew my knees to my chest and wrapped my arms tight around my shins. "Luke wouldn't trust someone from the council. He's not an idiot."

"It wasn't a water. A fire climbed out of a red sports car, said she was a friend of Sera's. He never had a chance. And after he was out, she burned the place to the ground."

Sera cursed and began pacing.

It took great effort not to rock back and forth. "A fire elemental did this?" If so, the situation was even worse than I thought.

Sera gave a terse nod. "No chemicals, no electrical failure. Those fires have a bitterness you'll learn to recognize. This was oxygen, rage, and magic."

I closed my eyes and fought a shudder. Despite the smoldering cabin, I was cold. Goosebumps rose on my skin. "They brought in outside help."

It seemed the council had, at last, accepted that my friends and I were stronger than they were. They'd given up their pride, their desire to keep my existence a secret, so they could even the numbers.

"At least it explains why the water council kept setting fires," Miriam said.

It was impossible to know how many elementals they'd summoned, or how many were fulls who could crush my friends.

I only knew one thing for certain. They would never stop, and it had already gone too far. A forest of shifters had been displaced. Our home was destroyed. Frank was in the hospital. Somewhere, Luke was trapped, his best-case scenario imprisonment and life-altering drugs.

To stop them, we had to destroy them. If they sent a dozen elementals after us, we'd need to eliminate one after the other until the secret died with them. My stomach clenched in revulsion at the thought, my mind rejecting the idea before it was fully formed.

Mac was correct. This was them, not me. The council was responsible for all its actions, and I wouldn't accept the blame.

Not being responsible wasn't the same as not being the cause. I was the reason our lives were being destroyed, and I'd keep being the reason.

I was also the only one who could end it.

EVERY SUITE AT THE LAKESHORE RESORT WAS BOOKED BY businessmen on a corporate retreat, so we settled for a couple of connected rooms on the second floor. Grams and the shifters met us in the lobby. While Grams mended Vivian's arm, we caught the others up on the day's events.

Those of us who lived in the cabin had nothing but the clothes on our backs, but there are advantages to having your name on the deed of a luxury hotel. The concierge ignored all the other guests to help Sera, and soon we had new clothes in every size, color, and fabric hanging in our closets, each item more expensive than the one before.

We ordered sandwiches, but room service decided we forgot half the order. The tray that arrived included a roasted vegetable salad and handmade ravioli. The hotel's restaurant had a Michelin star, but we could only pick at the food. Even Simon showed little interest in his tuna tartare.

We didn't leave the hotel. The group had developed a siege mentality, and after several hours that became a problem. I needed to be alone for a while.

"I'm going to the lake," I announced.

Grams stood with me. "Oh, that sounds lovely, dear. Lead the way."

I couldn't say no, so together we visited the pristine blue of Lake Tahoe. It was too cold for swimmers, and the winter tourists wouldn't arrive until the first big snow of the year. Only a few people milled around the lake, and they paid no attention to either me or Grams.

"No matter what happens, you'll get her out?"

My request didn't surprise her. "Of course I will. Fiona is my daughter. I wouldn't let her languish in some council cell. But nothing is going to happen, my dear." She caught and held my gaze, insisting I believe her words.

Ah, denial. As much a Brook family trait as our blond hair.

Dinner was a quiet affair, though this time I cleaned my plate. Tomorrow, things would change, and I suspected I'd need all the energy I could get.

Mac and I were given our own room. As soon as the door shut, I threw myself at him, claiming his mouth while my hands roamed his body, trying to touch every part. My urgency surprised him, but it wasn't long before Mac met me touch for touch, his lips just as demanding. We fell onto the bed, tearing clothes as our need built. We wanted to lose ourselves in the taste and scent and texture of the other's skin. For hours, we found relief from the day in each other's bodies.

At last, he drifted off to sleep. I waited a little longer than I should have. I wasn't ready to go. Not while Mac's arms were tight around me for what would be the final time.

I reached for the tiny thread of power he kept safe for me. It was so vibrant. We shared the magic, but it would never truly be his. It had been born within me, and its life was tied to mine. When my power was suppressed, so was his, and if I died, the magic would die with me. It was a small comfort, knowing Mac would be free.

I forced myself to leave the bed, and then the room. I saw no one on my way to the lobby, and the night clerk didn't argue when I asked to use the hotel's town car.

The driver dropped me at an office in central Truckee. The man who greeted me was yawning. My three a.m. phone call had been a surprise, but my lawyer knew it was bad business to turn away the woman whose fortune supported his entire practice.

An hour later, I returned to the hotel with a thick stack of documents. I pulled out the keys I swiped earlier. Sera had used that cartoon devil keychain as long as I'd known her, and seeing the silly thing made my throat tighten.

Her Mustang was in the hotel's underground parking lot. I put the folded documents that handed over my entire trust fund in her glove compartment. She'd discover them the next time she searched for her copy of *London Calling*.

When I reached Will's room, I slid another document under the door. This was the deed to the unused property I owned in Oregon, along with a request for him to pass it along to one of the now homeless shifters.

It was still dark when I snuck into the hotel room, and Mac's even breathing told me he hadn't noticed my absence.

The bathroom was connected to a walk-in closet, so I could close the door and dress without waking Mac. I still wore my outfit from that morning. It reeked of smoke, a constant reminder of what the council took from us.

I pulled on a new pair of my favorite brand of jeans. There was a bite in the air that wouldn't vanish with the sunrise, so I added a royal blue sweater.

I studied myself in the bathroom's full-length mirror, trying to memorize the image—the woman I'd become, not the one the council believed I was.

The shades of blue in my outfit evoked the pure color of Lake Tahoe, the body of water that had fed and powered me so many times over the years. It was where Mac cried against my neck while telling me about his family, where Sera had fought to keep me sane, where my mother and I began rebuilding our relationship after years apart.

It was home, and I didn't think I'd ever see it again.

All I saw in my reflection was water. Gray eyes like river pebbles. Gold hair, the color of the sun reflecting on the ocean at twilight. A tall body as slim and fluid as a stream merging into a river, and then into a lake, growing in power with each transition.

I'd been a stream, and I'd grown with each person I added to my life. Now I was an ocean.

The woman staring back at me wasn't complete.

A makeup case lay on the counter. I rarely wore any, but Sera did, and she'd asked the concierge to purchase several items. They'd given me a set as well, just to be thorough.

I dug through the plastic case until I found a thick black eyeliner.

I rimmed both eyes. The look should have been startling and unfamiliar, but it felt like my face became my own. I wrenched off my blue sweater and rifled through the clothes hanging in the closet. The concierge hadn't known our preferences, so the shirts were in a rainbow of colors, orange and pink and purple.

There was also a bright red sweater with a deep v-neck. It fit like it was custom made.

Gray eyes blackened by soot. The body of a water covered in the heat of a fire.

Whatever future remained for me, I would never again deny who I was.

I was ready.

I picked up the flip phone and dialed the number from earlier. Deborah answered on the first ring. She sounded wide awake.

"You win," I told her. I added several conditions, and she didn't hesitate before agreeing to every one of them. After I gave her a time and location, I hung up.

The meeting was hours away, but I needed to escape before anyone woke. They'd try to stop me, because that's what friends did.

Friends also did anything they could to stop psycho-bitch council members from destroying lives and property or kidnapping people. Today I needed to be that kind of friend.

The door slid open on silent hinges. I walked toward the bed, unable to leave without seeing Mac once more.

The bed was empty.

Wincing, I turned to face him. He wasn't alone. A small black cat known for his spying skills crouched at Mac's feet, and my sister stood at his side.

"Hey, Ade," Sera said. "You got anything planned for today?"

CHAPTER 26

The council told me to come alone. My friends made an alternate plan.

I'd agreed to meet the council at noon. My friends decided that didn't apply to them.

While they altered one thing after another, there was one part of the plan they didn't try to change. No one attempted to stop me.

"You're really going to let me do this?" I asked. We were studying a map of the planned meeting spot. It was a large clearing several miles northeast of Truckee, in a section of the forest best known for the illegal parties college students held on weekends. It was familiar territory. I wanted to face Deborah on home turf.

"It's not a question of letting you do anything. You've made your choice, Ade. I've been trying to keep you from being an idiot for months now, and it never seems to work. We're still in this position. If I stop you, you'll try it again, and you'll be smarter next time. At least this way you won't be alone. We'll have your back."

I didn't want them to risk their lives by coming with me. They wished I wouldn't go at all. This was the closest we'd get to a compromise.

Mac grumbled his very reluctant agreement. I'd say this for my friends. They understood exactly how stupid and stubborn I could be.

They also thought it was only a meeting. I knew it was

a surrender.

The shifters arrived at the designated spot five hours before the scheduled meeting. They scouted the entire clearing and several miles of surrounding forest, confirming that no elementals were already there and planning a double cross. Vivian and Jet arrived an hour later and, with Simon's help, scanned for any transmitting tech. Deborah might not understand technology, but we had no idea how many others were involved by now.

When the council appeared five minutes before noon, I stood in the middle of the clearing. Behind me sat a couple of SUVs and a Mustang. The vehicles had transported two bears, an otter, a mountain lion, a cat, a fire, an earth, a water, and one human. They all stood behind me. I'd been surprised when Jet asked to come. She said it sounded like fun.

Deborah rode in an enormous SUV. If it was any larger, people would try renting it for special events. The behemoth rolled to a stop a safe distance from me.

Four full waters climbed out of the vehicle. Deborah and Michael, of course, and two women I recognized from a photo in which they threatened to torch the homes of those I loved.

They all looked wan, their hair and skin a bit dull. The chase had taken its toll on them, as well. Good.

Grams had told me the Ponds were in disgrace, so none of their family had been invited when the council was reformed. That meant the new members standing before me were Ruth Strait and Harriet Lake, if Grams' gossip was correct. Both women had relatives who'd died on the Brook island, and both of them stared at me with a simmering hatred that boiled over when they saw my shifter company.

There was a weighted pause. It felt like a decision was

being made, then the other rear door opened and Allison Ash, the leader of the fire council, stepped out.

We weren't off to a good start.

"Are you kidding me?" Sera was at my side faster than Usain Bolt. "You're the water council's bitch?"

It didn't surprise me when Allison took no offense. A few days in the Blais compound had reminded me that fires seldom mince words.

"I've known—knew—your father for centuries, Sera. I considered him a friend. He talked about you often, which is why I know he desired the best for you. This path you're on will lead to incarceration or death. In Josiah's memory, I will help his daughter any way I can, even if you reject my help. It's what he would want."

"You knew him that well and never learned that no one was allowed to fuck with his daughters?" Sera sneered.

I raised my hand. "Please note her use of the plural. Daughters. Both of us. You didn't try to help me avoid incarceration or death?"

Allison's lips tightened. "That hasn't been confirmed."

"He told a roomful of people!" Who were all either dead, standing behind me, or a council member. Not an impartial witness among them. Frustrated, I chucked a small fireball at Allison as proof.

"That doesn't prove you're his daughter. Another full fire could have impregnated your mother."

The other thing I remembered at the compound was that fires can be stubborn to the point of irrationality. I gave up. This wasn't a battle I would win, and it was an unnecessary distraction.

"Where's Luke?"

Deborah gestured to Sera. "She needs to move back. No joining powers."

I glanced pointedly at the other council members.

They took three steps away from each other. I nodded at Sera, and she put the exact same distance between us.

Deborah called over her shoulder. "Now."

The back of the SUV swung open. Two men emerged, both over six feet and more muscled than a full water. They were blond, but a shade darker than the rest of the council. I'd guess they were halfs at most. The men looked like twins, the only distinction being one wore a sullen expression and the other appeared flustered. Neither seemed entirely sure why they were there.

Together, they maneuvered a gurney out of the backseat. A sleeping Luke was strapped to it.

"Place him over there," Deborah ordered.

Obligingly, they carried him to a grassy spot far from the rest of us. They unstrapped him, rolled him off, then returned with the gurney.

"I've upheld my end of the deal." Deborah's eyes gleamed with anticipation.

Next to me, Sera tensed. She'd heard nothing about a deal.

I asked Grams to check on him. She confirmed that he was alive.

"My mother?"

"Is no longer in a council cell." Deborah's voice was as perfectly modulated as ever, but I thought she was fighting the impulse to rush her words. "Also, we will leave Tahoe the moment you take the other man's place on the gurney."

I studied her, looking for any sign she lied. So far, everything she'd said had been the truth, or at least her version of it. Even her threats hadn't been empty.

Sera vibrated with agitation. "Ade, please tell me this doesn't mean what I think it does."

A rustle of feet told me the others were walking toward

me. I glowered at them until they stopped moving.

"I know what I'm doing," I called.

They paused, uncertain, hoping I had a master plan I'd forgotten to share.

My friends were about twenty feet away, and I raised my voice so they would catch every word. "This has to happen. If you're honest with yourselves, you'll know I'm right. You said I got to make my own choices, Sera. This is it. I've chosen to hand myself in, and I'm not going to change my mind. None of you have to agree with my decision, but you don't get to stop me."

They wanted to argue. I saw it on their faces, the frustration and rage and resistance to this horrible plan. It was everything I'd felt the day before. In the end, they reached the same conclusion I had. We couldn't spend the rest of our lives running.

Agitated magic encircled me, and the shifters' eyes were more animal than human. Mac was already half bear, his eyes feral and cunning. He hadn't agreed to this plan.

I tried walking toward Deborah. The air felt heavy and thick, like it was holding me in place. It went against everything I'd fought for these last months, to give in to this wretched woman.

I moved forward three feet, then paused. If there'd been a force field between us, it wouldn't have made it any harder to reach her.

Deborah wasn't evil. She was like so many old ones, disconnected from the human world and its ever-changing morals. Josiah had been no different, and Sera and I still mourned him.

All her threats, every act of destruction, was intended to draw me into the open. Malice had never informed her actions. No one was dead because of her, which was more than I could say.

Deborah wasn't unreasonable. She'd released Luke. He might be a dual, but he was also cured and hadn't killed anyone, so far as they knew. They could ignore his existence if it meant they got the bigger prize.

My mother had been set free. Soon, the council would give up any claim to Tahoe, leaving the shifters and elementals who lived there to build their own peace.

My life was a small trade for an end to constant conflict, destruction, and fear.

I wouldn't have believed that if we were talking about Sera's or Mac's life, or anyone else's for that matter, but there was a key difference between us: I deserved it.

I didn't deserve it because I was a horrible person. I no longer felt the need to wear a hairshirt. This wasn't the same impulse that had placed me under the cairn.

A drunk driver who kills someone is no less culpable because their judgment was impaired. The robber whose gun accidentally goes off when it's waved at the victim still committed the crime.

It was impossible to make amends by wallowing in the past. All I could do was choose my path going forward and choose it well. I stood before Deborah and the council because this was the best choice I could make. It was the choice that would do the most good, and I wouldn't shy away from it, no matter how difficult it felt at that moment.

I hadn't expected it to feel quite so difficult.

"Is there a problem?" Deborah lifted a single eyebrow. As waters aged, they went in one of two directions. They either became more flighty and easily distracted or they grew cold and merciless like the Arctic Ocean. She was solidly in the latter category.

I forced myself to keep moving. Deborah glared over my shoulder. My friends kept their distance, but they also matched me step for step. If I insisted on doing this, they would be with me the entire way.

"To the gurney, please."

The thing was fitted with straps that would wrap across my shoulders, waist, thighs, and ankles.

"The Hannibal Lecter treatment isn't necessary," I said.

Sera's agitation flowed around me. I sent my fire backwards and found hers, pulsing in waves. I tried sending her the message to just chill already, but her magic refused to calm.

"Precautions."

The more twitchy lackey held up a syringe.

Bile rose in my throat. "Do you ever run out of that stuff?" I took an involuntary step backwards.

Deborah's eyes narrowed. "You should welcome it. It's the only way we can justify imprisonment rather than your execution."

With Deborah's words, a bit of Sera's tension eased. If I was alive, there was hope.

Her words only increased my fear. Too late, I began to think the council leader might be a liar after all. She had no reason to keep me alive.

"If it's not too much bother," I said, keeping my eyes on the syringe, "could you remember that I'm here willingly?"

"You are here under coercion," Deborah corrected me. "Let's not pretend otherwise."

I didn't accept her logic, logical though it might be. "If I planned to destroy you, you'd already be dead. I'm in control of my power, and I have no desire to hurt any of you."

The man holding the syringe started shaking at the reminder of what I was, but Deborah remained unaffected. "Precautions," she repeated.

I didn't move. There was no mercy in the woman's eyes.

"Control means nothing." She bit off the words. "We've seen cured duals before who developed a taste for killing." Her mouth snapped shut and her eyes widened.

Michael studied the trees, searching for a good place to hide.

"You've… seen cured duals?" I repeated, my voice flat. "You knew there was a cure." I sifted through my mind, grabbing at memories from the last few months and finding understanding where there'd been none before.

The council was, collectively, thousands of years old. Josiah had known about the firsts. The dozens of pets who visited the island or the Utah hilltop knew. There was absolutely no reason someone on the council wouldn't have been aware of their existence.

Deborah and Michael had shown no surprise when they encountered the first on the island. Vivian had needed both the files on Sera's mom and Luke's explanation about the first to discover where Eila lived. The council had access to Josiah's files, but not Luke's knowledge. Those files would only make sense to someone who'd heard about first magics—and our trip to the island would only make sense if they knew firsts could heal duals.

We'd assumed Jet had found us through satellites, following us on an unknown path across the desert and ocean. No one thought to ask her if we'd assumed correctly.

The council had followed me to the island because they hoped to stop me *before* I found a cure.

I bared my teeth. "You've got some 'splaining to do, Deborah. How long have you known?"

Her eyes darted between my friends, and whatever she saw made her nervous. "Not long," she insisted. That could mean anything from a week to five hundred years in elemental time.

"You can start by telling us why this isn't common knowledge. If it was, any child of two different fulls could be healed long before the madness starts."

Deborah's mouth opened and closed twice without a sound escaping.

"Next, you can tell me why there's a death sentence on all duals, instead of an offer of a cure. Encountering a first is dangerous, but it beats a guaranteed execution, doesn't it?"

She spread her hands in supplication, begging me to listen. "Can you imagine the chaos if the existence of the first magics was common knowledge? Elementals would be desperate to see them. The creatures' power would be unimaginable. We would lose our strongest to their hunger."

It was a compelling argument, but I found myself uninterested in any solution that relied on secrets and half-truths and a system where knowledge was disseminated only to the most powerful.

"People should know," I said. "They can make their own choice and, yeah, some of them will choose the wrong one. It happens every day. Hell, elementals already learn of the firsts, but they hear some ludicrous fantasy of perfect magic. If they learn it's likely a one-way trip, a lot fewer would try to make it. Just the really stupid ones."

"Elemental Darwinism," Sera added.

I warmed to my argument. "The firsts may grow more powerful for a while, but they're tethered to the land where they were born. It doesn't matter how powerful they are if they're trapped. Plus, I'll bet their food sources stop seeking them out once it becomes obvious few survive those meetings. If I understand it right, if firsts aren't fed, they cease to exist. That's what we all want. Cured duals and no firsts. Once the firsts are gone, the cure will vanish as well, but maybe we'll learn another way to fuse the magic by then."

Allison didn't appear nearly as certain as she had before. Deborah hadn't shared news of the cure with everyone.

Ruth and Harriet exchanged wild looks.

Panic crawled into Deborah's eyes. She scanned the clearing, noting the position of each person and reevaluating the success of that day's mission.

I wasn't done. "And finally, perhaps you can tell me why it was more important to chase me thousands of miles, to try pumping me full of drugs, to terrorize my friends and family, and to harm an innocent human man—why was that more important than telling me how to cure myself?"

The henchmen stepped away from the gurney. They seemed to realize they weren't going to need it that day.

"Sera, will you…?" I mimed the action.

She rolled her eyes at my ineptitude, then put her fingers to her mouth for a shrill whistle that caught the others' attention. My friends closed the remaining gap between us.

I turned so that I could see both my friends and the council. "We all know it's about power, Deborah. Healthy duals disrupt the elemental hierarchy, don't they? They could bring about some real change."

Next to me, Sera grinned. When Mac appeared at my side, he wore the same expression, and his bear had been reined in. In fact, every single one of my friends and family looked pretty damn pleased.

I was a bit slower to understand what they'd already figured out. I wasn't going anywhere. None of us were.

I spun back to Deborah. "That's it, isn't it? It's why you never really cared about Trent Pond. He was under your control. You could have offered me the solution ages ago, but I was already too dangerous. If I was cured, I'd be one of the most powerful elementals in the world—and I'm friends with shifters. Unlike the old ones, I believe the races are equal and don't mind saying so. How long till you would have gone after Luke again? He's also fond of shifters, you know."

Deborah's lips thinned. I laughed, loud and harsh.

"We're stronger than you are. It's not because we have more power, though we do. It's because we have more knowledge. We can tell elementals about shifters and firsts and dual magics. If I'm free, we'll change everything, and you'll do whatever it takes to prevent that." I pointed toward the other old ones. "Are you willing to fight for her now that you know what she's done?"

Ruth Strait held her head high and sneered at the shifters, but it seemed more a habit than a deeply held belief. Harriet Lake bit her lip, uncertain.

A low moan carried to us. Luke was waking up.

Allison moved away from the council and stood next to Sera. I wasn't certain she was welcome, but I appreciated the gesture.

"Go," I told Deborah, my voice more tired than triumphant. "Leave us alone, and we'll leave you alone. We can figure out the rest later."

Deborah hesitated, undecided.

"Aidan?" My stomach dropped. The voice was as familiar as my own.

A tall blond woman was being carried out of the SUV by the twins. Fiona Brook. My mother. I should have asked more questions when Deborah told me she was no longer in a prison cell.

I took back everything I'd thought earlier. Deborah really was evil.

It didn't appear that my mother had been harmed.

She did, however, look so angry one could be forgiven for thinking she was the one with a fire side.

"Aidan Brook, don't you dare give into this woman." She glared at Deborah. "She…"

A hand clamped over her mouth. My mother continued to struggle, kicking out and connecting with more than one shin. It occurred to me that maybe all my temper hadn't come from Josiah.

"Deborah." I broke her name into three careful syllables. I would not shout. I would not throw things. I would not incinerate people. "What is this?"

"This isn't what I wanted," Deborah said. "Truly. I only asked that you come in. I would have freed her."

"Why is she here?"

"Insurance. I've discovered you are more compliant when those you love are at risk."

The twitchy lackey placed the syringe against my mother's neck. Each time his hand shook, my heart jumped.

The sullen one withdrew a tranquilizer gun from the vehicle and leveled it at me.

I didn't know what I expected next, but I sure didn't expect Vivian to step forward. The movement was uncertain, and her voice shook when she spoke. Deborah barely turned her head enough to acknowledge the weak earth requesting her attention.

"How much of the serum do you have?" Vivian pointed toward the man with the gun. "If we add the number of syringes we had in the case—the ones we grabbed from the Brook family's island—to the ones you left behind in the other tranq gun, and the ones required to keep Luke unconscious for a day, and the ones shipped to Trent Pond's facility in Eureka, then calculate the time you've been making the drug and factor in the weeks required to source the ingredients and produce a quite complicated serum, I don't see how it's possible for you to have more than one vial left. That tranquilizer gun isn't loaded." By the end of her speech, her voice didn't wobble in the slightest. "Math," she said to me.

"How could you...?" Deborah's eyes narrowed. Vivian had her complete attention now.

"Your lab shouldn't keep the serum's formula and its operations schedule online. Anyone could find it." Vivian's lips turned up, the bare beginning of smile. "If my calculations are right, and they always are, you have enough for Aidan. If I forgot to carry the two, which I didn't, you may be able to get Fiona as well. Even if you could knock them both out, which you can't, that would leave you in a lopsided battle against us. If you could somehow defeat a full and another dual and several angry shifters long enough to escape with Aidan, you won't be able to control her without the drug—and I suspect her offer to be compliant has expired. If you hurt her, you wouldn't be able to stop us when we hunted you down and destroyed you, which we would."

"We can always make more," Deborah lifted her chin, fixing on the smallest part of Vivian's argument.

Vivian rattled off an address in Tacoma.

"What did you do?" The words were strangled.

"In the future, I recommend not pissing off people who can access shipping, health and safety, and property records. Between all the illegal ingredients and the workplace violations, it was only a matter of time before the lab was shut down and sold to new owners. They were quite efficient. It only took a few hours this morning." The small smile was now a triumphant grin. "The neighborhood will welcome the new community center they're about to get."

Deborah wasn't the only one gaping at her at this point.

Then Vivian, the quietest, gentlest person I knew, said loud enough for everyone to hear, "Aidan is my friend, and you are kind of a bitch."

Before anyone could respond, she took a confident step backward.

"How many times are we going to go through this, Deborah?" I tried to sound bored. Boredom was a better negotiating position than fear, even if it was impossible while they threatened my mother. "You don't have the strength. You don't have the people. Apparently, you no longer have the drug. Despite what you think I am, I don't want to kill you. We only want to live in peace."

A muscle twitched in her jaw. "Someone must pay, and not just for David. For Lana Pond, who will never recover from what she witnessed. For the council lives lost because of Josiah's search for your cure."

"A search that wouldn't have been necessary if you'd shared your knowledge." My attempt at a bored facade shattered. "If you're going to blame someone, remember this all started when a dual magic needed to hide from a council that would rather kill her than cure her."

I marched to my mother. I was done with this. With all of them. We could talk in circles all day, or I could end it. I liked door number two better.

The man holding my mother refused to release her, so I set his arms on fire. He let go pretty damn fast. I glared at the second man. He dropped the empty tranq gun with no further urging. Only when my mother was far enough away did I douse the flames. Magic whispered around me as he pulled on the water in the air to heal his burns.

Deborah stepped toward me, and I snarled.

I wrapped an arm around my mother, supporting her. When we reached the group, I pushed her forward into Grams' arms. For the first time in my life, I watched my mother accept comfort from another.

"Someone must pay," Deborah repeated, an inch from my ear.

When I felt the pinch on my neck, I wasn't even surprised. She'd fought me too long to walk away. There would be no peaceful resolution, not for her. Glorious failure was better than useless defeat.

I yanked the syringe out of my neck before more than a drop or two could spill into my blood. It smashed on the ground, the last of the hated drug soaking into the earth.

I hadn't been fast enough. Those drops raced through my blood, seeking out magic that was stronger and purer than ever before, and they began to snuff it.

I had seconds before I crumpled to the ground, and I turned to my friends. They stared back, shock and horror on their faces.

That was no good. They needed different expressions.

"Show these idiots who we really are." Before I could say anything else, I slumped to the ground.

CHAPTER 27

It was the smallest dose of the drug I'd ever received, and I was no longer fractured. With my power at full strength, the anti-magic serum never had a chance. I wasn't sure how long I'd been out, but it couldn't have been more than a few minutes. No one was dead yet, though it didn't appear to be from lack of trying.

Someone had hauled me to the side so I wasn't in the middle of the battle. I was at least two feet away from it.

It was a struggle to hold my eyes open. The fatigue pulled at me, and I blinked several times before I understood what I was seeing.

The council was strong, and they'd joined hands to concentrate their power. Even the henchmen worked with them. Whatever doubts I might have stirred up about their alliance with Deborah, for now they'd chosen the devil they knew.

My friends fought four old ones, fulls with an immense amount of power. Together, they could drown us all with a thought.

Except for a couple small problems.

First, my mother and Grams were also old ones. While Deborah and the others had panic on their side, my family had rage. These people had threatened their daughters.

The council tried to force water directly into the shifters' and Sera's mouths and lungs. Each time, the streams redirected, falling impotently to the earth.

Twenty-foot waves rushed toward those on our side. Before they reached my friends, my mother and Grams turned them into harmless things a child could body surf.

The waves transformed into a flood. The water rose four feet and would have kept going if my family didn't resist. When the council forced it up three inches, my mother and Grams lowered it one.

Eventually, the flood would have risen above the others' heads, except for the other problem.

There were a lot more of us, and we weren't playing by any rules I'd ever seen.

Miriam swam through the flood as easily as any water elemental. Her sleek otter form slid between the council's legs, and she sank her teeth deep into their flesh as she passed. The wounds weren't life-threatening, but they required the elementals to divert some of their power to healing. The rising water slowed, a fraction of an inch at a time.

Carmen wasn't a natural swimmer, and her movements were sluggish. Even so, the younger men saw her coming, her immense paws churning through the flood, and they knew sharp claws were attached to her feet. More of their attention wavered while they kept an eye on Carmen's progress.

Luke stood on the edge of the clearing. He looked ragged and worn, as if he'd woken from a week-long bender, but he held his hands before him, using his dry desert heat to devour the flood.

Vivian stood next to Luke, her face a mask of concentration. Her power was so slight she could only convince the earth to absorb a tiny fraction of the water, but every bit counted.

Jet sat on top of the Bronco and cheered.

A constant stream of fire poured from Sera and Allison.

All they could do was slow the water, give it something to do besides drown us, but it was enough. The flood was holding steady. With a little more power, we'd be able to reverse it.

Simon crouched in a tree in his human form. From his position, he could observe the entire battle. He yelled warnings and commands to those below, and no one hesitated to follow his instructions.

Mac was nowhere in sight. I struggled to my elbows, terrified I'd find him lying on the ground somewhere, incapacitated or worse.

Instead, he emerged from the trees that ringed the clearing, his arm gripped around a massive tree trunk held against his shoulder. Will ran behind him, holding the other end.

Grams and my mother redirected their power, creating a clear path between the bear shifters and those we fought.

Will stepped forward, and the men adjusted their grip at the last moment. Together, they swung the tree trunk like an enormous baseball bat. It slammed into the elementals' backs.

The council flew through the air, losing their connection to each other's magic. They landed in a broken heap. None of them moved. All their energy and magic was needed to repair their internal injuries.

The flood dissipated instantly, though the earth remained drenched. The soil was dark, slippery mud. Fat puddles of water dotted the clearing.

The fight was over. Our enemies lay on the ground, gasping for breath. My friends watched them with wary eyes, waiting for any sign they planned to resume the battle. The council offered none.

I'd never considered this option. I'd expected them to leave once I surrendered. Things would return to normal.

I hadn't expected them to fight us, not when we were so strong, and I sure hadn't expected them to lose and leave us to decide their fate.

We couldn't let them go. Deborah would return again and again, each time with more weapons. She'd build a new lab, arrange for the creation of more drugs.

She would never accept defeat. She couldn't. The best case scenario was she'd eventually capture me.

The worst case scenario was all-out war.

I rolled onto my hands and knees, fighting a wave of nausea. My head pounded, and I stretched some magic toward the nearest puddle, absorbing its power.

I attempted to push myself upright. It didn't work so well, so I crawled instead. My mother walked toward me now that the fight was done, and when she saw me struggle she ran. She helped pull me to my feet, and I staggered against her. She held me until I could stand on my own, then we joined the others.

The twins rolled on the ground, groaning in pain. It would take them longer to recover. Deborah had managed to pull herself to a kneeling position, her white pantsuit covered with thick streaks of dark mud.

Grams' power slid past me to examine Deborah's injuries.

"How is she?"

"Her internal organs are mush. That's true for all of them. They will heal, of course, and sooner than we'd like."

Everyone heard the underlying warning, including Deborah. Whatever we were going to do, we needed to decide before her power returned.

"You can't murder us." Deborah's face was expressionless, but her voice wavered.

"Can't I? I keep hearing I'm a killer. You said so yourself."

"The cost will be too high. If I go, I will not go alone."

Ruth and Harriet huddled together, wide eyes pinging back and forth between me and Deborah.

My body felt leaden. My heart felt pretty much the same. Even my magic was heavy and dull from the serum. "Can you let this go? If we release you, can we trust you to drop this?" I asked the other council members.

Harriet's head bobbed up and down. Ruth seemed less certain. "Yes, but…"

"Yes or no?" I interrupted. I was in no mood for conditions.

"We won't try to hurt you," Harriet confirmed.

"Or shifters. They're not your enemy unless you make them so." I spoke to both women, daring them to reconsider an ancient prejudice.

Carmen remained in feline form. She sniffed the women, as if searching for a lie. Whatever she found, it made her snarl.

Then again, Carmen hated elementals. She wouldn't miss an opportunity to snarl at them.

Michael was trying to crawl his way to freedom.

"You need some help there, Mikey?" I called.

He turned and sat hard on the muddy ground. There was a loud squelch as he landed. "I'll do whatever you want," he said, without a hint of guile.

Michael followed power. Deborah no longer had it.

There was one thing left. I couldn't ask the others to do it. They'd already done too much. I knew what it was to kill. It was awful, and I'd never recover from it, but it needed to be me.

This was the last price, then. The cruelty of the moment struck me, that my sanity meant so little. One way or the other, death found me.

I summoned two fireballs, one in each palm.

My hands dropped. The weapons disappeared. I couldn't do it. I couldn't be that person anymore.

"If we can contain Trent, we can contain her," I decided. "We'll move her to the middle of the desert. Brew up some of the drug, just in case. It doesn't need to end in death."

Grams tilted her head, considering. "That's noble, dear, and I can't argue with you choosing your better angels, but it's an awful lot of responsibility."

"Particularly for someone who wants to see you dead," Sera reminded me.

"It won't be forever," I insisted. "It'll end when a new council is formed and we convince them we're not the bad guys. We'll figure out how information about duals and firsts will be handled. Deborah's greatest weapon has been secrecy, so we'll take that away from her. Then we can move her to the fine accommodations my mother and Grams got to enjoy. Michael, Ruth, and Harriet agree, right?"

They very much did. "We'll help you," Harriet added.

Carmen seemed annoyed that there'd be no bloodshed that day, but I felt a tiny bit lighter.

A coil of water snapped around Vivian's ankle and ripped her backwards. Her fingers dug into the earth, but it was too wet for any purchase. She slid through the mud and fell across Deborah's legs. The water's fingers wrapped around Vivian's throat.

Jet screamed and ran toward us.

Water was useless against Deborah, and I couldn't burn her without torching Vivian as well. Other than Jet, who was beyond Deborah's reach, Vivian had the most human- ity of anyone in the clearing. She was the easiest to kill, if that was the woman's intention.

Deborah's eyes weren't on Vivian. They were locked

on me as she issued a twisted challenge. Prove I was a murderer, or watch my friend die.

I could melt Deborah's organs without touching Vivian. The woman's fingers squeezed while Vivian thrashed.

My cheeks wet with tears, I called the fire.

I never used it. Mac stepped behind Deborah with only his hand shifted. He didn't look at me as he slashed a sharp claw across her throat, cutting deep from one end to the other. The movement wasn't savage. It was precise and clinical, nothing more than a means to an end.

Her skin split open, the arteries cut. Blood rushed down her neck, staining her white shirt red. She didn't seem to notice when she released Vivian's neck and the earth scrambled away from her.

Deborah didn't die immediately. She remained upright while her blood pooled on the ground below. She was as calm and poised as ever. She made no attempt to heal herself, though she could have.

Instead, she let herself die, and when she fell over at last, she was smiling.

Ruth and Harriet watched in utter horror. "You can't… you didn't."

"It was self defense." The words were sharp as a blade. The last thing we needed was panicked witnesses. "Keep an eye on them?" I asked Carmen, indicating the council members and their employees.

She bared her teeth in pleasure at the assignment.

"Don't eat them." It seemed worth saying, just in case.

If we didn't handle this right, we'd end up with a whole other set of enemies and a brand new death sentence.

Sera stood over Deborah's corpse, obviously thinking the same thing. "What the hell do we do now?"

———

THE ELEMENTALS ACCESSED EARTH, WATER, OR FIRE TO HEAL their damage. The shifters resorted to more traditional methods like antiseptic and bandages. My mother and Grams offered to help them, but they all refused. They might be learning to trust some elementals, but that didn't mean they wanted us digging around in their bodies with magic. At least their shifter blood meant a speedy recovery.

Once no one was bleeding, it was time to deal with the hostages and Deborah's corpse.

Vivian hung back as far as she could and still be able to hear the conversation, wanting to keep her distance from the white-faced corpse. Simon and Jet stood next to her, offering silent comfort.

The shifters showed no sign of discomfort. Perhaps something in their ancient DNA understood that the body was now only meat, nothing to either celebrate or fear.

Most of the elementals, while not exactly squeamish, were still uneasy. As long-lived as we were, death was rare among our kind. We never truly became accustomed to it, even with the recent practice we'd been given, and we all knew a sense of wrongness. If different choices had been made, Deborah should have lived another thousand years.

Flames sparked from Sera's fingers. "Damn it. We had no choice. We weren't all going to walk out of this clearing. I know you decided to flake on the big fight, Ade, but it wasn't a practice match for them. Was it?" She rounded on the lackeys we'd strapped to a tree.

The ropes were a token gesture, as it did nothing to limit the men's magic, but it made us feel better. Besides, all their power was focused on repairing the damage caused by the tree trunk.

The scowling one stared at his toes with great interest. The other shook his head so fast his cheeks wobbled.

Michael cleared his throat. "May I say something?"

"No." Miriam's expression was black. For once, she didn't appear even a little cute. She spat, just missing Deborah's corpse. "I second Sera's opinion. Fuck 'em. That bitch was going to kill Vivian. If Mac hadn't finished it, I would have."

I watched for Mac's reaction. His face was stoic, but it wasn't frozen. He understood exactly what he'd done, and why, and I saw no sign of regret.

I considered the corpse and the five waters that had tried to kill us only minutes before. "The way I see it, we have a few options. Burning is the best way to dispose of the corpse. We can get it hot enough to leave no trace, but someone will come looking for Deborah, particularly if this lot decides to talk once they aren't scared for their lives."

They still acted pretty damn scared. Their eyes darted around the clearing, seeing threats in every tree.

"We could try to frame the rest of the council, but then they'll be executed under elemental law. That wouldn't be good for our karma."

Grams tapped her chin. "Those aren't great choices, dear."

"There's another option." Carmen bared her teeth. "We can tear her flesh into tiny pieces and spread it through elemental homes up and down the coast as a warning of what happens when they attack shifters."

The shifters didn't look as appalled by that suggestion as they should have.

"No." I managed not to shout. "We *don't* want a war, remember?"

"What's left then?" Mac watched me. "Don't you dare say you're going to turn yourself in for this, too."

"I'm over that particular impulse," I assured him.

"There's another choice."

I inhaled, preparing to say what no one expected to hear.

"We tell the truth," said a voice behind me. Well, no one except Simon.

I spun to face him. "How did you…?"

He lifted his shoulders in a delicate shrug. "It was the only option that remained. It is not a bad idea, either."

The others disagreed. I was assaulted by a cacophony of voices, each wanting to tell me, in great detail, why I'd clearly gone insane after all.

I tried waiting them out until it became obvious that several would grow hoarse before they stopped arguing.

Instead, I found my phone and dialed. Everyone quieted enough to hear the conversation.

"Carmichael? We've got a dead elemental here. One of theirs, don't worry. Can you guys get here right away with whatever forensics tools you have? I know that's not your specialty, but you're all we've got, and we need you to read a crime scene." I gave him directions and hung up.

The others waited for my explanation.

"We need to prove we acted in self-defense. The waters might be witnesses, but I wouldn't count on them. Maybe, if we have enough facts and graphs and charts, someone will listen to us. We'll need evidence that Deborah knew about the cure. That part won't be easy. I mean, even Josiah didn't know about it." I paused, considering our options and finding few. Deborah was a technophobe. She wouldn't have kept an online diary with all her secret thoughts.

"Would this help?" Vivian raised her cell phone, the speaker turned to maximum volume. From several feet away, I could make out Deborah's voice informing me that she'd seen cured duals before.

My mouth opened, and I didn't close it right away.

"When Deborah started making promises she might not keep, I thought it would be good to have a record."

With great effort, I didn't run to her, tackle her to the ground, and shower her with kisses.

"I'd really like to speak," Michael called. Somehow, he'd managed to place himself thirty feet away from the group while we were distracted.

"In a minute." I turned to the henchmen. They'd healed enough that their breathing was stable, and I wanted to hear what they had to say.

"How long have you been with Deborah?" I asked.

"Not long," said the nervous man. "Um. About three weeks?"

The other kept staring at his toes.

"Tell me what you saw or heard. Anything about us or her plans."

Even the nervous one shut his mouth. It wasn't loyalty, I realized, not for either of them. It was fear.

A shadow fell across me. The lackeys tilted their heads up, then up some more, until they saw the very black expression on Will's face.

I crouched on my heels so I was eye level, then took a cue from Vivian and hit record on my own phone. I didn't trust these two to tell the same story when interrogated by a bunch of old ones, and the truth was our only defense. "Let's try this again. What did you see?"

Inspired by Will's presence, the nervous man couldn't talk fast enough. "They had us bomb the bar. We researched how to make it on the internet."

My lips tightened. At least we knew who'd be paying Frank's hospital bills.

"And?" I pushed.

"And we know about the fire in the forest. We didn't do

it, though. She did." He pointed at Allison Ash.

"What else?" I pushed. The faster he spoke, the more I sensed he was withholding information. The quieter man had started to shake.

The twitchy one shut his mouth. "That's it. Can we go?"

I sat back on my heels. Something was missing. There was still too much tension.

"They hired us in Hawaii." The quiet man spoke for the first time.

"What were they doing in Hawaii three weeks ago?" I had a strong suspicion I wasn't going to like this answer.

"Waiting." He raised his eyes to meet mine. "Waiting to see if you got off the island."

"And when I did?"

"They took a boat out. They returned a day later, and there was something with them."

My stomach dropped to somewhere around my knees. Four fulls visited the island of a creature who avoided all fulls.

"May I speak now?" Michael asked.

Harriet and Ruth's terror continued to grow.

"What did you do?" I spat out the words.

"It wasn't me! It was Deborah! I didn't know it could be done, but she said we control firsts. Something about children always having power over their parents. A full can bind a first."

I'd been so wrong. Eila didn't fear fulls because they could destroy her. She feared them because they could master her.

"Why would that ever seem like a good idea?" Luke asked. His voice remained calm while terror filled his eyes.

"She said it was the only way her power could match yours. It didn't work. The thing was furious at being restrained and taken from its home. I haven't seen it in days. It's gone." His words were a fervent hope rather than the truth.

Eila wasn't gone. She was waiting—and with Deborah's death, she was unbound.

I raced for the cars. "We have to go!"

I managed to reach the Bronco. A heavy wave lifted me, slamming me against the metal doors.

I knew what I'd see when I turned. What Deborah had brought.

What she'd been willing to die to unleash it upon us.

"You did not keep your side of our deal," said Eila.

CHAPTER 28

Eila didn't seem weak, despite the days spent away from her home. Now I understood why the council's faces were drawn and tired. She'd been feeding.

However, she didn't look entirely healthy, either. There was a thin and brittle quality about her that I'd never seen on the island.

This time, she didn't float to us. She appeared in one place and then another, buzzing in and out of focus. Her eyes were a black that didn't exist in nature, unleavened by even the hint of light. They were more void than color. Her hair rose from her scalp, twisting and curling according to the whims of a maniacal wind, though the day was quiet.

She was utterly terrifying and the most powerful creature I would ever encounter, and at that moment all I could think was I was so tired of this shit.

"Can you really not find a boyfriend of your own?" I asked. "I mean, you're crazy, and your narcissism would require a team of shrinks to work on you for a couple centuries, but you're not an unattractive woman. Go find someone else."

She expanded several inches in every direction. If I was smart, I'd stop talking now.

Smart was such a subjective term.

"I'd think any self-respecting first would find a guy who would worship them as a god. Bathe your feet and offer nightly massage, that sort of thing. Instead you're here, begging for scraps?"

"I was brought to this place. This is not-home." Her voice was different. Sharper, but also hollow. Discordant.

"Is that the problem? Cause we can arrange for someone to return you."

Eila gave no outward sign she heard me. She spun in a slow circle, though I never saw her feet move. She studied everyone in the clearing, registering each elemental, shifter, and human. She only glanced at the dark sedan pulling into the clearing, showing minimal interest in the FBI agents. Johnson slammed on his brakes when he saw the first, and both men stared slack-jawed through the windshield. At least they stayed inside with locked doors.

The rest of my friends were too far away. I stepped away from the Bronco, hoping to close the distance between myself and the others. I was too exposed on my own.

I was flung backwards. Once again, I crashed into metal. My breath escaped in a rush and I had trouble drawing the next breath.

Before I recovered, a lumbering beast rose before me. It had no mouth, eyes or ears, but it had arms and legs the size of tree trunks and hands as large as frying pans. Every part was formed from the earth. Eila had created a freaking golem.

I stumbled away from the vehicle. The thing grabbed my shoulders and pushed. It put forth no more effort than I'd use to flick a speck of lint from a shirt, but my body vibrated with the impact.

I called on the water surrounding me, but before it could wash away the golem, the thing wrapped an enormous hand around my wrist and shook me like a rag doll. My entire left side hit the SUV three times before it released me. I crumpled to the ground, unable to do more than whimper. My shoulder had been dislocated and several ribs were cracked.

I redirected the water to healing. The golem gripped my thighs and lifted me as easily as it would a pillow. It heaved me onto the Bronco's roof. My spine struck the edge and shattered. I slithered to the ground, my legs useless.

The golem disintegrated and returned to the earth.

"Be quiet," Eila said. My mouth filled with earth. I retched, thick clods landing on the ground as I cleared my lungs.

I pulled water from the puddles in the clearing, urging it toward my broken spine.

"No." Eila wrenched it from me and sent it shooting over the trees, an enormous wave flying beyond my reach.

Mac roared and Will joined in. Sera screamed my name.

I caught Grams' eye. "You're a full," I mouthed.

She understood right away. Grams turned to Eila, already sending thick streams of magic toward the creature.

Eila swatted it away like an annoying bug. "I have been unbound and brought to not-home."

Apparently, controlling Eila was a first come, first served kind of thing.

I stretched my power outwards, searching for nearby streams. There was always water in Tahoe.

But the winter rains hadn't begun yet. The creek beds were dry, and we were too far from the lakes and rivers. All the strength in the world meant nothing without my element. I grasped at the tiny drops clinging to the air or buried in exposed tree roots. They only healed a few scratches.

"There are more of you." Eila glided toward Mac, hands outstretched. He wasn't a man anymore, not entirely. His shoulders hunched and his shirt split open as his torso and arms morphed into a bear. One huge paw swatted Eila.

Her midsection disappeared. Mac's paw swung through empty space, but a single claw made contact. It tore into her flesh. Then she was whole again, the wound already healed.

It wasn't much, but it was more than we'd seen on the island. Away from her home, Eila could bleed.

A surge of water punched Mac in the chest, lifting him off the ground. His head smacked against a tree and he dropped to the ground, unconscious.

"He is unhurt," she said, using a different definition of the word than the one I knew.

I moaned, both at his pain and my own. As quickly as she called the water, it disappeared. I had no more than a second to grab its power. My ribs knit together, but the rest remained broken.

Eila seemed to have forgotten me. She moved down the line of shifters, examining them as she had the rest of us when we arrived on her island.

"You are as he is." She lifted her hand from Will's chest and slid to Carmen and Simon next, touching each of them for only a moment. "You are different." Her eyes grew unfocused as she recalled mental images she'd stolen from the islanders. "Cats," she announced. Normally, Carmen would be livid at being lumped in with a small house cat, but all I saw in her face was confusion and fear.

Miriam shrank back when Eila approached. It took her longer this time to find the appropriate name. "Otter," she said at last, with a hint of relief. "River otter."

With each shifter she discovered, Eila's expression grew more and more pleased.

Sera lunged toward Eila, stumbling to the ground when she tripped over the mound of earth that appeared from nowhere.

There was a small nudge against my skin, then a familiar touch slid into my body.

While Eila examined the shifters, my mother had taken five steps toward me. She sent her healing abilities to my shoulder. It popped into the socket, and I couldn't hold in the yelp of pain.

Eila found my mother's magic immediately. She removed it, then, for good measure, she used the ground to push my mother twenty feet away.

"I have been given a gift," murmured Eila. Nothing would distract her for long from her true obsession. "I needed to come to not-home to find so many of the lost children."

Lost children. Shifters.

Perhaps too late, it occurred to me that she hadn't desired Mac because he was a towering bundle of manly perfection. She hadn't tried to sleep with a shifter because she was bored of elementals.

She wanted shifters. Any shifter.

I rushed to put the pieces together, knowing their lives depended on the answer to this puzzle.

Like elementals, shifters were born from the firsts. While we'd remained in communities, both human and elemental, shifters functioned much like the animals whose skin they shared. They could be social or loners, but their community rarely extended far beyond their own families.

They never would have chosen Eila's camp, and if they'd found themselves in such a place, nothing would have convinced them to stay.

Now Eila had a veritable buffet of the animals she'd long been denied, and she was thrilled at the prospect. There was no way this ended well.

Simon screamed, wrenching my attention back to the present. Eila stood before him. Though she didn't touch his body, her hands moved in the air, conducting his magic as she once had mine.

Simon fell to the ground, face pale and green eyes devoid of life. The features I knew so well blurred, unfamiliar shadows filling the hollows and lines. It was still his face, but I was reminded of children around a campfire, holding flashlights beneath their chins. The slightly tilted eyes drooped and his cheekbones grew less pronounced.

For an instant, Eila took the form of a small, black cat.

"No!" I pulled myself forward, crawling on my forearms and gasping with each movement.

For the first time, Eila seemed truly happy. "Desire. Fight. More." she whispered to herself. Eila tilted her head, studying Carmen. "Not yet. Not strong enough yet." She moved to Miriam.

Miriam screamed. She fell, her face as dull and unknown as Simon's. An otter appeared where Eila stood, then vanished.

Eila disappeared. A ring of fire surrounded her, hiding her from view.

Eila stepped through the flames, and Sera and Luke rebuilt the circle again and again. It made no sense. They could never harm her that way.

They could only distract her.

Power slammed into me, my mother and Grams working as one. They didn't bother to be gentle, choosing speed over finesse. Bones and nerves healed beneath their touch. It was surgery without anesthesia. I shoved my fist into my mouth to stifle the screams and bit down hard enough to cut skin.

Then it was done, and I was whole. I reached for Sera and Luke's flames, recharging my fire side, then pulled myself to my feet.

"Why?" I called.

Eila faced me, giving no indication she was surprised to see me standing.

"Why?" she repeated, as confused as if I'd asked her to recite prime numbers in order.

"Why are you taking them? You're pure magic. Why can't that be enough?" I was angry, but I was also terrified, and my voice revealed both.

Something flashed across her black eyes. It might have been pain. "There is no pure. Pure is unchanging. It is frozen. Magic is not that. Magic is life. It grows. It moves. It returns. I will not return."

I turned her vague sentences over in my mind, trying to find sense in her riddles.

"What are elementals?" I asked.

"They are life."

"And what are shifters?"

She sighed, like a contented human after a large meal. "They are desire."

Eila didn't speak of passion. I'd leapt to that conclusion, so blind with lust for Mac that I believed even an ancient being would feel the same. She'd never craved his body. She'd wanted his bear, but she was too weak to take it on the island, the same way she'd been too weak to take Carmen. Mac needed to give his power willingly.

She was building up her strength. Simon and Miriam were such little animals.

I dragged my mind back. If I thought of Simon and Miriam, I'd go catatonic.

There had to be a reason. I recalled everything I knew about shifters, settling at last on the most basic detail. Shifter magic was animal magic.

Animals spent their lives with a single goal: to continue

living. Every instinct guided them toward survival. It moved them toward food and protection, and it told them whether they were the hunter or the hunted.

Within each shifter was a beast, and that beast held a feral magic that would fight to stay alive at all costs. A *desire* to live at all costs.

That was what Eila sought.

Elementals were power. Shifters were wild, untamed life. One kept her going. The other made her want to keep going. Without that desire, she would return to the earth.

"You want their life force."

"I will live," she answered.

All the people on the island, all the losses, because this damned creature was afraid to die.

One way or another, I would help her get over that fear.

I gave her no warning. I grabbed every drop of power I possessed and threw it at her. Both fire and water rammed into her core. Her stomach clenched at the impact, but that was her only outward response.

"I know your magic," she said, calm as ever. "You cannot use it to hurt me."

Eila considered Will and Carmen. Their chins were lifted, their spines straight.

She walked toward Mac, unconscious and unable to defend himself.

Once again, I formed creatures of fire and water and surrounded her with the small army. They attacked, and she absorbed them.

The magic didn't return to me.

Panic scratched at my chest. My assault strengthened her and weakened me, but if I didn't fight, she would devour Mac. She'd take them all, every shifter in the clearing, before claiming the rest of us as her new pets.

I wasn't strong enough to stop her. Not even cured.

The effects of the drug gnawed at me, weakening power that should have been absolute.

The others still fought. Fire and water and hot desert air rushed at Eila. She didn't seem to notice.

I felt along the cord of my magic, admiring the perfect fusion of the two threads. It was a work of art, even if it was Eila's work. That thread had given me hope, and it had given me time. It had given me long nights with Mac.

Now it would save him.

Magic could create. Water and fire, beauty and life.

It could also destroy. Ruin, desolation, and a madness that tried to claim me.

I took one last look at my mother and Grams, at Sera. "Don't hate me," I told her. Maybe she heard.

Eila placed her palms on Mac's shoulders, and I made the only choice I could. I claimed the madness.

I grabbed that loose thread and ripped the fire and water apart in a single, desperate motion. I let it all go. My mind and my heart, and everything I'd ever loved or trusted. The years I planned to wake at Mac's side. The comfort of knowing I was loved. The forgiveness I'd promised myself at last. The hopes I'd clung to during the darkest days when my control hung by a thread, when my friends believed in me though I no longer believed in myself. All that I'd ever wanted, I gave it to the magic, and I let it be destroyed.

I destroyed it all, knowing it was the last thing I'd ever do. There was power in grief and in the rage of loss.

I pushed past the encroaching madness, seeking memories instead. I recalled a childhood with a mother who loved me, the wild university years spent with Sera, and the quiet nights in the cabin with my family of choice. I'd helped people. I'd saved a few, and I'd loved so many of them, one so much I would rewrite the rules of magic itself to save him.

I claimed everything that made me good, all the best parts of me, and I let them explode.

I annihilated myself, and I sent the atoms of power created by my obliteration toward Eila.

She was in her solid form, and I wrapped the wreckage around her, grabbing onto her flesh and slicing into the skin. Blood welled to the surface and slid down her arms and neck and face, and still I cut, burrowing into her, seeking whatever organs lived within and crushing them.

Eila gasped and faced me, her movements sluggish. She was covered in a thick veil of my ruined magic. It slowed her, as water would a human, and I dug in deeper. I coated her in my destruction and waited for her to be destroyed in turn.

Ozone filled my nostrils, stronger than anything we'd found on the hilltop. That first had been decaying slowly. Eila was dying before our eyes.

I felt rather than heard her howl. I staggered as her power detonated, causing my own to rocket through the clearing. I gathered it for another strike, but it was already gone. Destruction happened in an instant. It was only the fallout that lingered.

I had nothing left to give. Aidan Brook no longer existed.

A shell dropped to the earth, bones and blood and flesh, but that was all. When Eila reached for Mac, it meant nothing. My eyes drifted shut.

My head jerked up as energy rushed into me, a magic so familiar I latched onto it without thought. It belonged to another, but it came from the same source my own once had.

Sera's fire ripped into me and became my own. Josiah's magic belonged to both of us, and she shared hers with me. Her fingers dug into mine so hard I thought she would break bones, but I felt nothing but the fire.

She panted with the effort, and sweat rolled down her temples and cheeks, but she held nothing back. She knew something I'd forgotten.

I was an elemental, not an empty husk. I was meant to be magic, and my body knew it. It grabbed hold of her gift and fed. I had no right to it, but I took it anyway.

I shuddered at the second onslaught, as water rushed to meet the fire. My mother and Grams stood on my other side and poured their power into me. As I'd been born from them, so I would be reborn.

In my core, the fire and water danced together, father and mother reunited in my body.

The single thread formed again, knit more tightly than Eila had ever managed. Hope and love and belief collided, and they rebuilt me.

It was pure creation, the first gift the universe gave us. I let it fill me. I let it make me stronger than I'd ever been. Stronger than the woman who knew how to kill, stronger than the woman who thought destruction was the answer.

As my magic was created from nothing, so was my knowledge.

I reached for Eila and found the gaps, the lost parts where her magic had weakened as the gift of creation faded, and I filled her with all she'd lost or perhaps never had.

I would never understand the original magic, but I knew the other kind. I knew the human side, and the elemental side, and I gave her both. All her missing parts, I patched with love and faith, sacrifice and forgiveness. All I'd learned, I shared with her. Everything the firsts had given us when they joined with humans, I returned it, and I took away the loneliness and fear that had torn at her for more millennia than I could count.

Eila's form was one we'd never seen before. Ethereal and glowing, a thousand stars held together by invisible threads, she expanded before our eyes.

I whispered to this oldest of creatures that it was her turn. Her chance to create one last good thing in a world that hadn't needed her for a very long time.

She didn't fight me. I felt only peace as her magic burst. The ethereal shape faded as one thread after another came loose.

Something shoved me, and I fell to the ground. My family lost their grip on my hands, but it no longer mattered. It was my own magic crashing into me, and as it soared through my body, it found the single thread my family had built. My restored power followed their lead, creating a perfect cord of both fire and water.

Memories returned, and everything that made me what I was, and I could only shake at the wonder of it all.

My family's gift unwound and returned to them. That wasn't the only power filling the clearing. All that Eila had once been filled us, curing our pains before rising into the sky. It hovered for a long moment before exploding, a white firework that coated the entire sky.

As magic rained over Lake Tahoe, the shifters' eyes opened just before I let my own close for a long time.

CHAPTER 29

I died. It was the only explanation. I died, and I went to heaven.

If I wasn't so comfortable, I might have been a little sad about being dead, but it seemed a small price to pay for the absolute peace that filled every cell of my being.

Oblivion faded slowly. As my senses returned, it occurred to me that heaven—my heaven, at least—probably didn't ask the celestial choir to cover The Clash.

I was, however, floating on a cloud. I pried my eyes open to find a white ceiling rather than blue sky, and four walls, and a mattress that cost more than many cars underneath me.

Next to the mattress sat a chair that had likely cost the same, though it barely held the man sitting in it.

"Where?" I croaked.

"Your hotel."

"I have a hotel?" It took me a minute to figure out what he was saying. "Sera didn't die and give it to me, did she?"

"Pfft." I blinked toward Sera in the doorway. "It was always half yours. Now it's official. Besides, you need a home, what with the cabin not being there anymore."

"Why not the trailer?" I asked, though I wasn't complaining. In fact, I was wondering if it was feasible to live full-time in this bed.

"The trailer wasn't big enough for all of us." The bed became even more appealing when Mac sat on the edge.

"Move over."

I didn't argue. His arm wrapped around me, and I melted into him. "I'm sorry you had to do that."

His face was blank for several seconds before he understood. "You mean Deborah? I'm not."

"But..."

"We know what it would have done to you to kill her. You're finally climbing out of the pit. I'm not letting you fall back in."

"Now you have to live with the guilt, though."

Mac circled a strand of my hair around his index finger. "Yes. It helps that I don't feel any."

I started to argue, but he dropped my hair to put his finger against my lips. I met his gaze, and his eyes were the same chocolate brown they'd always been, warm and full of quiet certainty. Mac wasn't at risk of falling into his own pit.

I curled in closer, just because I could. I might have stayed there for quite a while, had my stomach not chosen that particular moment to growl as loud as Mac ever did.

"Room service," I announced. "Pancakes."

"No pancakes," Sera said. "Pizza's on the deck, so get your lazy water ass out of bed."

"Half fire," I corrected. I'd worked too hard for that side of me to let anyone forget it. "You guys have to stop watching me sleep. It's getting creepy."

"Then stop passing out," she said. "Come on. People are asking for you."

"Wait." I stopped her from leaving. "How long was I out this time?"

"Two and a half days. We'll let it slide, but if you do it again now that you're healed we'll start thinking you're a drama queen."

Fair enough. "Are you all going to yell at me if I go up?

Cause if so, I'm staying put."

"Why would we yell?" Sera furrowed her brow.

"Cause I did that whole sacrificing myself thing. You're not a big fan of that." I braced for the lecture.

Instead, she shrugged. "It was the only choice left."

My chin dropped, and I used a hand to lift it back into place, in case she missed my utter shock.

She rolled her eyes. "Please. You used to go all martyr at the first opportunity. You waited this time. I think that's an improvement. And if I'd been able to do what you did, I'd have done the same. We all would have. What you did is why we're here now."

"We're all here?"

She called over her shoulder as she walked away. "Come to the deck and find out."

I bounced out of bed after her, surprised at how easily I moved. In the clearing, I'd broken myself completely and been put back together. I assumed that would come with some scars.

Instead, I felt like I'd slept for a week, then spent the day at the spa. I felt fresh and awake and new.

I showered and pulled on a clean pair of jeans. My red sweater hung in the closet in a dry cleaner's bag. I put it on. I was going to need to shop for a new wardrobe.

While I slept, we'd moved to the hotel's premium suite. It had been Josiah's home when he was in Tahoe, which meant a sheikh or monarch would feel perfectly at home with its amenities. If I recalled, it even came with a personal assistant/butler.

Later, I'd abuse that power with requests for three bonsai trees and a VHS copy of *Xanadu*. Right then, I needed to see my family.

The suite had a spiral staircase leading to the deck. I began to feel at home.

I climbed upstairs. Mac was behind me, taking a little too much pleasure in pinching my ass to make me go faster.

It wasn't so much a deck as a rooftop patio, complete with high-end barbecue, lounge chairs, pool and hot tub, and a large dining table. Everyone was gathered around the table, their plates piled high with pizza from the mountain of cardboard boxes stacked on the bar. I was greeted with a chorus of hellos when I appeared.

Sera stood at the front of the table. She tapped a metal knife against her beer bottle to get everyone's attention. "Now that she's here, let's do this once, for the record. Aidan is as normal as she's ever going to be. Still a freaky dual, still more powerful than she has any right to be, and she'll likely make a mess of it, but she's okay. That loose piece of fire is all sewn up now. From here on out, any crazy is all her own. Those two threads aren't coming apart, not ever."

Some cheered. Some smiled. Some teared up. No one appeared to doubt Sera's proclamation.

I waved, making sure it looked like a sane wave, then moved to the railing, gesturing for Sera to follow. Lake Tahoe stretched below us, blue and pristine and filling me with life.

"How did you know?" I asked.

"About the neat and tidy magic mix?"

"Yeah."

She was a little too proud of herself. "Who do you think made sure the fire behaved itself this time?"

I grabbed her beer bottle so I could toast her with it. "You're never going to let me forget that, are you?"

"Hell no."

"So, I've been thinking."

"Since when?"

"They're all here. Everyone we love is on this patio right now. Well, everyone we love and Jet."

Sera's eyes softened. "We've waited a long time to get here, haven't we?"

"There is one person."

They hardened again damn fast. "No. I'm not ready to talk about it."

"I'll make it quick. I've been trying to figure out why she changed her name from Helen to Ani. Maybe she was trying to start over, forget her old life, but it's an odd choice, isn't it? I think my brain spent some time on it while I was sleeping, cause it finally came up with something."

Sera didn't answer. She watched me, her expression inscrutable.

"You've seen me play with letters when I'm bored. Did you know my name works both ways? I'm Nadia backwards. Most names aren't that good. I don't want to date Cam or hang out with Mairim or Nomis. Probably not Anifares, either."

It took her a second. After her mother left, Josiah was the only one to call her Serafina.

"I'd probably end up calling you Ani for short."

She gave no indication she heard me, which told me she was considering every word I said.

"Told you I've been thinking," I said, trying not to look smug.

I left her at the railing. I grabbed a slice of veggie pizza and perched on a lounge chair next to Simon. "So fill me in. What have I missed?"

The pause was longer than it needed to be, with a few too many meaningful glances.

"Seriously? Something happened in two days?"

"It's not exactly bad," Luke said.

"More unexpected." Vivian stretched her legs before

her. After her little speech to Deborah, her movement had a certainty I didn't remember from before. She even appeared taller.

"Oh, just tell me," I muttered, with as little grace as possible.

Sera answered from behind me. "Michael, Ruth, and Harriet held up their end of the bargain. They told the truth. So did Allison Ash. The FBI's report and the voice recordings helped prove we were innocent. Deborah's being blamed for everything she did, particularly how reckless she was releasing Eila, but there are still a lot of questions about duals and firsts. Other council members are heading here to get answers. You'll need to answer them."

That did sound pretty dreadful. "I'll deal. We should probably rehearse something, though."

My mother leaned forward, her eyes a little too serious. "It's not only the water council, Aidan. They've told the other elements. Members of every council are about to descend on Tahoe."

"I'm not seeing the problem. They'll ask questions, I'll answer, I'll be all sane and stuff, and we'll figure it out. If we can handle Eila, we can cope with an interrogation or two. We've got truth on our side, right?"

Vivian began to speak, but Miriam cut her off. "Just show her, Johnson."

The quieter agent walked toward one of the potted succulents near the pool.

He touched its leaves, and it grew two inches.

"Vivian?"

"I'm not helping."

"But… the… Johnson, when did you figure this out?" As far as we knew, he was descended from earth elementals, but separated by several generations from any true power.

Everyone watched me, waiting.

"No," I announced. "No. Not again. Everything is good and happy and whatever doom and gloom you're about to unload on me, take it back. I don't want it."

I glared at the lot of them. I may have been rebuilt in the clearing, but it seemed a gift for denial was encoded in my DNA.

Simon rested his fingers on my forearm, a calming gesture. Mac sat beside me and took my hand. I had the distinct feeling I was being managed.

"When Eila's magic exploded, it didn't go away, did it?"

I studied Johnson, then looked at Vivian, who was definitely taller than I remembered, her eyes a shade closer to an earth's dark brown. "It went…"

"To everyone in the Lake Tahoe basin," said Simon. I was pretty sure he'd waited to speak so he could make the big reveal.

I grabbed the nearest beer and took a long swig.

Luke was the one who said it out loud. He made it real. "Every human with any elemental blood and every shifter who was born without the changing gene, they've all been boosted, I guess you'd say. Elementals and shifters are appearing everywhere we turn. We've been out the last two days trying to find anyone who's been acting out because they don't understand what's happening to them."

"But this could be okay. More magical races are good. We like shifters. And elementals. Well, the ones who don't try to kill us. This could be great, really." I was babbling. I planned to keep babbling until this all went away.

Mac squeezed my hand. "It could be great, yeah, but the balance of power is changing. No one knows how, but everyone's on edge. There were several fights between the races last night."

"Plus, we aren't sure what other effects the magic will have," added Vivian.

I tried picturing the new world forming around us. "And the elemental councils are about to walk right into this mess and light a freaking match."

The shifters, humans, and elementals in Tahoe had existed in a tenuous peace formed from a web of ignorance, denial, and contempt. It wasn't pretty, but it worked.

It was all about to change.

I walked to the bar, then picked up my own drink and wrapped my hands around the cold bottle, thinking.

When I set it down, I was ready.

"Cancel all hotel reservations. Keep only the employees with some magical heritage. Get everyone you care about under this roof. No more spreading out. No more separation. We're better together. Safer. We all know this. So, from now on, we are officially hunkering down until this is over."

Sera shook her head. "We can't ignore this till it goes away."

"That's not the plan." I rejoined the table, surrounding myself with the people I loved. "We've got two magical races fighting to build a new Tahoe where they get to be dominant. Screw that. We're not letting elementals and shifters and crazy council members tear apart our home. No, we're not ignoring it. We're getting in the fight."

The room's energy changed, quiet doubts giving way to strength.

As much as I longed for peace, it wasn't over. My friends and I still lived in a world that didn't want us. It didn't want shifters and elementals to be friends, let alone lovers. It didn't want duals to exist, and if we insisted on doing so, it wasn't sure it wanted us to live.

I sent my magic to my mother and Grams for a moment, then moved on to Sera and Luke, greeting their fire. I tested our joined power, reminding them how much we shared. I fed my strength into Mac, using the remnant of water magic he'd always hold. I looked at the friends and family who all, in their way, helped me achieve the impossible. I was here because of them. There was nothing they couldn't do.

It was a damn good thing, considering our new situation. We might need to do the impossible again. When you lived in a world that didn't want you, there was only one option.

You had to remake the world.

Acknowledgments

As always, I must thank my incredible group of readers and editors who were so generous with their time and support: Kaari, Carrie, Jess, Rachel, and Shelly. This is a far better book because of their feedback.

In addition, my Texan friend Kate spent much time trying to explain to this native Californian the proper use of "y'all." The fact that Luke never says it is proof that I was a terrible student, but she tried her best. In an alternate version of this novel, Luke says "y'all" often and in the proper context.

Thanks as well to Paul Taylor, my tech wizard. He somehow still likes me despite all the panicked emails I've sent his way. I shudder to think what my website would look like without his help.

I'm lucky enough to have two wonderful cover designers. Alisha at Damonza outdid herself this time, and Cynthia Fliege continues to create art with her gorgeous illustrated covers.

Finally, an extra special thanks to the readers who had to wait a bit longer than expected for this book. Your patience and kind words while I was sorting through life stuff helped more than you know.

About the Author

Mia Marshall is the award-winning author of the Elements urban fantasy series. She lives somewhere in the Sierra Nevadas, where she is surrounded by a small but deadly feline army.

To learn more, visit her online at http://miamarshall.com.